I'VE GOT MY MIND SET ON BREW

I'VE GOT MY MIND SET ON BREW

A Novel

STEPHANIE
JAYNE

alcove
press

Copyright © 2024 by Stephanie Jayne

Published in the United States by Alcove Press, an imprint of The Quick Brown Fox & Company LLC.

Alcove Press and its logo are trademarks of The Quick Brown Fox & Company LLC.

Library of Congress Catalog-in-Publication data available upon request.

ISBN (trade paperback): 978-1-63910-649-3
ISBN (ebook): 978-1-63910-650-9

Cover illustration by Sarah Horgan

Printed in the United States.

www.alcovepress.com

Alcove Press
34 West 27th St., 10th Floor
New York, NY 10001

First Edition: April 2024

10 9 8 7 6 5 4 3 2 1

For everyone working at crafting their own happy ending.

I've Got My Mind Set on Brew features supporting characters suffering from chronic illness. There are also conversations in the story about the sudden death of a family member (in the past).

CHAPTER ONE
ENGLISH-STYLE PALE ALE

A mix of earthy and fruity flavors and herbal hops, its color ranging between golden and amber. Medium to high hops and bitterness.

Four little words. Four words taunt me, no matter how hard I try to put them out of mind.

I found someone else.

Not the most self-affirming four words. At least not when said by your boyfriend. The supposed love of your life.

And, dammit, today the man who told me those words eleven months ago (but who's counting?) felt the apparent need to give me an update. Four more words with essentially the same meaning:

We're having a baby.

One more someone in the "someone else" category. Another else.

What am I supposed to say to that? *Cool, cool. I'm sure that master's degree in poetry will come in real handy for day care and diapers in the city that never sleeps!*

I should have switched out my phone. *Who this?* I could have responded, seeing the untagged number and pretending we had no connection. I should have changed my number entirely. Finally ditched suburban digits for a coveted 312 prefix, like I should have ditched this dude instead of letting myself get strung along. Nearly a year later, and I still freaking care.

I never learn.

Another text arrives. I stare at the phone. I stare some more.

It's an honest-to-goodness ultrasound image. Created by my ex and his trust fund darling. From a hospital in Brooklyn, because of course a jobless poet now lives in Brooklyn. Coasting on his new girlfriend's family money.

I fling the phone like it's fire itself.

"Incoming!" a coworker yells. He shifts left from the projectile, still carrying a tray loaded with pints, and proceeds to a four-top table.

Welcome to Resistance Brewpub.

My phone, meanwhile, has slammed against the edge of the bar, knocked into a glass, and tipped that glass onto a lap.

The owner of the lap jerks from the barstool, backing up in a *something wet is touching me* dance. He looks my way. "Hey! What are you, crazy?"

I gape in horror. *I have thrown a phone.* In my place of employment. My sole place of employment, mind you, where I depend on a crucial debt-reducing paycheck. I can't afford to squander this job. To squander a five-year career path. Never mind said career path is plan B career path—it is now my only career path.

"I'm . . . I'm really sorry." All I can see is wet crotch. I want to look away, but the horror of what I've done keeps my eyes lasered on it—the crotch, I mean. A man's crotch. This is worse than flinging a phone, staring so intensely at a stranger's soiled nether regions.

My phone. My phone! It's facedown against the floorboards with our best-selling IPA eagerly pooling around it. I snatch it up. A nervous laugh escapes as I shake beer from the protective case and wipe the device against my comparatively dry jeans.

Wet Pants Guy grimaces at me. I cringe. I mean . . . this is so my fault.

Then I remember what he said. *What are you, crazy?* Does this guy even comprehend mental health stereotypes?

"What on this holy green goddess earth are you doing?" Alex, the voice of reason and forewarning of airborne cell phones, storms over. His apron is dotted with an assortment of rainbow pins, including a *Trans Rights* pin in black letters on a bright-yellow background. His forearms reveal a sleeve of tattoos ending at pale-skinned hands as his knuckles grip a now-empty serving tray. "Are you okay, sir?" he asks.

I play it cool and sling my arm along the bar. "'Sup."

Alex looks from me to the phone to Wet Pants Guy. "We're very sorry. We'll clean this up." He steers me from the scene to behind the bar, where a bin of rags is stashed. He lowers his voice. "Explain?"

I blink. *Get it together, Kat.* Thankfully, only a few patrons are in the bar to witness my tantrum as we wait on our all-staff meeting. The meeting where I'm supposed to hear about moving up to a brewer position. I've been shadowing the brewers the past six months, splitting my time between serving food and drinks in the brewpub and finding any chance I can get to work with the brewing equipment. I've done whatever tasks needed to get done. Mostly cleaning tanks and kegs.

I'm ninety-nine percent sure I'm moving up. Okay, ninety percent. Maybe eighty-five. Regardless, I don't have time today for my ex flashing back into my life.

Alex moves in front of me. He lets his head fall one way, giving me a capital-L Look. Explanation required.

I turn the phone screen toward him. "They're having a baby."

"Who, Magda?" He squints at the blurry fetus. "If Magda is finally pregnant, she'll expect a party. I call you for planning it."

"No, not Magda!" Our coworker recently admitted she and her husband were trying. "Magda would tell you herself. This is Alden."

His expression falls like a sheet of ice collapsing in one solid chunk. "I refuse to engage in this conversation." He hands back the phone.

"Can you believe he texted me this?"

"Yes. And you're reading it. And you probably already wrote back your congratulations with a sunshine emoji."

"That is *not* true." I mean, I'm probably going to respond—it would be rude not to—but I haven't figured out what to say yet . . .

"See—look!" He points at me. "You're thinking about what to write back!"

I stuff the phone into my back pocket. "I swear, I won't this time."

"You're like a glutton for punishment. No. Hangry for torture. Forget his mess and be done." He shoves a rag at me and takes one for himself.

It's not like I want to hang on to Alden. He's made it clear as crystal he's moved on. One visit to NYC, and suddenly he was in line for a poetry residency at a Brooklyn makerspace. WTF that even means, I may never truly know, but reality was bye-bye Chicago and hello someone else to fund his life.

I wipe down the sides of the bar, the stool beside it, the floor. Wet Pants Guy is nowhere. Well, probably the bathroom. Maybe a good soak to the rest of his pants will even out the stain.

I toss the wet rags into the bucket by the trash. They miss, of course, so I have to go back around and pick them up off the floor.

"Kat." Alex has the *What's really going on?* tone set aggressively high. "Don't spiral. Alden isn't worth it. His pretentious name alone gives me hives." He raises a tattooed arm. "Look! Visible bumps!"

It seems more like his skin reacting to the ever-present chill in the old building, worse since it's winter, but I'm not about to argue. I take out my phone again and stare at the dark screen. "It was supposed to be my turn."

He sighs. "I know."

That had been the deal. I would work to support us while Alden went to school, then it would be my chance. My goal had been to get my master's in public health so I could climb the chain of command at the health alliance I'd worked for by day. Then I could finally quit my bartending job.

Ha. Life sure has a way of thumbing its nose at best-laid plans. Here I am nearly a year later, having lost the health care job, with the bar as my full-time gig and an added bonus of crushing debt.

It's all Alden's living expenses, everything that wasn't covered by his small stipend from student teaching. We didn't live extravagantly, but I also only made a starting salary, emphasis on *starting*. The apartment lease was in my name—two bedrooms, to give Alden an office to work in—and all the utilities were in my name. If something couldn't get paid, it was my name on the line. The credit card was willing and waiting. In my name.

There's a lesson I learned going uphill backward. At the time, I let the romance of a poetry degree sweep away fiduciary concerns. What did it matter which bills were in whose name? After all, we were going to be together forever.

Alex takes the phone from me, swipes up, and taps the screen. He hands it back.

I pull up my messages. The texts from Alden have been wiped away. His contact listing too. A blank slate.

Alden's number no longer taking real estate in my phone is a good thing. Right? No, right. It's good. "Thanks, Alex." I should have deleted the number ages ago. Like when I buzzed one side of my head in a moment of reclaiming control over my life. Yes, cliché, but at least now I have a badass haircut. Even if the cut initially came as an act of defiance after Alden left.

I can see the strain in Alex's face as he holds back an eye roll. "No prob. Now let me see if Mr. Hottie has left the building. Maybe I can do some damage control."

Gah. The blunder with the customer is peak Messy Kat, and I swore those days were in my rearview.

I excuse myself to the bathroom. I need a sec to get my mind straight before our staff meeting. The water scalds as I scrub my hands. My *Live well* wrist tattoo reminds me of what's most important: looking ahead and living my best life.

Outside the bathroom, I don't get far before I butt up against something solid.

"Oop!" I step back. Instantly, my shoulders slump. It's the Mr. Hottie Alex referred to, though I'd been thinking of him as Mr. Wet Pants. "Your pants are wet." Why this obvious statement flies from my mouth, I have no answers for.

"They are." His face is stoic, unmoving.

"That's my fault. I'm sorry."

He gives this a beat. "Are you?"

"Wha . . ."

"I watched the whole thing. You chucked that phone at the first guy you saw."

I scoff. "I didn't *aim* the phone. It was an accident. An accidental chuck." This is going well. "Besides, you called me crazy. That's offensive, you know."

He has the gall to laugh. "I heard what you told that guy. You're mad about a boyfriend."

Emphasis on *boy*, like a child. This is exactly what I hate, being reduced to a woman scorned. And yet I'm the one who flung a solid object with no regard to my surroundings.

Words aren't typically this difficult for me, but beyond my own brain scramble with Alden's pending baby-daddy status, Alex was right—this guy is alarmingly attractive. Like, gut-punch, incite-a-street-fight hot. Which is not helping.

I mean, he's not at all my type. My type being broody soul searchers with piercings and tattoos and side-hustle garage bands. And that guy Knife I once dated. His last name was actually Kniffen, thus the nickname, but he did ride a motorcycle.

Hottie here is one of those guys I see briskly walking in the Loop, dressed in a crisp blue business shirt and overcoat like a real adult. Clean-cut hair spiked enough to be stylish without being edgy. Dark-blond hair, golden-brown eyes, hints of beard shadowing an angular jaw. What is he doing in the outer rims? We're south of the Bucktown and Wicker Park neighborhoods where trendy bars and bookstores fill the blocks. Farther west than Lincoln Park or West Loop, where this guy would blend.

He's said something else, and I've been literally speechless. My ex is busy procreating, and here I am trying to form one full sentence to a live human male. "I'm sorry, what?" I ask.

"I said, unless you have a blow-dryer, we're done here."

I snort and cover my mouth. "I'm sorry. That was funny. Unexpectedly funny. I wasn't prepared."

"Clearly." He walks off, back to the bar.

I close my eyes and let the embarrassment flood over. My therapist suggests I accept these moments and experience the emotion. Name it, own it. I'm naming a lot of things in my head right now, and most of them are obscene.

Opening my eyes, I see him at the bar, grabbing his coat from a stool. A black wool one with a plaid scarf so soft I'm sure the tag says Burberry.

I watch Mr. Hottie Wet Pants leave the building. I almost feel bad he'll be waiting for the bus with wet pants in below-freezing temps, but who am I kidding? That guy drove here. No public transit, no rideshare, no cab. He drove and he parked.

"You okay, dear?" It's Prairie, my boss. Born of hippie parents, Prairie and her partner Joe (not born of hippie parents) started Resistance over twenty years ago, first as just a bar, then expanding their home brew to a small but legit brewing operation. The day I walked into Resistance looking for part-time evening and weekend work, Prairie sat with me, asking about my life, family, passions. She didn't bother with whether I had serving experience. I got the job the same day because, she said, I had wise eyes.

More like a wise ass. And not very wise at that.

I run a hand through my hair, the side that falls against my shoulder with black and fading flame-red streaks. "If the guy who just left complains about the service, please know I never *meant* to throw my phone."

She nods past me. "He left a tip. If he was as mad as you say, he wouldn't have left anything."

Fair point, but later at home I'll run through the encounter again fifty times and feel worse about it.

Her light hug of assurance means everything, just as it has time and again this year. "Come on back. We have a lot to cover today." She looks worried.

"Hey, is everything okay?" I've been so focused on myself.

Prairie makes a *hmm* sound through her lips.

I hope it's not a bad batch. Sometimes a batch goes sour, though it's been ages since that's happened and Joe is consistent with sample testing. He's a chill guy with a sharp eye for detail. Hopefully, this won't set us back. Chicago is a city with a lot of beer, and people come here for unique offerings. When there's no discovery, or a chance to brag about off-the-beaten-path small-batch brew, we lose that customer.

I cross through the glass door to the brewing area, which is situated in partial view of the pub. Customers love to see the operation in process. Joe sits on a stool in front of the brew kettle and nods to me in greeting. Beside him is a wheeled cart with sample-size glasses. The sample is Sunrise, our signature wheat ale.

I take one and sniff. The subtle fruit scents hit first. The beer is thick and hazy, with a faint amber glow. I sip and let the liquid coat my tongue. It starts sweet, with a medium body—not heavy but not watery thin like what I drank in college because it was cheap. The barest hint of a dry note surfaces in the middle to curb the sweet. The aftertaste is smooth and bright, exactly like Sunrise should taste.

I grin at Joe. "Gold medal. World-class beer."

He laughs and casts a glance at Prairie, who paces the length of the brew tanks. Fruit and field, light and crisp, is how I see Prairie and Joe. It's this game I like to play, to match beer types to people. Take me, for example. I like to think of myself as an American amber lager. A good balance of malt and hops, an easy beer that's generally liked. Reality is, most days I'm veering toward less balanced and let's just say a shade more bitter. An English pale ale. On particularly sassy days, an ESB—extra special bitter. I'm complex like that. I can be bitter and extra special.

Looking through the window into the pub, I see Luiz, Magda, and Anya enter and stomp snow from their boots. They join us as Alex comes in from the kitchen with the line cooks.

I'm finally feeling something shift, like I'm ready to embrace what's to come. The same sensation I had that night after closing as I talked with Prairie and Joe about what I wanted from life. Back then, I didn't know. "I like beer," was what I'd blurted, through tears, after incurring an unfortunate overdraft charge when I accidentally double-paid a bill. "I love it here. I love it so much I want to marry it."

Which still brings us laughs.

"We can do you one better," Prairie said then. That's when she shared how they were looking to train another brewer. Eventually, with apprenticeship, it could lead to a brewmaster role, if that interested me. Apprenticeship wouldn't require going back to school. Maybe just a few courses online or weekend workshops. More importantly, no debt.

Sign. Me. Up.

"You can marry the beer," Joe said. "Make whatever new brews you want. We'll show you how."

That did it. I'd be the creator. I could share a piece of myself, my favorite flavors, with the community who'd built me back up.

I tend to forget those things when I fall back to thinking of Alden. Today is a reminder, right here, of what I'm working toward. All I have to do is let myself believe it.

Magda hip-checks me, taking a sip of her own sample. I see Magda as a Baltic porter. Deep in color, like her dark hair and signature crimson lips, the porter typically has high alcohol content and is big in body. Magda is five feet nothing, but you'd never know it from her attitude.

"Good afternoon, everyone," Prairie begins. "We have news."

She and Joe exchange glances. Thirty-plus years of communicating, and they have it down to a look.

Prairie steps closer to Joe and squeezes his shoulder. He's the one to speak next. "Afraid it's not good news, and it's my fault."

A few titters scatter through the crew. Joe can turn anything into a joke, usually about himself.

But I'm not laughing. My insides coil tight, waiting for the drop.

Joe heaves a sigh. "Well, folks. Turns out I'm sick."

All movement ceases. Only the tanks hum in response.

"It's not the kind of sick I can shake off, sorry to say. So, we had a tough choice to make." He and Prairie grip hands. "We're going to sell."

CHAPTER TWO

FRUIT AND FIELD BEER

Beer made using fruit or with vegetables and herbs added
during the brewing process, for a little bit of whimsy.

I still remember the day the magic happened. My first taste of
creation, of crafting beer.

I'd been working at Resistance part-time a few weeknights
and every other weekend. When I lost my office job, I had more
time to spend at the pub. I found the science of making beer interesting, but it was the creative side that fascinated me. How each
tiny adjustment in the process could alter the flavor and texture.

Joe could talk the craft for hours. He knew labels and limited
runs from memory, could call up recipes he'd used a decade ago.
He was always proudest of his best seller Prairie, named after his
favorite companion. But he liked a challenge. An experiment. We
started tinkering with one, he and I, and called it Heartbeat.

We argued over the name as much as the adjustment to the
hops. Heartbeat, the center, the livelihood, the driving impulse.

The goal: create a beer pleasing to every person on the Resistance crew. An impossible task. A worthy challenge.

We started with mini-batches of his baseline Prairie recipe, a lager using warm fermentation. We tweaked the hops, waiting on the process to complete before tasting and adjusting again, over weeks, months. I researched on my off hours, learning everything I could about dry hopping and the home brew process from You-Tube and home brew forums. I loved the moment of tasting—both for my own pleasure and for the expressions on people's faces, my coworkers', my friends'. Aiming to please them, inching closer to a brew that captured the essence of who we were.

We never got to perfection. Maybe that was the point all along. Heartbeat will always be a work in progress.

Now, I'm numb as the announcement sinks in. *We're going to sell.*

Four even worse words than the ones I heard earlier today.

A sick feeling washes over. Resistance is my quirky, mismatched family. Without Prairie and Joe, what are we?

"Pancreatic cancer," Joe offers. He wheels his stool closer to Prairie and wraps an arm around her back. "Same as my dad."

I can't move. The word marches across my mind in bolded font.

Cancer

"I've known for . . . a while. It's why I've had a few days here and there away. It's why you've seen Ed back here more than me. And Kat here's been filling in as she learns."

I flinch at hearing my name. Everything I've done is nothing compared to Joe and Prairie building this place from scratch. Turning a run-down bar into a neighborhood favorite. Keeping the brews small and catered to the community. So many of us are here because of who Joe and Prairie are and the unique brews they've crafted. Otherwise, we could work anywhere else. Bars that aren't as cold inside, for starters.

I look at Edwin, Joe's longtime brewing assistant. Graying black hair, slightly weathered brown skin. He doesn't look much older than his midfifties, like Joe, but he recently told me he's sixty-seven. Did he know Joe was sick?

He wipes his eye and keeps his gaze to the floor. Seems he didn't know either.

How did we all miss Joe's been sick for months? He's thinner, now that I look at him more closely. A little worn, like he's gone a week without enough sleep.

Prairie holds up a pale-skinned hand. Delicate freckles float along her arm. "We appreciate you all so much. Please know this hasn't been an easy decision. But we're doing what's best for us."

Comments burst around the room. Anya launches into an explanation of how her cousin was taken out of hospice and is in full remission. Luiz is speaking in Spanish, and I catch only a few familiar words. I barely hear Alex, the other servers, and the kitchen staff. Everything they're saying may as well be in another language, because I don't understand any of it.

I pull apart from Magda, who's sniffling into her sweatshirt sleeve. I need space, but I don't dare leave. If I leave, that means I accept what's happening here, and I don't.

There has to be something we can do so they don't have to sell. To give them time for Joe to get better. Then they can return to what they've worked so hard for.

I step forward. "We'll pick up the slack. You can trust us to be here and do the work." I catch Alex's eye, and he nods. "I can fast-track my brewing certification and work with Edwin more."

I have no life outside Resistance, so what does it matter? I'll sleep here if needed. Heck, save on rent and live a squatter's life behind the tanks.

Okay, not really, because that's a massive health code violation. Though I could sleep in the back office.

"I can work doubles," Luiz offers. "I'll take Kat's shifts."

Alex raises his hand. "I can book local music. I have contacts."

"I'm taking accounting classes," Anya reminds everyone. "I can learn the books."

Prairie clears her throat. "You all are wonderful. We're so grateful. Always have been. Selling is the hardest part. Maybe even harder than the diagnosis."

"Speak for yourself," Joe adds with a laugh. The cavernous room swallows the sound.

"People use words like *warrior* when they talk about cancer," she says. "Fight this, battle that. But sometimes a body doesn't have the fight, even if the will is there." She looks at each of us. Her usual resilience is colored by blue notes. "You all know I'm not good at talking around a thing. We will fight, but we can't do that running the bar. It's not good for Joe to be stressed. We need to focus on the days we have left."

My limbs go heavy. *Days left.*

Magda clutches my arm.

Prairie's laying it out plain. This isn't something we can patch up and work through.

She tugs at the end of her long braid, a blend of faded blond streaked with silver. In her worn leather biker jacket, she's as badass a lady as ever. "You know we love you all dearly, but this place takes more than a forty-hour workweek to run. We need to use this time for us, for family. The money from the sale will help us with the medical bills, to care for Joe right."

My head is full of enough asterisked-out swears to short out a network TV mute button. Their medical bills have to be bananas. That's what this is coming down to. Back when I had a vision to save the world, I wanted to be a public health advocate. I had a bleeding heart after seeing what my sister goes through to manage her lupus.

It was a huge blow when I was laid off. Corporate cutbacks, simple as that.

"I'm sure you all know, investors are eager to buy craft breweries," Joe continues. "Back in the late eighties, not so much. We were the freaks playing with home-brewing kits. Now it's a multibillion-dollar industry. Resistance is small potatoes with no wide distribution. Everyone has ideas for what they want this place to be. It's hard to find someone to trust to hand over the reins to."

Prairie steeples her hands together, shifting weight from one foot to the other. "We're fortunate to have friends in high places. A close friend has been interested in investing—"

"Benny Burrito," Joe interrupts. "Met him at UIC. He graduated with honors, while I dropped out to run a diner down on Cermak near Racine—"

"Joe." Prairie levels him with a look. "This is hard enough."

"Yeah. Don't I know it."

"His name is Benjamin Bennett," she tells us. "I don't know where Burrito comes from."

"See, there was this one night—"

"Joe, please."

My heart aches at their usual banter in this unusual circumstance.

Joe waves a dismissive hand. "Ask me about Benny later over a pint. Point is, Benny invests in businesses like ours. Has a whole investment firm or what have you. He's a white-collar guy, but he never forgot his old friends. Offered to go in with us years back to expand distribution, but we told him we keep business and friends two separate things. He's been bugging us about it now that every bathtub brewer thinks they're the next Goose Island."

Prairie nods. "We'll still own the Resistance label, and we'll still have a stake. The day-to-day operations will shift to the new owners. Because we know them, it feels like the best option."

They stumble through an explanation about the exchange, clearly emotional but hopeful. My stomach lurches. They're talking about this like the deal is made. Like it's signed and hands have been shaken.

Joe looks at the assistant brewer beside him. "Ed here, well, he has an announcement too."

Edwin steps forward. "It's been a good twenty years together." He claps a hand on Joe's shoulder. "I'd like to go to Atlanta by my daughter and her family. If I don't go now, I may never leave."

My stomach drops again. With Joe and Edwin gone, who's brewing the beer?

"That means more change," Joe says. "Opportunities, if you look at the pint half-full."

He looks at me and smiles. It's a sad smile, but a smile nonetheless. My five-year plan, my plan B—I'm not ready to see it go up in fumes. I'm also not near enough ready to take over brewing. I don't have the experience or any certification.

I can't marry the beer. Not yet. I'm still courting the beer. Learning its side of the bed and what not to say around its parents. What I have is work ethic. I know the brewing process, and I can clean a fermenter tank well enough to make a health inspector blush. But none of that matters right now. Joe . . . he's leaving. It sounds like they won't be back, even if—when—he gets better.

Chatter fills the air as everyone reacts to the news. I join the line where our crew take turns hugging and spewing awkward affirmations to Joe. It's like a receiving line for the terminally ill.

Oh God, terminal? They didn't use that word, but it fits. *The days we have left. Sometimes the body doesn't have the fight.*

"Katri—" Joe starts.

I hold up a hand to stop him. "If you call me Katrina, I'll punch you. Lightly, of course."

He isn't fazed. "Kat, I'm not worried about you in the least. You'll spring right back from this. Keep doing what you're doing."

Questions flood my brain. Keep assisting the new brewer? Keep doing what I'm doing here, at Resistance? Spring back into what? I can't think of any of this now.

"I can tell that mind of yours is racing," he says. "I can't say what things will look like, but you're resilient. You're a hard worker. You'll find your way."

"Stop, don't worry about me." The fact he's even thinking about me at all right now says everything about who he is. "You just get well, okay?"

I cringe at my own words. Is it terrible to offer such a bland affirmation? Like sheer will can cure disease? It's not about me, but I feel terrible. I'm operating like a body full of loose bolts.

He pats me on the back. "Take care, Kat. Life has a way of working out."

I only wish I believed it.

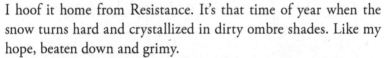

I hoof it home from Resistance. It's that time of year when the snow turns hard and crystallized in dirty ombre shades. Like my hope, beaten down and grimy.

It's selfish, but I feel cheated not knowing Joe was sick. I thought he and Prairie trusted us—me—enough to be real about their life. I can't quash the shock. I hate feeling helpless.

I pass by a modern condo beside the pre–World War II Eastern Orthodox church on my block, the details of which my roommate Sadie frequently finds opportunities to share. She wants to marry architecture as much as I want to marry craft beer.

I'm aware I fit into the gentrifier category in my neighborhood, being white and a transplant from the suburbs. I came here after college, finding the cheapest rent I could, and have watched million-dollar condos replace hundred-year-old multi-family households. Some have hung on. Alex and his Ukrainian family have lived in this neighborhood for four generations. I love seeing the old mixed with the new. But maybe more of the old. Sadie is rubbing off on me.

Through the iron gate, it's a half flight of steps to the front door of my three-flat apartment building. Upstairs is our landlord, Sadie's aunt. Downstairs is a basement-level apartment shared by a single mom and her daughter.

Neither of my two roommates is home. Sadie has become my closest friend outside Resistance. My other roommate, Neil, is a ship passing in the night. He works for an airline, and when he isn't flying cross-country, he spends his time at clubs living a life I dare dream of. Most importantly, Neil cleans up after himself and pays rent on time.

My head pounds. I toss back two ibuprofen with water and close the door to my bedroom, then fall back against my bed. Outside a siren wails, followed by a cascade of honking.

I'm wide awake. I sit up.

I wander from my room at the back of the apartment to the living room as Sadie comes in.

"Hey, darling!"

Sadie is wearing a vintage powder-blue hat with a feather along the side and a wool coat that swings. She looks like the chick from that *Mrs. Maisel* show.

She unloads her coat and bag and collapses into a tweed armchair.

"We should see about getting the fireplace working," I tell her, falling into the chair across from hers. The cushion sinks from decades-old springs. Both chairs came from the vintage-and-antiques shop where she works.

"I'll ask my aunt about it." She looks at me more closely. "What's on your mind?"

"I was thinking of all the things I could burn."

"That kind of day, huh?"

I tell her about Joe and c a n c e r. About the sale and Edwin's retirement.

She whistles low. "Rotten news."

"You're telling me." I gather my hair and scrunch it into a ponytail, holding it there. "I feel so bad for Joe and Prairie."

Sadie picks at a pink polished nail. "What's this mean for you?"

"I guess I see what the new brewer wants. If I can keep apprenticing. Maybe even get hired."

My phone buzzes. The name *Karrie* with my sister's picture flashes on the screen.

"I should get this," I tell Sadie.

"Hungry? I can heat up the leftover takeout in the fridge. Enough for two."

I nod and tap answer as I head to my room.

"Mom is driving. Me. Crazy."

"Nice to hear from you, Karrie."

My younger sister lets out a huff of frustration on the other end. The bratty six-year-old she once was is forever embossed in my brain, not the twenty-three-year-old she's become. "Kat. You don't understand. You have a life. I do not. I'm *so bored*."

"You have more of a social life than me. All I do is work." Only now, maybe not? The brewing will probably pause until a new brewmaster is hired and I—

"Are you even listening?" Karrie asks, busting into my thoughts. "I'm like a prisoner here. Can I come stay with you? I seriously can't manage Mom right now. She's refusing to let me move out with Addison."

Oh, so nothing new. This is the never-ending debate within my family. My parents insist Karrie live with them so they can help her manage her lupus and other related issues—celiac and skin flare-ups that are probably eczema but possibly something else. A carnival of doctors have suggested different theories. Karrie is in her last semester commuting to a liberal arts college two towns over from my parents and has been living at home the whole time. My parents had to understand Karrie would want to move out eventually.

"You know you're always welcome here," I tell her. "Maybe then Mom will return my calls."

"You're so dramatic," Karrie shoots back. "You don't know what it's like having her *literally* breathing down my neck."

Now there's a truth. I really have no idea what that feels like.

We talk a few minutes more until Karrie's venting loses steam. "I'll text you if I end up driving out to the city."

Usually, she doesn't. She just wants the option, I think.

When Karrie was a high school freshman, she felt drained to exhaustion when she was outside, leading her to quit softball. For months she complained about random aches. My parents thought it was lingering effects from a nasty respiratory infection, plus Karrie had always been a bit of a whiner. She was the first to tattle if things got rough between us. She never wanted to get dirty or run rabid through the neighborhood's connected backyards with the other kids on the street. My parents would say she needed more one-on-one attention. More affirmation and recognition.

By the spring of Karrie's freshman year, my senior year, it was clear she wasn't exaggerating her symptoms. Tests led to more tests and finally a referral to a pediatric rheumatologist. Diagnosis: lupus.

None of us really knew what lupus was until the doctor went through the details. I hated how people defined her by it. The sick girl. And me? I became the girl with the sick sister. Neither of us could escape the label.

It was as if our family scooped up our entire existence from its familiar cozy bowl and dumped out the contents, refilling the bowl with everything Karrie. Monitoring Karrie's diet, which was thought to contribute to inflammation and fatigue. Monitoring her medication. Getting work sent home from school, getting a private tutor to catch her up. More appointments, more medications.

Back then, Karrie needed my parents, while I was mere months from heading out the door to college. At the time, less hovering from Mom and Dad about where I went or what I did at which hour was like a backstage pass to the good life. Only most of the time I was exactly where I said I'd be: at my BFF Andrea's house or with another friend. A lot of times I was down the street at the home of Mrs. B, a retired teacher who used to babysit me and my sister. She owned an impressive vinyl music collection and had tubs of ice cream on standby.

I had plenty to do: debate team, literary journal, the school play where I ran tech behind the scenes. I just wished my parents had time to scoop those things into their mixing bowl along with everything else.

Things moved along like that until graduation. The day of the ceremony, I posed in my navy-blue cap and gown in front of our fireplace. Mom snapped the pic, but the photo never made it into a frame. Not that I ever saw.

I drove ahead with Andrea to get to the rehearsal before the ceremony. Since my parents and Karrie would be sitting in the bleachers outdoors at the school football field, they wanted to arrive right at the start to reduce her time in the harsh early-June sun.

The ceremony felt both silly and meaningful, a milestone the adults in my life had sworn would be memorable. I suppose it was, but for the wrong reasons.

After the ceremony, I headed to the bleachers with my friends, each of us peeling off as our families called out to us. I never heard my name. Probably my parents had ducked out to somewhere offering shade.

I walked the length behind the bleachers, checked the restrooms, and circled back to the stands, looking over each face in the mingling crowd. My phone wasn't the greatest after I'd dropped it near a lake (not in the lake, but close enough that water lapped over it—oops), so I restarted it. When the home screen flashed on again, two texts appeared from Dad.

Karrie is having a flare up. Sorry, Kitkit, we'll be there when we can.

Followed by:

Going to the ER. Call us.

I would be a massive jerk if I complained that my parents missed my high school graduation to take my chronically ill sister to the emergency room. My sister was probably mortified. We'd avoided emergency medical care all this time, but her condition was new enough that we just didn't know everything. It had to be bad. She was suffering, and there was nothing I could do.

And yet, knowing all of that, I was angry. *They missed my graduation.* This milestone, memorable event they'd talked up for so long, and they simply hadn't shown up. The one day of the year focused on me, and now I was expected to go find them at the hospital.

Saying any of this out loud to anyone couldn't happen. And while I'd felt the changes for months, how Karrie's need for one-on-one time had become essential, her need for attention not selfish but lifesaving, it was that day at graduation where I felt the shift in real time.

Our family had downgraded to a smaller bowl, one where my existence simply spilled over the edge. There was only so much room in there.

I'm staring at my phone, reading over Karrie's last texts to me. A few silly memes, a question about when Grandma's birthday is, a book she read as part of a course she thought I might like. All normal. It feels sometimes like we have separate families. Like I'm looking in on hers and she's looking out at me. Alone.

I plug the phone into my charger and join Sadie in the kitchen. Two warm plates of leftovers wait on the counter.

Sadie opens the fridge. Glass bottles clink into one another as she reaches for our filtered water pitcher.

"Uh, sorry about all the beer." I squeeze beside her and pluck a Pilsner and a wheat, each with a colorful label. "Alex gave me two from a four-pack he wasn't into, and I picked up these bombers at Clap Your Hands." Our favorite neighborhood liquor store and more.

She closes the door. "I can look for a mini-fridge at an estate sale. You could have a whole second fridge for your collection."

My own stash fridge? Maybe in my bedroom as a nightstand. "Yeah, that would be great, actually."

"Say no more."

I set the bottles in front of her on the counter. "You pick first."

Sadie inspects the labels. "I like this one."

She chooses her beers by label aesthetic. If she doesn't like the taste, she drinks it anyway. She's found a lot of favorites this way. I figured she'd like the one with the 1920s-inspired line art.

"You know what I don't get," I tell her as we eat. "You get a college degree, pay for it, and the job you get is totally unstable. Then you're still on the hook for the student loans after you're let go, and your new *salary*"—I throw up air quotes—"doesn't allow for paying it off. But if you don't get the college degree, you can't get the job to begin with." I shake my head. "Or you build a job from scratch, work for decades on making it a success, and cancer gets you."

She has the heart to give me an empathetic look. "Life is unfair. I agree."

We're both quiet. It's not like I'm only now realizing the unfairness of life. People have it worse than me. My sister, for starters.

Sadie opens her twenty-two-ouncer. She sniffs the open bottle, pauses, sips. I watch her face for her reaction. Sadie is an Irish red. Low on bitters with that reddish hue to match her brassy hair.

"It's not as fruity as I expected. It's a little—hoppy? Is that right? And smooth. It's yummy."

My own beer is light but bready with a touch of honey sweet. Not nearly the bitter I need tonight.

I sigh. "I need something in my life to work, Sadie." I try not to look sad as this next piece becomes clearer. "There are too many unknowns now, and it's making me nervous." Even Karrie calling saying she wants to move out reminds me change is inevitable. I typically like to know what's ahead.

"It's a trust thing," Sadie says. "You trusted Joe and Prairie. It sounds like maybe you feel let down—"

"I can't," I interrupt. "Joe has *cancer*. It's not about how I feel."

"You can feel let down at the same time you feel empathy for his situation. Both can exist at once."

It's hard to justify. It still feels like a contest between my feelings and their situation. How can I complain when I'm able-bodied and not saddled with a chronic illness? Or a terminal one? My issues are solvable. Find a new career. Ditch the deadweight boyfriend.

Sadie leaves me to my thoughts as she clears the dishes. A saint, she is.

I can't imagine Resistance without Prairie and Joe. They're baked into the foundation. They kept Resistance small because they liked being hands-on with the business.

Each shift I worked, I saw them take time with customers, with staff. They're good people. They were my sounding board and never claimed to be too busy. My whole plan B career was an idea we came up with after hours over craft brew. *I'll marry the beer.*

Working with them, I felt like the daughter they never had.

But I was the one who filled in those blanks. Now what I'm left with is just that: blank.

CHAPTER THREE
AMERICAN PALE ALE

A golden to light-brown ale with medium to medium-high hop flavor and aroma. Classic.

I'm back at the bar working a serving shift. The lights in the brewing area illuminate the tanks, but no one's back there tonight. I want to be, even if it means sanitizing an already-spotless mash tun. It would at least feel like progress toward my end goal.

My end goal is not to serve drinks for trivia night. Yet here I am.

It's *Seinfeld* trivia. Me and trivia—not such great pals. I'm more a visual learner versus a memorizing-facts type of gal. Learning about beer brewing from Joe has been perfect, since I've been able to see everything as it happens.

Joe isn't here tonight. He's doing okay and starting intensive treatments, according to Prairie. For now, it's business as usual.

"Now look who showed up." I stop in front of a table left of the trivia leader, who's reading a question about candy falling into body crevices. *Ew.*

One of our regulars, Anthony, gives me a chin nod as greeting. "I've never seen a *Seinfeld*," he says.

"I've only seen a handful of episodes myself. I'm more of an *X-Files* or *Star Trek: TNG* fan when it comes to older TV."

Anthony gives me a full smile—a rarity, since Anthony is self-conscious about his teeth. Well, about the missing ones, anyway. His knuckles are chapped and weathered worse than I've seen in a while. "I'll take whatever's on a special."

"You got it." I linger. I have to ask. "You doing all right? Keeping warm out there?"

"I'm good. You know I'm always good." Anthony rubs his reddened, chapped hands together and blows on them, making a show about the staying-warm comment.

I knock on the table once, signaling I'll be back. I slide a small basket in front of him with two rolls made from our spent grain.

I can't help but worry. In the summers, Anthony drifts around the city, sleeping in parks and doorway alcoves. Sometimes he stays with friends. He has friends here at the pub but swears he'll never outstay his welcome with any of them. Now, in the winter? I don't know what he does. Neil and Sadie agreed Anthony could crash with us a few weeks back when the temps dipped to single digits. Anthony refused my offer. He insisted he could take care of himself.

I add a pint of Dragon's Scrag IPA to Anthony's tab. The tab is for inventory purposes only, as Prairie insists on paying his tab herself every month. Most of us chip in to cover when we can. Anthony is young, but he's steady, regularly bringing in friends who settle their bills the same night and often take care of his too. He's helped us book a few local bands. He's good people.

A group of dudes with gray beards in biker jackets high-five each other after scoring a win about the actor who played George Costanza's father. I bring them all Wizard's Keep, a single-hop pale ale packaged in a fantasy art label. It goes well with our chili cheese fries.

Magda has full rein at the bar, while Alex runs tables along the front wall by the entrance. Trivia night brings in the foodies. We've got our beer cheese dip for house-made pretzels, which are always a hit. I zip to the kitchen and back three times with orders before I have a moment to catch my breath.

"Excuse me."

I turn to a table who must have seated themselves while I was in the kitchen. "Yeah. What can I get you?"

The man is my parents' age, in a black business suit. Ruddy face, but probably a looker back in the day when his scowl wasn't his primary feature. He blinks, then squints at me. "Marcus?"

"Huh? Oh, my apron." The name *Marcus* is written on it with permanent marker. I never knew a Marcus who worked here; it's just an apron I grabbed. "Sorry, I'm Kat. We don't have name tags here." Resistance Brewpub T-shirts make up our uniform, paired with whatever pants we want. Tonight I'm wearing black leggings—with safety pins zigzagging the outer seam—underneath knee-high black boots that look badass and hide my comfort insoles.

The man manages to scowl harder, like a real deep dig into scowl country. I shift tactics. "We have our winter brew on tap. That's a wheat with low hops and light fruit sweetness. We also have our custom IPAs, which will be more bitter and hoppy. Or a barrel-aged nut-brown, aged in a whiskey barrel with a real malt-forward flavor profile."

"Can I have a Budweiser? Or is that like speaking Chinese around here?"

My smile freezes. Racist shade aside, we can handle a commercial beer. "Of course. Would you like a menu?"

He stares blankly.

"For food?"

"You sell food in this place?" He casts a wary look at the bikers, then to Anthony's table, where he slouches over his pint, layers of clothes piled on top of each other. His gaze swings the other direction. This one group of Gen Xers still repping their 1990s goth culture absolutely crushes at trivia night. The sight of their black hair, black eyeliner, and the guy in a cape might be too much for this customer.

I set the menu on the table in front of him. "I'll leave this right here."

Grabbing the beer he wants from the bar fridge, I pour it into a Resistance-branded pint glass. All kinds of patrons stop through the bar, including grouchy guys. It happens. We bring in locals all week, suburbanites on weekends, sometimes families with kids. You never know when you'll find a repeat customer who loves the beer or the atmosphere.

I have the distinct impression Grouchy Suit Guy does not dig the atmosphere.

Resistance's vibe is nonmanufactured rustic. Exposed brick outer walls, ancient hardwood floors. High ceilings with pipes running along a painted-black ceiling. Our decor is primarily band posters—the Grateful Dead, Joy Division, Tina Turner (from *Thunderdome*)—mixed in with framed prints of our custom Resistance-label art commissioned for the small-batch brews. Joe and Prairie are big on using Chicago artists for the labels. They send press releases around to the media to feature the artists' work when a seasonal brew is released. Whose job will that be when they're gone?

Gone.

I add as much sunshine to my personality as allowable as I serve Grouchy Suit Guy. I make a point to check on him extra times, though he seems more interested in his phone than anything else. The goths are a fountain of *Seinfeld* information every time I stop by. I almost forget the crushing reality of c a n c e r and career uncertainty.

I finally get another second to myself and lean my elbows against the bar, watching Magda's magnetic smile enchant another sucker. She's so taken, and these guys never want to believe it. I pull my phone from my apron and check my messages to see whether Sadie is stopping by or if she's suddenly gained a life and abandoned me.

"Careful with that."

The comment stills me. Not the comment, but the voice who says it. I turn against my better judgment, even though I prefer not to.

It's Mr. Hottie McWet Pants. When the *Mc* got added, I don't know, but that's his name now.

"Uh, hi." I summon my sunshiny, good-customer-service face. "I see you have the winter lager. Nice choice."

I'd like to say he laughs and all is well, but he's staring at me in a way that indicates he's categorizing my faults, of which there are many. Visible ones, too. The Marcus apron, for starters. Dried ketchup on my sleeve, for second. A zit on my chin I stupidly picked, so now it's red and covered over with too much concealer (a misnomer, if you ask me, since all a concealer does is clump around the part you're trying to smooth over). Meanwhile, Hottie McWet Pants is as frustratingly good looking as he was the first time he came in.

"I'm surprised you don't have the game on." He nods to the two TVs over the bar. One is tuned to MMA fighting, the other to an action movie I can't name.

"Which game?" The second I ask, I know it's the wrong question. I lean over the bar in search of the remote. It's out of reach, so I crook a knee onto the stool and scoot my body to lay across the wooden bar top and grab it. I slide back to the floor and hand him the remote. "Here. Turn it to whatever you want."

He looks at the remote in my hand, then at me. His mouth is parted. I wouldn't call it a gawk per se, since this isn't a guy who gawks. At least not with his mouth hanging open. No, this is a judgy stare. And I'm being decimated by it.

The guy swivels in his seat, taking in the bar's clientele. Then he takes the remote and clicks a few buttons. A basketball game shows up on screen.

"The Bulls! Hometown team." I try to come up with another sports thing to say but come up empty.

Magda slides over. "Everyone good over here?"

The guy does that thing where it's part laugh, part haughty huff. Haughty. That's the right word for him.

"Must not have hated it here that much if you came back," I tell him.

He looks at me again, his brow furrowed. This guy is a golden ale, if I've ever seen one in human form. Smooth, easygoing, no dominant malt or hops. Just somewhere in the middle and generally restrained. One might say boring, but he made the blow-dryer joke the other day, so he has to have some sense of humor.

"Let me know if you need a blow," I say with a quirk to my smile.

His chiseled jaw gapes. Now there's a reaction. Not a gawk, but it's close.

"Uh, Kat? You okay?" Magda is likely not horrified but loving the awkwardness. It is *very* hard to ruffle Magda.

"A *blow-dry*," I say, as if this is super obvious. "To the *crotch*." I laugh in a way that lets them know I'm in on the joke.

He doesn't laugh.

"The other day, when the pint spilled—"

"You mean when you threw your phone," he says.

"Yes, when the phone knocked into the beer and it spilled—"

"The phone you threw that knocked it over."

This guy. "Right. It . . . you know what? I'm sorry. Again, I'm sorry."

His mouth forms a thin line. Even like that, his lips still have a fullness to them. His hard stare only makes him look more like a guy from one of those unintelligible designer cologne commercials.

Suddenly, Grouchy Suit Guy is standing next to me. "Finally, someone with sense turned on the game." He tosses down a handful of bills. Singles, from the looks of it. "Too late. Though it's probably not as interesting as what's on your phone," he reprimands me. He puts on a hat and starts for the door.

I twist to look back at his table. An empty glass and wadded napkin remain. Dang it. He cashed himself out and thinks I was ignoring him.

"Excuse me." Hottie McWet Pants snags the sleeve of Grouchy Guy. "Did you tip?"

The man turns with a full-force grimace. "Sorry? You're asking if I left them"—he points menacingly at me and Magda—"additional money? For the service they didn't provide?"

"It's okay," I tell Hottie.

"It's not okay. I saw you bring his food and a beer. A few bucks doesn't cover the bill, let alone a tip."

The man sneers at Hottie. "What, is she your girlfriend?" He digs into his coat pocket. "If you're chained to this train wreck, you need this more than I do." He turns to leave, but not before tossing a few more crumpled singles at Hottie.

I have very stable tracks, thankyouverymuch. Only a mild derailment today.

"Don't let the door hit you," Magda calls out through a red-lipped smile.

Hottie flattens the bills on top of his own cash. He hands the stack to me. "Some people are just assholes."

He drapes his luxurious scarf around his neck and stands from the stool.

Magda and I both watch him leave. I can't fully explain it, but his walk is both confident and communicates severe disappointment. It's an exit worthy of a movie.

"That is a beautiful man," Magda says.

I sort through the cash left on the bar, feeling the sting of responsibility for two customers walking out. "Here, let's split this." I divide the cash and slide her share across the bar.

She pushes it back. "Oh no, that's all you. The man was defending your honor."

Today is a cold one. Single digits, gray sky, searing wind arrowing between buildings. Trudging across the road to Resistance fully mummified in a puffer coat, I couldn't be happier.

One more down. I paid off a store credit card and sliced it for my debt-busting collage. My found-objects art hangs above the key holder at the apartment, so I see it every time I come home or leave. Mod Podge lingers on my fingertips from the latest victim. Sure, I could cut up the card before I pay it off, but there's something cathartic and downright joyful about snipping into a string of numbers now that the debt doesn't own me.

My main credit card is a different sitch, but that sitch is a worry for a different day. I pay more than minimum payments every month, and I'm doing my level best. Celebrate the victories. And I'm celebrating today.

"Hey, girl, you're almost late." Magda gives me a stern look from behind the bar as soon as I'm in view. Silver rings line each finger above short, painted-red nails that match her lipstick.

Crafting with credit cards maybe took longer than I thought—and I was supposed to be in early for a staff meeting. "Good thing there's no such thing as *almost* late." I smirk at her. Magda hates tardiness.

"You doing okay?" she asks me.

I missed a shift for not feeling well—winter-crud cold. The last couple days have consisted of lying on the couch watching old *Star Treks*. "I popped some vitamin C and ate chicken soup. I'm good."

She gives me a skeptical look. "You sure about that? I texted to ask how you were doing, and you went off about how the women of the *USS Enterprise* were the united force holding space exploration together. I had to Google the *USS Enterprise*, by the way. And did you fall asleep on your phone or something? Because the rest of what you sent was keyboard spaghetti and a link to a YouTube video about fermenting yeast."

That sounds about right. I drifted in and out yesterday, preferring to sleep if I couldn't do anything productive. I wasn't sure if I spotted Neil in his cabin crew uniform stopping by to sleep for a night or if it was a hazy memory of Commander Riker.

Magda comes over to me from around from the bar. I stand a good five inches taller than her, due more to her being short than to me being particularly tall.

"Hey, how are you doing?" I ask. "Your honey feeling better?"

Magda's husband—her *honey*, as she always refers to him—has been in bad health, but she's tight-lipped on details. I try to give her the space she needs.

"He's okay. We're filing papers for disability. It's a thrill a minute."

"I'm sorry."

She turns my body for me to look across the bar. "You ready to meet the new owner?"

"The owner is here?" It had to happen sometime. Avoidance tactics and Captain Picard can't stop reality. I sigh, resigned to this fate. "Okay. Let's talk to this burrito."

"Huh?"

"Benny Burrito? Remember?"

"Oh. No, that's the investor's name. There's a different person coming in to run the day-to-day stuff. Like Prairie spelled out in the email. Did you even read the email?"

"I skimmed it." Obviously, I read the part about being here for a meeting. I didn't care to read details about the person they'd sold their livelihood to. It was pretty easy to mentally press my back against the brain door and not think about any of it. While simultaneously also thinking about it.

I'm not *fully* in denial—just dipping a toe in, then maybe a foot or another limb. I like testing what it's like to pretend nothing will actually change and seeing how long it holds.

I mean, the chances of this new owner being a mentor for me are basically zilch. Those days are over. I never knew I needed a mentor until I had one. Joe challenged me with learning new skills at a time when all I wanted was to hide from the world (but couldn't, because bills) or sleep (which isn't good in fifteen-hour stretches if you want to escape depression).

I suppose he was a father figure, though I have a father I like quite a bit. He's different from Joe. My dad golfs and watches guys yell red faced about finance on basic cable news. I can't say I've ever had a conversation with him about my passions. A good-natured "You're doing great, honey. Don't be so hard on yourself!" is about the extent of our deep talks. And that's fine, because that's who he is. And my mom's attention is so focused on Karrie, I don't like to bother her.

There's been something about coming to Resistance all this time, how it's grown from part-time work to a place I see myself investing in long-term, that feels broken now. I can't see weeks ahead, let alone months or years, and it scares me. I don't want to think about it, but here I am. Time to face what's next.

Change and I have a beef with each other. Or I have a beef with change. Change, I imagine, does not have an opinion of me, because it is not sentient.

This is how my brain works. It's a fun place inside this skull.

Magda looks past me. "There."

I whip around and scan the pub. Several older women in suburban going-out uniforms cluster by the door. Black tops, jeans, black-heeled boots of varying heights. A thrill sings through me. "Which one?" I didn't expect an aging boomer mama to take over the bar, but it makes sense, given Prairie and Joe's connections. Maybe an ex-hippie or a veteran of the women's movement? I could be down.

"Not them. Over there."

I angle to look beyond her. Besides the women, a bearded regular sits by himself with a laptop open at the table. Another guy I've seen once or twice stands at the classic pinball machine, wearing an open flannel over a Soul Asylum T-shirt paired with baggy jeans and Doc Martens. The nineties may be alive in Portland, but they breathe in pockets of Chicago too.

The only other person in the bar has his back to us and is talking to Alex. Close-cropped hair, blazer and medium-wash jeans.

Magda winces. "I'm sorry, Kat."

"Why? I only see a Chad."

"His name isn't Chad. It's Ryan."

"I don't mean his name is Chad but that he is *a* Chad. The type of guy who would be named Chad."

Given the blank-stare response, clearly I'm not explaining this right.

I try again. "A guy likely to be named—"

"I'm pretty sure it's Ryan. And he's going to run Resistance."

The words she says are in English, but it's like they're arranged in the wrong order, so the syntax is off.

"That's the new guy," she says again, since I'm like a woodland creature blinded by an oncoming car.

"He's too young," I blurt. I still have only a back view, but the guy looks too young to be an owner of a brewpub. Not to be ageist or anything; I'm young, and I want to be a brewer. Okay, I'm young*ish*. Twenty-seven and still on the young side of life if I don't venture to Pitchfork Fest. Everyone there is so painfully obviously of the next undefined generation that I'm like their babysitter.

"Calling Major Kat. Come in, Kat."

My thoughts scramble to push that proverbial door shut again, but it's flung open and it's windy outside. Or whatever. The door is staying open. "Sorry."

"We should introduce ourselves. The guy hasn't even started, and we're already judging him."

Well, obviously. That's how judging works. You base your opinion on zero real information and flashes of impressions. "So our new boss is a Chad who wears faded frat-party shirts from ten years ago to the gym. Not because they still fit but because he doesn't realize it's been a decade since undergrad."

"You're such a snob."

"I'm not a snob. I just know how to call them. I can profile a white, middle-class bro who graduated from a state school to a frightening degree. I guarantee you he was in a fraternity."

She should be glaring at me or tossing back a sassy quip. She looks pitying. A little worried.

I freeze.

The guy across the room shifts position to a profile view. He's like an image in a J. Crew catalog. Or one of those cologne . . .

Aw, shoot. A chiseled jaw like a movie hero. The hero who wears a Burberry scarf, not a faded fraternity shirt.

The Chad turns fully toward us and makes eye contact. I stare. Not a Chad. A Ryan.

"Maybe time to make a good second impression?" Magda says.

"Third. Third impression."

Mr. Hottie McWetPants is named Ryan. And he's our new boss.

CHAPTER FOUR

IMPERIAL INDIA PALE ALE

A pale ale with more hop bitterness than an American
pale ale, gold to light brown. For when you want all
the bitters.

Magda is herding me toward Hottie Mc—Ryan, our new boss.
The guy I've gotten started with on a foot so wrong it's an elbow.

"Get a hold of yourself, woman," Magda says. "You know we
run this place."

We *did*. Under the easy guidance of Prairie and Joe, who let us
be who we are. We were treated like family. And like in a family,
something horrible and tragic happened, upending the very roots
I cling to.

"Good afternoon." He nods at Magda first, then me. "I'm
Ryan." Then he does a thing that shocks me.

He smiles.

Oh dear god, is it a good one too. A prodding pokes at me
from not so deep within. It's Tween Kat, popping up to make sure
I notice Hottie Ryan's smile and how he looks like he should be

on TV. A medical drama, because TV doctors are the ones with those defined jawlines. Or a serial killer profiler on a premium cable show. Yeah. He could be either.

It's never too late for a third chance at making a lukewarm impression. "Hello. I'm Kat. I don't believe we ever formally were introduced." Holy passive word salad. I smile and feel my teeth tighten.

He's still smiling. It's practically vacuum-sealed to his face. "I disagree. It was a memorable introduction." He has an honest-to-goodness twinkle in his eye.

I am murderous. "Should we turn on the game?"

Magda kicks me in the shin.

Ryan laughs. Not a drop of tension on his face either. Why should he be tense? He's taking over Resistance. He has the power here.

But who appointed him? And why? I really should have checked my email.

He clasps his hands together and looks past us to the brew tanks. "Let's get everyone together."

Magda shoots me a glare and mouths *Be nice* before she drops by the table of women in black tops.

Ugh. *Nice* is a state of being that gets a person stepped on, used, forgotten. Being nice is still texting your ex when he's so clearly moved on, he's creating more humans to move on with.

I stop by Bearded Laptop's table and let him know we'll be in a meeting in view through the big window. "Wave if you need anything." I pause before I join the others. "No, really. You should wave in maybe three minutes. I'll stand near the door."

Inside the brewing area, I take a spot beside Luiz. He arches a brow at me without moving an inch elsewhere. "Looks like Zack Morris is our new manager." He rolls his eyes.

I snicker. I can always count on Luiz for petty comments. Except he's wrong. "Zack Morris has way more of a rectangle face."

"I don't mean the actor, gata," Luiz says, calling me the Spanish name for cat, aka Kat, his nickname for me. "I mean, like, his overall thing. He's Preppy. Like Slater called him."

Luiz is older than me and must have actually watched *Saved by the Bell*. I've never gotten past the outdated clothes and how there were only eight other students in the whole school. Still, if Luiz finds this guy suspect, I'm for it. I chuckle and make a show of it. "Yeah. Preppy. Like Slater said."

Ryan positions himself in front of the gleaming stainless-steel fermenting tank, and it's like a brochure on the art of craft brew itself. He's wearing a soft blazer over a T-shirt with a graphic print. I think it's stars and abstract lines. Professional but not stuffy. Generic enough not to offend anybody. His jeans are fitted but not skinny, and his black leather boots shine without a hint of salt or snow scum. He's the kind of guy who stashes a travel shoe polish kit in his messenger bag.

"Stop. Judging." Magda's stage whisper comes at me from the right.

"I'm not—" I stop. I am. I'm letting pettiness get the better of me, and it's not a good look. I know it isn't and I know better. I should give this guy his shot. Or at the very least, the appearance of giving him a shot.

"Hello, everyone," Ryan says from a comfortable wide stance. "Prairie said she filled you in on what's happening with ownership and the daily running of Resistance. She wanted to share the news before I came in. She also suggested I meet with you all without her here. By the way, she says Joe is resting and doing well. They'll be in touch."

I clench my fist so hard my nails dig grooves into my palms. We are all perfectly capable of staying in touch with Prairie and Joe.

Luiz tosses another exaggerated eye roll my way. Luiz, a true imperial pale ale. A stronger-hopped IPA substantially more bitter than his counterparts.

"I imagine you have questions. First, if I can say, I'm so pumped to be here. I've never lived in the city of Chicago proper but have always loved it. I'm here just about every weekend—"

"In the Viagra Triangle," Luiz side-chats to me.

I bite my lip to keep from laughing too loud.

"And being family friends with Joe and Prairie," Ryan continues, "it means so much to have this opportunity. My family is so honored to be able to invest in the brewpub. You're in good hands."

Wait a sec here. So Ryan is friends with Joe and Prairie, and so is the investor. And he said his family is honored . . .

I lean toward Luiz. "What's Ryan's last name?"

He shrugs. His brow rises again. "It's same as the Burrito guy. Not Burrito."

My eyes widen. "Bennett? Are you kidding me? He's the son of Benny the Burrito Bennett?"

The room is silent. I look up, and everyone is staring at us. Ryan's mouth twitches as his gaze darts around the room. It's the first sign I've seen that he may not have full control of his cool.

Ryan is the investor's son? So, what, they just handed him this bar to run? How does that work? Though—I could be being hasty here. He obviously has restaurant experience. No investor would hand over managing a brewpub to someone who doesn't have restaurant management experience. I wave my hand to signal for him to continue, feeling heat in my cheeks over causing a distraction.

I glance out the window to the customers. Does Bearded Laptop need a refill? Some cheese fries? A listening ear?

No one in the pub looks our way. The black-topped ladies are laughing and drinking, oblivious to us. I wish I were them.

Ryan is back to talking, and it's all about the rise of craft brews and Chicago's rich beer history. He's not saying anything every single one of us doesn't already know.

I shoot my hand into the air.

Ryan shifts to angle toward me. "Uh, yes?"

"You said we might have questions. I have one. What's your experience working in a brewpub?"

Luiz snickers beside me. Magda, I'm sure, is sending me death rays, but both of them should be wondering the same thing.

"I'm a fan of and support brewpubs and taprooms. I have great respect for small brewers. Like I said, I'm grateful for the opportunity. As I was saying, in Chicago, the number of microbreweries and—"

My hand goes up again. "Excuse me."

Ryan's mouth twitches again. "Of course. How about let's open this up to questions."

Yes, let's. "Have you run a restaurant before?"

He has that plastic-sealed smile on his face again. "I have not. This is a first for me."

The air in the room grows heady and thick.

Anya raises a hand. "Will you post open shifts online? To our group chat, I mean? Prairie never kept up with it, but it would be a huge help. I don't always check my email."

Ryan blinks. "Uh, yeah. We can talk about that. I have a lot to learn, so that was going to be my next point. I'll need to learn from you all. I'll be shadowing each of you and asking a lot of questions. You'll be the ones teaching me."

A cough sounds from across the room. It's Alex, and I'm pretty sure the word *bullshit* was uttered within it.

The air has thickened to curdling. I feel sick. This guy has no experience. He knows nothing. His father, Benny the Burrito, used his Big Burrito money to buy out Resistance and stuck his son in charge of it. How did that conversation go? *Hey, son. You know the hippie bar in Chicago our friends run? Yeah, we're buying it to help them out. Want a job?*

Like, imagine being handed a business to run. Just handed it. With zero experience. And *we're* supposed to teach him? In what universe is this okay?

I raise my hand again.

"Kat," Magda warns.

I don't wait for anyone to acknowledge my hand. "Who is brewmaster?"

Everyone is looking at me, and this time I know it's because they've got my back. This is what my mental door has been keeping shut. I need to know who I'll be working with. Who I'll need to contend with.

Ryan perks up. "We have open postings now. I think we'll find some great candidates, given the climate for craft brews in the city."

Open postings, plural. "You said postings, as in multiple. Which jobs are posted?"

Ryan is slowly nodding. "Good question, good question. We'll have a few open spots for experienced brewers, since Joe and Edwin are both leaving."

"Git 'em, Kat!" Luiz whisper-shouts.

Ryan blinks, looking between us. "Is there something . . . anything else I can answer?"

Hands rise everywhere. I shake my head no and step back, signaling I'm done. The questions continue about hours, shifts, schedules, booking bands. Ryan's go-to is "I'll look into that."

I have what I need. I can apply for an open position and bring my expertise and grunt work to the new brewers. There's still a chance I'll get what I want. I'm going to trust what Joe said. Life has a way of working itself out.

CHAPTER FIVE
BLONDE ALE

Light to medium ale with low hop bitterness and spiced
or subtle fruit notes. Pretty basic, just sayin'.

The past few days, an anxious restlessness has surfaced. I'm worried about the job application and my experience. My seeming lack of experience on paper.

I stack an empty crate too hard, causing it to topple over.

Alex peeks into the stock room. "Need help?"

"I'm fine," I snap. "Sorry. I'm . . . on edge."

"Tell me it's not about Poetry Daddy."

I snort. Now there's a nickname I'll immediately adopt and never give up. "Uh, no. I haven't thought much about him. I'd rather be brewing." I sound like a bad T-shirt slogan. "I'm not trying to be helpless about it. I've been searching courses to take for brewing certification, and I just . . ." How do I say this? "I don't want to go back to school. Like, at all."

Alex leans against the doorframe. "So don't go back to school. I'm taking a break, and the world didn't end. Besides, you can work at a brewery without being certified. People do it all the time."

He's right, but I can't quell the uneasy feeling cropping up every time I think about this. "Nothing was official with Joe and Edwin. I was just helping them out. And I have tons to learn." It's almost easy to find reasons my dreams won't work.

"You know a dude would apply for the job and make the rest up."

"I'm not going to lie on a job application. The posting states at least a year of brewing experience, and I've only been helping out here for six months."

"You've done more than *help out*, Kat. You've done the whole process with Edwin. You invented a recipe with Joe. You filled in days Joe wasn't here."

All I can hear are the qualifiers. *With Edwin. With Joe. Filled in.*

I run my fingers along the apron hem. "It's one thing to be Joe's sidekick in training, but I don't know who we're going to end up with." I want to say I'm simply not ready, but maybe that's life, happening regardless of whether anyone's ready.

"You're overthinking. Apply. See what happens. Go from there."

So simple. So impossible. "What's it like to not overthink?"

"Beats me. That's why I tell other people what to do."

Fair enough.

Alex's eyes water at the sides. "I'm real bummed about Joe."

"I'm sorry." I lean toward him, a gentle side lean that's part hug, part *I won't crowd you and your feelings.* I see Alex as a Bohemian Pilsner with a distinct, comforting flavor. Maybe it's his Eastern European roots. His great-grandparents immigrated here from Ukraine and his remaining family still lives in the neighborhood.

So do his parents, and Alex with them. Alex is sensitive and strong with a fierce commitment to family.

Alex slouches against the wall. "I don't know what this place will be like with the new owner. It could get . . . different."

This disruption has unique effects on each of us. "We'll watch out for each other." With Ryan not knowing anything and Investor Daddy at the wheel, maybe things won't change all that much. We can keep the culture. The vibe. "Hopefully, things will stay the same, just with someone else paying the bills."

We leave the storeroom together and each do a quick scan of the bar. Alex circles back to me. "You're not naïve enough to believe that, though, right?"

"What do you mean?"

"Joe and Prairie ran this place like an *Oliver Twist* stage production. We're their little orphans. No one else coming in is going to care like that."

"You don't know what it will be like. Ryan could be moldable. He certainly looks like he was created from a mold."

"True." Alex shifts weight from one boot to another. "My feet are killing me. Anyway, stay strong, Ponytail Girl." He playfully tosses my side pony. "Don't worry about your qualifications. Just apply for the open job and don't doubt. You've come too far to regress."

I give him a light shove. Here's Alex giving me therapy tips when he's been through hell and back fighting his own severe depression. That his family accepted his transition from the jump when he was a teenager helped him carve out a safe place at home with his parents. His break from college is going on three years now, a fact he's sensitive about but determined not to obsesses over.

"I won't let the new guy ruin what we have," I promise him. "All I know is, this is the only place I've truly enjoyed working. I hated working in health care. I liked *having* health care, but

working in it? No. I don't want a master's degree in public health."
Not anymore. That much I know for sure. "If it takes everything I
have to keep Resistance the way it's meant to be, I'll do it."

Already I feel better about the day. I have a goal and a purpose. Once I get going, I'm a force near unstoppable.

Later that night, Ryan strolls into the pub, his steps fast and deliberate. He stops, looks at the bar, and proceeds to the back office.
Magda and Luiz are both off tonight, and Anya is in her own
world memorizing stats during her downtime for a test tomorrow.
Her soft black Afro bobs in time to the music in her headphones.
I've agreed to take on her side work. A nice stack of flatware rolled
in napkins sits on the bar, ready to go.

Ryan emerges from the office after five minutes and joins me
at the bar, sitting on a stool like a customer. Something about this
feels unexpected. He could have come right behind the bar and
pulled a drink from the tap, given he's Top Cheese now. Or more
like Top Burrito. Though I don't think of burritos when I look at
Ryan. I can't imagine an aged-up Ryan who can eat a burrito as big
as your head, or whatever the legend of the college burrito tale is.

Ryan is definitely more on edge than I've seen him so far. A
little jittery. A touch twitchy. Face still perfect, but everyone has
flaws.

Ryan swings his attention to the TVs. I intentionally put on
basketball and a golf documentary. The golf TV looks like the
program switched to an infomercial on Instant Pots. I grab the
remote and land on a crime procedural. Ryan really does look like
he could fit with the cast.

"Kat. How are you doing?"

I keep my voice light. "I'm good."

He glances around the bar. "It's dead. Is this usual?"

"It's a Thursday in the middle of winter." I think back to the past few weeks. "Seems about right."

Ryan is still looking over his shoulder at a customer sitting at a corner table with a laptop open. "Is that guy even ordering anything?"

"He had Prairie Wheat thirty minutes ago. Anya checked on him, and he's good for now."

He sighs. "This isn't free office space. If they're going to sit here, they should be drinking. Or eating."

Alex's words float back, his worries about how the pub might change. Pestering people to order more or make them feel unwelcome if they don't would be a direct violation of everything Joe and Prairie have built. Regulars hang out here because nobody bothers them.

"Go through a typical day for me." Ryan gives me his full attention. "Working here, I mean."

I hold back from commenting on the mild insult—where he felt he had to clarify that he meant work and not, like, what soap I use in the shower in the morning.

Having Ryan's full attention feels a bit unnerving. The man's eyes are a honey golden brown and the white parts very, very white. Like bleached of all redness.

I've been waiting on this conversation since he said he wanted to shadow each of us. He hung around Magda last night, and she later reported he had asked similar questions about low customer patronage and slow nights. He'd also questioned whether young people came here on weekends or at all. To which Magda commented he wasn't allowed to look at her state ID card to check her age.

I nod to the customer in the corner. "He works out of an office on Sacramento. He's with an environmental justice nonprofit. Sometimes he comes here to unwind, but unwinding for him is still answering client emails. They're short-staffed and working on needed causes."

Ryan's with me but looks confused. "Okay . . ."

I point toward the other end of the room to a couple in their thirties. Two women. "They had their first date here in October. We did an Oktoberfest party, and one of them dressed in lederhosen. The other had on a German celebrity T-shirt. They were falling over themselves laughing from the start. They've been coming in a few times a month and always order black bean burgers and onion rings. When the fall lager went out, they switched to our winter ale."

I gesture toward the pinball machine. "That used to belong to a bowling alley up the road that was torn down to build condos. Joe rescued it. He salvaged wood used in the lanes and had a buddy make tables and those benches over there out of the reclaimed wood."

Ryan shakes his head. "What does this have to do with how you do your job?"

I finish the full stack of rolled flatware and step aside, leaning my arms against the bar top. "That's what Resistance is. We're our regulars and we're the history of the neighborhood. We're small and local. That's what Joe and Prairie wanted."

People often asked them why they hadn't expanded distribution. They did test limited distribution a few times over the years, but what they truly loved was this pub, the people, and keeping business small. They didn't have interest in growing so large another company had to buy them out. Though that's exactly what happened. Only it hadn't been their choice. Going with a family friend for the sale, they probably hoped the family would know enough not to question their direction. To maintain and preserve it.

"You want a drink?" I ask Ryan.

"No, I'm working. Why, are you drinking?"

"No. I'm working." I take a sample glass and go to the bar fridge. I find what I'm looking for and flip the cap off using the bar-mounted bottle opener. I tilt the glass and pour the straw-colored beer into the small glass and let the head settle. I move it in front of him. "Try this."

He takes the glass, pauses for perhaps a half sniff, and downs it shot-style. Swallows. Blinks. "Is this some kind of test? You want me to describe the flavors?"

"You can if you want. I thought you might like it is all."

"Kind of plain. Not bad."

"It's a golden ale—blonde ale. It's simple, crisp. We try to please a variety of beer drinkers."

"Can I see?" He reaches for the bottle, and so do I. Our fingers graze.

We each spring back. For a hot second we're tweens who've dared hold hands on the bus. He looks one way and I look the other.

"This isn't one of our ales," I tell him, to get us back on track. "It's from a microbrewery in the city. We tend to keep some on hand."

He's looking at me like he wants to say something, but he doesn't. I'm looking back at him like I want him to say something, but I'm not sure I do. He is nice to look at, though.

"So," I say.

He straightens on the stool. "So. Yes. Local beers on hand. Got it."

I kind of like seeing him nervous. Or whatever his state is. It's . . . sweet. No, he's not actually a *sweet* kind of guy. Maybe fermenting glucose. "Since you know Prairie and Joe as a family, you know their commitment to community. I imagine that's why they chose you for the job."

He doesn't respond, instead drumming his fingers against the counter. "You've been working with Joe. On brewing."

It's not a question, but I treat it like one. "Yes."

"You've been here a year or so?"

I nod. This is my chance to ease in about the job. How Joe had me in the books but not officially, because that would have required writing something down. Okay, not fair to Joe. He's great at brewing, but he's been doing it so long it's second nature. Brewing guidelines? Yes. Miscellaneous paperwork? Not so much. One might say he has a *life has a way of figuring it out* approach to paperwork.

Ryan continues. "I know a lot of you here consider Joe and Prairie like a second family. You're obviously closer to them than I ever was. It's my parents who know them. I hardly do."

I have no idea where this is leading. "Alex says we're like their band of misfits." I squeeze my eyes shut. "I mean, a highly functional band of individuals from differing backgrounds. Functional misfits."

"Yeah, that feels accurate. I'm seeing some things here I think could be done differently. Like, at a personal level. More surface things to help with branding and the image of Resistance. Starting with the staff."

"I thought you were shadowing me. Now you want to give advice?"

It's as if little tufts of steam rise from his collar. A periwinkle-and-white-striped button-up collar more fitting for a cubicle job than here. "I asked you about the job, and you told me life histories of your customers and about a torn-down bowling alley. Then you poured me a beer. I don't think you comprehend the state of Resistance, Kat."

The way he tacks my name onto the end of his little reprimand makes me want to roll up my sleeves and say *Yeah? You and what army?* In my imagination I'm a scrappy do-gooder ready to brawl.

"All right, then. Since you seem to understand the state of things, please go ahead and suggest your personal-but-not-personal recommendations."

He stands and takes out a notebook from his back pocket. He flips it open and clears his throat. "For starters, uniforms. I'm thinking polos with the Resistance logo embroidered here." He touches the upper left of his own shirt. "Or a button-down in denim with the logo."

I choke on air. "A *denim embroidered shirt*?" Those three words should never be strung together. "That . . . that's a clothing item that exists?"

His cheeks color beneath his beard scruff. "A classic polo or button-down shirt is professional. Denim is casual. It strikes a balance."

"Would *you* wear embroidered denim?"

He opens his mouth and shuts it.

That's what I thought.

"It's not like the whole thing is embroidered," he says. "Just the logo."

He actually looks energized by this point, as if he's blocked my shot with a defensive move.

"What's wrong with the T-shirts?"

He makes a show of looking around. "Which T-shirts? I don't see any Resistance emblems on the front or back."

I tug at what I'm wearing. I have a long-sleeved waffle layer beneath a plain black shirt. All of it clean. "My Resistance shirts are all in the laundry."

"Anya doesn't have on a branded shirt either. Hers has a line drawing comic on it about taxes."

"She's studying to be an accountant. We can't save everyone."

He doesn't join my attempt at humor. "The staff looks sloppy. It's hard to tell who works here. Some of you wear aprons; some of

53

you don't. The aprons you do have look like rags tossed out from another restaurant."

Do I tell him? That he's right? How Prairie thought she'd won the jackpot when a nearby restaurant went out of business? Boxes of secondhand aprons, dishrags, towels, and extra bar supplies all became ours.

Something tells me Ryan wouldn't appreciate any of that.

"What else is on your list?" I ask.

He flips to another page. "More flat-screens, but that costs money. More branded glassware, but that costs money. More online advertising—also costs money."

"Almost like running a business costs money."

He levels a look at me. "I went to business school. I've been working in an actual business for five years postgrad. I'm not a total idiot."

He's exasperated. I've surely contributed to this, and yet it's hard to scare up pity. "If I can ask, what made you take this on? A love of craft beer and a heart of gold?"

His jaw goes to stone and he stares past me. All that's behind me is the bar and a giant, dirty mirror. The man is seeing himself reflected back. Symbolism, or a pretty image? I turn and take a peek. Damn, he is a good-looking guy. I turn back to face him. Damn Part Deux, he is *very* good looking.

He looks at me with a thread of determination hanging on. "I want Resistance to succeed."

"I would hope so. You're running the place."

"I'm not your enemy, is what I mean." He looks at his hands knotted together. "I didn't get the greatest first impression of this place, but it doesn't mean I don't care. I could have walked away. I didn't. I'm here."

I take this in. I'm being petty, aren't I? Miffed because . . . because I don't understand how we've gotten here. Joe is suddenly sick, though it wasn't all that sudden. Joe has been sick enough for long enough that he and Prairie were forced to tell us about it. They'd kept it from the kids all that time. Our parents hadn't been truthful with us. We're a family, and a dysfunctional one, after all. That hurts.

But that's not Ryan's fault.

I believed Joe and Prairie when they told me I could be their successor. A little time and elbow grease and I'd be running the joint myself. Maybe that was a lie. Or a platitude, more like. They might have told me only what I wanted to hear, being heartbroken and directionless. I gave up on a career I'd thought I wanted and instead found solace, joy, here with them. Maybe that solace was fleeting and temporary.

Maybe they never believed I'd marry the beer. Maybe it was simply a fun thing to say.

"I've been defensive," I tell Ryan. "I take everything about this place to heart." I look him over. There's more. He's legitimately stressed. "I know this is all new to you, but what's going on that has you so worried?"

"It's . . . it's nothing. It's not anything I should be talking to you about."

I fold my arms. "Something you'll get pretty quick, if you haven't yet, is we function like a family around here. For better or worse. If you keep information from staff, you're going to find it hard to fit in here."

He grumbles something under his breath. It's nothing short of amazing seeing him so flustered when the outward-facing product screams *put together.* He's the opposite of out-of-sorts. He is *sorts.* Or should be. Right now he seems confused by the very thought of being so confused.

"Look, despite our rough start . . ." Throwing phones, assigning him a pants-based nickname, and generally being awkward—all me. "I will help you. You think this place is a mess. I get it. If you're truly interested in learning about Resistance, I'll tell you what I know. I'll help you the best I can."

It does me no good to play adversary when I want him to hire me to work with the head brewer. He needs to recognize me as competent, knowledgeable, helpful.

I can almost see his guard step back. His shoulders relax, and he straightens. "If you can listen to my ideas, I'm open to hearing yours."

If I can listen? The nerve . . . I internally tell myself to chill. Ryan holds access to what I want. I admitted to Alex earlier I was intimidated by that very thing. But it's my own hurdle to get over. This current learning-from-each-other arrangement could be a real positive. I'll consider his ideas—hopefully better ones than denim shirts—and then he'll listen to mine. Since I nearly live and breathe Resistance, he'll come to see the true Resistance vision. Inclusive and a little rusty on the edges. We'll be like a shadow regime. *I'm the captain now.*

It's only a matter of time before he'll come around. "I'm guessing Joe showed you the brew tanks?" I ask.

"Yeah. I've seen them."

"Do you know how they work?"

He shrugs. "I mean, I couldn't explain it if this is a quiz. But we'll get someone in with experience who knows what they're doing."

Perfect. "Okay. Follow me."

While people make up the soul of Resistance, back here, where the beer is made, is the heart. Where the blood pumps through the proverbial veins. Only these veins are stainless steel.

Each craft brewery I've been to has its own unique, visceral feel. I don't have synesthesia, but I do sense things in vivid and almost tactile ways. A brewery can be round and comforting or cold, sterile, and precise. I once visited a microbrewery that made me think of loose cats. It was cramped in a tight space in the back of a nearly collapsing old storefront, but the brewers knew what they were doing. Their setup seemed to defy physics. The brewery had nine lives, having survived a couple floods.

Resistance makes me think of backyards and field grass. I see a peaceful green when I'm back here. None of the walls or the floor or the tanks themselves are green. It's probably because of Joe and Prairie's aesthetic. Laid-back and all.

I don't know how to convey this to Ryan, though.

The glass doors to the pub close behind us. "It can get a little intense back here when things get going. When we're cleaning or performing lab work, not so much." I keep saying *we* like I'm a brewer. Oh well. "A lot of the process is physical, and a team needs to work together. When we grain out, because we're a small operation, we physically shovel out the spent grain. By hand." I flex an arm. "Cheaper than a gym membership."

He laughs. Maybe a little louder than he should.

"Hey! I know I'm not exactly cut, but I swear there's muscle beneath this soft flesh."

His face visibly colors at the word *flesh*. Okay, maybe lay off talking about flesh.

I lead him to the tables along the back wall, where instruments and beakers are arranged, all cleaned and organized. "To knock out the kettle requires temperature monitoring and checking on the yeast. We check the oxygen levels with the meters over here. You have to watch oxidation. Oxygen is introduced during the chilling and transferring wort stage. If the yeast pitch is too delayed, the wort oxidizes. It will get stale."

He nods. "So, timing is important."

"Exactly. It takes a team to do this well." I clear my throat. "Anyway, Prairie and Joe liked to keep our tap list unique. A few mainstays like Prairie Wheat, the Sunrise and Sunset collections. As IPAs gained popularity, they were right on that wave. That's why you see so many of the older biker crowd here mixed in with the younger fans. They've been cultivating a market for a long time. Before it was cool to the Pitchfork crowd."

He arches a brow.

"The music fest. Not, like, rioters."

"Right. Well, it sounds like you know your stuff."

I stop and look at him. This is it. Here's my chance. "I've been apprenticing under Joe and Edwin. Joe and I had an agreement, which I understand isn't an agreement anymore now that things have changed. All that to say, I'm putting in my application."

He seems to be waiting for more information, and finally asks, "For . . . ?"

"The open position you mentioned. For a brewer."

"But you're a server."

Working as a server isn't in itself offensive, but in context, the way Ryan says it, it's like a hand slap across my face.

"I've done the dirtiest, grimiest work to put in my time back here. And I *like* it." Key point. "The new hires will need someone familiar with what's at Resistance already. I would be an asset to the new team."

He absorbs this. "But are you qualified? I can't just let you back here because Joe did."

Inner rage, can you take five? Hard five. Go on, I'll wait.

I breathe out. "A shift brewer doesn't require certification. I'd like to take more coursework—I'm working on it. It's part of my career path to brewmaster."

Ryan seems puzzled by this but eventually nods. "Wow. Well, it's great to have goals. Thing is, the job description Joe gave spelled out the qualifications. I cross-checked these with the industry standard." He slips his hands into his pockets and paces the room, looking up at the tanks and the ductwork snaking across the ceiling. "Just because you work here already doesn't mean you have a fast track to the job."

Just because a daddy has the money to buy an establishment doesn't mean his son knows how to run the business. I clench my fists. "I know Resistance. I deserve a shot."

He has the nerve to give me a pitying look.

I can't let this go. "Really, if I had a piece of paper, that's what would do it? A stamp of approval?"

He takes in a measured breath. "We can expand. Do distribution. Really get going with a whole market we're missing out on. I need a professional team in here to do that." He pats a tank, leaving smudges against the surface. "I'm sorry if that doesn't fit your career path."

Flags in assorted red hues stand at attention in my peripheral. "Aren't you getting ahead of yourself? Joe and Prairie intentionally kept Resistance small."

Again, that bemused look. It's part pitying, part smarm. "Look at this place. If this is the number of customers who come in, who are we making all this beer for? What's the point? Distribution is where the money is."

The money. That's what this keeps coming back to. Obviously, any business needs to make a profit to operate, but getting into distribution to afford more flat-screens and—shudder—denim embroidery seems massively shortsighted. "Joe and Prairie built a community. I hope you keep that in mind with your grand expansion plan. Resistance is for regulars."

"Well, maybe the regulars should be more regular."

We've all but stopped talking about my application. "I'm still going to apply," I remind him. It's an open position, and I imagine Joe will want a say in the hiring, since he and Prairie still own the Resistance label.

Ryan is back to pacing and looking over the tanks. "Sure. Of course. Definitely do that."

Why does it feel like I've asked to stop for ice cream and Dad has said *We'll see*?

"I was thinking we stock up on more of the big sellers." Ryan lists off the names of several popular beers bought out by larger distributors.

"Those aren't craft brews."

"Yes they are."

"They were before they were bought out."

"The buyers finance the product. They back distribution. It's hard for small-timers to keep up with demand."

I know all this, and it's not the point. "Customers at Resistance don't want what they can get anywhere else. They want what we have specifically. Or in a pinch, what other small-batch brewers are making with limited distribution. That's why they come here."

He nods toward the window overlooking the pub. "That niche of a customer base isn't packing the seats. More popular beers could bring in customers looking for more common options."

"That beer I gave you to sample? We recommend it when a customer asks us for something light, not bitter. A taste to go with anything. The difference is, it supports a local business. Win-win."

He chooses a bottle from the display shelf by the door. "Devil's Maw? I mean, look at this. There's a creepy horned guy riding a surfboard over lava into some black hole. Not exactly mainstream stuff here."

"That label is from a limited run with art commissioned by Ami Wang, a well-known Chicago artist. She got picked up by an animation studio and works on a show for Adult Swim."

"Cool. Do you sell a lot of it?"

I grab the bottle from him. "We sold out of this run. We had a packed house for the release with a David Bowie cover band. There was a great write-up about the event in the *Reader*."

"And yet." He looks out to the empty seats. "I'm not saying what Resistance has isn't unique. I'm saying it's not bringing in enough people."

There's that word again. *Enough.*

What is ever enough for anybody? I never have quite *enough*. Not enough to pay off the credit card in full. Not enough to get something extra besides basic grocery staples and replenish leggings and underwear at Target. I wasn't enough for Alden . . .

No—I can't let myself mosey along that road. Resistance *was* enough. Now Ryan says it isn't.

"We're going to have a lapse until the brewmaster position is filled," Ryan continues. "So we're ordering from other sources to fill the need. I'm looking at the order histories to see what sells best." He's still talking about his big plans. Business business something something. "I'll supplement the rest."

"With garbage commercial beer."

"No, with popular, best-selling beer."

"That no one here will drink."

"That people who don't already come here who we want to come here will drink."

"In theory."

"In reality." Steam puffs off his collar. "Offering more options makes this place less of a sideshow."

I freeze in place. "Is that how you think of us? A sideshow?"

He seems to realize he's gone too far. He holds out a hand. "That's—not what I mean. It's too niche here. This place can't survive on catering only to this neighborhood with only this beer and few others."

"Resistance *has* survived." I hurt for Joe and Prairie if they were ever to hear this. "You're arrogant and don't know anything." There. Come back from that.

He throws up his hands. "I'm here, aren't I? Showing up. Doing what I have to do."

I scoff, loudly, so he can hear himself being scoffed at. "Why *are* you here? Boredom? Tired of spending Daddy's money? I think you'd be more comfortable in freaking Crystal Lake or whatever far-off burbclave you exist in. Drive in on weekends and go downtown clubbing. That's the Chicago you know. Not us and not this neighborhood."

He straightens and, to his credit, says nothing.

"You know, I was new here once too," I admit. "I can't claim I'm born and raised in Chicago. But I did learn to respect the people who've been here. Alex's family has three current generations living in Ukrainian Village. Just . . . just make sure you respect people. It's not about me and what I think but about what Resistance has been and what it means to people."

Ryan walks to the door and pulls on the handle. He stands aside for me to walk through.

I hold my chin high and return to the pub. It's only when I reach the bar that I realize he hasn't followed. Ryan holding the door open wasn't him being polite. That was Ryan showing me the door.

CHAPTER SIX
PILSNER

A pale lager with a bit of a bite and a crisp, bitter end
note. For when you're a little sassy.

I'm wearing a green dress that makes me look like an upholstered
couch, and I don't hate it.

"I don't hate it," Sadie agrees with my mental assessment.

We're at the antiques-and-vintage shop where she works. It's
about a quarter-mile walk from Resistance down one major street
from the pub. Sadie's aunt is driving around the North Shore suburbs hitting up estate sales, leaving Sadie to run the shop and work
on the shop's online inventory.

The shop is crammed full of curated finds from every
twentieth-century era. A copper, pressed-tin ceiling peers down,
and the whole place smells like history in a way I like.

"I would hate this dress even less if it were ten dollars," I say.
It's not ten dollars, so I return to the fitting room in the corner
of the shop behind a similarly floral upholstery fabric curtain and

63

change back into my street clothes. A Boy George T-shirt—Prairie and Joe's eighties-and-nineties music taste has had an effect—over red ripped leggings, with tights underneath because it's fah-reezing outside. Heavy black boots because the snow out there isn't melting anytime soon.

"Your résumé looks good." Sadie slides off red-framed glasses on one of those granny chains for spectacles. It looks anything but elderly with her retro-meets-modern look. "I think you have a great shot. Especially if Joe is involved in the decision. The cover letter is adequately persuasive."

It needs to be more than adequate in the persuasive department. "Thing is, I may have told off my new boss. Who also has a say in who's hired."

I may have forgotten to mention that part. I'm currently in denial it ever happened.

Sadie winces. "Why'd you go and do that?"

"Because he deserves it." I imagine myself saying exactly that to Ryan's face. Only imaginary me scrunches her nose, losing momentum. Great, even my subconscious isn't cool with me chastising my boss. Whatever. I lean my elbows on the counter Sadie sits behind. "Basically, him telling me they can only hire a brewer with experience when he himself was handed a job by his rich father is, like, actual irony. He sees me as some unstable server chick playing at beer making."

"Kat, he doesn't know you." She taps her laptop. "He probably wants to be as by-the-book as he can to show he's being fair. Just apply. You have as good a shot as anyone."

I can't say the second-guessing is wholly a gender thing, because Alden would sometimes freak over a decision I considered a fairly obvious choice. On the other side, he thought it ludicrous he wasn't making bank doing poetry readings and working part-time at a bookstore that actively drove customers away if they bought something the staff turned up their noses at. Peak snobbery on all counts. The fact he was so entitled honestly baffled me.

And I wonder why it didn't work out between us.

Regardless, I have issues to sort through. There's a thing I want, within grasp, and this weird notion inside to sabotage it. Like I don't deserve to get the thing I want and have been working for. Like there's more time on my sentence to pay off the debt I was stupid enough to accumulate, and more years I should spend under the tutelage of wiser folk than me.

I have to believe my friends when they say to go for it. Sadie would set me straight if I were full of crap. Alex would too. I have people who believe in me. The person who's undermining anything at this point, if I'm being honest, is me.

"Send your suggested changes to my email," I tell her.

"Oh, I printed it out." She slides the paper across the refurnished vintage countertop beside the register and her laptop. "You know I prefer hard copies."

Her elegant script reads *Way to go!* at the top with flourishes only a fountain pen can provide. "You're too much."

"Or just enough."

"That too. Hey, what's on for tonight? I'm off." I decide to ask her instead of assuming we're on for movies and popcorn and whatever leftovers I still have from the kitchen at Resistance. I swear, I wouldn't eat nearly as well if I didn't work at a place serving food.

"Oh, didn't I tell you? I'm meeting up with Becca and Sofia. They're coming in from Tinley."

"Ah, okay. Gotcha." Coming in from the suburbs is no small feat on a weeknight with traffic. Wait. "It's Friday, isn't it?"

"All day."

I lose track a lot with a serving schedule. "I haven't had a Friday night off in . . . yeah, I don't know." Even when I was scheduled off, I usually traded with someone to get the hours. Enough Resistance crew with social lives were eager to take me up on the offer. Any extra hours I wasn't serving, I helped Joe and Edwin brew.

"You should go out." Sadie suggests this as if this is a normal thing I might do.

"With what money? My tips are going to my phone bill and groceries."

She adjusts her glasses, now perched back on her nose. "Maybe you could reverse commute and go to the burbs. Visit with your parents."

I make a stink face. I don't exactly pop in unannounced on my family. When I do, I either meet an empty house because my parents are out at some community event, or they'll be winding down by the time I get there after hiring a rideshare or borrowing Sadie's car and driving the forty miles.

My sister might appreciate a visit. I send her a text. Not thirty seconds later she responds.

> Karrie: *OMG why would you come here? You live by everything.*
>
> Karrie: *Mom and Dad are at that charity dinner thing and I'm going to a party. I can't believe you can't find something to do!*

Great. Confirmed a loser by my sister. Given our recent conversation, I know she'd kill to be living on her own in the city, with roommates instead of parents, not worrying about what she eats or how exposed to sun and stress she is.

> Me: *Come visit soon. You're always welcome.*

"I guess I'll head back home," I tell Sadie.

Sadie steps away from the counter and drapes an arm around my shoulders. "Someday you'll look back fondly on these times when you were figuring it all out."

Hmm, hardly. I like my life figured out past tense, *thankyoupleasedon'tcomeagain.*

She dashes back to the counter. "New business cards. It has our updated website and mention of our estate sale services. Tell your friends."

Fifteen minutes later I'm doing just that. "If you know anybody who needs to manage their estate." I tap the card against the bar top at Resistance and make a snapping sound with my tongue. "Here's your gal."

Magda crosses her arms. "What, am I eighty? I already know Sadie. Maybe give this to those goths."

I look across the bar. "That's great they're here. It's not even trivia night."

Magda gives me a maternal look I swear she's been practicing. "Kat. What are you doing here? You're not on the schedule." She physically turns me one hundred eighty degrees to face the revolving door. "Go! Be free! Enjoy your youth!"

"Come on. You're only two years older than me."

"And I should have done far more reckless things in my twenties."

I turn back in a huff. "I only ended up here *because* of reckless things in my twenties."

She spins me around again. "No, you did responsible things like help your sleazy boyfriend afford his broke-ass lifestyle. Now's your time to live. Go do it while your back doesn't hurt."

"My back always hurts." A side effect from being on my feet eight to ten hours a day.

"Ain't that the truth."

"I'm broke. I'm going to go back to the apartment to watch movies."

"With roommates?"

"Sadie's going out with friends. Neil is . . . Neil." We've never hung out other than for the occasional evening or breakfast when all three of us have been home at the same time. He said to text him whenever he's home and we can *do the clubs.* Not music venues like the Vic or Metro or, more often for cheapskate me, the Empty Bottle, but legit dance clubs with cover charges. I've never been a dance club kind of gal.

Besides, I never know where Neil is.

"I'll text Neil and see if he's on the ground here and not someplace like Tempe, Arizona." A few texts later and my suspicions are confirmed. Not Tempe, but Temecula. He sends back a snap. *Wine country!*

I text back: *You look like you're in a dance club*
Neil: *Yes. In wine country!*

So much for that. A familiar tune comes over the jukebox. It's early Taylor Swift and Magda is the reason it's playing. She's singing along and pointing at me.

The door from the brewing area opens, and Ryan emerges. He's walking fast and direct like he did the other night. "I'm going out." He pauses next to me. "What are you doing here? You're not on the schedule."

"Tell her to go out!" Magda pushes her small frame into mine, sending me forward.

I stumble and step directly onto Ryan's pointy leather shoe. My monster boots are caked with road salt and snow crust, of course. "Sorry!"

He utters a low-key grunt from my foot stomp. A ghosted salt outline of my boot tread remains on his shoe.

I need to smooth things over from our last encounter. "If you can use me here, I can always help out. Believe it or not, I don't have plans."

Ryan laughs that soft puff of air laugh. He doesn't seem to have trouble believing me. "Look at this place. I think they've got it covered."

More than half the tables are filled. A few are pushed together for a larger group. Also, the goths. "The goths are here, and it's not trivia night," I tell Ryan.

I expect him to understand this is good news for business, but his reaction is of the nonplussed variety.

Magda inserts herself between us. "For the love of all that is holy, take this woman with you!"

"*Magda.*" I seethe. *Not cool.*

She tilts her head. *Go.*

He's our boss.

Ryan looks between us. "Look, I don't know what silent conversation you two are having, but I'm heading downtown. Kat, if you're going my way, I have a car coming in five."

I start to say I'm not going anywhere but to my apartment, but I sense Magda's telepathic threats. What's one night of tips spent on a car share down to the Loop? I can always take the train back. Then walk a zillion blocks. In the cold. Ugh, I already want to escape beneath a heavy pile of blankets.

"She is going your way." Magda steers me toward the door.

I want to raise a stink, since that's a particular skill set of mine, but Magda's right. This is my chance to butter up the boss. To make amends for being horrible to him the other day. If I want Ryan to take my application seriously, I need to show him we can get along. The fact he's offering to share a ride together is a starting point. An olive branch of sorts.

I glance to Magda. *You're a genius.* This will be a perfect chance to sit with Ryan and share what Resistance means to me. Like a soft-launch job interview. A preview for the main event.

Ryan has one hand on the door. "You coming?"

I pull on my coat. "Yes. Yes I am."

Outside is predictably freezing. The kind of crisp, cold night where every detail is sharp and visible.

"Where are you going?" I ask Ryan as we wait for the ride outside Resistance.

He sinks his neck deeper into his scarf. "Where are *you* going?"

"Um, with you?"

"Weren't you headed my way already?"

I shrug. "Something like that." Be honest. "I meant it when I said I didn't have plans. I'd like to talk and make up for being so . . . outspoken the other day." It nearly kills me to say this, because one regret I never have is speaking up. "Or at least, the way I talked to you. It was . . . not appropriate."

He considers this as a shiny blue Ford pulls up. The wheels grind against a crusted layer of snow along the curb. "I'm going to a bar with mainstream beer and music from this decade. You okay with that?"

"I'm capable of nuance, you know."

He opens the back door. "No, I don't know. I've never seen you outside of here." He jacks a thumb toward Resistance.

"*You look surprisingly less snotty removed from your natural habitat*," I say in a dopey fake-guy voice. "*Almost approachable.*"

His nose scrunches. "Is that supposed to be me?"

Oh dang, that nose scrunch was pretty adorable. Smoking hot with a cute side too? Unfair. Somewhere in a parallel universe is a guy with negative hotness and no cute side to speak of, and here's this guy, hoarding it all.

Instead of responding, I wink and slide past him into the back seat.

Hold up. I *winked*. At my *boss*.

Ryan gets in beside me.

The driver, a guy who can't be a day over sixteen but has to be at least eighteen, taps at his phone, pulling up the rideshare app with our destination. "Is this off Clark?"

"Uh . . . I just know it's in the Gold Coast."

I lean forward and give the driver the cross streets. "You'll want to take Grand or Division over. Chicago Ave has funky construction by Halstead. In case you didn't know."

"I didn't, thanks." And we're off.

Ryan tugs his scarf tighter. The Burberry one. "You've been there?"

"No. I just know where a lot of stuff is."

"You know the city well."

He sounds kind of impressed. Curious, since he said he came to the city a lot. "I thought you said you were down here every weekend?"

"Yeah, but I don't know how to get downtown from *here*."

It bothers me the way he says *here*. A hundred assumptions leap into my thought feed like trolls ready to pounce. *Not a posh-enough zip code. Too working class. Well, who's working class now, eh, Ryan?*

I remind myself why I'm here. I need to build a relationship with him—respect and good vibes—or I'll never get what I want. The job is within reach with enough buttering. I need to channel a real Land o' Lakes vibe.

"Getting around is easy once you get the hang of it," I tell him. "The diagonal intersections always throw me with the zany six corners. Watch for buses too. They will run you down."

"That's why you call us," the driver says. "I've got business cards. Here, take a few." He reaches across to the front passenger seat and digs through a vinyl gym bag. A CTA bus turns onto the street in front of us. Our car doesn't slow the slightest bit, and the back bumper and taillights of the bus grow closer and closer.

"Bus!" I shout.

The child driver slams on the brakes, jerking us back. Ryan swears.

"You okay?" Ryan asks me.

I'm breathing hard. "Yeah."

"I saw it the whole time!" The kid gives a light punch to the steering wheel. "We're gold."

Does he mean we're golden? Or . . . I don't know. Whatever. We're fine, and none of us are crunched beneath the undercarriage of public transport.

Ryan looks at his sleeve. "You want to hold on the rest of the way?"

Oh. I unclench his coat, which I apparently gripped in momentary terror. "Sorry about that." I ignore that smarmy gleam in his eye.

Even smarm can't harm his hotness.

After another jerky stop at a light, Ryan shifts the slightest bit toward me. "How long have you lived here?"

I keep one eye out the front windshield as I answer. Just in case. "Since right after college. I got a job in an office a block from Michigan Avenue. I figured, when else will I get to live in the city?" Traffic is clear ahead, or at least enough car lengths ahead for adequate stopping, so I breathe a little easier. "I had a great roommate at first. A friend from high school, but she, like, immediately got engaged and moved in with her boyfriend, leaving me to cover five months of the lease. I found someone from an apartment-finding web forum, and that was . . . well, let's just say when you pay rent on time and don't bug people about their dirty dishes, you're far less likely to be murdered by your serial-killer-in-training roommate."

"Is that true?" The driver turns his entire body around to look at me in the back seat.

"Watch the road!" Ryan and I yell in unison.

He shifts back. "Fine, fine. Never once had an accident."

"In the two months you've been driving?" I mutter. A snicker sounds beside me.

I swear to all higher powers, if my life ends by this adolescent driver, I will negative-star him. From the afterlife.

"You were saying?" Ryan says, trying to distract me from back-seat driving.

"Oh, yeah. I can't prove my old roommate was a serial killer in training, but she was obsessed with true crime TV and was studying forensic science. In and of itself not an issue. But typically, people don't use crime scene photos as bedroom decor. Nor do they line up tiny jars on their windowsill filled with fingernail clippings."

"GROSS!" Kid driver is laughing and shaking his head.

I'm aware I'm talking a lot and stop to check myself. Alden used to say I sometimes filled silences that didn't require filling. Counterpoint: Alden is an ass.

"Anyway, I have good roommates now." I don't mention Alden. It's a lot, and I don't need to be within spitting distance of that level of *lot* tonight.

The next mile crawls until we're near enough to our destination that I spy the sign for the bar. Out the window, I can see what seems to be a safe enough place to exit. "Right here is good."

"Don't you want—"

Ryan palms the back of the driver's seat. "You heard the lady. We'll get out here."

We exit the car. The driver powers down the window. "Don't forget to rate four or higher for a satisfactory delivery!"

The sedan peels off. Ryan taps at his phone. "No way I'm giving him higher than a two."

"Technically, he did deliver us without an accident." I look over the business card. "His name is *Toben*? With a name like that, throw the kid a bone and give him a three. He's gonna need all the help he can get."

"You're too nice."

"Me? I thought I hated men. According to you."

His mouth evens out. He walks straight ahead toward a door with a line snaking out. Immediately, I realize I am thoroughly under-dressed. I still have on my Boy George T-shirt and leggings plus my puffer coat. I see nary a puffer throughout the line, only wool and leather coats and flimsy wraps barely covering women's shoulders.

All the women in line are wearing heels or boots with heels, their hair styled sleek or in those messy updos you know took forty minutes with high-end products. My hair is in its side pony. The other side of my head doesn't have any hair.

A burly rectangle at the door nods in recognition to Ryan. He lets us pass through.

I can't help but be impressed. We get to bypass the line?

"Well, well. VIP," I say as we make it inside.

Ryan leans in so I can hear him over the crowd noises. "I know him is all."

"Isn't *knowing a guy* what makes you a Very Important Person?"

He laughs subtly. Whether he's laughing at me or with me, I don't know, but a sense of warmth rushes into my veins. My veins don't discriminate. Making him laugh is now my night's goal. If my charm can chip away at his steel exterior, it will feel like a victory.

The bar is packed. Everyone mingling is a capital-P Pretty Person. I glance to Ryan. I am Pretty Person Adjacent, which works as a cover. Maybe people will think I'm the bratty sister he had to drag out of the house for the night. Which isn't too far from reality.

He's scanning the room like he's looking for someone. He notices me noticing him and moves closer. "This is what Resistance should be like on a Friday."

I don't know where to start with his comment. Okay, that's a lie. I know exactly where to start. "None of the people here would step foot in Resistance."

"Exactly."

"You understand what we'd be losing if this . . ." I circle my hand in the air toward a Kardashian clone. I forget what I'm saying because I can't stop staring. She looks *that* much like a Kardashian. One of the younger ones with the excessively gorgeous hair.

"The only thing we're losing now is profit. Come on." He angles through the crowd.

I follow him to the bar, which is slick black with chrome details. Narrow mirrored strips provide a backdrop for shelves lined with bottles. It's fitting for this scene but lacks any sort of character. The bar top is far too glossy. Where are the worn patches and carved initials from pocketknives?

I scan the tap offerings and see the flagship commercial beers. The local Chicago favorite—the one that's owned by Big Beer at this point but still has the reputation of a hometown brew. A seasonal commercial ale.

There has to be a drink list with better options.

"Looking for this?" Ryan hands me a skinny, leather-bound menu.

I look over the small scripted font on laminate pages. Our drink menus back at Resistance are printed on recycled cardstock with bottle rings stained across the pages. I scrunch my nose at what's listed. Is it really so hard to throw something mildly artisanal in the mix?

"I told you—" Ryan starts.

I hold up a hand. "I know." I flip to wines and spirits, but who am I kidding? I don't care about whiskey or vodka or whether it's top-shelf. Those are fine and all, but I want a beer. A good one.

"What are you having?" Ryan asks me. He has the bartender's attention.

I squeeze past a guy on a stool and a *Vogue* cover model and lean forward to speak to the bartender directly. "What do you have that's aggressively hoppy with earthy or citrus notes?"

He doesn't blink. "Two blocks over on Dearborn and it's called Alfie's."

Another bar. I grin. I always appreciate a smartass. "I'll have the winter seasonal on tap."

"You got it."

I take out my wallet, and Ryan visibly recoils. He slides a credit card across the counter. I expect him to say *Your money's no good here* or something similar. He's my boss, after all. He probably thinks it makes him look weak if his underling pays her own way.

Having started a tab, he swivels to face me. "What is that thing you took out?"

Or not. "Do you mean my wallet?" I hold out the vinyl money holder with a Velcro closure. "This?"

He looks as if I've shown him a handful of fish bones coated in pocket lint. "What's on it?"

"The design? This is from an anime series."

"The duct tape is an animated series?"

"No, the tape is holding it together. The faded design has characters from a series. See, this is one of the rich boys and his chibi dragon pal—" I stop, given the disgust on his face. "This is a respected anime series. I bought this wallet at C2E2."

"I don't even know what that means."

"Massive convention? It takes over McCormick Place. It's like a Comic-Con. Trade show vendors, cosplay competitions, workshops."

His response is a nonresponse. It's pretty loud in here, so he either hasn't heard me or, worse, he has. Checkmark in the Not Impressing Ryan category. But hey, there's one mark in the Impress Ryan category for knowing Chicago city streets. One to one. Not so bad.

I exhale, looking out at the bar. This was a stupid idea, tagging along thinking we'd have a chance to talk about anything serious. If he's put off by my wallet, wait until he sees my T-shirt.

I sip my beer. It's mild but sweet, easy on the taste buds, and generally a smooth, satisfying choice. I don't hate it. I don't love it either. I like a beer that has some bite. Something that talks back.

There aren't any free tables. A lot of people are standing and don't seem bothered by it. Their main reason for being here is probably to be seen, like fame-thirsty mannequins who can imbibe liquid courage.

About that courage. "So, Ryan—"

"We should talk about Resistance." He moves in close so I can hear.

"Yes!" This is good.

He runs a hand across the cut-close side of his hair. I imagine for a moment how it would feel against my fingertips. The hair is longer than mine on the side where I've recently clipped it, so it's still short enough to give a light sensation across the fingers when run against the grain.

Hello, he's my boss, so no. I order my mind to stop the hair-touching fantasy. What was it he just said?

"Come on." He hovers a hand at the back of my shoulder, not touching me. "There's a spot over there we can stand until a table frees up." He points, making sure I see it until I nod. His hovering hand moves to light pressure at my upper back to guide me through the crowd.

I'm kind of into the idea that it looks like he and I are together. Is this what it's like to be one of the surely gorgeous specimens he dates? The experience isn't half-bad.

A silver-fox type runs his gaze up and down me. *Ha—not much to see beyond my unzipped puffer coat but an oversized T-shirt, you fool.* He won't get a back view either, since this is my heavy-duty puffer. The coat nearly reaches my knees.

Beyond him a woman with amazing sculpted brows and matte-red lips lingers her attention on me. Nope, not me, on Ryan. Well, yeah. He's pretty much standard gorgeousness, so I can't blame her for staring.

The hand guiding me pulls away, and the woman is right next to us now. She looks like that one actress, the blonde who's young and suddenly in everything? Her.

"You didn't call, you bad boy." She speaks past me, to Ryan, with those classic MAC red lips. Sadie owns more red lipsticks than I knew existed, and this looks exactly like one she has on her vintage vanity dresser.

I whip around to face Ryan. No easy feat in the puffer, which whistles its presence against someone else's back.

"I . . . things have been hectic," Ryan tells the actress double. "I'm between places now. Have a new job." He gestures to me, looking grateful I'm there for some reason. "Kat here, she works with me. We're here to discuss business."

The blonde's expression kaleidoscopes with impressive nuance. It lands on polite acceptance. "Business. How . . ." She looks over my whole deal. "Nice of you," she finishes.

To her, I probably found Ryan through an ad: *Local loser seeks business tutor.* Instinctively, I yank the scrunchie from my hair, smoothing the bob-length strands to my shoulder.

"I'll definitely hit you up later," Ryan is saying.

The woman is liquid sexiness with her hot aura tentacles wisping around him. He's being reeled in. "Don't wait too long. I'm in LA all next month."

Maybe she *is* that actress? I squint and try picturing her roll-diving from a car fire.

I'm being steered toward a precious corner standing spot as a two-top table clears. I snatch the free chair nearest me and slip into it, hooking my feet around the legs of the second chair and scooting it up to the table. Ryan circles around the table, and I let my feet fall to the floor.

I peel off my coat. "Ryan, is she the actress who was in that comic book movie? The one who was also up for an Oscar the same year?"

"What? No. Her name is Jillian."

I can't remember everyone big in Hollywood, but I don't think it's a Jillian I'm thinking of. "Were you supposed to meet her here or something?" I hope I'm not third-wheeling this situation.

He shakes his head. "Definitely not."

Shade me skeptical. "She's seriously beautiful. It's weird you don't seem very interested. *I'll hit you up later* is like guy-speak for *never going to call you again.* Or so I've heard."

"I'm not the kind of guy she wants. Believe me."

"I don't believe you. I mean, look at you."

He tilts his head a fraction. "Look at me what?"

"You! You're . . . you. She's . . . that." Words. Not easy. "You two belong in an ad for a tropical vacation."

"I'm not sure what you're saying, but we're not compatible. She's looking for someone with—" He stops himself. "Not me." He removes his own jacket, revealing a lightweight long-sleeved shirt in a pewter color. He angles an arm on the table, and the sleeve tightens around lean muscle.

I am beyond curious about this compatibility assessment but have the sense enough not to press. Again, *boss*. Potential job advancement on the line. The desire to make a good fourth impression. I need to play this more professional.

"Is that Boy George on your shirt?"

I lean back for a top-down view of the giant face across my chest. "Yeah. It came through Sadie's thrift shop. It's not their vibe, since they do more classic vintage. Sadie's my roommate."

"Not the serial killer with the fingernail clippings."

I bite my lip. "Nope. That chick is living in a windowless bunker somewhere."

Ryan smiles, and I can't lie, it's pretty great. Keeping him smiling, getting him slick with that buttery vibe . . . Nope. Don't go there. Definitely don't go there.

Recenter. "I'm glad we have a chance to talk outside of Resistance. Being in a different setting is . . ." A driving bass pulses so intensely I can feel my hair. "Is refreshing."

"I've been thinking about what you showed me the other day, with the brewing." He thinks through his next words. "Does Resistance offer tours?"

A good question. "Not anything consistent. We've done open house–style events where customers are allowed back by the brew tanks. Joe would share about starting the brewery, things like that. It happens maybe once or twice a year if it makes sense with an event."

He folds his hands together. "Let's look at upcoming holidays. What can we tie in that's maybe different this year?"

We go back and forth like this for a while, and I'm feeling pretty good about having answers to all his questions. We aren't talking about me, though.

"So, as far as brewmasters go, I wanted to tell you how much working with Joe has meant these past months." I finish my beer, and within a minute, a server is at our table offering a refill. She is crisp and put together, and I can't help comparing her to how I serve drinks in a secondhand apron and whatever's-clean clothes. "I've had a difficult year, and brewing has become a passion for me. An unexpected passion. I'm so grateful I landed at Resistance and with the people there. They make who Resistance is and what we stand for."

Ryan nods. "Yeah, I can appreciate that. Community is hard to build. I can see how close you all are. I hope that continues."

"There is a sense of uncertainty," I venture, being careful with my words. "People are worried things will change. I was hoping I could provide some consistency, continuing to work in back."

He nods again. "Consistency is good." He looks at me and it's different this time, like he's searching my face for something specific. "It means a lot for you to be a part of it?"

"Joy found in serving drinks has its limitations. Creating the drinks themselves—that's something I never knew I wanted until I had the chance. I'm so grateful for the chance Joe gave me. That's why this has been . . . a lot to deal with. Everything happened so suddenly."

His expression shifts, seeming clouded. He finishes his drink and sets the empty glass on the table. "I'm glad we've had this chance to talk."

I feel my tension ease. The butter is greasing what it needs to grease. "Communication is key."

"Totally."

We're both smiling. This is good. Things are going to be okay.

CHAPTER SEVEN
SPECIALTY BEER

A catchall category for brews that don't quite fit in
another category. Much like that one friend in every
group where you just say *They're special*.

Ryan and I both finish our drinks. The server comes by, and Ryan
starts to order another but pauses, catching my eye. He looks back
at the server. "Can you circle back in a minute?"

She leaves, and Ryan leans his arms against the table. "You
don't really like this place, do you?"

"It's fine." Between the pounding music and my pounding
head, and the fact that I haven't eaten since . . . I don't remember?
I've been better. But that's not a fair assessment. "It's not really my
scene, but the place is clean. I'm sure they pass their health inspections. And the server is attentive."

He sits back with a grin. "Is that how you think of your Friday
nights? Passing health inspections and attentive servers?"

I want to swat him. "I was being diplomatic. My personal
preference doesn't mean there's anything wrong with this place."

"But you're not enjoying yourself."

Enjoy might not be the most accurate word. I've attached myself to Ryan tonight without invitation and so far managed to be critical of just about everything. I'm supposed to be establishing a professional rapport to get the job I want.

"It's interesting to see where you like to spend your time," I say finally. "Maybe I can understand more about what you want to bring to Resistance."

The server stops by again. Ryan tells her he'd like to close out the bar tab. He looks to me again. "Where would you like to go?"

I reach behind me for my coat. "I can take off."

He makes a show of looking at his watch. "No way. It's early. Let's go somewhere. A bar where you don't have to hold your nose drinking what's on tap."

"Come on, I'm not that much of a beer snob." I point to my empty glass. "Look! I drank the whole thing!" As far as where to go, I don't know bars in River North or the Loop very well. "Where do you go when you're here for the weekend?"

I think he flinches at that. I didn't mean it as an insult, but I imagine how he spends his time in the city is different driving in for a night than it is for someone who lives here. Or maybe I'm making things too complicated in my head. A very Kat-like thing to do. Want things simple? Then never tell me something and leave me to sit a spell. I've got plenty of available brain synapses ready to party.

Ryan signs off on his tab and stands. "I know where we can go. Come on."

Vultures descend on our table within seconds. Two guys grab the chairs but seem to be focused on my puffer. The coat swings across the table as I pull it around me and tips my empty pint glass. My reflexes kick in, and I grab the glass before it rolls off the table.

"Nice catch," one of the guys says. He looks me over. "Going to the Arctic?"

The other guy snickers.

"Actually, the Arctic is on my bucket list. An environmental research trip. And I have just the coat for it." I finish donning the monstrosity and find Ryan watching us.

"Everything okay?" He's glaring at the two guys.

"Yeah, yeah." I nudge him forward. "Let's go before this becomes Testosterone Showdown."

We make our way through the crowd to the door. Once we're out front by the street, Ryan spins, walking backward. "Did you say you want to go to the Arctic for a research trip? Like Antarctica?"

"I just made that up. I'm not sure what the survival rate would be if I'm in prolonged cold that extreme."

"You mean whether you would survive?"

"No, everyone else." I rub my mittened hands together. "I'm kind hard to be around when I'm miserable. Being cold for too long makes me super miserable."

He nods as if thinking this over. Probably wondering if I've peaked at *hard to be around* or if we're just getting started.

"Are you okay to walk a few blocks?" He nods toward the curving street that bends along the Chicago River. "The place I had in mind is that way."

I sink into the comfort of my coat. "I don't mind. I love walking in the city. Even in winter."

He does one of those double takes, where his head actually jerks back after he's started to turn away. "I don't always know when you're serious."

"Oh! I wasn't being sarcastic. I really do like walking. Even when it's cold—thus the extremely warm coat. I walk to work, and part of each walk is seeing how the houses change over time and how landscapes shift in the seasons." I sound like an ad on HGTV, my parents' favorite channel. "Anyway, no sarcasm. I find sarcasm to be annoying and often overused. Clever and witty, I'll take. Melodrama, sure. But sarcasm a lot of times feels lazy without any added wit."

We fall in step together with Ryan taking the outer edge aligning with the street. "So, sarcasm should be limited unless it's witty. Got it."

"You don't have to take notes about me. I'm just rambling."

"I'd probably run out of paper if I did."

I check his expression and he's grinning.

He angles around a streetlamp. "Most girls—women—" He coughs and starts again. "They don't like walking far when we're out. That's why I asked. It's usually the shoes."

"These are all-weather boots." I mash a crusty snow mound with my sturdy tread. "I save heels for summer." Well, mostly I save heels for my closet floor. And date nights. Of which I haven't had any in recent memory.

We haven't gone far when Ryan slows. A storefront picture window tinted amber with old-timey script gives a glimpse of a warm, cozy interior. "I don't know what they have on tap, but I've been wanting to try this place. The food is supposed to be great."

"Good. I'm STARVING." The declaration bursts from me.

Inside, the atmosphere is polished speakeasy with heavy, dark wood and industrial fixtures. A dry note makes it feel like the heat's sucked all the moisture from the room.

Behind the bar, rows of ornate glass decanters mix in with bottles of all shapes and sizes in clear to caramel hues. "Is this a distillery?" I ask Ryan.

"I don't think they distill on-site, from what I can tell. Looks like their options are mostly whiskey and spirits. I'm sure they have beer." He doesn't sound too certain.

My stomach growls. A host shows us to a table along a back wall covered with black-and-white framed photos that look like 1920s Chicago. Sure enough, the menu is all vodkas and whiskeys and other spirits.

A guy moves toward us, and Ryan does the chin nod of recognition, motioning for him to come over. The guy is Asian, has black hair, and is around my height and super built. Probably a fitness trainer or professional stud muffin. *Shut up, brain, before you say that out loud.*

"Ry! Hey. It's been too long." The guy shakes Ryan's hand. He looks to me. "Hi, I'm Michael."

I smile. "I'm Kat."

"We work together," Ryan explains.

Michael nods. "At your dad's?"

Ryan's brows rise as he speaks. "Actually, I'm down here now. I'm managing a bar in Wicker Park."

It's not in Wicker Park, but I hold back from correcting him.

"Nice. Which place?"

"Resistance Brewing."

Michael squints. "Huh. Never heard of it. Is it on North Ave?"

"No, further south." He gives the cross streets.

Michael nods. "Ah, okay. I'm not down that way much."

I can almost hear Ryan filling in a response. *Exactly. And that's what needs to change.*

But he doesn't say that, and instead the conversation shifts to a friend they have in common.

Michael takes out his phone and taps at it. "Hey, listen. A group of us are heading to the lake house next weekend. You in?"

"Next weekend?" His focus darts between different clusters of people around us. "Maybe. I'm working most weekends now."

86

"That's gotta be a change for you." Michael claps Ryan on the back. "Mr. Three-Day Workweek doing weekends? Who will be our full-time party captain?"

Ryan laughs, but it sounds forced.

Meanwhile, I'm over here dying to hear the duties of a party captain. And whether there are part-time slots if he's given up his full-time role. Also, three-day workweek? I can't remember when I've even had three days *off* during a week.

"I won't keep you." Michael finishes a text and slips his phone into his back pocket. He gives me a friendly smile. "You're welcome at the lake house. We're near the Wisconsin border. Snowmobiles, hot tub, lots of top-shelf options. I restocked the gin and found some amazing tequila."

The guys say their goodbyes, and Michael returns to a table across the room.

"Old friend," Ryan tells me.

"You should take Resistance brews with you. Mix it up from the gin and tequila. Then get your friends to visit the pub."

He grabs a menu from the edge of the table. "I'm not going."

"Then how will I get to snowmobile?" I send him a playful grin.

"Oh." Awkward pause. "You want to go?"

I must be weak on my playful game tonight. "I'm kidding. That would definitely be weird."

"Because of snowmobiling? And here I thought you wanted an arctic adventure."

"Not the snowmobiling. Because of you."

He looks puzzled.

"Because you're my boss. That's all shades of inappropriate. Lake house? Hot tub? Top-shelf liquors? It's a prime setting for debauchery."

He starts to laugh but still has that confusion marking his features. "Yeah, but I'm not, like, your *boss* boss."

I tilt my head.

He gestures between us. "We have to be close in age. It'd be more like hanging out. Like tonight."

"You're my boss tonight too."

"But do you think of me that way? As a boss?"

"Yes. Yes, Ryan. You're my boss."

He straightens in his chair. "I've never been anyone's boss. I was hoping to come in and be more of . . . a peer, I guess." He blows out a breath. "No wonder no one really talks to me. I'm the *boss.*"

I open my mouth, and he holds up a hand. "Hold on. I know how that sounds," he says. "I understood I was coming in to manage. It just didn't sink in what that meant. That's all I'm saying."

I hold back further commentary. I deserve a sticker for good behavior.

Since this conversation is making Ryan squick out, I take my own menu and look it over. "I bet those lake house friends are good to have when you need an escape."

He slumps behind the menu. "Unless you're sick of that scene."

Well, well. There's clearly more to that story. My stomach demands to be fed, so I get to searching the options. They've got mostly small plates of heavy pastas and wood-fired vegetables and smoked meats. All at prices I'd prefer to spend on groceries for several days' worth of meals.

I scan the spirits and cocktails section. I'd kill for a reliable stout, a nice gut-filler, since I'll be waiting until I'm home to eat.

"I'll take a whiskey, neat," I tell the server when he arrives to take our orders. The heat of drink can trick me into feeling less hungry. I slide the menu back across the table.

Ryan looks up. "That's it? How about the charcuterie plate? It's supposed to be amazing."

It looks amazing, but the price nearly tips me over. It's half my cell phone bill.

"I'm not really into fine meats or cheeses." My skin reacts with physical pain at the lie. "I mean, the cheeses, yes, but it's probably all goat cheese here. Not a fan."

The server cuts in. "The cheeses featured tonight are an aged cheddar, a port wine spread, and a smoked gouda."

I would smoke a gouda right now I'm so hungry. "That's okay. The drink will be fine."

Ryan hesitates. "I'll have the rigatoni and smoked salmon plate. How about the hand-cut wedges with aioli and sauces. Kat, you like fries, right?"

This is becoming uncomfortable. "Sure. Great." Someday, I will look at a menu as more than dollar signs that take from my utility and grocery bills.

"If the fries aren't enough, when he comes back, we can get something else," Ryan says after the server leaves. "I feel bad. There's no beer here, and the food doesn't seem your style either."

I'm holding back actual drool thinking of those cheeses. The problem is, I want to pay my own way. I just can't bring myself to pay these prices when I've worked so hard to save money. I'm proud to live on my own without borrowing from my parents as a safety net. With Karrie's medical issues a constant drain on them mentally and financially, I'm the last person they need to worry about. All because I want to toss my money away at luxury cheese plates.

"Are you all right? Is it the boss thing still?" Ryan is asking.

Tension inside me simmers to overflowing. "I wasn't planning on coming out tonight. Now I'm getting in the way of you hanging out with friends. You dissed Jillian Hollywood and now your Michael friend, who you're saying you don't have time for. I don't want you to resent me. I'm getting the idea tagging along was a mistake. Me being here probably reminds you of work, so you're not able to get a break."

I hadn't planned to say any of that. It's messy and convoluted, but it's out and no take-backs.

"Kat, it's fine. If I didn't want you here, I'd tell you." He levels a look at me. His eyes are whiskey colored and incredibly compelling. "I'm sorry I didn't take the boss-employee thing more seriously. I didn't think it was a big deal." He raises an eyebrow. "After all, you said you were coming my way."

I'm mildly mortified he's teasing me about coming along. Then again, I tend to get in my own way over things like this. And truth? It's not so bad being out with him. In fact, I'm rather enjoying our time together.

And that's a turn I hadn't expected from tonight.

It's been three days since Ryan and I had our night out over commercial beer and club music with a whiskey chaser. He hasn't called me for an interview, despite my sending him my résumé the next morning. Yes, on a Saturday, but we work weekends in this business. And now Ryan works weekends instead of playing party captain with his bourgeois friends.

I'm at Resistance with Alex, both of us lurking near the window overlooking the brew tanks. Keeping out of sight from Ryan on the other side of the glass, we peer closer to spy on his meeting.

A guy with a light-brown handlebar mustache and a bowler hat stands with Ryan. The guy has on a white shirt with black suspenders and black skinny jeans. They're both nodding and smiling.

Alex gasps. "What *Back to the Future* nonsense is this? Paging Marty McFly!" He amplifies his voice, calling into the bar.

Gary, a line cook, chuckles into a vape cloud. We're not supposed to use e-cigs inside, but we're technically not open yet, so all bets are off. Also, I'd like to see Ryan attempt to tell Gary no about anything. Really, that sounds like a fun show.

"I haven't seen an old-timey variety hipster like this since Alden sent me pictures from a farmers' market in Brooklyn." Before Alex says anything, I interrupt myself. "*Months* ago. I swear I haven't heard from Alden since you deleted his number."

We both look back through the window. I grab a clean dish tub filled with rolled flatware and napkins as a prop in case they look over. Clearly, I'm busy. Carrying this tub.

"My guess is he's hiring a brewmaster first," Alex says. "I can guarantee we can't afford this gentleman."

"What? How do you know?"

Alex smirks. "Ryan's mentioned nearly every time he's here how dead this place is. Even some of the regulars have been holding off. They don't know what to make of it with Joe and Prairie gone."

I haven't heard the chatter. I guess I've been too focused on myself to notice, or I'm talking to the wrong people. "Anthony was here. He's still around."

"Yeah, until his tab comes due." Alex looks at me plainly. "You know covering for him won't fly under Hottie Ryan."

I shush him instinctively. "Don't call him hottie."

"Why? I know you check him out. Everybody does. The man looks good."

Don't I know. "There are more important things to focus on here." I've already told Alex about Ryan's plans to expand to distribution. He didn't seem as irritated by it, which annoyed me. "He wants to change *everything*. That's a huge red flag."

Alex notices me holding the tub. His brow furrows, then he shrugs it off. "Honestly? I'm lying low. Whatever works to keep this place going is fine by me. Did I tell you I'm enrolling at Columbia College in the fall?"

"Columbia? That's fantastic!" I can't help a small hop of joy.

His grin is sheepish. "Yeah. I know it's kind of a cop-out being so close to home, but I'm excited. My family will be nearby."

"Nearby? Are you moving out too?"

He sucks in a breath, still grinning. "Maybe? I'm asking around with friends. I've got time to figure it out. For now, I need to keep weekend hours. I don't want to be in debt for years—" He stops. "Sorry."

"Don't apologize. I made dumb choices."

"You also worked your heinie off. I'm only saying I want to keep my student debt as low as possible. It's why I've been saving and doing the two jobs."

"Never say *heinie* again."

"Fine. Hein*er*."

"Just say *butt* or *tush* like the rest of us."

"No one says *tush*. And it was a joke." He gives me a light shove, just enough for me to catch my balance. He's about my height but leaner. I'm more solid, with hips that swerve out and my strength concentrated in my legs.

"Okay, sure," I tease.

Butt terminology aside, a lot of us need more than one job to get by. I decided to focus on Resistance once I started shadowing Joe brewing. Otherwise, I would have taken part-time office work to supplement working here. Something with health insurance, if I was lucky enough to find part-time work that included it.

The joys of modern adulthood.

The doors open, and Mustache Bowler Hat glides out. I half expect him to be on a high-wheeler, but he just has a loping step. He also has on orange socks with canvas boat shoes.

Ryan stands at the brewery door, watching him exit through the pub. No escort out seems a little discourteous. Ryan shakes his head and retreats to the office.

"Can't afford him." Alex snaps his gum, which comes off hilariously immature. "I bet they can afford you, though." He levels a look at me.

"Hey! Are you saying I'm cheap?"

"Not cheap, but you'll take any offer to work back there. Don't pretend you won't."

I can't pretend and don't. I'm at the bottom of the barrel. Actually, that would be better, because it would be a beer barrel and that's where I want to be anyway.

That seems pretty pathetic, though. If Ryan offers me the assistant job, I at least need to ensure I'm getting a living wage. What would a dude do? Ask for what they want to be worth, that's what.

"How do you ask for a set amount of money when you know the person doesn't think you're worth it?" I ask Alex.

"You're asking me? I work *here*. Ask . . . I don't know, that roommate of yours who jet-sets everywhere."

"Is that a verb? Jet-set? As in, to jet-set to a place? Or is somebody part of a jet set?"

Alex gives me a bored look. "It feels like you're avoiding dealing with this, Kat. Go talk to Ryan. Ask him about the job."

I'm sure he's right, but Resistance is about to open, and I'm working a serving shift. "I will. Once we get up and running."

Alex and I get tables prepped and check in with the kitchen. We open. Business is deceased. Not even life support can save the nonexistent business happening here. Finally, a couple of the bikers come in. Only two, when usually it's a group of five or six.

A guy in a Great American Beer Festival T-shirt gestures to the room. "It's not the same without Joe and Prairie." It's a guy named Wolfston, which I imagine is his last name, but even if it isn't? Bitchin' name.

I set their beer bottles on the table with cold pint glasses and work on pouring the first. "Yeah, they're missed, for sure. Doing okay, last I heard."

"You've still got the Wizard brew?"

"Of course. We've got barrels on standby until the new brewer comes in." It hasn't been that long, and Resistance doesn't feel significantly changed yet. "Does it feel different already?"

Wolfston stretches his back. "It's them I miss, checking in. Now this young kid is in here. Looks like he stepped out of a catalog. Soon enough this'll all change. You'll see."

I feel vindicated with the catalog comment, but my denial about change must be showing, because his friend pipes up. "Why're you still out here? New boy doesn't want you working in back anymore?"

I press back a flinch. "Oh, you know. Changing of the guard." My smoothing-it-over laugh comes out nervous and brittle. "I'm applying for an open position. I should get an interview any day now."

"Who's that?" Wolfston nods past me. "New brewer?"

When I turn to look, a man is shaking Ryan's hand over by the bar. He looks like a dad type: early forties, soft middle, ball cap and plaid shirt.

"He's probably here for an interview. Head brewer, I'd imagine. I guess they want the brewmaster in before they interview the assistant. That makes sense, right?"

Wolfson levels a look at me. "They don't tell you much, huh?"

My cheeks go nuclear. "So far, not so much."

I know he doesn't mean it as an insult. They've followed my journey to marrying the beer, always eager to ask about new brews we're putting on tap next.

I'm sure I'll be up soon for an interview. They need to find a brewmaster first. I need to be patient.

I watch as the man goes with Ryan to the brewing area. The door shuts and the two walk side by side, looking at the tanks.

It's a single pane of glass, but the separation feels like an impenetrable wall.

CHAPTER EIGHT

SAISON

A highly carbonated pale ale that often uses wild top-fermenting yeast and a variety of grains. Great for experimentation.

Waiting on an interview at Resistance is pure, undistilled torture. With perpetual gray skies to match my mood, I'm feeling restless.

It doesn't help that with every glimpse of Ryan during my shift, he looks more stressed. At one point I thought he'd left, but he emerged from his office looking like he hadn't slept in days.

What I really need is something to make my résumé stand out. Since working with Edwin and Joe is apparently not enough to land me an interview.

That night at home, I scroll through online courses. Some are part of college programs, some are attached to specific beer-brewing schools. I'm good at this part—the scrolling. The consuming of information, the tracking down of programs. I imagine myself enrolling. Being surrounded by other beer lovers learning the science of brewing. Taking field trips to farm suppliers to see their agricultural practices.

I click on a degree program at a university in Michigan. Sustainable brewing. It's only a three-hour drive from here. The hands-on coursework sounds amazing.

Four years of amazing with tuition costs to go with it.

Predictably, I close the browser window. I don't want to go back for another degree. All the broken promises from Alden pretty much ruined me for higher education. To be honest, it's not even solely about the money at this point. The idea of waiting to brew beer for another two to four years is maddening when I could be doing exactly that right now, working my way up the chain. That was the appeal of working with Joe. I would learn on the job.

I can't quell my restlessness, so I click a new internet window open and check a favorite craft brew forum. The posters are into learning the craft, making home brews, or looking for first-time jobs in brewing.

Mindlessly scrolling, I stop on a topic titled *Your best way into the industry*.

I reach the most recent post.

Hands down, this is the best class I've taken. Full-day workshop, hands-on stuff. Open to anyone. Flat fee. So many brewers trained under Sam—get in on this class!

I click the link. It leads to a microbrewery in Wisconsin outside Milwaukee.

I know this beer. Sam Giddeon, brewmaster, does a series of workshops every few years. One is coming up. On Saturday. *This* Saturday.

I can't read the details fast enough. *Biochemistry and Artistry: How the Science of Brewing Meets Creative Exploration.*

My heart screams. This is exactly what I want! A hands-on workshop that isn't part of some massive university curriculum designed to drain my bank account. This is what I want to learn. Artistic craft and the science to make it happen. *Exploring sensory skills along with science to make informed choices in brewing.* Yes and yes.

The price isn't nothing, but I can make it work. This is an investment, and it's a reasonable cost if I keep my expenses lean the next month or two. I click the *Enroll Now* button.

Nothing happens.

I click again, and a red line of text appears beneath the button. *This class is currently full.*

I let my head fall back. "WHY?" I ask the world and my empty apartment.

Of course it's too good to be true. A workshop where I could learn precisely the content that excites me, with a bonus of adding experience to my résumé.

I hate you, Universe.

My gaze falls back to the screen. Tiny text below the button lists a phone number and mention of a wait list.

My phone is in my hand dialing before I read the final digit. Someone picks up. A young-sounding guy.

"Hi. Hello." He picked up really fast. "Um, this is Kat. I'm calling about the workshop Saturday. If I can possibly get on a wait list for it."

"Oh yeah," the guy answers in an easy tone. "No prob. Someone canceled yesterday. You want in?"

I pump my fist in the air and kick my legs out in silent celebration. "Yes! I want in."

At work the next day, my confidence surges. I head straight for Ryan's office. I'm enrolled in a class I'm excited about, and that can only help my chances of getting the assistant job. I need to stop being such a scaredy-cat and just lay it out for Ryan. *I know Resistance, and I am an asset to this team. You need me.*

I open the door to the brewing room and realize Ryan is talking with the dad-looking guy from the other day. I hadn't seen him from my angle walking in.

No one has noticed me yet, so I silently let the door close and wait for an opening. A second man, an older white guy with graying hair in a low ponytail, is also there talking to Ryan and Dad Guy. In his tie-dyed Pink Floyd T-shirt and faded jeans, he looks like someone Joe and Prairie would be friends with.

My stomach kicks back. *Nope, be confident.*

I head for them, walking in a curve to get in Ryan's sight lines first.

He's upscale professional today in a dress shirt, dark jeans, and those ultra-shiny leather boots. "Kat! Good to see you. I'd like you to meet our new brewing staff. First, this is Kurt, head brewer. And our new brewing assistant, Randy."

New assistant.

An *assistant.*

The assistant.

They've already been hired.

Ryan's breathing ticks up, as if he's finally clued in that I'm not one hundred with this situation. The situation where he entirely skipped me in the interview process. I know my résumé made it in. I received an automated response from some third-party tool thingy. I even sent it a second time to his Resistance email. Ryan knew I was applying. I told him. He knew.

I'm not certain which expression my face lands on. What I know is my attempt at control fails. My mouth is in the shape of a smile while my throat snatches it back. My eyes fight an impending tsunami. Kurt the Dad is smiling and saying pleasant introductions. I find myself shaking his hand. Randy gives me an easy nod like everything is Matthew McConaughey *all right all right*.

"I've heard good things, Kat," Randy tells me. "It will be nice to work together."

I'm so confused. I shift to look at Ryan. "Work together?"

"The tours," Ryan is saying.

I blink at him. "Tours?"

Excitement practically pounces out of him. "I'm going to have you partner with Randy to host tours for the public. He'll tell you what's going on with the batches, and you can work around the brewing schedule. I'd like to make it part of the Resistance package."

"Tours," I repeat. The smile is still hanging out, and it must be a horror. "This is a paying position? The tours?"

Ryan's pause speaks volumes. He lets out a nervous laugh. "We can discuss compensation opportunities later." He looks to Kurt, but Kurt is on his phone discussing pickup time for the kids. Randy is chatting with Gary from the kitchen. They seem to be old buds.

I finally shut my craw and swallow back everything I'm feeling to get through the next few minutes. "Can I talk to you?" I say to Ryan.

His composure is rigid. "Sure, later, after we're done here." He glances to the other men.

Randy and Gary hunch over a smartphone watching a video that causes them to excitedly talk over each other. I've never seen Gary act so friendly with anyone. Usually he's yelling at one of us for being ungrateful end-of-the-alphabet-generation imbeciles. Truly, Gary needs those e-cig breaks.

Ryan's shoulders rise and settle. "Okay. Now is fine."

We walk a few steps for distance. "Why didn't I get interviewed? I have confirmation my résumé was received."

He holds up a hand. "Kat. When we talked the other night, I thought we were on the same page. The tours?"

The words he's stringing together don't make sense. "What about me telling you why I care about Resistance and my passion for brewing made you believe I didn't want to be involved with the brewing? As a paid staff?"

"Look, I told you we needed someone with experience. I thought you understood. Randy knows Joe and Prairie. They recommended him."

The fermenting tank is my only focus as the edges of my vision blacken. Ryan is a blur. "They recommended Randy . . . and not me." It's humiliating to admit out loud, but I have to confirm. It doesn't feel real.

"Randy knows his way around craft beer, and well, he's not exactly demanding. He falls in line and does what's needed, no questions. Just a solid guy. For head brewer, we needed someone who gets my vision."

His *vision. His* vision?

I keep my voice low. "Which is?"

He inches closer. "I came here with ideas, and I'm just getting started. There's real money on the line."

I might need an emergency trip to the eye doctor; this anger is incinerating my retinas. "You knew I wanted a fair shot at this job. I deserved an interview. Even if it was to tell me you're going with someone else. That's what a professional does with their staff."

Ryan's mouth twitches, and he presses his lips together. He knows he messed up, but I know just as quick he won't admit it. He never planned to consider me.

Another thing. "You said Randy isn't demanding. Is that because I am? He's solid, but I'm not?"

Ryan keeps his voice low. "I know this feels personal, Kat, but it's not. It really isn't."

How can this not be personal? This isn't just my job but my future. I envisioned wedding bells back here—me and these tanks in holy-hopped matrimony. Now I'm the forever bridesmaid holding a tour pamphlet. Like we even have pamphlets.

Before I say something stupid, I remove myself from the scene. I leave the brewing room for anyplace else.

I end up in the bathroom. It's clean, at least.

I lean back against the door. What the even is this? I can't words, I'm so mad.

My chest constricts, and I have to breathe through the hurt. It's not really my chest; it's deeper, much deeper. Like the wind knocked out of me, and that wind is my whole spirit.

After everything with Alden, supporting his dream, working dearly to pay for it, it was supposed to be my time. I hadn't dreamed big enough. My job in health care administration had been fine. There were certainly worse jobs out there. A master's in public health was the next logical step to the career I'd wandered into. I figured a higher degree would take me to that magical next level. I never thought too far ahead to what waited at that level. It was the next thing. Every year in school, you look ahead to the next. Look ahead to college, look ahead to jobs and graduate school. What else was there?

My first week at Resistance, Joe made me try one of his experimental brews. The face I gave him after one sip sent the man into hysterics. I wasn't much of an IPA drinker then, let alone into saison. He told me how the saison's dry and earthy spice flavor came from yeast and not hops or malt. It was so strange on my tongue, so different. And wow, with that nine-percent ABV, the stuff nearly knocked me out.

I found myself needing to know more. Asking Joe and Edwin how they determined each recipe. The level of dryness, the fruit notes. All of it fascinated me.

It didn't take me long to realize I couldn't drink these beers the same way as the beers I'd been used to. Craft brews deserved attention and care. Each of them needed the right food paired with it, like a fine wine for an everyday Jane. I loved that about craft brew. It isn't fancy, but at the same time, it has a sophistication. Contradictions, which I love. Joe loved that too. His favorite flavor profiles played with contradictions.

That's what made Heartbeat such a challenge. A single beer everyone likes? Nearly impossible.

With each new batch, Joe taught me more. He and Edwin had been making beer so long together they finished each other's sentences. Stress from life and boyfriend troubles faded while I worked. I felt special when I made beer. Needed. It was a feeling I hadn't experienced with my own family for years. A feeling I craved.

Caring for Alden had filled that need for a while. Providing for him while he did grad school meant I was essential. Important. Obviously, that didn't turn out well, but my Resistance family was there for me when the relationship fell apart. This family didn't have expectations of who I should be. They embraced me where I was. They loved the things I loved. They cared that I cared about those same things.

But the family I trusted has been fractured. Joe and Prairie are who I've gone to the past two years. They listened. They heard me. And now they aren't here.

Now they have more to worry about. It's not their fault. Just like it's not my parents' fault that Karrie needs so much attention. It's just life, and the reality is, I don't come first.

A new thought arises. *If you're not happy with the plan, change the plan.*

I let the thought sink and shift through my body. Thankfully, we're low on customers, because I'm reaching a pretty chill meditative state in our public bathroom.

It's not the plan that's the problem.

That's new. I thought I had to change the plan. If it's not the plan, what is it?

I wait for this still, small voice to speak again. Nothing.

No burst of wisdom surfaces, so I use the bathroom and wash my hands.

I have my hand on the bathroom door, ready to open it, when the rest comes to me.

No one said the plan has to mean staying in the same place.

If I stay in motion, I don't have to lose more time.

Leave. I could leave Resistance.

And I might have to if it means doing what I want.

CHAPTER NINE
GERMAN MÄRZEN

A lager with deep malt flavor, varying from pale to dark.
American-style Märzen is often called Oktoberfest.

Because life doesn't always suck, Sadie offers to drive me to the brewing class in Wisconsin.

"You're sure you're fine going to estate sales all day?" I ask as I buckle in.

"Are you kidding me? I have the company credit card. My aunt explicitly told me to, and I quote, *go nuts*."

I fill her in on the past week, since our schedules have been off. She already knows I was passed over for the assistant brewer job. I told her that immediately.

"I'm glad you're doing this class, Kat. I think broadening your horizons is a good idea. What I'm not getting," Sadie says with one hand on the wheel, the other holding a breakfast sandwich she made at home, "is what is this Ryan guy's passion? You told him brewing is a passion you discovered, but what's his?"

"We don't exactly have those conversations."

"What type of conversations do you have?"

When I'm not throwing my phone at him or blubbering at his dumb perfect face? "The ones where he says we need to change this or that about the pub. I doubt he'd describe his *passions* in detail." Though I admit I'm curious. What does an Adonis male in the prime of his life aspire to? "He was barely interested in Jillian Hollywood the other night. She was laying it on real thick, and he gave her the line he'd hit her up later."

"*No.*" Sadie punctuates the word with added drama. "Guys only say that if they're not interested. Or if they just want to call on the booty."

I laugh at her phrasing. "I wouldn't know, because I don't get calls for my booty. But yeah, I've heard."

"I'd prefer a handwritten note to a text any day."

"Of course you would." Sadie deserves someone who will put pen to paper for her. A full sentence in terrible cursive. Heck, I'd take a note too. Even a dirty one, so long as the words are spelled right.

"Wait, who is Jillian Hollywood?"

"Some model or something. But his friends seem loaded. One of them invited us to their lake house."

She raises a brow. "Ooh, that sounds promising."

"I'm not going with my boss to someone's lake house."

"Maybe you could meet someone else there. A sugar daddy."

I snort. I haven't dated anyone since Alden. He and I were together three years, so it's been four years since I've tried to find somebody. I've made no attempt at tossing a line into the dating pool. No one calls it that, which is proof my fishing pole is rusty. My internal-monologue metaphors are rusted out too.

"I was joking about the sugar daddy," Sadie says. "Trusting is hard, especially after what you've been through."

Maybe I'm not meant to fall in love. Someone as skeptical as me with a bitchin' case of the bitters is too much for most guys.

"I don't think you should pressure yourself either," Sadie tells me. "I've never had a serious boyfriend, and I'm just fine."

"You're wearing a hairnet in public, but okay."

"I told you, it's a snood. It's a period piece of clothing women have historically worn outside of the home."

She's too easy a target, but I don't push. Sadie has never once pressed me about jumping back into dating after my breakup. And in turn, I never prod her to share details of who she's dated—or hasn't.

"Maybe we could go in on this dating thing together," I offer. "How about we each sign up for different apps and make a friendly wager." I lower my glasses and waggle my eyebrows.

"You're broke, Kat."

I consider that. "Fair point."

My mind drifts to Ryan. I doubt he has to use a dating app. Maybe he does anyway, solely for the stats. It has to be a boost to the ego to see all those swipes and upvotes and gold stars and whatever the apps are using these days. Again, I wouldn't know. My boyfriends came from old-fashioned means like football games, mutual friends, and a bookstore poetry reading that I now deeply regret.

We roll into the brewery with plenty of time. This is a microbrewery for craft beers, so not a massive operation by any stretch, but significantly larger than small-time Resistance.

"Don't forget your lunch!" Sadie powers down her window and hands me a paper bag. I wish this was a joke, but I legit packed a lunch in case the food options here are scarce. Also see item A: broke.

I stuff the sack into my massive woven shoulder bag, and I'm off like a kid in the school drop-off zone.

Inside, the space has an industrial look with stainless-steel high-top tables and polished wood stools. Glass windows cover the length of one wall looking into the brewery. Tall and gleaming silver tanks line up like soldiers. They emit a faint hum this side of the glass.

A group of ten gathers near the door to the brewery. Behind me, more trickle in. Oh, hey, I'm not the only woman!

The lone other lady sees me and walks over. She's athletic and probably in her forties, though I'm terrible with telling anyone's age. She has long black hair and bronze skin and gives off an outdoorsy vibe in a red plaid shirt paired with a utility vest.

"Hi. I'm Jana." She holds out her hand. "You're here for the course?"

I shake her hand. "Kat. I came up from Chicago."

"Nice shirt."

I'm repping Resistance in a T-shirt from last year's fall seasonal release. "Thanks. We're a small operation. Maybe even nanobrewery sized. Nothing like this." I nod toward the rows of tanks. "No wide distribution. You?"

Jana hands me a business card. "I'm at a microbrewery about a half hour's drive from here. My boss trained under Sam. Told me once when Sam opens his workshops to the public, go take it. Otherwise, you have to enroll in the university course he teaches. Not my thing."

I'm impressed she has business cards. Should I have one? What would it say, *Resistance staff server, want fries with that IPA?*

"The university route isn't my thing either," I admit.

"I got into this from beer judging." She flashes a goofy smile as she peers through the glass at the massive tanks. "This is all so cool, huh?"

The lights are bright and the tanks look spotless. "Yeah, I want to get back there."

The group is nearly twenty strong now. A man steps forward—pretty cut build, bald head that's pink hued and shiny. He's all smiles and shakes each of our hands. "I'm Sam Giddeon. Welcome to my brewery."

We do a round of introductions, including why we're here. About half the class look to be in their twenties, all working in breweries or advancing in home brew. The other half range from midthirties to gray haired.

When it's my turn, my mind races with how to sum up why I'm here. "Kat Malone. Resistance Brewpub in Chicago. I've had the privilege of working with a brewmaster the past six months and decided I want to keep doing this. For good."

A look of recognition hits Sam's eyes. "Joe and Prairie. Good people. Great brewers."

He moves on to take us through a tour. Any nerves I had coming in here siphon off. I'm still hurt Joe and Prairie didn't vouch for me with Ryan, but at the same time, now that I've heard their names spoken by this brewer, it's like a little piece of them is here with me.

The morning is full of information with little downtime. I'm absorbing every shred, taking notes. Sam reviews how to evaluate core raw materials for brewing. Sustainable sourcing is a big topic, as are material supply chains. Where your raw ingredients come from—including getting the best hops you can—matters to the end result of the product.

"From grain to glass, brewing is resource intensive," Sam explains. "Large amounts of water and energy are used for the end product, so innovation to reduce waste is something our brewery aims to excel at. We then teach other brewers how to do what we do. But raw materials aren't the only way to be sustainable. Who can tell me additional ways a brewery can manage resources?"

A bearded guy with a starter beer belly raises his hand. "Lean processes to eliminate time waste. Mapping processes to cut inefficiencies."

Another hand rises. "Energy-efficient refrigeration."

"Solar power," a man dressed all in black says. "And repurposing spent grains into food."

Sam nods and talks about repurposing opportunities. He looks around the room again. "What else?"

"How about social sustainability?" I offer with a raised hand. "Jobs in the community and investment into other local businesses and charities."

A snicker comes from behind me. "Breweries aren't charities."

That's not what I said, but whatever.

Sam nods at me. "Equipping staff with valuable skills is investing in the community. Build a solid foundation, and you build a business that lasts. Less waste from turnover to different businesses, and that consistency leads to further community development, like charities, as you mentioned."

Beside me, Jana nudges me and winks. "Nice," she mouths.

We move to a makeshift classroom space at one end of the brewery just short of the cold-storage doors. Long tables with stools and a variety of instruments have been placed along each table.

After another two hours, it's time for a lunch break. We're free to leave and come back or eat at the establishment.

I catch up to a guy named Matt, the one with the beard and the cute little beer belly. "Hey, I liked what you said about breweries not expanding too fast. You're right how the demand can get so high with wider distribution and then the supply can't keep up."

His face lights up. "Yeah. Happened the last place I worked. They ended up laying us off and selling." He points a thumb toward the pub part of the brewery, where customers fill most of the tables. "You eating here?"

I think of my sad sack lunch. "Um, I can, maybe. Let me see what Jana's doing."

Jana is talking to Sam, but they wrap up by the time I get to her. "Hey, want to eat together?"

She smiles brightly. "I was planning to go to a place down the block. Get some air. You're welcome to join me."

"How about here? With the class?"

She peers past me. "Are there any tables left?"

I turn to where she's looking and see the group has pushed two tables together and every chair is full. Moving closer, I realize the space is tight. Customers at other tables are seated close, so there's no room for more chairs.

Matt walks over. "Hey, sorry. Looks like the table's full. Maybe you and the other chick can sit over there?"

Jana makes a guttural sound behind me. The table Matt points to is on the other side of the pub. Totally separate from the group.

Okay, this isn't a middle school cafeteria. "You know, never mind. I think we'll head out."

Jana gives me a light tug to the arm. "Good move. I'll drive."

Her well-loved red pickup takes us to a café not three minutes away.

"So, tell me what you like to drink and what you want to brew," Jana asks when we sit to eat our sandwiches—hers café bought, mine covertly unearthed from my bag. I made sure to purchase a drink to support the café.

"Have you had Total Turkey? It has this sweet pop at the jump, with a moderate malt in the middle. The bitter end lingers and makes me want to knit a sweater."

"Nice. You knit?"

"Drinking that beer makes me think I *could* knit."

She laughs. "I have one that makes me think of jump roping with my best friend when we were kids. It reminds me of summer and skinned knees. The flavors I associate with summer."

That sounds lovely. Except for the skinned-knees part. Then again, I like it when a craft brew stings a little. "It's interesting how emotions and memories connect to taste. That's what I want to develop—unexpected flavors that take you somewhere, whether somewhere new or familiar." I dig into my mini tangerines. "So, do you like where you work?"

"It's okay. I'm in production and packaging. Moving pallets and putting bottles on the line, that sort of thing. The kind of work to put hair on your back, my mother would say. My partner and I plan to open a taproom with our own brews."

"Yeah? What kind of beer?"

"We have an ale called Earthmaker named for a Potawatomi myth—that's my Native heritage. My partner is white with family from Wales, so she named her first IPA Branwen for the Welsh love goddess. We're going with a mythology theme. You know, hashtag *ladybrewer* and all that."

I laugh. "Or just *brewer*, sans the *lady* part."

She sighs. "Yeah, I get it. Sometimes self-labeling as a woman sets us further apart."

She and I are literally apart from the rest of the class. In a different building, even. Though we could have stayed and made lunch work, so maybe I'm overthinking, like usual.

"We already have to prove our competence to people who don't believe we can do it," Jana is saying. "But don't listen to me. I'm old and jaded."

"Your plan sounds amazing." I'm instantly envious of the mythology aesthetic. "How did you find a business partner?"

She finishes her sandwich and folds the paper wrap into a neat square. "I married her."

"Oh, wow!" I'm even more intrigued. "The people I work—worked—for are a married couple. They were in business for twenty-something years before they sold."

"What happened?"

I fill her in. And then keeping filling with all that's happened since, including my failed attempt to move up at Resistance. "Sorry. I didn't mean to dump that on you."

"Don't apologize. That's a lot of change, especially when you're starting out. You're young. People will screw with you."

She says it so directly it takes me aback. "Prairie and Joe would never hurt me. This all came up so suddenly."

"You said they promised you an assistant job. Then they didn't recommend you to the new owner?"

I fumble for a response. "That's what Ryan—the new manager—that's what he told me."

"You haven't been in touch with the old owners?" She holds up a hand. "No, I get it. The health problems. That makes sense." She shakes her head. "But they shouldn't have made you promises they knew they couldn't keep. You got your hopes up because they dangled that offer to you. Then they turn around and suggest someone else for the job."

I can feel an ugly sensation surfacing. Bitter, grotesque resentment. I hate this feeling, when all I want is to wish good things for Joe. Edwin deserved to retire and be with his daughter and grandkids—I can't be mad at him for that. What kind of cretin am I for feeling even a hint of betrayal, when Joe could be dying?

I just can't entertain these thoughts.

"Sorry," Jana says. "I poked a sore spot. I speak too plainly sometimes."

We're both quiet. The pause doesn't feel awkward, even though the conversation turned difficult. I need a minute to process.

I look up from my lunch, and she seems to be waiting to speak. "You didn't ask for my advice, but I'd hate to see you lose more time. You'll need to fight for your chance. These breweries will lowball you on salary, so watch for that." She gathers her things, since we're due back at the course. "That's why I'm going into business myself. It's time for me to be my own boss."

That sounds incredible and terrifying. Running a brewing operation from scratch. Nobody to tell you what to do. No one to trust but yourself.

We return to the brewery. The group is gathering again, chattier than this morning.

Matt approaches. "Hey, sorry about the table thing. My bad."

That ugly sensation of feeling forgotten and left out crawls back. Sometimes I have epic levels of FOMO. That's my issue, not his. "It's okay. Food good?"

He pats his gut. "Burgers and brews. Can't go wrong."

He gets pulled away by someone else from the group. Maybe I should have stayed. I'm too far off from starting my own mythology-themed taproom myself, so I probably need an in with these guys if I'm going to be scouting for jobs.

Ugh, job searching. If I'm even ready for that. *You can't put off these thoughts forever*, I remind myself. It's good that I'm here and thinking about possibilities.

The afternoon session is just as detailed as the morning's, with more hands-on work. By the end of the workshop, I'm tired but filled with inspiration.

After class, Matt finds me again. "I'm in the northern suburbs and go into the city a lot. We should meet up sometime."

Yes! This is exactly what I need—connections. "That would be great. I don't have a business card or anything."

"Oh." He laughs, scratching at his beard. "Neither do I. I just mean, we can hang out, you know? What's your number?"

We exchange numbers, and he slides his phone back into his pocket. "You don't have a boyfriend, do you?"

"Sorry?" I'm still finishing putting his contact in my phone. "Why do you ask?"

He shifts his weight in his Chuck Taylors, laughing softly. "I just mean, I don't want to encroach or anything."

"You won't encroach. We'll be talking business over beer."

An expression I can't name passes across his face. "Right. Sure. Uh, it was nice to meet you." He nods awkwardly before joining a few lingering classmates by the door.

He absorbs easily into their group, a homogenous glob of pale skin and beard scruff. Matt and another guy look over at me, then back to their group. Laughter follows.

I'm being paranoid. They aren't laughing at me. My brain is simply very skilled at torture. After a confidence-building day where I feel energized, why not imagine it all crashing down? Brains are downright savage sometimes.

"You heading out?" It's Jana, standing nearby. Probably wondering why I'm muttering to myself.

"Um, yeah."

She hooks an arm through mine. "Come on, then."

The whole exchange with Matt leaves me with sour notes. In beer, that flavor would be welcome, but I'm finding I don't like the taste.

CHAPTER TEN
WHEAT BEERS

An easy entry into craft beer, wheats can use ale or lager
yeast. American wheat differs from German wheat, with
increased hops and fewer fruit notes. A little more arrogant, one might say.

I'm on shift again today to serve at the pub, and I'm determined
to lift this funk of a mood. I can't let myself get dragged down
over my stalled brewing career. I just need a little time to figure
out a plan.

So for today, I'm going to blast some 1980s goodness at the pub
and do my thing. I mentally put together a playlist on my walk to
work. The Cars, Echo and the Bunnymen, Siouxsie and the Ban-
shees, and Whitney Houston. Prairie had a real soft spot for Whitney. If Luiz is on, he'll want Selena going. I'm humming "Bidi Bidi
Bom Bom" and any of the words I can remember with my terribly
busted Spanish as I enter Resistance from the back by the kitchen.

Gary loiters outside, vaping. He opens the door for me.

"How's it going, Gary?"

"Peachy. Wait till you get a load of what Playboy is doing."

I'm guessing Playboy is Ryan. I brace myself for what's next, but the Selena track in my head demands I not let anything spoil my mood.

I set my coat and bag in the employee space beyond the kitchen and head out to the main pub. Right away, a few things are noticeable.

Item the first: A new flat-screen TV is mounted above the area where we host open-mics, live music, and the trivia guy.

Item two: It's a really big flat-screen. Turned to basketball.

Item three: The music playing is a pop song that sounds like Pixy Stix and methamphetamine ground in a blender with a girl-child singing over it.

Item four: There's a woman I've never seen standing by the front door in micro shorts and a jersey top with a bottom hem reaching just below her chest. Not exactly active sportswear. Her hair is in pigtails, but there's nothing childish about her. She's rubbing her bare arms and stamping her feet. A tray of shot glasses sits beside her on a table.

A shot girl? Honestly?

Alex walks my direction. He sees me and stops.

I point to the TV. "There's a—"

"I know," he says.

"And the music—"

"I know."

"And a girl by the—"

"Yup."

"When did—"

"Yesterday." Alex continues toward a table and sets down a beer with such force a whole sip sloshes out. "Ask the boss."

Oh, I will.

Just as I think it, Ryan emerges from the kitchen carrying a tray of pints. Well, this is interesting. I stand back to watch.

He has on a blue button-down rolled at the sleeves and faded jeans. The type you pay money to buy faded, mind you. He and the tray go straight to a table of dudes. Young, unfamiliar faces, all guys, angled toward the massive TV. A chorus of cheers goes up.

"Drinks on me," I hear Ryan say.

So, these are his friends. How convenient he bought them a new TV to woo them here.

I'm on shift now, and this is my section, so I roll on over. "Hi, boys. I'll be your server today. The name's Kat." I point to the name tag pinned to my shirt, which Ryan is now requiring of us. "Is there anything I can get you?"

Ryan runs a hand through his short-clipped hair, and while I'm very much not thinking how his hair would feel against my fingers, I notice he's a little stressed at my presence.

"Yes, uh, this is Kat, everyone. These are some of the guys who offered to—"

One of them shoots from his seat, jutting out a hand. "Chris Knox. Pleasure to meet you."

The rest of them cackle at the gesture and call him names. I play along and shake his hand. "Kat Malone. Pleasure is mine."

A crass joke comes from one of them, probably because both of us said the word *pleasure* and these men are twelve. I don't get their game yet, but I imagine it's not hard to figure out.

I take out my trusty order pad and start down the line.

"We're covered," Ryan tells me. "This round is on me."

"This *round*?" Chris Knox parrots. "You said you'd hook us up, bruh. I'm here *all day*."

I'll just take note of this is all. I squiggle on my notepad: *Total bro hoes*

"Any food?" I ask, turning my tone extra perky.

The orders come fast—nachos, burgers, all the staples. Ryan is looking a little green in the face but promptly adjusts as if everything's cool. He's a good faker. I need to remember that.

At the bar, Alex beckons me. "Look at this." He shows me his phone. "This doesn't even look like Resistance."

It's a Facebook ad promoting one free pint with any order if the user tags us on social media and likes a post about Resistance. Our usual ads, which ran inconsistently, showed off the brew tanks or the front sign with its neo-psychedelic font and rainbow colors. A rainbow flag hangs in the window with a sign taped below it reading *Hate Has No Home Here*.

This ad features the new flat-screen TV and a generic picture of guys holding up pints. It looks like a stock photo.

I take in the pub. No biker jackets, no goths. It's not like those groups are here every time I work, but usually some of them are.

More mainstream beer, more mainstream advertising. More mainstream customers. I blink and flash back to the pub last summer during our Happy Birthday, Jerry celebration (Jerry Garcia, RIP). The place was packed with gray haireds and purple haireds, tie-dye shirts and faded denim. The Grateful Dead rocking the jukebox. I blink again, back to the big screens turned to basketball and sports news. To the people I don't recognize.

Does it matter if things are different if the customers are paying?

A wave of sadness passes through me. It's so strong I place my hand against the bar.

Alex is still lingering, watching me.

"Sorry, I spaced out. Getting nostalgic over here." I shake it off. "I'm surprised the ad bothers you. The other day you said whatever Resistance has to do to stay in business, you're cool with it."

"The ad is whatever. It's . . . I don't know. It's probably in my head."

"Hey, that's my turf. What's all in your head?"

He turns so his back faces the customers. "Would you mind taking the table by the kitchen? Those balding guys with the gold chains?"

I peer past him. "What, you think I can kick them over with these boots or something?"

Alex shifts with an uneasy laugh.

I look closer at him. "Did they say something to you? To, like, make you feel threatened?"

He shakes his head. "Not directly. But there was a table yesterday who left after I took their order. I came back, and they were gone. It could have been anything."

My unease grows stronger. A few one-star online reviews have marked Resistance down for being "too political." *Keep your politics at home. I came here for beer.* As if a person's identity is itself political and can be easily stuffed into a duffel bag in the break room before shift. Those reviews have happened since I've been serving here, though they've been occasional, not frequent.

It could have been anything that caused those customers to leave, but I'm protective anyway.

"And this table?" I look past Alex again. "You're getting a vibe?"

"I'm getting a vibe."

The regulars who come back time and again are like a buffer. A table full of bikers who will stand up for any server here brings a sense of security. This isn't a pub with bar fights. A few times fights have broken out on the street outside the bar, but inside, people protect the space.

With a new owner and new advertising, who's to say what we're dealing with now?

"I'm on it," I tell Alex. "If you feel unsafe at all, come find me."

I stop by another table first. "I'm glad you're here," the customer says. He and his friend are shaggy-haired, bearded types with T-shirts featuring craft beer label art. "What's going on with this music?"

The song switches to another pop song. Possibly a modern boy band. "Good question."

The jukebox isn't lit up like usual. What the . . . Okay, so the music is being piped in through the PA. That's all fine and good, except the music coming out is wrong for Resistance.

I march over to the jukebox. Crouching, I fish for the cord, bringing out the loose end of the plug. Great.

The customer calls over. "Bring back the Skynyrd!"

"Dang right, bring back the Skynyrd," I say to myself. The jukebox is massive. I can't move it myself to get at the outlet.

One of the shaggy beard guys appears at my side. "Here, I'll help."

Together, we pull at the machine. It budges enough to give me space to wedge my arm behind it. I connect the plug into the outlet.

The interface lights up at the same time as his face. He holds up a fist to bump. "You're awesome. You pick first."

I bump his fist back. "I've got a good one." I tap a few buttons, watching the menu pages manually flip through options behind the glass panel until I find my pick.

A crackling guitar riff bursts through the jukebox speakers. The riff jams again, and my bearded table pumps their fists in the air. "'Cult of Personality,' yeah!"

Never mind dialing to eleven; this baby is cranked to thirteen. Breaks in the guitar give way to the generic pop song still playing on the overhead system. It's like one of those music mash-ups, only the pairing isn't clever and the sounds don't go together. It's insane and my brain hurts.

The bros turn in their seats. "We can't hear the game!" one shouts.

A bearded guy strums an air guitar at the bro.

The boy band on the overhead speaker croons *Bayyybyyyyy*.

Guests at another table rock their heads in time as the jukebox rages with the song's political lyrics. The sports bros shake their heads. One of them stands and grabs his coat. Ryan appears at the table, talking to his friend, who eventually sits down.

Ryan scans the room Terminator-style until he locks on my location. He bullets toward me. "What are you doing?"

I rock a hand at my hip. "Putting on some real music."

"They can't hear the game."

"Put on closed captioning. These customers over here love it."

The beardy guys have a full show going on—lip syncing, air guitar, air drums. A group behind them rises from their seats for the guitar solo, five of them air shredding along with the music. It's impressive! I'm bopping along, enjoying the show.

"Kat!" Ryan yells to be heard over the music.

Ugh—reality. "Okay, I get it. The *game* is on." A few other tables look confused, and some lady is holding her hands to her ears. You can't win them all.

Ryan mashes buttons on the jukebox. "We can't have on two channels of music."

"So turn yours off. This is what the customers want to hear."

"Not all the customers."

"You mean your friends?"

He grits his teeth. He pushes the edge of the jukebox, aiming to move it away from the wall.

Oh no you don't. I put my hand on the machine and lean my weight into it. "Ryan. I know you're trying something new, but our regulars hate this." I nod to the overhead speaker in the corner. "If anything, let's find a happy medium. There are plenty of streaming options besides this garbage." Ryan can be butt hurt all he wants, but I'll riot if I have to stomach eight hours of candy pop by child stars.

He turns his face to me, his hands still gripped against the jukebox. "It's not. Your. Call."

I flinch and step back. He pulled rank. About a freaking jukebox.

The jukebox song hits its crescendo with guitars wailing behind it. I give Ryan a final hard stare and spin off toward the kitchen. With this bitchin' soundtrack and my bitchy look, it's a worthy exit.

On my way, I glance between the tables with the bearded guys and the bros. Craft brew dudes and Ryan's friends. They're probably close in age but couldn't be more different. Different is fine, but this different feels off. Unsettling. I don't like where these changes are headed.

But I'm not paid for social commentary, and apparently not paid for my opinion on the music we play either.

Luiz is talking with Gary and the other cook, TJ, when I enter the kitchen. Their conversation fades.

"Hey, crew." I toss down the food orders, using our favored gender-neutral greeting. "What's up?"

Luiz looks me over. "You're like a tornado, gata."

My thoughts whirlwind, not far off from a tornado. "Did you hear the music out there? It's like a food court at a sixty-percent-occupancy mall. Our customers hate it."

Gary gives me a chin nod. "Everybody hates it."

"This guy, right? Coming in here with his sports and flat-screens like it's some kind of miracle. He's going to be the end of Resistance. He can't do this."

The kitchen door swings behind me, and the crew looks over my shoulder. Their faces wipe free of discernible expression.

"He's behind me, isn't he?"

Gary, who's smart enough not to tick off a new boss, douses the hot cooktop with oil so the sizzling destroys the awkward silence. TJ walks to the refrigerator. Luiz starts whistling and moves past me out the door.

"Actually"—Ryan officially announces his presence—"I can do exactly what I'm doing. That's why I was hired."

"By whom again?" I keep my tone sweet tinged with my patented extra-special bitter note.

He flinches.

Ha. Got 'im.

I move to pass him, but he shifts into my path. "We can't function like this."

I stand tall. "No, we can't."

"I mean you can't act like you're calling the shots because you're mad you didn't get the job."

I'm glad the grill is hot and sizzling, because if Gary could hear this, I'd be mortified. "I'm not discussing this." I leave the kitchen.

Ryan is right behind me. "Don't walk away from me."

He probably thinks he sounds authoritative or menacing, but he's more like a kid tugging at his parent's coat sleeve. Which is probably all he did to get this job. "I'm working."

"This . . . we can't . . ."

His insecurity is giving me life. I check on two tables, take more drink orders and drop them at the bar. The jukebox is now playing Lynyrd Skynyrd, and the beard guys are content. I deliver the drinks and bypass the bros, since Ryan so conveniently gifted them free beer. I could see if they're doing okay, but I honestly don't care if they come back.

I circle back to the kitchen.

I swear under my breath. Ryan is here. "Kat. You and I. Talk now."

"No." I fold my arms.

Gary chuckles at the grill.

"This isn't funny," Ryan seethes to me.

"Do I look like I'm laughing?"

He's not going to reprimand Gary for laughing. Gary will knock him to the floor faster than he can fire up an e-cig. Those are the things Gary does fast. Those two things.

Ryan walks ahead to the narrow hall and stops by the room we use to stash our coats and belongings. It's more of a glorified closet with coat hooks along one wall and a beat-up folding table pressed against the other with a couple of chairs pulled up to one side. He waits.

Reluctantly, I follow, arms folded.

He has a desperate look in his eyes. "I need those guys to come back. They won't if they hate it here."

"Do they get unlimited free beer each time they grace us with their presence?"

He presses his fingers to his forehead. "That's not the point. They'll bring friends. Who pay. They know a lot of people."

I note he didn't say no on the free beer. "So your master plan is to have your friends come here and save Resistance one pint at a time?"

He shakes his head, his jaw firm. "You." He points at me. "You've been nothing but judgmental toward me from the start. In any other situation, a person in authority wouldn't tolerate it."

I can't help it; I snicker. "Sorry, you said authority like you have any."

A whole lot of something cycles through that disturbingly good-looking noggin of his. A roulette wheel of responses, I imagine, spinning and spinning. I want to hear it. I want to hear the best he's got.

"I mean it, Kat. There are people who've been fired for less than this."

And the wheel stops on threatening employment! "Oh, *I've* been fired for less than this. I lost a full-time salaried job because the numbers weren't good enough to keep me. I was simply a data point that didn't work out."

He breathes in and lets it out. "I'm sorry."

His apology stalls my momentum. "It doesn't matter. The music—it's a whole thing here. People like the jukebox. They like to pick the songs. Yes, they're old songs. No one has ever complained we don't have current pop songs playing. They can go literally anywhere else for that."

"Okay. We'll talk about the music. But I don't think this"—he gestures between us—"is only about the music."

Fair. So let's do this. "You made your point clear. You're not interested in investing in your staff. If you were, you'd listen to what's important to us. Anya is already asking around to switch shifts to work with her school schedule. She's the easiest person to manage so long as you work around her schedule. And Alex. He just asked me to take a table because he's getting unsafe vibes. He's never asked me to swap tables before. Your marketing attempt seems to be attracting quite the assorted variety."

He seems taken aback by what I'm saying. Good. He needs to hear it.

"Is that it?" he asks, his tone hard as his granite stare. "Are those all my mistakes? I think what you're missing is I don't invest in staff because I didn't hire you. You're not just mad, you're blaming me. I'm another reason for your life not turning out the way you want."

It's like a hundred paper cuts slicing my fingertips. I can't show him it stings. He doesn't get to tell me how I feel or why I feel it.

I inch into his space. "I didn't even get an interview."

He stands straighter. "You can't see how entitled you are. You assumed the job would be yours."

He said entitled. He called *me* entitled. When his own father handed him this very job! "I deserved a shot. I won't back down from that. Ever."

He stares. I stare. I refuse to flinch or blink or breathe.

The room shrinks and the air with it. We're close. The energies our bodies are putting out slam against each other and pull out switchblades. Somebody calls out, "Street fight!" Or maybe my imagination is hyperviolent right now. I'm glad my energy is doing the work, because the fight in me is dwindling. I can still smell, and he smells good. Frustratingly good. Woodsy but laced with a familiar grainy scent from working near the brew tanks.

He balks first and steps back. A small victory. An empty one, though. Nothing is different.

Wait, maybe that's not true. Nothing has changed about my situation, but what's between Ryan and me feels different after this confrontation. More charged. More tense.

"I want to get along." He speaks in a softer tone. "If you have a problem with anything I'm doing, come to me. Don't let it play out in front of the customers."

Since I have his attention. "I do have a suggestion. Let your shot girl put on some real clothes. She's freezing standing by the door."

"Is this some kind of feminist thing?"

Can blood boil? I think blood can boil. I think mine is boiling. "She's a hot girl. It's feminist to look good and own it." I can't believe I have to explain this. "The girl is *shivering*."

He nods once, probably reluctantly. "We can station her away from the door."

"Fine."

"Okay, then."

We look at each other some more. I'm drained. It's six hours until close. Ryan looks weary and grateful this conversation is likely ending.

And yet it's near impossible to pry myself from the room. This energy, whatever it is, glues my boots to the floor. I urge my feet toward the open door. "One more thing."

"Yeah?" His response comes across eager, hopeful even. I have to believe he wants us to get along and listening is his way of showing that. A low bar, but I'll take it for now.

"Load the shot girl with beer samples. *Our* beer. And send her to me for coaching."

With that, I return to the floor and focus on my job. For as long as I'm here, I'll let him know exactly what I think.

CHAPTER ELEVEN
KOLSCH STYLE

Light and crisp, this style balances lager and ale quali-
ties. Pairs well with heavier fare like sausage and cheeses.
And angst.

The next night, those of us on shift cash everyone out. We have closing down to a written procedure with bullet points. In fact, I drafted
that exact procedure and provided it to Ryan, formerly Hottie
McWetpants, He of Soured Golden Ale, and my Nemesis Overlord.

I open the door to the brewing room, which is empty at this
hour. I miss being back here. The class in Wisconsin reminded me
of what I'm missing.

Jana, my buddy from the class, texted earlier to check in.

Jana: *How's it going, lady? Getting your time in with the
brewers?*

I'm instantly frustrated with myself. I've made no progress
connecting with Kurt and Randy other than a quick review with
Randy on my processes.

I text back that I've been busy. It's a BS answer I'm sure she can see through.

Jana: *If you want to talk strategies, I'm open. Things are moving faster than expected. We have a potential investor. Looking to make our goddesses operation happen soon.*

I should at least take her up on talking career plans. Otherwise, I'll get bogged down with daily work and won't plan further on an exit strategy. Being busy is a good excuse for putting off hard decisions.

Me: *Thanks. I'll text you later. Really appreciate it.*
Jana: *Stay strong! Take care for now.*

Ryan comes out from the back office. "Do you need something?"

A new job at a different bar. Or, better, him gone and replaced with anyone else. "What are you still doing here?"

For a split second he looks like he's going to snap something at me, but then he appears to think better of it. "There's a lot to figure out."

"Well then, I'll let you get to figuring."

"Hey. Hold up."

I already have the door open a crack when Ryan shoves his foot against it. The abrupt closure causes me to flinch and step back.

Ryan's hands fly up. "Sorry. I didn't mean to—just, if you want to go, go, but I wanted to say something. No, um, show you something. In the back office."

Heat crawls across his neck. The way he's stumbling over words could be viewed as endearing except for how he tried to trap me here. "You want to go to the back office to *show me* something?"

His left eyebrow twitches. "To review something, yes. For business purposes. Obviously."

Of course obviously. Did he think I was flirting? I wasn't. I was pointing out how unbusinesslike what he said sounded, but now I sound like the perv. Should I bother to explain any of this? "It's weird you blocked the door."

"I know. Sorry."

"You could just ask me what you want to ask me."

"It's less of an ask and more of . . . it's better if I show you."

I'm curious now, I can't help it. "Okay. Fine."

He makes a point of opening the office door as wide as it can go, craning his neck to see into the brewing room and beyond. His gesture confirms that yes, we are alone in this office, but in full view of any staff should they choose to look this way. They're all going home, so it's pointless to care.

Ryan taps the desktop computer awake. The thing is old enough to drive and maybe old enough to drink. If I hadn't sold my college desktop to replace my old phone, I'd have donated it to the office. At least mine was from the past decade.

"Definitely need an upgrade in here," he mumbles.

"But that costs money," I add with a smile. He doesn't acknowledge my comment. "Sorry. Couldn't help it."

"Did you ever—" he starts. "I know you were close with the owners. Being part of making the beer and all. Did they ever let you in on the numbers?"

"The finances? Not really."

"I had a tough conversation today." He sinks into the chair. The faux leather is worn through on the armrests and peeling all along the back cushion. "There were suppliers Resistance had a tab with. We had to get those paid down or . . . I mean, I don't have the relationship with those suppliers like the other owners had. I can't let them extend us free credit indefinitely." He shakes his head. "I'm sorry, I didn't mean to drag you into the details. I'm trying to get a sense of what we're looking at given where we're starting."

I'm really listening now. "What are you saying?" Prairie and Joe have big hearts, but they've kept this place afloat for over two decades. You don't do that with sloppy bookkeeping.

"I talked with Prairie about the money owed to the suppliers. She's taking money from the sale to cover funds owed, but . . . they obviously need that money for medical costs." He sighs. "They've been sliding with some bills here. I can't figure out what's up with the electric—they're paying it, but there's always a balance."

A solid drop hits my gut. "How bad?"

"It might not be as bad as I think. Prairie was getting protective, defensive. I want to trust her—"

"Of course. It's Prairie."

He looks me over. "That doesn't mean the same thing to me. I don't know her. I see these numbers, and they don't add up."

My heartbeat wakes up. "I'm sure it's a mistake. Neither she nor Joe would leave this a mess on purpose."

"I'm not saying it's on purpose."

He's talking to me like how someone calms an animal. I don't like this feeling, this—this overturned idea of who Joe and Prairie are. They're good people who ran Resistance the way they wanted for decades.

"Kat, I have to do this right. I sent the books to my family's accounting firm for a full audit. It's going to take some time."

A chill runs over my skin. My mind goes to Anthony's tab. One guy's tab paid off every month by the bar isn't much to sneeze at—only their generosity wasn't limited to Anthony. They paid me part of my check in advance a couple of months ago and still paid me again on payday. They told me not to stress; it would all even out in the end.

The suppliers have known them for years and drank for free here when they wanted. We knew them too. But they were still owed their money. The electric company doesn't owe us favors. And here in Cook County, right in the heart of the city, taxes are high. The state of Illinois is no joke when it comes to licensing costs. In that it costs a fortune.

I know this, and from one look at Ryan's pleasantly symmetrical face, he knows it too.

"And meanwhile, you bought a new flat-panel TV," I remind him.

"Yeah."

"And ads giving away free beer."

"Do you think it's working?"

"I'm giving away a lot of free pints of beer we don't make. Is that what you consider working?"

He leans back in the chair. "Look, I know you're loyal to Resistance, but what was going on here wasn't going to work long-term. I had to do something else."

"What you could have done was come to us for ideas. Instead, you want to turn this place into a sports bar."

"Everyone likes sports."

"Everyone does not like sports."

"Most people."

"A lot of people. Sports are fine. But we already have TVs by the bar. The people who come in to watch football sit there."

"There are eight seats at the bar. I'm talking a whole bar filled on game day. There are bars in the Loop packed when the Chicago teams play. Bars in Wrigleyville at capacity during Cubs games. Pubs on the South Side are crowded with Sox fans."

"And Resistance fills a gap for those who don't want a packed bar on game day. Who'd rather do trivia while they listen to retro rock and drink wicked-good beer."

"A quiet place to use as an office for their side hustle while they drink one beer over two hours? Surfing the internet doesn't pay the very real bills here." He grabs a stack of papers to gesture with. "Trivia nights can't save this place. I can't hold off those suppliers forever."

What's the name for when you know someone makes a fair point and you don't want to admit it? I hate it, whatever it is.

"So why show me this?" I ask. "You brought me back here, for what?"

He lets the bills fall to the desk. "You care about Resistance. Probably more than anybody here. It's not simply a paycheck to you."

"Lots of people care."

He props his elbows on the desk and lets his head hang a second. "You're the only one who talks to me."

Which is sad, because most of my talking toward him is pretty snarky.

"The servers barely give me a second glance. Don't get me started on the kitchen."

I know that's not entirely true, because we've all given him a few second glances. But I hear him on this. The staff aren't talking to him. If he's reduced to man candy, that's not a relationship. No real trust built. And he's right about the kitchen.

"It's because I want to marry the beer," I tell him.

"I'm sorry, what?"

"It's a thing I used to joke about with Joe and Prairie. You know how kids say *If you like it so much, why don't you marry it?* I said once . . . never mind, it's dumb."

"I need your help, Kat."

I look at him. No smirk, no scowl. Genuine worry. His guard is very much down now, and it's me he's letting it down for.

Me.

I have to admit, he's around a lot. He's in over his head, but at least he's taking a crack at a plan to get Resistance in a better place. Even if his plan sucks, it's better than doing nothing.

He rubs the back of his neck. "I need to get this right."

Curious. "Why is that? You don't have any strings here. Other than your folks know Joe and Prairie."

He considers this. "When I talked about opportunity, I meant it. This is my chance to prove myself. Do you know what it's like to be on a fast track where everything is working out, until suddenly it isn't?"

I realize I'm leaning forward, rapt with attention. Immediately I sit back, picking at a nail. "Maybe."

"I always had a plan. I knew I wanted to go to Iowa State when I was fifteen. My brother enrolled there, and I idolized him. I studied business like my dad. They made it easy for me. Maybe too easy."

I feign a yawn, but I'm consuming every word. He's been so freaking closed off all this time. I know next to nothing about him.

"After college, the place where I'd done my internship chose a buyout and relocated to Texas. I wasn't interested in moving with them, and they didn't offer anyway. My dad wanted me to work for his investment company, but it felt like a handout, so I told him no. I moved home with my parents to look for work, only they never pushed it. Mom liked having me back in the house. My older brother, he—never mind, doesn't matter. Anyway." The corner of the electric bill is like a mini accordion from how he's bent and folded it. "I started working for my dad after all. It never felt like a real job, because I barely had any real work."

"The three-day workweek, like your friend said."

He stares at the desk. "Not quite, but I did spend a lot of time golfing with clients. I hate golf. I usually took off early on Fridays to spend my weekends downtown in our spare condo."

Whatever twinge of empathy I was feeling for him drains instantly. "A spare condo. In the city. Don't tell me it's lakefront."

His face colors. "It's not *on* the lake."

I keep my gaze trained on him.

"I can see Lake Michigan from the bedroom window, okay?"

"Is that where you're living now?"

He nods. "It's temporary. It's not mine."

I grip the arms of the hard chair I'm in. "Must be nice to be handed a place to live and a business to run. I'm sure if things go sour, you can start again with something else."

I peek at him. He's not scowling or readying a defense. He looks shamed. "Not this time. This is it."

"What do you mean? Your parents kicked you out? To the spare lakefront condo?" Honestly, I'd take that deal.

He stands and walks the length of the small room. "If you really want to know, my parents got into a huge fight. Lines were drawn. My mom loves having me in the house. I mean, it's pretty great—she cooks for me, kept my room clean—" He stops talking. "Yeah, I realize how it sounds."

"I didn't say anything."

"You were muttering. I heard you."

I was probably muttering. "So Daddy wasn't happy that Mommy was extending your childhood. What next?"

He bypasses my sarcasm. Which he should, because I already told him sarcasm is lazy. "It wasn't fair to them. I knew it, but I didn't know what else to do. It's . . . complicated. I tried. I really did. I would apply for jobs and get turned down. Or I'd show up for an interview and it wouldn't be anything like the listed description. And paid barely anything."

I actually laugh. Out loud. I shift in the chair and look at him. He's serious as a funeral. "Welcome to *jobs*. That's, like, the entirety of adulthood for a majority of people. The jobs never pay enough, and they're never what you think they're supposed to be."

He presses his lips together. "You know what? Never mind." He walks to the computer, bangs a few keys. "You think I'm a spoiled rich kid who hasn't worked a day. I have worked. I *want* to work." Now he's shaking the mouse because the screen is frozen.

"Look, Ryan." I take the mouse from his hand and set it on a Resistance Brewpub mouse pad so faded in the middle only the *R* and *B* are left. "I did health care administration before this. I even made enough money to live in an apartment with hot water eighty percent of the time. I didn't hate the work and thought I'd make a go of it with a master's degree. Climb the ladder and all that. Remember how I said I lost my job?"

He's calmed and back to sitting. "Yeah?"

"I was laid off. My whole division lost two or three people in each department. My job no longer existed."

"I'm sorry."

I take a second to make sure I'm still calm. A company I did everything right for who couldn't find space for me. "I'd already started here at Resistance nights and weekends, so at least I had something. Just like you, I started applying places and getting turned down. When a server quit here, Prairie gave me their hours. This became my full-time gig. My fascination with brewing became a new path forward." I flit my hand toward him. "We were talking about you. Tell me more about what's going on with your family."

He stills. "My family."

"If it's relevant."

"It's nothing. Forget I said anything." He checks his watch, a large-faced Apple watch pristine enough to be a recent Christmas purchase. "It's late. You should go."

So, that's it? What a cheat bomb. Just when we were making progress. I get up and head out the wide-open office door.

Inside, I'm a mess of emotions warring with aching feet and a body begging for seven hours with a pillow. But I stop at the door, because Ryan was real with me tonight. He cares about this job and is lost on what to do. He asked for my help. It's tempting to stay bitter, but I know better.

Too many people get hurt if Resistance is in bad shape. If all I can think of is how to get a zinger in on my privileged boss, who am I, really? That's not the person I want to be.

I return to the office and place a palm against the desk surface. "You made a guy tip me."

Ryan startles at my reappearance. "Sorry, what?"

"The grouchy guy. Before I knew who you were. You told that guy to tip and then called him an asshole."

"Some people are just assholes."

"That's exactly what you said! You didn't have to do any of it. And that was after I threw my phone at you."

"So, you admit it. You threw your phone at me."

Did he just do a gotcha? At me? "I didn't target you with intent. It was passive rage, I guess."

"You guess you had passive rage." He laughs softly. "That's quite a skill."

"If I was skilled in passive rage, I would have way more control over it. Subconscious, even, since the rage doesn't require deliberate thought." What am I saying? "Anyway, we were talking about your family." I sit to show him I'm listening. "It sounds like they're a part of why you're here trying to make it work. I think it's worth hearing you out so I can help you."

Ryan slides back from the desk but stays in the chair. "Here's the thing. With my parents, we've had . . . issues. I realized I was part of the problem and it was on me to make a move or my parents would never last. I couldn't do that to them after thirty-five years of being together. When I heard how our company planned to invest in Resistance, I knew this was my chance. I had to do this."

"To prove you're not a freeloader. Except for the whole spare-condo part."

He leans forward with his elbows against his knees. "I understand what it must sound like. You changed careers once already. You're getting yourself out of debt, on your own, from a job that pays tips."

I don't remember telling him about my debt, but I talk about it enough that he must have heard.

"My dad agreed to give me six months to make measured improvements. The bar can't be in debt. It has to remain fully staffed. I have to show marked increases in sales and revenue or he's going to find someone else to run the pub. If it's too much a loss, he'll sell."

I take this in. "Your father invested because he cares about Joe and Prairie. He wouldn't sell Resistance to someone for the sake of selling it. That was the whole point of them choosing Benny the Burrito."

"Benny the what?"

"The whole burrito thing. You know. From college?"

Ryan covers his face with his hand. "Only Joe calls him Benny. I don't think I've ever seen my dad eat a burrito."

Must be a fantastic story to have made him quit burritos for life.

He goes on. "My dad's bottom line is always the bottom line. After going through the books, it's not looking great. Depending how Joe's health goes—"

I stand. "You know what? That's enough. I don't want to hear about what Joe's health has to do with anything."

He's eyes fall shut. "I'm sorry." He opens them again. "Truly, I'm sorry."

That Joe's health could even slightly factor into the future of Resistance under the new owner—his college buddy—appalls me. Resistance is in trouble. And Ryan needs my help.

Oh, the irony, after not hiring me as a brewer.

If only he'd hired me, then the crew would have seen it as an investment. I'd be part of the process to help us move in a new direction.

I could go somewhere else. There are tons of other pubs and breweries around the city.

Something scratches at me below my racing thoughts. I'm invested here. I care about the staff, my friends. I don't want to see Resistance mismanaged, or worse, go under. Even if there are other jobs out there, I can't do that to the people I care about. If Ryan thinks I can help, it means he may be ready to listen to our ideas.

I look at Ryan. If he didn't care, we wouldn't be having this conversation. If he didn't have even a handful of crumbs of respect for me, he wouldn't have pulled me in.

"If you want my help," I tell him, "this has to go beyond proving to your family you can be an adult. It has to be about investing in what Resistance has been and what it can be. If it's not that, then you'll never build trust with the crew or the community. The people coming here for years want to feel welcome, even if you're importing half the North Side to slum it with us."

His face is stoic. Unmoving. He breathes, and the facade collapses. "I'll do whatever it takes."

This is promising. "Okay."

He angles forward. "Really? You'll help me?" The relief on his face is almost comical. He's at once boyish and perfectly handsome and oh my, did he say he liked that his mom cleaned his room? A woman somewhere exists who would love to clean up after Ryan. A supermodel who likes to vacuum, I imagine.

I scoot the chair around to the end of the desk so I can better see the computer, which has now thawed from its frozen state. "Pull up the file that says *Bands*." I point with a pen toward the screen.

He scrubs a hand over barely existent beard scruff. "Now? It's nearly one thirty in the morning."

My body screams for my bed. "Whatever it takes, dude."

CHAPTER TWELVE
COFFEE BEER

Roasted flavor often added to stouts and porter bases and increasingly found in more styles, like IPAs. Beer or coffee: Why choose?

After five hours' sleep, I stir awake. My brain won't shut off. Ideas keep prodding at me. Ideas to turn Resistance back into a profitable business.

Ryan and I only stayed another twenty minutes at the office last night. Turns out one forty-five AM is my drop-dead time. No more all-nighters for me. I don't know what it is about that magic one-to-two-AM hour, but all my energy collapses and I'm jelly. I'm swiftly surpassing the age where an energy drink can fix that kind of tired.

And I'm clearly entering the age of early risers. Why fight it? I get coffee started in the kitchen.

My phone buzzes with a text. Jana again.

Jana: *The investor is in! We're a go!*

Wow, things really are moving for her. Fast.

Meanwhile, I have a notebook open with the word *IDEAS* at the top underlined with nothing below it. I pour myself coffee and wait for inspiration.

Nope, nothing.

I underline a second time.

I could spiral about my lack of progress, or I could do something. I call Jana.

"Hey girl," she answers. "Sorry if I'm bugging you with my texts. I'm just excited."

"It's great! I'm happy for you." Pause. "You said if I wanted to talk strategies . . ." I trail off, because I don't know where to start.

She tells me to go ahead and share what's up. I give her a high-level overview of my talk with Ryan and the state of Resistance. The high-level devolves into details and speculation and maybe a few things more suited for a therapist.

Jana utters an occasional *mm-hmm* on the other end. When I finish, she takes a moment; the line is quiet. "It sounds like your mentors had a rough go of it with the business. Maybe things weren't as sunshine and rainbows as you thought."

My protective guard activates. "They're good people."

"My best friend is a good person. She would also be terrible at running a business. She gets overwhelmed easily and focuses on details that don't matter. She's adverse to conflict."

"I realize people have different strengths. Prairie and Joe were great at bringing people together. I don't want to lose that."

"One thing you can't change is how things will change."

"Yeah, but there are things worth preserving. I can't leave Resistance in the lurch when the very thing that brought so many of us together is being destroyed."

She utters a *hmm*.

"What?"

"You said yourself the finances were mishandled. It sounds to me like this sale did them a favor. The owners may have been forced to sell eventually anyway if they couldn't pay their bills."

This is obviously logical. But she doesn't know Prairie and Joe. She wasn't there with them listening to Alex break down about not believing he was good enough for a new relationship. She didn't see them support Anya through balancing work and school. Or with me, how Joe and Prairie stood in for what my parents weren't around to do. They gave me extra hours and taught me new skills. Gave me new hope and direction.

"They loved Resistance and invested in the people." I don't think Jana's arguing that point, but I want it said out loud.

"I know it's tough to hear," she goes on. "What keeps me going some days is to think how proud my parents would be of the business we're making. My own dad died in his fifties. My mother never got over it and was never the same."

"Wow, I'm sorry. Is your mother still alive? What does she think?"

"I know she loves me, but she doesn't understand my love of brewing. She thinks it's seedy. Underhanded. Like prohibition rumrunners." She laughs a little, but it's tinged with sadness. "I found myself seeking out other people to be a parental figure, you know? Other family. I'm in my forties now and still need someone to look up to."

I seem to have a knack for glomming onto parental figures too.

Maybe I made the mistake of coloring Joe and Prairie with my own idea of sunshine and rainbows when they were struggling just as much as anyone. Just as much as my own parents.

"Joe and Prairie listened," I tell Jana. "They cared. That matters to me. They were more than bosses. They were like family."

"And they hurt you like family."

I bite down on the inside of my cheek, willing tears to stay back. They did hurt me. They didn't mean to, but they did. They left me. I'm all but forgotten by the family I made for myself.

"Kat, I promise I'm not trying to press the wound," Jana says in a soothing tone. "I see a lot of myself in you. You can still care about them, but you don't owe them your time and career to fix what they abandoned." She pauses. "Thank you for coming to my TED Talk."

I actually laugh, which is a near miracle, since I'm feeling so low.

"Thanks for talking through this with me," I say. "I do feel an obligation to Resistance. I don't know that I can turn that off." Not now, at least.

Life is shifting, and I'm in the center of the shift as it's happening. I can preserve Joe and Prairie as faultless in my own memory vault, or I can start thinking about them as the flawed people they are.

What that thinking leads to, I don't know. The unknown is what scares me most.

I may not owe Prairie and Joe—though that's a hard concept to get over—but I do owe Ryan help. He asked, and I care enough about Resistance to follow through.

He gave the crew his cell for emergencies. This is almost an emergency. Especially when it turns out Mr. Not-Burrito is trigger happy to sell the business off.

Me: *Let's meet—brunch.*
Ryan: *Who is this?*

Ugh. He didn't bother to save my number?

Me: *It's Kat.*
Ryan: *You're up already?*
Me: *It's ten in the morning!*
Ryan: *I didn't get in until 3:15!*

I got in just after two last night . . . er, this morning. Ryan insisted on driving me home. I agreed, because safety first. I was so tired and the ride so short, I don't have much memory of our conversation. But I do remember something. His car smelled *great.*

Ryan: *It's my day off. And yours.*

Is this guy for real?

Me: *Anything it takes*

There's a pause where all I see are the little wavering dots indicating he's typing back.

Ryan: *Fine.*

Ha.

Me: *Where are you again? Give me cross streets.*
Ryan: *You're coming here?*
Me: *I'll find someplace close to eat. Otherwise you'll sleep until noon.*
Ryan: *What are you, my mother?*

Oh, he did not.

Me: *I'm not cleaning your room. Ever. Call me your mom again and the deal is off.*
Ryan: *I guess the joke part wasn't obvious?*

I don't laugh. I mean . . . this guy. This gorgeous, ridiculous specimen will not have trouble finding a woman who will gladly "clean his room."

I am not that woman.

I take his cross streets and plug them into an app for food options. I text him a place and time, then switch to my public transit app to figure out a route.

The route isn't direct and requires a bus and the train plus a two-block walk.

I beat him to the restaurant. I'm seated at a table by the front window and see him before he sees me. Even with him being wrapped in a black coat like half the population out there, I know it's him. The Burberry plaid scarf, for one. The sculpted cheekbones, for two. And three, I don't know—his face, I guess. He has such a distinct face. He's doing his fast-and-purposeful walk, like an escape in an orderly fashion.

"Oh, hey." He slips into the booth across from me, all rosy cheeked from the cold. "What even is this place? There's a breakfast café run by a celebrity chef a block from me. I thought maybe this"—he makes a face as the pleather booth seat squeaks in response to him sitting—"was a mistake."

I open my glossy laminated menu, which lists every breakfast food imaginable. "I saw the celebrity place on my dining app. There's a two-month wait list. For brunch."

He scowls. "Oh, wow. Sorry I'm late. I wasn't sure where to park."

The menu falls from my hand. "Park? You live two blocks from here."

"More like three and a half, plus—" He shakes his head. "I might as well have walked, because I'm parked two streets over the other direction."

I can't hold back my bafflement. "It's kind of the entire reason I came to you. To make it easy."

"Yeah, well, nothing about getting around here is easy." He squirms against the seat, which makes another, lower squeak. He yanks his scarf out from under him and bunches it on top of his coat. "Most of the parking spaces around here are permit-only zones."

"Where do you usually park?"

"My building has a lower-level garage."

I can't fathom how much enclosed, lower-level garage access costs. My bet is Ryan doesn't know either. "We should try something out. You should take public transit to work for your next shift."

He looks like a cat doused with water. "No way. There's no reason for it."

I could let this go. I really could. Except I'm feeling those extra-special bitters today. "Have you ever taken a bus?"

He's completely exasperated, looking at me like I'm on drugs. Or the War on Drugs telling him he can't use drugs—I don't know his stance on substances. "Stop talking to me like I'm a child. Yes, Kat. I've taken a bus. To school, every day from upper elementary until middle school."

Not too many years riding the yellow beast, but he answered my question and I've already pushed him.

Why does he do this to me? I turn salty the second we face each other. I need to scale it back. Like, majorly limit the sodium content.

He keeps talking. "Not that I have to prove anything to you, but I've taken the train into Union Station. I've taken the El. It doesn't make sense for me to use public transit to the pub, given my hours and where it is. It's easier to drive."

The server comes by to fill our coffees and I let her know we need a minute.

"You're right; the route isn't direct for transit, as I just experienced. It would take significantly longer than driving. So ignore me on taking it to work. But I do think it's valuable to see how different areas of the city connect. You get a sense for the people who you live around and work with when you're riding the bus or taking the El." I scan the menu, then set it aside.

He grabs his menu. "How are you ready? You've been talking the entire time."

The server is back, and she's absolutely checking him out. I don't blame her. I'd give her fair warning, though—she works on her feet all day, so she's not going to want to clean his room on her off time.

We put in our orders, and I pull a folder out of my bag. I've goaded Ryan enough, and it's time to get cracking. "Examples of promo for some of our release events. I'm sure you have most of this on the office computer, but in case you haven't seen it, I thought we could go over it."

He continually looks out the window, at his watch, and around to the bustling customers coming in for an early lunch while I'm showing him the materials.

"Sorry, is this boring you?" I wince at my own sarcasm. Apparently, I use that tactic often even though it irritates me when people use it on me. Something Ryan has made me acutely aware of.

"We can't achieve what we need with business as usual. It's not going to work."

"This isn't business as usual. These are special events."

"We can't rely on an occasional weekend of good business. We need to improve business every day."

Our food arrives, and both of us focus on adding condiments. "I'd love to hear your ideas." *If you have any other than shot girls and big-screen TVs.*

He digs into his poached egg and English muffin. "This is great." He drinks from his coffee mug. "Maybe we should do breakfast."

It takes me a second to follow. "At the pub?"

"Sundays. Do a brunch."

I'd prefer to immediately shoot this down, but . . . maybe not. Sadie and I joined a friend of hers for brunch a few months ago at a pub in the Loop. It was stupidly expensive for the amount of food I ate, but we attended with free tickets courtesy of her friend's company. The place was packed. Families, the influencer crowd, business types. An all-you-can-eat buffet with unique food choices at a venue not typically open for breakfast.

I finish chewing. "We should talk to Luiz."

"You could at least tell me my idea is bad before moving on."

"I'm not moving on. Luiz knows a lot of restaurant owners in the neighborhood—the neighborhood by Resistance. There was someone, I forget who, that catered an event at a taproom in Wicker Park. Luiz said the food was fantastic. We could host a vendor, like a pop-up event. They do the food, bring in their contacts, we host the event."

Ryan nods. "It could be a good way to cross-pollinate."

Now all I can think of is bees. "Did you have to bring pollinating into this?"

"You know what I mean."

I take out my phone and tap notes into an app. I type *bzzz* and delete it. "If we host another vendor, we won't stress our existing cooking staff. The vendor can use our kitchen. We can do that, right?" I look up. I don't know restaurant kitchen guidelines. "We can let other people use the kitchen?"

Ryan shrugs.

Of course he doesn't know. "Maybe put it on your list to find out?"

He shakes his head. "We're doing it."

Okay, then. "I'll talk to Luiz and get his suggestions on who to ask. Can I have him follow up with you?"

"Luiz? Uh, sure."

"It could be a chance for you to make a connection with the crew. Besides me, I mean."

He leans back against the booth seat. "Good idea. Thanks for this, Kat. I do need to get better at connecting."

All noise fades as he looks at me. A thread is forming between us. I sense the energy and see it taking shape. He's trying. Brunch is a good idea, especially if it's a recurring, regular part of business.

"It'll be good to find a vendor who's already part of the community," he says, breaking the connecting vibes. "You said that part was important—to serve the community." He digs back into his food with renewed gusto.

I watch him inhale half his plate. The guy can eat. "I also think it's important to define what we mean by 'community' going forward," I say. "It will shape what we do. You mentioned your vision for Resistance. How is community part of that vision?"

He's giving me a blank look, and I know I've lost him. Or he doesn't care. Or he's focused on breakfast, for which I can't blame him. This place rules.

"Let me go first," I say. "Community to me is having a place to go when everything feels in turmoil. People who will listen and accept you for who you are, right then and there. Not conditionally. People who will sit you down and tell you what's what, even when it's difficult and risks intruding." People who will delete a toxic contact from your phone, for example. "For me, Resistance is that place. They were my family when my own had no energy for me. I found my roommates because of people at Resistance. They're the community who showed me I had more to offer than what I was seeing in myself. They're the ones who trained me with skills I'll always have."

My chest tightens as I think of my earlier conversation with Jana. Maybe I don't owe Prairie and Joe, but I feel an obligation to continue what they started. I can put my own hurt aside.

"That's . . . wow." Ryan looks at me—fork down, even. "I don't have a community like you do. I'm starting to wonder if I ever did. My mom was always there for me. A little too much. My brother . . . it's not the same."

"Your family can be your community. There's nothing wrong with that." I wish I had that.

"Except they're not. Not anymore. We haven't been . . . close in a long time. Back in college, I had some friends, good friends. I can't remember ever telling them *everything*, though. Or having anyone, like, steer me in a direction." His eyes light up. "When I played basketball. Middle school and high school. That was a good community. Those guys—they were great. I think my brother, though . . ." He looks back at me. "Any siblings?"

"A sister. Senior in college. Though she's just past the typical age for seniors."

"What's her major?"

"World domination."

He laughs.

I point at him. "You laugh, but it's true. She wants to apply to medical school, which is a real accomplishment, since—" I stop. This is a hedge I get to every time I talk about Karrie. Half the time people confuse lupus with other *L* diseases like Lyme disease or leprosy. They think it's the one where your limbs fall off or whatever. Someone for real asked my sister if she was afraid of losing her toes. I don't want people thinking of my kid sister as diseased. So it only comes up when it has to, and right now it doesn't have to.

There's a line waiting for tables, so we square away the check.

Back out on the street, the sun is fierce and bright through the cold.

"Did you have more ideas?" Ryan asks, holding the door for an elderly couple walking into the restaurant. "We could go for coffee or, I don't know, back to my place. It's close."

"So close you had to drive."

"I'll never live this down, will I?"

At least he's smiling.

I am so wide awake it hurts. "If I have any more coffee, I'll be like that guy."

A man walks by us as the wind whips into his comb-over. The hair flaps at us in greeting, and he mashes it in a frenzy.

Ryan snickers. "Okay. My place."

We find his car, which I'm fairly certain is parked in a residential permit zone. The sleek black Audi smells like a room filled with leather chairs and books and whiskey. Like a dapper gentleman's home library.

The ride is short, because of course it is, and we pull into underground parking with a steep decline below the high-rise. Here's a black Audi, there's a black Audi, everywhere shiny black Audis. Oh! One bright spot. A yellow Honda with road salt coating the wheels and a Star Wars BB-8 sticker on the back window.

"That one's my favorite."

Ryan parks two spots down and shuts off the car. "What's your favorite?"

Oops, thinking out loud. "Nothing. Just that crusty yellow car."

We get out, and he clicks the doors locked. "A Honda whatever model that is, that's your favorite car?"

"Not the car, but the all of it. Look at this row. Everything is black or gray and then a burst of yellow. It's not slick yellow either, but lived in. I want to know how the person driving that car is living large on the lake."

"We're two blocks from the lake."

As if two measly blocks make much difference. "Who pays for covered parking for *that*?"

"A renter?"

Maybe. Rent has to be bananas here.

We enter the elevator, and Ryan hits the number ten. The doors glide closed. Suddenly, I'm aware of every sound my body makes. The whistle of my coat, the ever-present puffer. My breathing sounds like an avalanche. What was I talking about with that Honda? He has to think I'm such a weirdo. Who declares their favorite car in a parking garage?

We make it to floor ten without incident. I follow him to his door and into a small vestibule with a coat closet on one side facing a modern art painting on the opposite wall. I untie my boots and slip out into socks. I shrink at the sight of the dirty boots in the pristine hallway. I start to toss the puffer on top of them, but Ryan holds out his hand. "I'll take that."

The kitchen is on the right after the vestibule, open to a small, classy living room with windows looking out at more tall buildings. Everything is modern and clean, though it looks short on personality. Sadie would hate it, but I wouldn't hate on that stainless-steel four-door fridge. Or the—no way—second smaller fridge built into a lower cabinet.

I rush to the mini-fridge and nearly yank it open like a heathen. Instead, I squat and peer through the glass. "Why is this thing empty? We need to load this baby up."

Ryan hovers next to me. "The wine fridge? I'm not a big wine drinker."

"Fill it with beer." Seriously, how did this guy end up at Resistance?

He's shaking his head. "There's plenty of room in this beast." He pulls open the refrigerator doors. "I'll get us some . . . not coffee."

I wander to the fireplace and find a family picture on the mantel. I almost mistake the people in it for models advertising the frame—that's how freakishly good looking this family is. But there's Ryan in the pic, squinting into the sun, so unless he's had a job as a photo frame model, this is his family. His parents, Benny and Bonnie Burrito, and another guy who could be Ryan's twin, except he looks older than Ryan, with shaggier hair. Ryan's face is a little rounder and younger than it is now. His smile—wow. What a great smile.

"This is your brother?" I turn the frame toward him.

"Yeah," Ryan answers from across the room.

Holy hotness. I study the picture again. His sibling's eye and brow shape mirror their mother's, while Ryan's are more like his Dad's. Same defined nose and slightly full lips. Whew, these boys are smokin'. "He's got to be a lady killer. I bet the panties melt right off when your brother's around."

I look up and find Ryan standing in the living room holding two glasses of water, his jaw unhinged.

I'm an idiot. "Sorry. You don't want to visualize that when it comes to your brother. And I shouldn't assume. Maybe he melts boxers. Or boxer briefs. Grandma panties." *Stop it, Kat.* I don't know why this keeps happening around him. "That was a crass thing to say. Please ignore what I said and never tell your brother I spoke those words."

"Easy enough." He hands me a glass and sits in a modern ergonomic chair. "My brother is dead."

CHAPTER THIRTEEN
MILK STOUT

A dark ale with added lactose, also referred to as cream
or sweet stout. Probably okay to pour over cereal.

I am a terrible person. People who aren't great say crass or stupid
things, even to their bosses, but it takes a special type to combine
those things into a comment on a cherished family member who
no longer inhabits Earth.

I sink onto the couch nearest the mantel. I'm still holding the
frame in one hand, so I get up and put it back. "I'm so sorry."

"You didn't know." His words are tight, but he's not glaring at
me; he's looking past me to the photo.

"No, I mean it. That was incredibly insensitive of me. You said
there were things going on with your family. You hinted that life
hasn't been the same. I missed all the clues."

"Kat, it's okay. You didn't know." He drinks a sip of water and
sets the glass on a side table. "You're right—he was a good-looking
guy. As objective as I can be on that sort of thing."

It's on the tip of my tongue to ask what happened. I don't. It feels too intrusive, and I've already said many weird things today.

"If you're wondering how he died, it was a car accident. A stupid accident on icy roads where a semitruck couldn't brake fast enough."

I don't know what to say to something so life altering. I go with another apology. "I'm sorry."

Ryan cracks his knuckles. Aware of his actions, he clenches his hands together and taps his thumbs. "He graduated from college earlier that year. It wrecked my parents. It's been nearly ten years, and ever since then, we've been in this stuck place. All of us. My dad, he dives into work, and that's like his only identity. My mom, she liked having me at home after . . . which made it very hard to leave."

There's a lot of context now for why she was cleaning her adult son's bedroom. Maybe she's the type to hyper-caretake in a crisis. I can't imagine how that feels, having taken care of myself so long. It sounds great, but probably dysfunctional. His dad focusing on work makes sense—avoidance, distraction. Then there's Ryan's own lack of motivation. Probably depression and anxiety, but I'll save psychology for those outside an armchair.

"We all react differently to grief." It doesn't seem sufficient, but I want him to know that nobody acts in a predicable way after a tragedy.

"Everything feels like it has a piece missing now. It's amazing how much . . . space he took up in our family. I don't mean that as a negative—the space thing. Only that we can't ever be the same family. Nothing fits anymore. There's always a hole somewhere that can't be filled in."

I know acutely what this feels like—not fitting in the family's new footprint. I'm kind of stunned he described this so succinctly. It makes sense. It's also incredibly sad.

"He was four years older than me. I worshiped him, not that I'd ever admit it to his face. I'm sure he knew." He stands abruptly. "Let me show you something."

I follow him past the kitchen to a short hall ending in a bedroom. The walls and bedding are shades of gray with the also-gray curtains open to clear, sunny skies. A slice of Lake Michigan peeks from between the buildings. "Ah! Your lakefront view."

He laughs softly. I'm standing close, since the room isn't big, though the bed is, leaving us limited space to stand with professional distance. I back up anyway.

He pulls a photo album off a built-in shelf beside the closet door. Flipping through it, he lands on the page he wants. "This is totally my brother. Jesse, that's his name."

I move closer, into the range of Ryan's body heat. The energy between us returns, pulling me in, wrapping around us. I hold my breath.

His brother is in the center of a group, laughing. He's surrounded by a mix of people at an outdoor festival. Jesse is holding a beer.

"He knew Joe and Prairie better than I did." Ryan slides the picture out of the photo sleeve and holds it closer. "They came to his funeral."

My throat constricts.

"I remember them being there but not anything they said. I talked to so many people. Jesse knew everybody. You wouldn't believe how crowded it was." He blows out a breath. "I sound like I'm eighty. Anyway, Joe checked on my dad a lot after that. He'd call or drive out to the house. He invited us to the pub. I never went." He flaps the photo in the air. "I should frame this. Put it in the office at Resistance."

"Your community." It's out before I can self-edit.

Ryan looks at me, his eyes swimming. He blinks, and I must have imagined it; the tears are gone. "Yeah. I think he was my community. The guys from school are one thing, but my brother? He was a good guy. More than good—the best. He looked out for me." Ryan looks around the room, then at me, and steps back. "Sorry, this is probably not appropriate. To have you in my bedroom."

"I thought it was the guest room." I didn't, but it's an out.

He walks into the hall ahead of me to the kitchen, stopping at the high-top counter with barstools positioned against it. He places the photo of his brother on top of a stack of mail. He straightens it so the edge is flush with an envelope. "We should get back to planning."

That was quite a detour. I offended Ryan, saw him nearly cry, and touched his bed, all in the span of fifteen minutes.

"The brunch idea was a good start," I tell him. "Let's think through more options that could work for us."

Saying *us* feels different now. Just Ryan and me together, alone here, talking about Resistance like we can be the ones to save it. No, not save it. Keep it awesome. That's less like owing my time to Resistance. I'm helping because I want to.

"There's also the tours. You're good at giving the Resistance tours."

Sigh. Yeah. It's a pale shade compared to working as a brewer, but it could be a feature. "If we combine a small fee for a tour with a deal on food or drinks, that could be a draw. Don't forget, we need to include the staff in our plans if we want real buy-in. Resistance is theirs too."

Ryan is nodding, and it feels like we're back on track. "I think we should visit more bars. Like we did that one night."

"The night I forced my presence on you?"

"The night you said you were headed my way." He grins, but there's a sadness caught in his features not easily cast aside. "You weren't. Why did you go? Was it Magda pressuring you?"

Magda is always bugging me if she has the chance. "Partly. I thought I could sell you on hiring me. Only I botched it."

He moves behind the kitchen island. Picks up a glass, sets it down. Loads a bowl into the dishwasher. "I don't know what to say. I'm sorry. I was just trying to hire who I thought would work best. I hope it doesn't all fall apart."

I hope that too. Even though Petty Kat would want it to fall apart so she could take a job slot. Petty Kat needs some time on a beach or at a timeshare.

"Kat." He's looking at me with one of those hard-to-distinguish expressions. Guarded but not severe. Attractive, because he doesn't have to try. "Thanks for listening."

I'm flattered he credits me for listening, especially after I bungled my words so much. Which gets me thinking. "Hey. What else do you have going on today? I have an idea."

We are on a bus. Me and Ryan, cruising northbound to see where the wind takes us. Speaking of wind, it's awfully blustery out there. The bus windows periodically rattle in response.

I lean across Ryan to squint at the passing storefronts. "If you see something interesting, let me know and we'll hop off."

Ryan tugs his scarf up higher. Whether it's to warm his chilled nose or to mask the scent of a nearby abandoned chili dog wrapper is unclear. "I *have* ridden a bus before," he says through the scarf.

I catch the twinkle in his eye. He's teasing. "Think of this as our own pub crawl, courtesy of the Chicago Transit Authority." I sure hope he sees it that way instead of as me strong-arming him back into the bitter cold for an unplanned adventure. On his day off.

We ride in silence for bit, if silence includes noisy teenagers, squeaking bus brakes, and a guy in headphones with the volume so loud it may as well be a public address system. I'm beginning to regret this spontaneous plan when Ryan angles closer to the window. "Let's stop."

We exit at the next cross street and double back. I scan the businesses. "I don't see anything beer related." No taproom, bar, or even a liquor store.

"Here." Ryan nods toward a narrow storefront with an ancient sign jutting out from the weathered brick. He holds the door open for me.

I pause in the doorway. "A bookstore? I'm surprised. Should I be surprised?"

He shrugs. "I like books." A gleam from his eye hits me square in the feels.

Ryan likes books. *I* like books.

Kat can't think smart now.

I head inside, and a whoosh of warm air rushes at my face. It's a used bookshop—the type that boldly denies running out of shelf space when there's a perfectly good floor suitable for stacking.

Bookshelves line each wall in the slim space, with a set of low shelves dividing the middle of the room. Books stack across the top of the low shelves too.

I watch for where Ryan goes first. He drifts along the shelves nearest to the front—travel books, then history.

I wander past him. The store offers a wide mix of newer secondhand titles and old stuff dusting up the shelves. Anything I find, I'll have to take back on the bus, so I'm selective.

After a little while, I find Ryan. "I have twelve books. Help."

He looks up from an open book. "Check this out. A history of beer brewing in the Midwest. And this one is about the business of beer making."

My frosty little heart softens. He came here for research. About beer.

He eyes my stack with a questioning look.

"You're far more focused than me." I review my selections and pare the stack down to four books. All fiction in different genres. "I'll put these other ones back, and then we can check out if you're ready."

He snags me by the puffer coat sleeve. "Why are you putting those back?"

"I'm not lugging all these books around on the bus. We've still got hours of exploring left." Unless he's tapped out before we reach a tap house. Either way, I have a long way back to my apartment and these books aren't light.

Ryan looks at me like the solution is obvious. "I'll carry them. Just get the books."

I wave him off. "It's too many. I get greedy eyed in places like this. It's fine."

Ryan removes the pile of take-backs from my hands. Just straight-up takes them. "Consider it a gift. We're supporting a local business. I know you love that."

Something tightens in my throat. I *do* love that. And he knows it. *Ryan is buying me a stack of books and won't take no for an answer.*

It may be the sexiest thing a man has ever done for me.

Over the next week, we pull the first advertised Resistance Brewpub tour together, with a Peace and Love promotion to tie in to Valentine's Day.

For the tour, we end up with a few regulars and several craft beer connoisseurs who look out for that sort of thing.

Sadie comes because I begged in case no one would show. She's looking a touch interested in a guy who has questions on fermenting temperatures. Or maybe that's me wanting to pair them together. He's a dark stout, with strong dark hair and features.

Sadie bounds over after I wrap up the tour. "That was so informative, Kat! I learned so much. I was careful to keep my distance so you wouldn't be distracted."

"That's sweet." She smooths her dress, a fit-and-flare in bright pinks and reds to coordinate with Valentine's Day. A touch overdressed for a beer tour, but she looks great. Besides, Ryan is wearing a blazer and a button-down and the view is good.

Speaking of Ryan, he appears on the other side of the glass in the pub.

Sadie hugs me close. "That's him? Ryan?"

I nod, and she whistles low.

I knock into her. "Stop it. He's my boss."

"He bought you books, Kat. *Books.*"

"I knew I shouldn't have told you that."

Ryan looks up when I say it, even though he can't hear me through the glass. Our gazes connect, and it's like cold filtering through my veins. It never gets old, seeing him. Now that I've seen where he lives and I've seen his family in those photos and know their story, or part of it, I'm less sure on him being a golden ale devoid of deeper notes. Losing a brother, that's big. Feeling the weight of a business's success, that builds layers.

Besides, golden ales can be quite good. Their simplicity isn't bad just because they aren't screaming bitter with hops. Maybe a little less screaming is good for balance.

Ryan enters the brewing room and schmoozes with tour guests. He holds the door open as a gentle reminder that it's time to go. I herd Sadie and the dude I mentally paired her with back into the pub.

At the door, I stop beside Ryan. "I think it went well."

"Good. Since they registered online, we'll send them a feedback survey."

I laugh, but he's not joining. "You're serious? They're going to grade me?"

"It's standard customer service. We should be surveying the customers too. I thought about doing a random sample with a hard-copy survey when you give the final bill."

I try picturing Anthony filling out a customer feedback survey. It would come back with fire-spewing dragon drawings. "Whatever you say, boss."

He lets out an irritated breath and the door closes, leaving us alone by the tanks. "I know what you mean. It's your cue to get me to stop talking."

"Imagine that. A woman telling a man to stop talking."

"Ha. Ha." He speaks the faux laugh.

I gather the empty disposable sample cups and toss them in a closed-lidded trash barrel near the door.

"I'd like you to view me less like a boss."

"I thought you wanted me to recognize your authority?" *There are people who've lost their jobs for less.* I really deserve another sticker for not saying that last part.

"That was a necessary conversation, but hopefully we can move past it. I mean, I appreciate your help. I wanted you to know that. This week has been decent."

"Thanks." I can take a compliment. "Did you book the food truck people Luiz recommended for brunch?"

He shakes his head. "I haven't reached out yet. I was calling a few other places who do catering."

"His suggestion is a good one. We should check them out."

Dos Islas is often stationed a few blocks from here and parks at several other city locations too. They're Cuban and Puerto Rican owners with mash-ups of traditional dishes.

I follow Ryan to the office and slip my phone out to search their website. It links to an app with a live map of food trucks, noting how their hours can change. A colorful map with tiny truck icons fills the screen. We're in that midafternoon lull after lunch and before dinner. The timing is perfect. "Hey, they're open and only a few blocks from here. Let's go."

"Now?"

"Yeah, now. Come on."

He pokes his head out of the office to see into the pub. "What if something happens?"

"Our best servers are here. Magda's on the bar. She could run this place on cold meds and blindfolded. Come on. Get your coat, and I'll meet you at the back."

The cold air hits as we enter the alley. I circle around the dumpsters to a shortcut through another alley to end up on the next street over.

In a few minutes we make it to the small grocery lot where the food truck is parked. String lights drape from the truck to a portable awning positioned over two picnic tables. The truck is painted bright green and blue with images of two islands on the side—Cuba and Puerto Rico.

Everything on the menu looks good, and I'm starving. I've only eaten from here twice, both times when Luiz brought in food.

We're next to order. I unearth two bottles from my bag.

Ryan snaps toward me. "Hey. That's Resistance beer. You took those?"

"I paid for them." Or I will. Later. I smile at the guy inside the order window. "Hi! I'm Kat from Resistance Brewpub down the street. This is Ryan Bennett, the new manager. We come bearing gifts."

"Oh, hey!" He calls back to someone else in the truck, speaking Spanish.

Another head pops into the window. "Buenos días—hello, hello. Thank you for this! What can we get you?"

"Make it on the house," the first guy tells him. "I'm Nesto. This is Aaron."

"Great to meet you both," I respond. "I'd love the Cubano. And thanks, but we'll pay. We had an idea we wanted to ask you about." I give a short pitch on the brunch and mention how Luiz suggested their truck. "If that might interest you, we can discuss it more when you're not working."

They're looking at each other, nodding. They speak to each other in Spanish again.

"We'll get back to you for sure." Nesto nods to their business card in a little plastic holder on the edge of the counter. "Definitely interested. Tell Luiz we said hello."

"I will!"

"The special today is a two-Cubano meal meant to share. Would you like it?"

Little hearts are tacked to the order window with the deal advertised. "No," I say quickly as Ryan says, "Sure!"

"It's like a Valentine's thing." This is not a date. It's a work . . . thing.

Understanding hits Ryan. "Okay, I guess that's a no, then. I'll order mine separately." He orders, and we move to the side as a family lines up behind us.

Ryan rocks back on his heels. "You made that look easy. I contacted like ten places recently, and no one's called back."

"When did you call?"

"This week."

"No, I mean, what times? Was it when they were open, during service? That can be busy for a call. In person is better, if you can go when they aren't swamped. We're lucky we hit a lull here."

We get our orders and decide to hang out and eat. Neither of us speaks as we attack our food. It's like I haven't eaten in days. Not true—I've eaten, but the food was cheap noodles and canned vegetables at home. Not exactly flavorful Caribbean fusion.

"We'll be lucky if they say yes," Ryan says. "I should have trusted Luiz's suggestion."

"Why didn't you?"

"I don't know. I get a little intimidated around the crew."

"Dude! Work smarter, not harder. You have too much else to do. I bet Luiz would take over planning the whole brunch initiative if you let him lead it."

We finish our food and head back toward the pub. Ryan's shaking his head and quietly laughing to himself.

"What am I missing?"

"Nothing . . . just, you're right. Your idea is a smart way to handle things."

"Oh. Glad I could help."

A city bus struggles toward us and brakes at the stop we're approaching. I wave the driver off. Fumes linger behind as we cross to the next street.

Ryan increases his pace. "I guess I was trying to impress you. Trying to do it all myself."

I laugh, and my breath bursts into a white puff. "You didn't consider that maybe doing the thing I suggested might impress me? That listening to me might be what's endearing?"

"You'd find that endearing?"

I glance at him. "Are you being serious right now?"

"You're an intimidating person, Kat. Most of the time I get the sense you'd rather be anywhere else than talking to me."

My steps slow as I mull this over. He slows with me. "We didn't start off the best, that's for sure. And yeah, I get frustrated. It's not always you, but also sometimes it's you. Just being honest."

"You're the only one who is."

I hate how Ryan isn't gelling with the Resistance crew. It's almost like he's avoiding them by hanging out with me.

"A few things," I say. "I doubt myself all the time, but maybe I come off like I have it together. I'd like to think it's supreme confidence, but it might be putting my guard up. I do that sometimes."

"Would you believe me if I said I do too?"

"Yes."

"It's obvious?"

"Sometimes you look chiseled from stone. You make sculptures look like Jell-O. Granite like a pillow full of marshmallows. That's how guarded you come off."

He lets out a staccato *ha*. "Can you blame me? You all are like a family, and I'm the stepdad coming in after a divorce. No one wants me around."

"If that's true, it's on you to make the first step. It's not on the kids to make it easy for you to parent. The divorce has been hard enough. Okay, enough with that analogy."

We're now stopped on the sidewalk half a block from Resistance. The aged brick building is shadowed and unassuming from this angle.

"I know I'm not your dad or anybody else's. What gets me is the things that shouldn't be hard are the hardest parts. Just talking to people feels impossible. I used to do that all the time with my dad's company." He shakes his head, like he can't even believe his own situation. "The whole gig was talking to people about their companies. See if we should invest. But you all, you're so close with each other. And cool. Luiz has a neck tattoo. I feel like some blowhard dope from the suburbs coming in trying to take charge. It's obnoxious."

So he knows it's obnoxious he was handed this pub to run. Hearing him admit it shakes off more of my hardened shell toward him. And the part about the neck tattoo makes me laugh. So I do.

"A lot of us have tattoos." I scrunch up my coat sleeve to show mine off. "I wouldn't be surprised if you had one. Do you?"

He shakes his head. "I've thought about getting my brother's name. I don't know."

I think back to the brewing class in Wisconsin and how the guys gathered so easily. I hated that sense of feeling left out. Like the middle school lunchroom all over again.

Have we been the clique at Resistance? The roving band of misfits who didn't create space for a straitlaced bro? Then again, that bro was turning our ragtag joint into a classic sports bar. That was what I've been literally resisting.

"I'm sorry if any of us have been excluding you," I tell him. "Part of it is a power structure thing. You *are* our boss. It's not the same as a new server coming in."

He looks past me, his profile revealing soft creases at the corners of his eyes. He looks vulnerable. Not etched in stone. Adaptable. Open to be adapted.

"You were trying to im-*press meee*," I singsong the words to lighten his mood.

He shakes his head, laughing. "I should never have told you."

"I promise I won't hold it over you. You said you want me to see you less like a boss, right?"

"Maybe that's a bad idea."

I lift my arm halfway, gesturing for him to loop his through mine. "Let's have a drink. Play the customer at your own pub."

He hooks his arm in. "That'll go over well."

Heat travels through my body at his touch. "Step one to breaking through the clique. Let's give it a shot."

We head toward the corner and veer to the front entrance. "Does this mean turning the jukebox on?" he asks.

"You know it."

CHAPTER FOURTEEN
BALTIC-STYLE PORTER

A robust dark beer that's actually a lager based on the
cold-fermenting brewing technique. A tricky identity.

The key to breaking the ice with the new boss is to get him
drunk.

I wish I could say Ryan is three sheets to the Windy City, but
he's playing it cool and responsible, drinking ice water and taking
his time with his beer. It's a low-ABV lager, so he might as well be
drinking only the water.

For a Saturday night; business is decent. Most of the tables are
filled. There's a mix of regulars with a healthy dose of New Blood,
mainly younger men clustering by the new TV or at the bar keeping Magda busy.

Ryan ran to the back when we first came in to switch off the
overhead music. I turned on the jukebox, and immediately a line
formed to put in song picks. After a round of beer, I encouraged
Ryan to choose a song.

"This thing doesn't take money?" Ryan notices the bill collector has a plastic piece closing it off.

"Jailbreaked," I say. "If that's what you call a jukebox that doesn't require money. That's what Joe called it. What's your song?"

He lands on Aerosmith. "I always liked that song from the asteroid movie."

"*Armageddon*? No, you have to do seventies Aerosmith." I stop. "Sorry. Pick what you want."

"I'll do old-school. You said to do the whole Resistance experience."

A low guitar sounds with Steven Tyler's unmistakable yowl. The bikers seated nearby hold up their pint glasses.

"Hey, fam!" I walk over, dragging—er, leading—Ryan with me. "Have you all met Ryan?"

Ryan looks ready to bolt.

The bikers are giving off a frosty vibe. It's not me their frost is directed at.

One of the two women at the table lifts her glass again. "Nice to meet you. I'm Bess. Heard your family knows Prairie and Joe."

"Yes, they—we do." Ryan lifts his own pint, which is nearly empty. "Cheers."

The bikers love that and all clink glasses. I stay and chat for a little bit, watching Ryan guzzle the rest of his pint and slowly start to loosen up.

We mosey back to our table, where I provide commentary on our crowd. I point out who comes in a lot and what they order. Anthony is here with a friend. He nods our way, and I wave.

"Anthony—" I almost tell Ryan we take care of his tab but stop short. Probably best to keep Ryan away from that setup for now.

Anya has our table. She has an extra pen tucked behind her ear around the soft curls of her afro. Her apron is covered in book-related pins, one of which I particularly love: *Read Romance, Fight the Patriarchy*.

"What would you recommend if I like medium hops and not a high alcohol content?" Ryan asks.

Anya's eyes widen. She looks at me, panicked.

"It's not a test," Ryan says quickly. "This was my idea. To hang out for a night."

I know he's not taking credit for my idea but aiming to put Anya at ease.

"Oh, sure. If you want my opinion, I'd suggest our Wild Western." She points to the listing on the menu, named after a nearby major cross street. "Or this Pilsner is good, especially with the Loaded and Exploded Fries."

Ryan orders the Pilsner and the fries.

"She's good," he tells me, after she takes off. "I didn't even want fries. Did Prairie and Joe hang out like this, just drinking?"

"All the time."

"You're here and you're not on tonight," he remarks. "Why? You could have gone home after the tour ended."

"Like Prairie and Joe, I also hang out here." I shrug. "A lot of us do. But you don't have to if it's too awkward. Maybe mixing work and your off time doesn't mesh for you."

I can tell he's trying. But the thing is, he has to. Try. I don't get the impression he actually wants to be here.

Whatever sports game was on ends, and the TV is switched to a Vin Diesel movie. The barkeep handles the remotes. Magda loves a good Vin Diesel movie. Unless that's an oxymoron. She loves a Vin Diesel movie whether it's good or not.

A new group comes in and fills the seats nearest the TV. With an IPA in hand, the movie playing, and Fiona Apple on the jukebox, it feels like a slice of the Resistance I know and love.

Luiz joins us during a lull in service. We're on our third pints, and Ryan goes on about how great the food truck was and what a perfect suggestion Luiz made for a partnership. How glad he is Luiz has that connection and thought to share.

Luiz, to his credit, has coat-checked his sass for the night. He's hooked in and all smiles. "I've known Aaron for years. I worked with his truck to cater my parents' thirtieth wedding anniversary last year. We rented a room at Garfield Park."

"At the conservatory?" Ryan asks. "That must have been beautiful."

Luiz arches a brow. "It's a beautiful space. My parents wanted to keep the party to the backyard, but us kids, we insisted."

Luiz brags on his family for a minute, which is really sweet. Ryan knowing about the nearby conservatory and gardens probably shouldn't surprise me—it's fairly well known—but I find myself impressed.

This is what I've been waiting for. This glimpse of a connection. While they discuss the brunch idea, I hop to the jukebox to put in a few more song picks. INXS, because they're amazing. Wilco, because they're Chicago legends, and I sneak in the other Aerosmith song for Ryan. It's a love song and it is Valentine's Day weekend, after all.

Not that I need to play Ryan a love song. It's just a theme. Peace and Love and all that.

Ryan excuses himself, and on his way to the back he stops by two tables to chat. He's already shifting into a more natural zone I can see people here appreciating.

I know I do.

Over the next week, brunch planning comes together. Luiz and Ryan do the bulk of the organizing, but we're adding a brew tour to the ticket options, so I tag in on their meetings. We put together two flight options customers can choose from, with four generous samples of different beers. Recommendations of food pairings came from the food truck owners with detailed flavor profiles.

Kurt, the head brewer, has a say, of course, but he's focused on production. In fact, when I ask his opinion, he doesn't seem interested in discussing which beers go well with a Cuban and Puerto Rican brunch selection at all. His exact words were "Vaya con Dios" in a flat midwestern drawl. I think it's meant to be a permissive blessing?

Whatever. Any niche I can carve out for myself beyond serving customers, I need to pounce on. It's up to me to make opportunities happen if I'm going to keep on with my end goal. Which is brewer. Not brew *taster*.

Well, that too. But I want brewer as a title.

I sneak time in to work with Randy cleaning the tanks before a new run. Randy knows the drill from work at a microbrewery, but he says he appreciates my efficiency with our equipment and processes. Randy is easygoing and works quietly, though a few comments give me the impression he and Kurt don't get along. I do my best to stay out of it.

It's another night past closing, and I'm in the back office with Ryan. It's late, but we're both not interested in leaving until the images for our social media are ready to go.

I hold my breath as he clicks and drags the wrong text to the wrong spot. "Dude, that looks terrible. Keep it where it was, but change the font size and add the second line below the image."

"That's what I was trying to do." He clicks the mouse, and the font duplicates. Now it's two lines of text on top of each other, so it reads blurry.

"Move." I elbow him in the ribs.

"Hey, give a guy some room. I've never made graphics before."

Never mind that most places hire out for this sort of thing. I elbow him some more. *"Moooove."*

He huffs in frustration. As he shifts from the chair, my arm slides against his chest. He moves a hand up, cupping my elbow. Gently, he moves my arm aside. Heat from his body melds with mine as we switch places. I'd be an idiot not to notice his heat, his scent.

I'm an idiot anyway for jabbing him like an annoying little sister. Sometimes my maturity goes on break. This time it fell asleep in the car and forgot to clock back in.

My stupid heart is beating. Fast. Too fast.

A few more adjustments and the image looks pretty good. Yup, all fine and good and it's time to go home.

I scoot back just as Ryan leans a hand on the desk. His body angles toward the computer, toward me. You'd think after a day at the pub, he'd smell like the grease fryer and fermenting hops, but he doesn't. He has that Ryan's car scent again, the gentleman's library. His hip rests against the side of the chair, brushing against my arm. "It looks good."

You look good.

My back goes ramrod straight, and I shoot from the chair.

Please tell me I didn't say that out loud.

"What's wrong?" His voice ticks up, his hand off the desk and hanging out in midair, waiting to react.

"Oh, nothing. It's late is all. I happened to see the time."

"Two AM shutdown?"

I wince. "You remember that?"

"You were practically dead weight when I dragged you out of here last time. Hard to forget."

Right. Classic Kat, remembered for nearly falling asleep on a guy. At work.

He's right, though, I'm nearing my drop-dead limit, so it's time to call it a night. I'm not actually tired, but I'm acting weird and I know it. And I'm currently blocked in. One end of the desk is pushed against the wall, and at the other end is where Ryan stands. Looking and smelling divine.

"You don't look tired," Ryan says. "I know I'm not."

"You want to keep working?"

He angles past me and shuts down the computer. "We should go out."

I'm stone and can't move.

"Oh," Ryan says quickly. "I don't mean, like, go *out* out. Just, like, go somewhere and, you know, talk over things. Like we did that one night with Baby Driver at the wheel."

I snicker at the comment. I'm not sure if going to a second location with Ryan right now would do me any good. Something is shifting inside me.

It feels like . . . more is happening between us. More than a boss and his snarky subordinate. And it worries me.

"If you don't say something, I'm about to feel extremely self-conscious for asking you to hang out with me." He notices he's blocking me in and steps back, giving me a path out from behind the desk.

"Like you're ever self-conscious." Although he admitted he didn't feel like he fit in here, so he probably does have those doubts.

Here's the thing. I want to hang out with Ryan. I want to hang out with him not as my boss but as just us. But I can't do that. I'm in too weird a headspace, for one. He *is* my boss, for another. Besides, he already said this would be like hanging out the night we talked almost entirely about work.

Ryan walks to the door and leans against the frame. It's surprisingly sexy—the lean. It's this casual move that signals he's comfortable. Here, and with me. And he doesn't look out of place.

I'm getting used to seeing Ryan here. He's becoming as much a part of the pub as the woodwork.

An urge to reach for him pulls at me. His soft shirt, those warm hands. Who ever knew leaning was a trigger for me?

"What's still open around here?" Ryan asks, disrupting my thoughts.

I guess we're doing this. "A four AM bar. There's a few." Anthony often wanders to one in Logan Square after Resistance closes to use up another few hours before daylight.

"Somewhere in Wicker Park, maybe? You hang out there, right?"

"I did when I had money." I grab the puffer from the back of the chair. I want to destroy it by this point in the winter and would love to switch to something not so gigantic. Except—I slip it on—ah, so warm.

Ryan takes his coat from a hook behind the door. "You bring up money a lot."

"Kind of one of those foundational cornerstones of life."

"It's just a few drinks, right? Not too much to spend."

"Not too much if you have enough *much* to begin with." I could stop here, but I'm feeling ranty. "Eating and existing require cash or credit, and when the credit runs dry, well . . . it's more like when the credit *bleeds*. It doesn't dry up so much as it bleeds you dry."

His easy expression fades. "I'm not sure if you're being serious right now. How bad is it?"

I keep it vague. "I've made a lot of progress. Just one credit card left, the big one, and I pay as much as I can each month." Why am I telling him this? "Look. I'm an adult. I vent sometimes, but I can take care of myself."

"I would never question that. You're amazing."

My hand freezes on the coat zipper. Amazing, he said. About *me*. "You've been cooped up too long." I move past him to the brewing room, where the space isn't so confining.

Ryan closes the office door and follows me. "Don't short-change yourself."

Shouldering my bag, I find him slipping on his coat, and what can I say? Perfection. With the scarf, a Burberry ad itself. An Instagram snap worthy of 100k likes.

He jangles his keys. "Where are we going?"

Ryan insists on driving, because of course, though it is very late and very dark and very cold, so that makes sense. I suggest where to park, and we walk the block to the six-corner intersection of Damen, Milwaukee, and North Avenue. Huddles of vapers stand the exact distance from bar doors as required by law.

Our destination is a bar with black walls and scuffed floors with plenty of lingering late-night drinkers. It's the opposite of pretentious. Just a place to be with good beer that's not pretending to be anything other than that.

Ryan's attention darts from each corner of the room to the bar itself. "What are you getting?"

The brews range from commercial canned varieties to craft beers on draft. A mix of local and famous national craft beers. "Probably this porter. It's local."

Ryan gets the bartender's attention and orders two of the same. He lays cash across the bar. "Do you always drink local beers?"

"When I can." I swallow. "You don't have to pay for me. I know I talked about bleeding credit cards, but I was being eccentric."

"It's fine, Kat. It's only a couple bucks."

It's more than a *couple* bucks. This is good beer and we're in the city. And yet the dollar amount is insignificant enough that I know it won't set him back. It's monstrously ridiculous that it would set *me* back. I feel like such a leech.

"What?" Ryan asks. "Is it too loud in here?"

I can hear him fine, though the music is more the intense growling-and-yelling variety you'd hear at a punk show. "I'm good."

We take our pints from the bar and find a table. Groups in the back gather around pool tables and arcade games.

"I know it's dark in here, but this beer looks black." Ryan sips the porter. "Whoa. This is . . . huh." He sips again. "I don't know if I've had one like this before."

"It's not a slammer, that's for sure." I take my own taste. "This is a Baltic porter. Do you like it?"

"There's a licorice flavor, I think. I could see people not liking this, but I always liked licorice. And these old-fashioned molasses candies my grandma had at her house. My brother hated them. I always scored a whole candy dish full of the stuff because he wouldn't touch it."

I watch him enjoy another sip, and it's like a third wind of energy. "Jana and I talked about that—Jana is the brewer I met at the class in Wisconsin. We talked about beer that makes you nostalgic. How a taste can call up a memory."

"Huh, wow. I never thought of it like that. It's not like this tastes exactly like that candy or anything, but it's the first thing I thought of."

"I like the deep flavor. It feels satisfying to drink."

We talk about flavors we like as we further dip into the porters. The group behind me gets up to leave, and a guy bumps me by accident. I scoot my chair to give them room, moving myself closer to Ryan.

Instead of shifting his chair to give me space, Ryan leans in. "We should check out every bar in this area. See what they have on tap."

The air grows hazy and warm between us, like a comforting lager. He's looking at me now and I'm looking back. Noticing. He has a tiny scar above his left eyebrow. The brow dips a little lower than the other. A fine wrinkle creases the edge of his eye. He's real and close and moving closer.

I wish I weren't so worried about money. And Ryan paying for me. It blurs lines that are already out of focus. But if I can't have fun now, when can I ever?

"Sometimes I think I don't deserve to be happy." The words fly from my mouth before I can stop them. I run a hand through my hair. "I don't know where that came from. Forget I said it."

"No." He catches me lightly by the sleeve. Just as quick, he retracts, realizing he's made contact. "I get it. Ever since losing Jesse, it's been hard to find any direction. It's why I want this job to work. But every step forward doesn't seem enough."

He holds up a hand before I have a chance to comment. "I'm not looking for pity. Really. I just want you to know I'm trying. I have a lot of confidence that we can turn things around."

He keeps saying *we*. We, like me and him. I don't mind it. I don't mind any of this.

"I mean, look at this place." He tips his chin toward the pool players. "Everything here is so used up. The tables are worn, the aesthetic isn't really anything. But the address brings them in. And they're open late."

"Please don't make me work until four AM." I reach for Ryan's hands for emphasis. Electric current runs through me, and I let him go. The beer is hitting me. It's not even that potent, but I'm tired and my emotions are all over the place.

Ryan laughs that easy laugh. "Nah, I don't think we're the four AM type of pub. You'd be good at running things, though. If you ever wanted to run a bar."

My whole body reacts with a flash of heat. "I doubt that."

"You're good with people."

"I don't want to run the pub. I want to make the beer. I want my hands in the grain. My sweat on the floor. Okay, all of that sounds unsanitary. I mean I need to be back there brewing or none of this means anything."

Ryan looks past me. "I know giving the tours isn't the same thing. Maybe once business picks up, we put you on more with Randy and Kurt. I can see what they need help with."

"I've already been helping Randy," I admit. "It's hard to stay away. They can use the help now that we're back up and running."

He focuses on me. His eyes search, scanning my face. My whole inner self seems under scrutiny, and I don't hate it. It's like he's seeing all of me and taking notes. "This could work, you know. You and me, together."

My breath stills. "Yeah?"

The staff probably wouldn't care if we, well, hook up. He's close, and his heat is pulling me in. His breath is nearly my breath now, and I find I want this too. I want him closer. And then? I don't know what. I want to find out. I sip my drink again, letting the flavor wash over me as I take this in.

"We could run Resistance. Together."

I snap to reality. He isn't talking about him and me *together* together. "Like business partners? How would that work?"

"My father gave me those financial goals. I think we can do it. If this brunch goes well, and we do the brew release events like Resistance is used to doing, only ramped up, and maybe we partner with . . . I don't know, artists or whoever like you talked about, and we advertise more . . . we have a shot. You're invested here. Your passion . . . well, it's infectious."

Hearing him say *passion* sends a thrill through me. It's a bit tempered by his use of *infectious*, but I'll take it. But partnering? I'm still not sure what he means. "Do you mean a different job title?"

His face brightens. "Yeah, could be. I mean, let's talk. Let's see what you want. The way Joe and Prairie had things going worked for them for twenty years."

Neurons are firing all over the place. Middle school Kat resurfaces from the depths with heart-emoji eyes. *Chill.* "Joe and Prairie were married. Resistance was their life's work."

Ryan's cheeks flare, and he adjusts back in the chair. "Well, yeah. It's obviously not the same. I meant more that you and I have been making a good team and eventually we could take this on our own. Once we show my father what we're capable of."

I blink, and the heaviness in my eyes flips on like a switch. Suddenly, my limbs are like lake buoys and I sway in my seat. It's the beer and the hour, and this is a lot to take in.

Maybe this is how people are handed things. Want to run a bar? Just know the right guy! Here's a guy right now offering a partnership.

My pint is nearly empty after a hefty gulp. "Wow. I guess I hadn't thought about . . . running the bar. I mean, co-running. Or support for running. Whatever the terminology is. It's not like I went to school for marketing or bookkeeping . . ." Or beer making. "But maybe that's my own hang-up? This, like, idea that we have to go to school for the thing we end up doing as our career, when it doesn't work that way for so many people."

I wonder if I'm losing Ryan with my rambling, but he's right there with me. "Exactly. I have a business degree. *Business.* How generic is that?"

"You probably learned about bookkeeping, at least."

"I aced my accounting classes. My dad wanted to steer me into an accounting role at his business, but—" He makes a face. A goofy one that's funny but doesn't make him any less hot. "I don't know. I need something with more life. A moving, living organism that needs order and direction. Like Resistance."

I haven't really heard him talk about Resistance like this. Almost like he has a drive or a passion for it. "That's really cool. Taking a challenge instead of what could come easy."

He drains the rest of his pint. "I question that choice daily."

"I question everything daily."

He smiles at that. His face looks a little smeary, and I laugh.

Ryan almost looks pitying. "It's late. I should get you home."

I shake myself awake and check the time on my FakeBit, my trusty thirty-dollar version of a fancy fitness tracker. Yike on a bike. My blink comes slow. Crud, am I drunk? "I can't be drunk on one pint. This is absurd."

"You were pretty tired already, and I convinced you to come out." He moves back the chair and stands, holding out a hand. "Come on."

He takes my arm and guides me out front and down the walk. The vaping crowd has cleared out. Moments later, we're back in his Audi and I breathe in the rich, comforting scent. "Your car smells nice," I tell him. "Like you."

He chuckles softly as he starts the car. It's only after we've turned onto the street that I realize what I said.

"Oh. I only meant you smell nice."

"That's what you said, yes."

"I know, but I wasn't like, smelling you. Or memorizing your—" False. Falsehoods and lies. I absolutely have memorized how he smells. "You smell like your car, and I can't figure how you don't leave the pub without smelling like the deep fryer or sour hops."

"Do you want to tell me where I'm going?"

He's dropping me off. Which he's done before, but the guy can't remember directions. "Go straight, and I'll tell you where to turn. Are you okay to drive?"

"I'm good. I promise."

We get home fast. He remembers my building, because he slows at the right spot beyond the church across the street.

I turn to say good-night and find him looking at me.

"I hope I haven't made you doubt yourself." His fingers flex around the steering wheel. "When I didn't hire you to work with the brewers."

This is unexpected. "Because I said the thing about not being happy? Ignore that. I say weird things sometimes."

"You've been through a lot, and you were counting on that chance. I keep seeing you do the work, and I wonder why I didn't see it before."

I don't have much to say, since I'm doing free tours and working for tips still, but I appreciate the acknowledgment. "Having a guy with more experience looks better."

"It's not because you're not a guy," he says quickly.

It doesn't matter at this point. The idea of a business partnership is promising, but it means putting trust in someone I barely know. There are too many questions to answer right now to even go there mentally.

He looks at me. "I want to do better."

"Okay. Why are you telling me that?"

He flinches. "You have standards, of who you respect. And I'd like you—and the others, but mostly you—to respect me."

He wants my approval is what he wants. I'm not sure I'm the one to give it, or why he thinks I should approve of him. "I respect you . . . more now." I can't say I respected him from the start. Nothing can change the fact he was handed the job with no experience. I hate that it was so easy for him when it's so hard for the rest of us. "I see that you really care. That you want to see Resistance succeed."

"But you're not sure you want to work with me."

"I already work with you."

"I mean, on a different level."

And have it handed to me? It doesn't feel right.

If I resent how he got this chance, how can I seriously consider joining him as a business partner? Unless I'm entirely overthinking (likely). Those guys at the brewing class, would they care whether a potential business partner was funded by their own family? Probably not. They'd look at the business plan and the risk and move forward.

"I do respect you," I say again, and find that it's true, when I pick away the crust of resentment.

I'm not sure what we're doing in this car talking at nearly four in the morning, so close we can taste each other's last meal. Well, last beer. *Reminder: Kat, you've been drinking.* The best idea would be to say my good-night and get inside and go to bed.

I don't move.

He's here and I'm here, and it's been a long time since I've been in a close shared space with a guy who interests me. Who seems, the way he's looking at me, maybe interested back.

And never have I been so close in a shared space with a guy like Ryan. He doesn't look like any guy I've ever dated. His friends aren't like my friends, and his peeking-lake-view condo is a different world from mine.

"That guy who screwed you over must be the biggest jackass."

Ryan's declaration makes me burst out laughing. "What?"

"Your ex."

"He was . . ." I don't want to talk about him. I don't want to think of him when Ryan is within reach. This frustratingly privileged guy who I should loathe but don't.

Ryan lifts a hand toward me. Slowly and tentatively, he moves a strand of my hair.

The moment is here. The moment where everything between us can change. I've played things safe. So safe. I hang back, then regret it. Everything I do feels controlled, measured, cautious.

I don't want cautious. Cautious didn't save me from hardship or pain. I still lost my job, the safe job with the steady paycheck.

I still lost my supposedly dependable boyfriend. Lost my plan B. Doing the safe thing doesn't pan out for me.

I close the gap between us.

Our lips meet, and it's instant fire. Heat and energy pulse through me.

This is stupid, but I don't care. If he kisses back, I don't care. He kisses back.

I could ride a fourth wind and stay up until dawn breaks. Just here, with him, tasting the night on his lips. He angles closer and deepens the pressure between us. He's controlling this now, and I blissfully let him. It's time to let go.

His movements feel expert. I force from my mind the question of how many people he's kissed to gain this expertise. Who cares—I'm the one who benefits now. I'm the one taking a chance.

I let everything else fall away.

CHAPTER FIFTEEN

GLUTEN-FREE BEER

Yes, it exists. Yes, we need more of it.

I wake up in twisted sheets to my phone buzzing. A quick glance shows it's Karrie and not anyone from work. Work . . . what day is it? What time?

My lips feel funny. Swollen almost. I run my fingers across them as heat threads beneath my skin.

I gasp and roll over. My pale-blue wall stares back. I return to my back and let my focus rest on the ceiling. Ryan. Last night. His car. Our lips.

I made it inside last night, finally. Alone. A victory of sorts. I wasn't drunk, not off one beer, but I was tipsy. As much as I let go, I'm infinitely grateful for a sound mind that didn't jump into anything more with Ryan at three-o-nasty in the morning.

My phone buzzes again. There's an entire novel written by Karrie in text form.

I'm on the next train.

That's the message from three seconds ago. She's taking the commuter train from the suburbs into the city. She's coming here.

Scanning the earlier texts, I can't find that anything new or earth-shattering has happened. The girl just needs a break from our parents. Mom sounds like she's at Category Five Meddler.

I text her back that I'm home and tell her which El train and bus will get her here fastest, though I'm sure she knows.

I know, she texts back. *And thanks.*

I hit the shower, do a sweep of the apartment to spot clean, and pull out the bedroll and extra blankets.

When Karrie shows up, I have herbal tea and her favorite gluten-free cookies ready, which I'd snatched up just in case when I saw them on sale.

"Oh my gosh, Kat, you have no idea how much I needed to get out of there." She lunges for the tea, breathes in the steam, then sips. Her eyes flutter shut. "So warm. So good."

"Glad to see you," I tell her around a hug. "I'm off today, but I'll probably go in later to take care of a few things. We've got a brunch thing happening tomorrow—you can come, though I'll be running around and busy."

It's probably good Karrie is here, or I'd run to Resistance right now to see Ryan. Assuming he's there.

Assuming a lot of things, really. I kissed my boss last night. It was not accidental and not a quick peck. I'm not sure what that means for us going forward.

He kissed back, so there's that.

Karrie's shiny, caramel-brown curls look effortless peeking out of a white knit cap. She peels off her coat and hangs it by the door. Removing her boots, more fashion than weatherproof, she collapses into a chair in the living room. She isn't usually frenzied. That's my territory.

I give her a minute to breathe. Okay, thirty seconds. "Things got bad, huh?"

Karrie sighs and starts in about our parents controlling her schedule. Questioning her on everything. How she found a post-college internship but our parents shot it down because it's too far a drive. How the apartment lease is waiting to be signed and something about a guy named Jayden. Mom and Dad, but mostly Mom, don't approve of any of it. They think Karrie hasn't aged a day since her diagnosis. She's forever cemented as *the child who needs us*. Even though Karrie doesn't make that assessment out loud, everything she's saying points back to it.

"I'm sorry," she says finally. "I just busted in here and talk-spewed all over you."

"You had a lot to get out."

She tugs at her soft pink sweater. It looks new, with a stylish cut. "I don't know why it's so intense lately."

I count to three so I sound like I'm pondering a response. "It's because you're noticing it more. Their protectiveness bothers you now when it didn't used to."

She hunches over her tea and thinks this over.

I blink, and she's my kid sister again—the little kid. Growing up, Karrie preferred playing tea party and doing makeovers with pristine dolls. I liked older Barbies with hair gone to straw and nicks on their legs. My other favorites were collectible dolls that had their own book series written about them. Dolls who made their stamp on the world.

Karrie and I have always been different. My mom said I came out of her squalling, two weeks early—so, basically, loud and opinionated from the jump. As told to me, Karrie was delivered by C-section and merely whimpered, almost as if startled to be discovered. Karrie thinks things through. I think things to death. Karrie is even-keeled and always put together. I'm . . . not so much those things.

Now, Karrie is itching for freedom. She's cutting her teeth by escaping here, even if it's only for a night or two. It's doubtful my parents will let her move out without a fight. Doubtful her leaving will transfer any attention to me. Even if it does, I'm not sure I want their scrutiny. I used to be bothered by them ignoring me, but now? I'm used to how this family works. I assembled my own family in their place.

An ache hits my chest. I replaced my family. I've been doing it for years. Mrs. B, friends, roommates, Alden, the Resistance crew . . . Joe and Prairie. A new truth: replacement family isn't guaranteed to stick around either.

"You think I wasn't bothered before?" Karrie asks. "By Mom and all her research?"

"You never really complained."

"She's been great, mostly." She hedges. "I feel ungrateful if I complain, but then she just is *there* all the time. Constantly reminding me about things I already know. I'm not twelve."

"Kind of like how I reminded you which bus to take?"

She grabs a cookie. "That at least makes sense. I'm not down here *that* often."

Good; she's not annoyed by me. I try to treat her like an adult, but my older-sister vibes come on strong sometimes. "How's Mom doing?"

She snaps a second cookie in half. "She needs something to do besides manage my life."

"Maybe a career change." I probably shouldn't give advice on that front. "I'm sorry it's a stress. I can text Neil and see if he's in Amsterdam or something. You might be able to crash in his room if we change up all the bedding to my spare sheets."

Her eyes widen. "Like my own room?"

"Totally. With pink ponies and unicorns on the walls."

She sticks out her tongue. "Whatever."

I finish my text, but if Neil's flying, it could be hours until I get a response.

Karrie stands and stretches her arms above her head. She's thin but looks healthy, with round cheeks and a faintly pink nose from walking out in the cold. She resumes a relaxed position and tilts her head at me. "Something is different about you. You look . . . I don't know." She scrutinizes my face. "You're not as uptight."

"I'm never *uptight*." Ugh; that is the last thing I can be described as. I'm a woman who throws a phone in the heat of the moment.

"I don't even care enough to argue. I'm just glad I'm here. Tell me what's new. Please tell me you're dating someone."

My insides dance, and I blurt it immediately. "I am! Okay, not officially. I sort of am, maybe—*maybe*—possibly dating someone. Unofficially. Completely unofficial."

Her smile ignites. "Yeah? Who?"

"This guy . . . from work."

Immediately, she's skeptical. "He's not in a band, is he?"

"No."

"A painter?"

"Nuh-uh."

"Douchey content creator?"

"Nope."

Karrie has never been fond of my past boyfriends. My attraction to arty guys with a casual relationship to employment has more than once led her to lecture me on how I deserve better. Karrie is the type of girl who expects boyfriends to take her to both dinner and a movie and call it a date and not "just chilling." Having the guy pay is absolutely necessary. I tend toward rants about patriarchal roles that hold women back while I fork it over for both my and my date's tickets. Or grumble and seethe when they insist on paying, like Ryan.

"He's kind of more your type."

She holds up her teacup. "Now I'm curious. What's he like?"

"He's into sports—"

"Sports? *You're* dating a guy who's into sports?"

"Unofficially dating. So, yeah, sports, and his family has money. His social circle parties at lakefront cottages. That sort of thing. And he likes beer. Not the same beer I like, but I think he's getting there. We work together."

"Yeah, you said that. You sound, like, hesitant. Just because he's different?"

"He's . . . my boss."

Her mouth drops open with predictable exaggeration. "Kat! Are you allowed to do that?"

I smirk. "Who's uptight now?"

"Right, but like, how old is he? You said he has money. Is he balding? Does he have kids my age?"

I throw a tiny pillow at her. It's embroidered with a Loch Ness Monster in lime green. "No. He's my age. Maybe a year older."

She mimes wiping her forehead. "Whew. I thought you might have given up on your starving-artist phase and gone right to old daddy."

I look for another pillow to throw at her before she squeals and runs off.

For a moment, things feel right where they need to be.

CHAPTER SIXTEEN
HYBRID BEER

Half lager, half ale based on the technique (lager yeast
is fermented at warm temperatures and ale yeast at cool
temperatures). For when you want it all.

The next day's brunch event brings in a mix of Resistance famil-
iars and, more importantly, a slew of new faces. Families, multi-
generations, heavily Latinx—thanks to the reputation of the food
truck and Luiz's personal promoting—plus a younger demo-
graphic skewing bearded and tattooed. Lots of food pics posted to
Instagram with our new hashtag *#ResistanceDoesBrunch*.

There's an energy here I can tell has been missing since Prairie
and Joe left. Not their same energy, but one I think they'd appreciate. The community is coming together.

Alex, Anya, and Luiz are working while I cycle guests through
tours. Kurt isn't here—it's his day off—but Randy is, hanging out in
the background, out of the way, like part of the brewing system itself.

Between tours, Ryan swings by, first shaking hands with
guests and thanking them for coming. He hands out flyers for

the food truck with their posted locations, part of our partnership deal to promote them.

Seeing him, I run my fingers across my lips. I snap my hand away. *You're in public, fool.*

I didn't end up coming out to the pub last night after all. I texted Ryan to check in, and he responded with *Hey, things are good. We've got things under control.*

No flirty banter. No *Was it good for you?* Or maybe people don't ask that for just kissing. It's honestly been so long I've forgotten what dating is like. Or not dating, as I'm starting to realize the case may be.

"How are you?" Ryan asks after the guests trail out.

I'm feeling a little run-down and sniffly, but I'm loaded up on vitamin C and otherwise feeling positive. I tell him about the morning tours and which beers guests seem to be digging. All shop talk.

Ryan nods. "Good."

"Yeah. It is!" I pitch my tone to indicate everything is great. And it is. Mostly. "Oh, and over there, that's my sister, Karrie. Want to meet her?"

I point to the table where Karrie sits with a friend she convinced to come out for the event. Apparently, her friend lives in Bucktown just north of us. Gotta love a sister who hustles for you.

"Your sister?" Ryan takes in a breath, his eyes flicking back and forth between us.

"Yeah, I know. She looks like a put-together human. I promise, we are actually related." I start to walk to her table, expecting him to follow.

"Actually, I've got to check back with the kitchen." Ryan is already stepping away. "We're winding down. I need to make sure Nesto and Aaron have support."

O-kayyy. So, I have a choice here. I can read into his dissing my sister. Not to her face, but still. I can shred those thoughts to death until I'm convinced he doesn't want to be around me, let alone acknowledge that we kissed.

Or I could be reasonable and assume Ryan is focused on running a brand-new event with staff unfamiliar with our kitchen, and he genuinely needs to check on them.

I'm going to act grown and go with option two.

Certainly, there's no time to talk further about the business proposition. Though today, I've seen glimpses of what that might look like. Working in tandem, communicating through glances across the pub. I can see it.

I check on my sister and her friend. They've made plans for the rest of the day, so I don't have to entertain Karrie.

We have a little downtime as we transition out of brunch. I find Ryan in the back office, standing behind the desk, looking down at papers.

I knock on the open door. "Hey."

He looks up with a flicker of something beyond *I'm your boss and busy* in his eyes. The softness there puts my doubts at ease. "Hey yourself."

I relax a little. "People loved the food. They seemed to enjoy the beer pairings."

"If the Dos Islas guys agree, I want to plan this as a regular gig. I was thinking we could have them park their food truck here. Maybe in the alley at the end of the block just off the street."

"Permits," I remind him. "City of Chicago has rules about where food trucks can do business. But it's not a bad idea to check."

"Right." The response comes out tight. "They're exhausted from today, but pretty sure they want to continue."

"That's fantastic!"

His attention drifts back to the papers. He taps a pen in an odd rhythm as he reads.

Yeah, something is off between us. Or maybe I'm bugging him.

I find myself moving in slow motion through the rest of my shift. My tray weighs a metric ton. I'm so wiped I can barely stand. Maybe the "something off" is me.

Alex catches my arm. "Kat, you all right? You look sick."

The second he says the *S* word, all my symptoms congregate together and strike as one. *Dammit*. Extreme tiredness, congestion, low-grade headache. It's the end-of-winter crud I always get.

I stumble toward the coatroom. My body feels drenched in fatigue.

"I'll walk you home," Alex is saying.

"No, thanks. How are you doing?"

Alex rolls his eyes. "Get your coat, and I'll meet you up front."

I'm heading out when Ryan meets me at the coatroom door. "Alex said you're sick. Oh, wow. You look awful."

"Awesome. I'm so very glad we had this conversation."

His earlier distractedness seems to have burned off. "Hey, I mean, you look ill. Not that—you know what I mean."

"I'm sure it's a cold. I'll sleep it off and be back tomorrow."

"I don't want you here if you're contagious. It's bad enough you were here today feeling like this."

"I wasn't . . ." I wasn't sick like this earlier. Just some sniffles and the usual aches this morning when I peeled myself out of bed.

He's right, though. All the people I came into contact with today. What if I got other people sick? What if I got Ryan sick? We kissed! Not that he seems to want the reminder.

Talking feels like too much, so I keep it to a nod.

Ryan looks impatient. "How are you getting home?"

"Alex said he'd go with me."

"He's driving you?"

"Alex doesn't have a car."

He rolls his eyes, which is rude, but I don't have the energy to argue. "I'm driving you."

Now I'm the one eye-rolling. "Please. I'll be fine. I'll feel better with fresh air."

"Meet me out back, I'll take you."

"No." This irritates me beyond reason. "I'm not helpless. I can walk home on my own two feet."

"Kat, I have my car here. It will take five minutes there and back. Just let me do it."

"You're my boss."

I've got him now. He's thinking about all the things we aren't saying. How I kissed him and he kissed me back and now he's going to drive me to my house.

He's close, but not within-breathing-space close. Still, his voice softens. "Let me take you home, okay?"

Alex pops his head in. "Kat, you coming?"

"I'm taking her," Ryan says.

Alex shoots me a saucy glance, and I shrug. Behind me, Ryan throws on his coat and whips the scarf around his neck. My foggy brain shows me an alternate version with Ryan in a captain's chair, swiveling toward me and ordering me to beam out to safety. I let out a low, dumb laugh. "Captain Ryan."

"Kat?" Alex squints. "How much did you drink during the tours?"

I didn't sample any beer, which is sad, because I definitely feel tipsy.

Alex walks me out the back door, where fierce wind rips at my skin. Okay, so I'm grateful for the ride.

He parks me in the open seat of Ryan's car, which is waiting in the alley. Like I'm a hospital patient being wheeled out for curbside pickup.

"This was not necessary, but thank you," I tell Alex.

"Take care. I'll text you later." He looks past me at Ryan in the driver's seat, then at me again, and winks.

I swat him. Alex gives me a devilish grin. I hate him for it.

Here we are in the car again, me and Ryan. The world is spinning. I've only once before had a vertigo sensation, and it was three years ago when I had a nasty bout of the flu. I thought a flu didn't have sniffles, though, and I have sniffles. I'll look it up when I can remember how to type.

Ryan is talking at me, but I kind of don't care. How was I upright for so many hours today? All I want is sleep.

"Kat? I'm going to help you into the house."

Oh. We're here. I fell asleep in the car. In the four-minute ride.

Ryan has the car door open, and I heave myself out. I stand on my own and head to the gate. Something is missing. That something would be my purse.

I pull on the iron gate in case by chance it was left unlocked. It fights back and stays shut.

"Where are your keys? I can get this."

"My purse. At the pub."

He scrunches his neck further into his collar. "Ah. Well, we can go back and get it."

My vision blurs, and I sway on my feet. I feel so gross.

"Are you dizzy?" he asks, steadying me.

"Yeah. It's . . . real weird. I can't get back in the car. I have my phone. Let me see if Sadie answers."

She doesn't answer. Right, because she's away for the weekend, which for her extends into Monday when the vintage shop is closed. My sister has a key, but she's downtown somewhere shopping.

I try our landlord. She answers and tells me she'll be out in a minute.

The wind isn't as fierce with me huddled by the gate with large trees overhead, but it's still cold. Ryan gathers me close, and I swear I almost fall asleep again.

The front door opens, and Sadie's aunt scuttles down the steps in slippers and a quilted vintage housecoat. It's a glamorous stay-at-home look.

"You poor dear." She lets us in the gate. "Here's another spare key. Hello," she says to Ryan.

They greet each other and take care of opening the apartment for me.

"You call up if you need anything." She heads back upstairs.

The door closes behind me, and somehow my coat is coming off. Ryan. He's still here. He hangs the bulky puffer on the coatrack.

"Your car . . ."

"The spot in front was open, remember?"

I don't.

"Nice place," he's saying, taking in the front sitting room with the nonworking fireplace, mismatched armchairs, and plaid davenport. Sadie insists on calling our coach a davenport, after what her aunt calls it after what her aunt's parents called it. This thing is third-generation velveteen with a horse print in varying shades of brown.

Our place has a good amount of space and feels cozy, but all I can focus on is how threadbare it looks compared to Ryan's modern condo. That slice view of the lake. I'm embarrassed and don't enjoy the sensation. I mean, who likes feeling embarrassed? Other than YouTube stars, and they have an edit button.

"Where's your room?"

I realize I'm standing in the doorway just sort of existing. "I really am fine. It's a head cold. Hit me all at once."

I head past the kitchen down the hall to my room. At the bathroom, I turn ninety degrees. I make it to the toilet in time to empty what's in my stomach.

CHAPTER SEVENTEEN
HONEY BEER AND BRAGGOT

At the crossroads of beer and mead. Honey beer derives
its sweetness from malt with honey added in. A little
dose of sweet can go a long way.

I wake to darkness. My head feels like a brick soaked in day-old
water. My pillow is damp from sweat. My back and body ache
with dull throbs. The taste in my mouth is beyond unsavory. A
full glass of water sits beside the bed with an assortment of plastic bottles filled with bright-orange and -purple liquids. A single-
serving package of cookies and two mandarin oranges wait on a
plate. Next to that is one of my new paperbacks from the used
bookstore.

"Karrie?" Shoot. What a bummer for my sister to come here
for an escape and I'm passed out from plague.

I drink some water, take the nighttime syrup, and head to the
bathroom.

Ahead of me down the hall, someone leaps into view. I scream.

"It's just me!" a male voice calls out.

I wait for my bones to settle back into my body. "Ryan? What are you doing here?"

The light in the kitchen flickers on, sending dim rays toward me. Ryan's hair is perfect and trim, but his clothes are rumpled. "I stayed to make sure you're okay."

"Where's Karrie?"

"Your sister is staying at her friend's in Bucktown."

Thanks a lot, Karrie.

I must have muttered that out loud, because Ryan responds. "I sent her away. I didn't want her to get sick."

"But you're still here."

"I don't have an immune disorder."

"How did . . ." I could have sworn I never mentioned my sister's illness to him.

"She told me." Ryan fills in for my incomplete question. "We talked a little before she left. You've been conked out for hours."

A pleasant sensation floats through me. Ryan is being . . . thoughtful. Attentive. I don't have so many words now. Too groggy. "I threw up, didn't I?"

"You did."

I nod to myself. "The highlight of your day, I'm sure."

"I've seen worse."

"Frat parties?"

"Am I that predictable?"

Whatever judgment I have left over from state university bros during my own college days, I can't seem to apply to Ryan. The only real sign of bro-ness I've seen in him was when his buddies came to the bar for free beer.

"How are you feeling?" he asks.

"Just need to sleep this off." I stumble to the alcove by the kitchen as a sneezing fit comes on so hard I have to lean against the wall.

Ryan's right there, holding me up, his face pointed away from me. "Did you take the cold stuff? I wasn't sure what you had, so I got a bunch of stuff."

This is . . . a trip. Ryan playing nurse. "I'm fine." A round of coughs has me hacking until my throat shreds like a pop-metal guitar solo.

"You were sweating through the sheets."

"You were *watching* me?"

"I only noticed the sweat when you called out in your sleep. I went in to check on you. I swear I was going to leave after dropping off the medicine. And your purse." He gestures to the kitchen counter.

Good news: my purse is here. Bad news: I apparently bark out words in my sleep.

"Did I say anything interesting?" My eyes are closed in case this can spare my dignity.

"Nothing that made sense. Just words. Fragments."

Brilliant. At least my fragments didn't add up to anything mortifying. Or if they did, Ryan's not saying. "I'm sure this will pass. You can go, and I'll see you at the pub tomorrow."

"Kat, you can't go to work like this. You need to rest."

"My bills say otherwise."

"Missing a few days of work can't possibly be that bad."

I stare at him, groggy eyed, but hopefully he catches the glare behind the grog. "I don't have anyone paying for my life."

He's thoughtful for a moment. "I can float you money if you need it."

"No. I can't take money from my boss. If anyone found out—"

"Advance on your paycheck."

Joe and Prairie paid me ahead once, and I swore I'd never be so irresponsible again as to need it. I'd never judge anyone else for asking, but to me, it felt like failure as an adult. Besides, this feels different. It's not the married couple I see as stand-in parents; it's Ryan. A guy who's here in my apartment, nearly holding me upright. It feels too close to asking . . . whatever. It's not right.

"Thank you, but I'll be fine." I catch the time on the oven: 2:47 AM. "I can't imagine you're interested in round two of this, so please, go home. And thank you. You've done more than enough. I appreciate it."

He's quiet for a beat. "I should stay. What if something happens?"

"I've got medicine and snacks." My toes curl thinking of the little package of cookies and the oranges on a plate. "That was thoughtful, thank you."

Ryan tugs at his zippy sweatshirt. The tails from his dress shirt hang out the bottom. "The couch up front is comfortable. Anyway, I'll get out of your hair."

I imagine him then, fully tangled in my hair, and don't mind the visual one bit.

"You wouldn't have done this for Alex," I say.

"Huh?"

"Or Magda. Or Anya or Luiz."

"Probably not."

Definitely not. And I want to hear him say why. I want to know why he insisted on driving me home. On seeing me inside, and running errands for me, and why he's still here hours later.

We're both quiet. I'm a little dizzy still, but more alert than earlier. Still bone tired. I don't want him to leave, but it's ridiculous to expect him to stay. Grown adults take care of themselves when they're sick. I can do this on my own.

"I did this for you because I wanted to," he says, as if hearing my unasked question. "Is that okay?"

It's a lot okay. Even the checking on me in my sweaty sheets—I'm glad there was someone here to do the checking.

I'm also glad it was him.

I want to kiss him . . . again. I want to, but I'm sick and my mouth tastes like wallpaper glue. What I imagine wallpaper glue might taste like. Which is revolting.

Ryan is staring at me. "You're so pretty."

I stifle a laugh. "I'd like to say I've looked better."

"Even now. Especially now."

We sit in this moment, so quiet, so ordinary. It's lovely and sad in a hopeful way.

He takes my hand. "I would kiss you now if you weren't sick."

Curse this crud. I step back so I don't breathe sick fumes on him. He looks tired. "Since it's so late, don't leave. If it's easier to stay, I mean. On the couch. Or you could crash in Neil's room, since he never sleeps there. I'll wash the sheets later—"

"The couch is fine."

"We call it the davenport. I can fill you in later."

He smiles. "Okay." His hand finds my elbow, which feels intimate and appropriately distanced.

"I don't want to get you sick."

"I wiped everything with those bleach wipes."

The strangest thing happens then—and it comes on with a quickness. Tears. Tears are here, and they're shedding fast.

"Oh my god, Kat, what is it? What's wrong?" Ryan is near enough, but no longer touching me to give me the space I need, which sends me into another emotional burst.

I flail a hand in the air. "It's not what you think. I'm fine, I'm fine." I steady myself and wipe at my eyes. Moving into the kitchen, I take in the scent of lemon cleaner and bleach. All the dishes that were cluttered in the sink are drying on a mat.

Ryan moves with me, utterly perplexed.

"Did you do these?" I point to the dishes. No way my sister did. She's too used to Mom cleaning up after her.

He nods.

"A man who cleans. I guess it got me a little emotional."

I doubt I've convinced him I'm stable, and I haven't exactly convinced myself either. What I know is Ryan cared enough to clean my kitchen. I've lived with guys who did less when it was their own house. I'm sick, and it's one less thing for me to do. Sending my sister away, it was the right thing. I don't want her to be sick, and my parents . . . none of it matters now.

Right now it's time to head back to bed.

Turns out this isn't the kind of sick you can easily shake off. Herbal tea and cough syrup get me through the next day, but neither is making this go away. My bones ache. I'm like the Cryptkeeper shambling in a haze when I head to the bathroom.

Ryan texts to say everything's great at Resistance, no worries. Rest and get well. He offers to stop over again but sends the offer when I'm dead asleep. By the time I respond, he's already back at the pub.

Ryan: *You should see the doctor*
Me: *What doctor?*
Ryan: *Your doctor. A medical doctor . . . Sorry, thought that was obvious?*

This is amusing, this idea of a named doctor at my disposal. I'm a full-time server who uses a state-backed health plan that is essentially like insurance behind a glass case: Break Only in Case of Emergency.

Me: *I'll be fine in another day.*

I'm not. I have to call in again. I couldn't go in to work even if I wanted to. Not with this hacking cough and runny nose, when I work with food and the public. Certainly not around the brewing.

Sadie makes a drugstore run and offers to wash my sheets for me in the machine on our semi-insulated enclosed back porch. It's all I can manage to strip the bed and put on the spare sheets. But the cotton feels cool and comforting, and I'm grateful for the suggestion.

My phone rings. The actual ringtone, not on vibrate. I must have knocked into the wrong button because wow, this ringing is terrible.

"Is Karrie there?" Mom's voice demands when I answer.

Um. "It's Kat, not Karrie."

"I know, I called you. I'm looking for Karrie. She's supposed to be with you."

This should be fun. "She was here, but I'm sick. A she-devil cold with flu-like symptoms. My nose is running like a faucet, and—"

"Where is your sister?" Her question comes out shrill. Panicked.

"She's with a friend! Mom, relax. She's like a mile from here."

"Which friend? I don't know of a friend of hers in Chicago. Who is it?"

I describe the girl, poorly, because I've forgotten her name. "Sorry, my head still hurts. This cold thing is really dragging me down."

If I expect a soothing *Aw, honey, I'm sorry you're sick*, my money is on the wrong horse.

"This is incredibly irresponsible, Kat. I can't believe you don't know where your sister is. She's not answering her phone."

Probably because she knows it will lead to this conversation. "Karrie is fine. My b . . . my friend who was here, he sent her off. He didn't want her to catch what I have."

"Well, of course we don't want that. Obviously. But she was only supposed to stay with *you*. I thought it was just for one night, maybe two most, but she's not answering now. I don't know when she's coming home."

I don't have the bandwidth to tell her Karrie brought her big suitcase. She didn't say it outright, but my guess is she's planning on more than a couple nights away. The real question is *if* she's going home.

Mom is still talking. "If she has a flare-up, you know how bad it gets. How will she manage while she's hanging out with some random friend all the way out there in the city?"

Okay, I need to summon the bandwidth. "Karrie is an adult. She knows her body, and—"

"*Knows her body?*" We're at peak exasperation here. "This isn't some feminist manifesto. This is your sister we're talking about."

I match her intensity, best I can through the head fog. "Her friend isn't *random*. And believe it or not, there are stores and hospitals and restaurants out here just like where you live. She's not lost at sea."

"You know how your sister is. She can hardly manage a part-time school schedule. She sleeps until noon."

I have so many thoughts right now. So many. I could bite my tongue.

I could.

But I came out squalling, and I'll go out that way. "Mom. I love you. But you need to hear this: Karrie *needs* to be allowed to grow up. She needs to make her own way. I think she's been . . . depressed. The sleeping a lot could be because she's bored and doesn't see a way out of her confined life. You won't let her take more than part-time classes. It's why it's taken her extra time to get through college."

"You don't understand her condition."

"I don't know what it's like to live in her body, no. But I've seen Karrie excel. She's doing great. She has goals. She wants to move out with Addison."

"Absolutely not. Addison spends her weekends partying. She *bar hops*."

Oh, the humanity! My eyes fall shut. Me moving full-time to Resistance wasn't a popular choice with my parents. Neither was my quest to brew beer, but they largely don't bother me about it. Mainly because they don't bother me about anything.

"It's pretty typical for people in their early twenties to go to bars," I tell her. "She's legally allowed to drink. Besides, you remember I work in a bar, don't you? It's insulting for you to assume—"

"Don't give me that line, Kat," she spits out. "You know exactly what I mean. Karrie needs to follow a strict diet. Beer isn't on that diet."

I'd like to remind her gluten-free beers exist, but I don't think that will help. "You need to let her live her life."

"I don't need to do anything. I'm her mother. *I* say what I get to do."

Well, Karrie wasn't overreacting, that's for sure. "You're right. I can't tell you anything. I'm not sure why I'm bothering at all, since you never listen."

"Stop being so dramatic."

I've stayed out of their way. Made space for them so much that I've shrunk myself into nothing. And for what?

Long-simmering resentment surfaces. It's hot in my chest, the hurt. The memories are there, so easily called up. "You missed my graduation."

There's a pause. "From what? Are you in school again?"

I fight myself, wanting to hold back the words. The conversation we've never had, because I knew it would go like this. My gut compels me. "No. From high school. You missed it."

She sputters. "What does this have to do with anything?"

"Nothing else has mattered to you since Karrie's diagnosis. It *consumes* you. And Dad goes along for the ride. Anything happening to Karrie has been more important than literally anything else."

"Of course. She's sick. What else was I supposed to do?"

I don't have an answer for that, but I need to press forward. "I think you did your best at the time. Even if you stopped paying attention to me. But Karrie is more than a sick kid. She always has been. Now, she's an adult. She's nearly a college graduate. She's creative and funny and deserves to be looked at like she's those things."

"I'm sure you have life all figured out." Her tone is anything but complimentary. "I'm sure it's easy to dismiss the work I've done as some kind of obsession. You don't know what it's like to be a mother. Or what those nights looked like with Karrie exhausted and crying and barely able to eat. You *weren't there.*"

The words prick just like she intended. I wasn't there. I spent a lot of nights at friends' houses senior year and that following summer. Then I was off to college. I didn't go home every other weekend like so many students at my state school. I stayed on campus or went with friends back to their hometowns. I knew my place.

Just like I know my place now.

"Sounds like you have it all figured out," I say. "Drop me a line when you find Karrie. If you care enough."

I'm about to do a thing I've never done, but I hold off. Hope is a hard thing to cast off. Just in case, I wait a beat.

Turns out I don't have to do the thing after all.

My mom hangs up first.

I wake to movement in my room. Something presses down on the bed near my legs. I open my eyes.

Ryan. "Hey." His voice is soft, and the room is nearly dark, with only light from the hall coming in. "Sadie let me in. I've been sitting over there but saw you moving."

The chair across the room, usually piled with clothes in the worn-but-not-quite-dirty category, is now cleared, with a soft dent in the cushion.

He squeezes my foot through the blanket. "What you said about not having a doctor. I didn't want to press, but—"

"I do have a mother, you know. I just talked to her." Which is really disingenuous, because that was not a pleasant conversation. "Sorry. I get snippy when people tell me how to take care of myself."

"Understood." He considers his next words. "If there's anything I can do . . . I'm feeling useless is all."

He's anything but useless. Ryan's been at Resistance every time I've been on shift that I can remember, and he's usually there before me and after. He's been showing up and doing the work. Speaking of. "There's not work to do at the pub?"

"They've seen me enough." He shrugs. "Our cost per click is decent on the Facebook ads. I wish we had more money to dump into them."

"Maybe we do something fun on the main page to get organic reach. What's coming up?"

"Saint Patrick's Day. We can go all out."

"We have beer. That's already a draw. Put shamrocks on some ads and maybe a happy hour special. What else? What's the sports thing that's big right around now?"

He gives me a pitying look, then immediately brightens. "March Madness. College basketball."

"What's the thing with the brackets everyone's always obsessed with? Can we do something with that?"

"Like . . . custom brackets? About beer?"

I snap my fingers. Ow. Snapping. Not good when the body aches. "A craft beer bracket challenge. On the Facebook page."

He scratches at light beard scruff, which looks good on him. "That's a good idea." He jumps from the bed and digs through a leather messenger bag on the floor by the chair. He pulls out a tablet and a fold-up keyboard.

"Fair warning: I don't know how to bracket."

He smiles. "I do. And you know beer." He sits on the end of the bed with the laptop and starts typing.

A fog still coats my brain, but this is better than lying here alone. "IPA can be one category. Then we'll do a wheat, Belgian, and maybe stout. No, Pilsner?" I grab my phone. "Let's do a mix of Resistance beers and keep the other choices all smaller craft beers, all local. We can gain a lot of interest with that market. Chicago craft beers, and we network with other brewers."

He nods along, still typing. "Yeah, it's fun, but you have to know your beers."

"We can link to our website with the detailed descriptions of our beer. There's a lot already on our website we could highlight."

"Why didn't I think of this? Even when you're sick, you have good ideas."

"It's almost like being sick doesn't change me as a person."

He stops typing. "Okay, either I'm an ass or something just got more serious."

"It's nothing." My thoughts are half-baked, like I'm waking up from a hangover. "Okay, it's something. That call with my mom. It didn't go well. She's mad Karrie isn't still here. She can't get a hold of my sister, and she blames me for it. My parents want to control her life." I do a high-level summary of the conversation.

"I'm so sorry. If I overstepped by sending her away—"

"You didn't. You did the right thing. Karrie isn't missing. She texted me herself. She's exactly where she said she'd be—at her friend's. Besides, Karrie is twenty-three. She's not a teenager."

He shakes his head. "Sure. How is any of this your fault?"

It's not, but it still feels like my fault, a little. I shrug. "Karrie doesn't want lupus to define her. I don't want that either, but it's like all my parents can see." I press my hand to my head. "Maybe this is too big a conversation for now."

He sets the laptop aside. "I'm listening. We all want to be known for what we do, not what people think we are. Like a spoiled bro whose daddy hands him a business."

I raise a brow. "You *do* have a business degree."

He grins. "It's like we've come full circle and switched sides." He leans against his elbow across the narrow end of the bed. "I don't know much about lupus, only that it affects the immune system."

"Yeah. She has flare-ups from time to time that can be debilitating. She almost didn't get to go back to college sophomore year. My parents were freaking out. She's good about taking care of herself most of the time, but she's still young. She was trying to keep up with her friends and . . . couldn't."

"That's probably hard to watch."

I sip water from a cup on the bedside table. It's cool, meaning it hasn't been sitting there long. "With my family, I feel I'm in the way and excluded at the same time. Even though it was work, Resistance was my escape."

He rubs my foot over the blanket, and I let out a moan.

He retracts. "Sorry, too much?"

Not enough. "It's good. Keep going. I mean, if you want." A warm sensation coats my skin. A good warm that can heal me better than any doctor visit. Okay, wishful thinking, but I'll take the cozy vibes helping me relax. We were talking about something important . . . "You told me it seemed like your mom didn't want you to leave home. After your brother . . ."

He lets his head tip back. "Yeah, but I don't blame her. I could have moved out sooner. I could have tried harder. I was making things worse sticking around."

"Maybe we're too hard on ourselves."

Ryan is at the other end of the bed, but I've never felt closer to him. Seeing me bleary-eyed in pajamas with runny-nose stains, he's still caressing my feet and looking at me like he maybe wants to jump me.

"What are you thinking?" I ask.

His grin turns sly. "Do you really want to know?"

I nod. Desperate is an understatement.

"When you're feeling better, I'd like to show you."

CHAPTER EIGHTEEN
BELGIAN STYLE

Ales focused on malts and fruit flavors. Varies in color
and hops, depending on differing techniques. A dependable choice.

It's Saturday afternoon by the time I return to Resistance. I've
missed nearly a full week of work. It pains me to calculate the lost
income, but the idea of being on my feet for eight hours serving
food and drinks was enough to drive me back under the covers.

Ryan coming by every day didn't hurt. He brought me food and
tissues, and we finalized the bracket challenge. We looked up the
websites for every craft beer bar in Chicago, then the sites for other
bars, seeing what they offered, what stood out. What we could learn.

It made me miss working. Not serving drinks or making ads,
but working in the back. Brewing beer. Tinkering with Heartbeat.
It's the first thing I want to do when I get back. With Kurt and
Randy's permission, obviously.

My time with Ryan wasn't all work for Resistance. He has
accounts for nearly every streaming service—a gold mine of

sick-at-home entertainment options for me to poke around on, given I was too out of it to read for more than ten minutes at a stretch. When he returned to check on me, I'd landed on a space drama series I'd never seen, and we dug in. Who knew he was a sci-fi fan?

As we embraced the couchbound life, Ryan lay behind me while I snuggled into him. Spoon-style, no kissing—and he never once complained over the no-kissing part. Even when I mimicked his voice and put complaining words in his mouth, he told me he wanted to keep me company while I got better.

It was like existing in this strange little cocoon with the rest of the world on pause.

Only the world wasn't on pause. Now I'm back at the pub, and already I can tell the kids are not all right.

The plastic pop music is on, the jukebox dark. The pub is nearly half-full, a good sign for midday before the evening rush and night crowd. Alex, carrying a loaded tray, visually takes in a breath when he sees me. Something about him is off. He's wearing odd clothes, but I can't fully examine the look before he abruptly turns and heads toward a table.

I head to the back and nearly collide with Ryan.

"You're here." He doesn't look relieved to see me. Annoyed, more like, and not cutely rumpled and adoring like in my apartment. "Are you serving?"

Why thank you for asking if I'm feeling better. "Isn't a tour scheduled?"

"It's canceled. Didn't you see my email?"

"I didn't get any texts."

"I said email." He huffs out his breath. "Official work notices go through email. Not texts."

Oh, okay, we're playing boss-and-subordinate today. "I see. No, I have not checked my email today."

That's when I notice Kurt and Randy milling around behind him, looking stressed.

"What's going on?"

He looks past me, distracted. "You mean besides the deep fryer going down? A bad batch. The customers were saying the beer tasted sour. Too sour. It shouldn't have even gone out like that. I don't know; Kurt said there's microbes or something in the tank."

That's not good. I should have been here to help Randy. *To do the job right.* I push the thought aside—it's not fair. Kurt and Randy have experience, and this can happen anywhere.

"Sorry, Ryan. It happens. Bacteria in a hose or lingering in the corner of a tank."

"Right, that's what Kurt said. We have to ditch the whole batch and sanitize everything." He checks his phone and looks back at me, almost like he's seeing through me. "Can I help you with something?"

I'm sure I flinch at his abrupt tone. "I see you're on edge. If there's no tour, I'll help in the back." I wave toward Randy.

"I need you on tables. Anya called in."

I shake my head. "No, I'm better used here. They're testing, right? To find the contaminant?"

He shifts his weight to lean an arm against the wall. "I don't mean to be short with you. I just really need you on tables. That's what will help most."

I take a measured breath. Serving drinks is not the best use of my time. "Ryan. Think about this. I know this equipment. I've worked with Edwin and Joe on the plating tests. Unless Kurt has a rapid test kit?"

Ryan rubs at his forehead. "They're the brewers and they know what they're doing, okay? I hired them to do a job, and that's what they're doing."

I don't need him to fill in the rest. I'm already walking away when he catches up.

"Kat, I'm sorry I snapped." His tone is softer now, apologetic, but still tense. "We've got a special group coming in, and this doesn't look good."

"What special group?"

He exhales. "My dad and a couple of his friends."

"Benny Burrito?"

He looks confused until he remembers the nickname. "Uh, yeah. He should be here any minute."

What's weird is this will be the first time his father has been by since the ownership switch. At least that I've seen. You would think he'd be around more, given he's the investor.

Time to fetch an apron and get to work. Only the apron box is gone. On the table in the employee coatroom are stacks of . . . I hold back a retching sensation.

Denim shirts.

The Resistance name and logo are stitched in pumpkin orange against the denim. Buttons all the way down and buttons at the cuff. A stiff, ugly dress shirt. They are worse than I imagined.

Alex appears in the doorway. I nearly choke.

His expression is lethal. "Don't."

It's the shirt. It's like seeing Alex's face but on a body not his own. A body in head-to-toe denim. His dark jeans are missing the usual patches and frayed accents, further solidifying the altered look. The shirt looks decent on him, considering, but different. "If anyone can make this shirt look good, it's you. And maybe Magda."

I gingerly poke at the remaining shirts on the table. There's a small, which for sure won't fit because these boobs moved me out of small sizes for good, and an XXL. I can wear the small unbuttoned over my black plain tee or swim in the oversized shirt.

"This week might do me in, Kat." Alex breaks my focus over the shirts. "Ryan's been a wreck. It's like with you gone, he doesn't know what to do."

I snort. "That's an exaggeration."

Alex isn't smirking like I expected.

"What? You can't think he's a worse boss because I'm not around."

"That's what everybody thinks."

"Everybody? You all have been talking about me and Ryan . . . together?"

He rolls his eyes. "We all know. Give us some credit."

How could they know we kissed? I've told no one. And no one should know Ryan's been at my apartment. Well, except for Alex, who practically carried me out to Ryan's car.

"He only took me home the one time." No. "Well, twice. Three times, but those were before I was sick." Not to mention stopping by all week and bringing me food from the kitchen.

Of course they all know.

Now Alex is grinning a grin full of gloat.

I glare at him. "Stop that! Stop giving me that look!"

Magda appears, wearing the new work shirt. It looks good on her despite the horrid orange logo. "Yeah, it's there," Magda says to Alex. "It's all over her face."

I expand my glare. "Nothing is on my face. Besides, he wants nothing to do with me right now." Which, admittedly, annoys me. I'd probably be stressed too if my boss who was also my father were planning to stop by when we'd discovered a bad batch and the deep fryer was busted.

Magda curls a strand of hair around her finger. "Don't fight it. Maybe it will get you places." She spins off toward the bar.

My face flushes. Exactly what I don't want anyone to think— that hooking up with Ryan will give me an advantage because we're together. Especially if anything pans out with this supposed business plan that we haven't actually gotten around to further discussing. That's going to look worse than scandalous if we're hooking up on the side. What's worse than scandalous? Hooking up on the side, apparently.

Alex moves in front of me. "Ignore her. We were teasing. Don't let it upset you."

"You don't need to manage me," I tell him. "I know I'm a mess, but I'm not your mess."

I grab one of the shirts and head to the kitchen to wash my hands. I towel off and find Alex behind me, looking ready to pounce. "Hey, what's up?" I ask.

"Maybe consider people care about you before you go telling them who and who not to *manage*."

I wince. "Sorry for how that came out. I don't want you to waste your energy fixing me."

"Last I knew, caring about someone didn't mean fixing them. Do you see it as a waste listening to my problems?"

"Of course not. Your problems are more . . ."

"More what?"

Severe? Important? "I don't know. This feels like middle school and I'm the dope with a crush on a boy I'm scared to talk to."

"I've felt like that, you know. When I doubted every word I said and every new person I met because I thought they were judging me. When my thoughts were so dark they went goth."

I laugh at that.

"Being here, around people like you, that helped," he says. "My folks, they annoy me to no end, but they're right there telling me anyone who doesn't like me is an idiot."

"Hard agree on that."

Hearing about his family makes me miss my own. Not the version of my mom who hung up on me, but the mom who used to take us to museums and parks. Who set firm Friday night plans with takeout pizza, movies, and board games. I miss how my parents invited the neighbors to sit around our fire pit on summer nights. My birthdays that were remembered and celebrated beyond a card in the mail.

I put on the shirt—the XXL size. If this is the uniform now, what choice do I have? I tuck the shirt ends into my pleather leggings. Yikes. Giant folds of denim bunched into tight leggings? No. The shirt will have to hang out like it's summer vacation.

"Can't have loose tails," Gary calls over from the grill.

Alex has his shirt tucked in. Crap.

"Try this." Alex unbuttons the bottom two buttons of my shirt and ties the loose ends together.

"That's cute. Am I cute?" I turn for inspection.

"It's a health hazard to have the shirt tail dragging."

Alex is not one for fashion advice. We leave the kitchen and cross to the bar. Ryan stands beside it with three older men. I slow and lean toward Alex. "I've only seen Benny Burrito in a photo. Is he the taller one?"

"Yeah. The guy in the middle. You haven't met him?"

"You have?"

He nods. "The first time was maybe a year ago. Prairie introduced me. Then he was here a few weeks back. I recognized him, but he didn't say anything to anyone. Ryan wasn't even here."

A chill races across my back. It's frigid in here, but that's not why. "How was business?"

He half shrugs. "Hard to say. It was dead in here, but nothing went wrong. Not obviously, anyway."

A hundred more questions beg to be asked, but they're probably better suited for a time when there aren't customers looking our way with empty pint glasses.

"Do you want to go over there?" Alex asks. "Or is this like a meet-the-parents thing? Are you nervous? You must be nervous."

"Well, when you put it that way." Yikes. No pressure. "One of us needs to hit those tables." I make a move, but Alex traps my arm.

"I'll go. You go introduce yourself to Mr. Bennett."

I'm grateful for the offer. And for the reminder of Ryan's dad's real name. The last thing I need is to blurt out *burrito*.

The men are headed toward the brewing area. The one that's a mess of parts and cleaning supplies.

Ryan shoots a grand smile my way. "Kat! Come on over."

If I turn the other direction, he'll drag me back. That's how much his face is pleading with me to stay now that his dad is here. I straighten my shoulders and look as professional as I can wearing a knotted denim shirt over pleather leggings. I thrust my hand out. "Kat Malone. Good to meet you."

"Benjamin Bennett." He shakes my hand, seemingly unfazed. I'm worrying for nothing.

He introduces his friends. Ryan is stiff, his movements stilted. It hurts my heart to see him so nervous in front of his own father. My parents are annoying a good seventy percent of the time, but I'm never a nervous wreck around them. I save that wreckness for later when I'm alone obsessing through my thoughts.

"Kat, what do you think about putting together those flights we had for the brunch event?" Ryan is attempting to steer his father toward a table, away from the brew tanks.

"That's a great idea. We have two options with four beers each at four to five ounces."

"We were going to check out the brewing." Mr. Bennett cranes a neck toward the tanks. "I'd love to see the changes since I've last been back there."

I'm not sure what changes he's expecting. There isn't room to expand with more equipment, since the space is tight. Though it makes sense he'd want to go through the area.

I notice Ryan's panic. It's probably best to be forthright with his dad. Hiding the truth doesn't accomplish anything.

"How about we take a look through the window and give the brewers space?" I walk ahead and don't give them the option to say no. "They're doing a deep clean of the tanks to root out an issue that soured a batch. The sampling process throughout brewing is pretty fascinating. There are test kits on the market that are more and more precise about sourcing an issue." I give them examples from what I saw in person at the Wisconsin brewery and explain the process. The better, faster test kits cost more, of course, which I mention as delicately as possible. Older, less expensive methods are what Resistance has typically used, mainly since it's what Edwin and Joe were used to using.

Mr. Bennett's friends ask more questions I'm happy to answer.

As they shift to talking among themselves, Mr. Bennett pulls me aside. He has a similar gentleman's library scent like his son, but more polished wood and bourbon. His face is etched in fine lines in that way that only makes older good-looking men more handsome. The nerve. "Are you the young lady who gives the tours?"

"I am," I answer brightly. I stifle a cringe at *young lady*. It's not offensive on the surface, but it rubs me like pleather on my thighs. And yes, these leggings were a bad choice today.

"I can tell you know brewing. Excellent work."

It's like a teacher handed me an A+. "It's easy when you love it."

Ryan inches into my peripheral, still looking on the edge of bolting. I send him a reassuring smile, but his return grin is forced to the point I almost laugh.

We get the men seated with menus. Mr. Bennett turns, looking around. "Where's that jukebox? Why isn't it on?"

I press my lips together as Ryan sputters a response. "It's been on the fritz. The thing is ancient. I'll see if it will turn on."

Ryan leaves to tend to the jukebox, which I'm sure he unplugged. Mr. Bennett looks at me. "How long have you worked here, Kat?"

"A few years." I tell him how I increased to full-time and how much I enjoyed working with Prairie and Joe.

"You certainly know the brewing process. I haven't seen your level of knowledge with the other servers here. An interest of yours?"

Since he asked. "Yes. I want to be a brewer. To do what Kurt and Randy do."

Ryan is back, and the plastic pop has been replaced by Nine Inch Nails. Interesting choice for present company.

One of Mr. Bennett's friends nods his head to the beat. "Great song."

Things seem well and good here, so I make a move to leave, only Ryan snags me by the giant shirtsleeve. He looks at me for a beat. "Please. Don't go," he says so only I can hear.

Mr. Bennett is hardly a beast. How bad could he be? He's a legend for eating a burrito, for Pete's sake. "You'll be fine. I need to run these orders to the kitchen."

I leave Ryan to his own devices, drop the orders off, check on a few tables, and eventually find Ryan by the bar with Magda on the other side.

"Need a drink?" I ask him.

Magda drums her nails against the bar top. "I already offered. Guy's a ball of nerves."

"I'm glad you're both amused by this," Ryan says. "He's judging me right now. He's impossible."

"He is the investor. Of course he's going to be checking on things." I try to imagine what it's like for Ryan, but there are too many variables different from my own for me to fully grasp. Or maybe that's the key. "He wouldn't have given you Resistance to run if he thought you'd immediately jack it up. He obviously trusts you enough to do the job."

"Or he's waiting for me to fail."

"That seems vindictive."

Ryan shrugs. "He's been focused on work the past few years. He gets bored easily. Finding new investments is a thrill to him."

I don't know what to make of this revelation, so I don't reply.

The rest of the afternoon with Mr. Bennett and his friends passes without issue. He and Ryan disappear into the back office together around the same time business picks up. An hour later, Ryan tracks me down.

"Time for a break yet?" he asks.

"Always."

We head through the kitchen outside to the alley as Gary returns from a vape break. The door closes against the brick doorstop.

"I think it went well—" I say at the same time Ryan cries out, "This did not go well."

"What?" I ask.

"The audit came back."

Oh, right. The audit. "How do the numbers look?"

He tilts his head toward the night sky. Overcast, no stars in sight. "Worse than we thought."

CHAPTER NINETEEN
AMBER LAGER

Malt and hops both featured with toasted malt flavors.
Low to higher hops and a golden to copper hue. Also,
the name of that girl you once knew in college.

My gut drops. "How much worse?" We already know Joe and Prairie had past-due payments and owed money to the vendors. I thought they'd settled those debts with money from the sale.

Ryan leans against the brick exterior. With the light by the door casting shadows, he looks older, more like his father, but with hints of his brother too. I know how much he wants this. Also, how complicated it is to run a business.

"I had all these ideas to expand the brewing. Distribution. It's going to cost huge bank to upgrade the machines and do expanded bottling. Plus those fancy test kits you were talking about."

"I hope you're not blaming me for explaining how the faster test methods cost more. Any brewing operation needs to invest in its process."

He nods. "That's not what I mean. He wants to see these plans in action. He's impatient and thinks I haven't, as he says, *taken the initiative*. Our walk-in freezer maintenance came due and they're advising a new system. We could use more servers, as business is picking up, but I'm not sure how to pay them." He pushes out from the wall. "Resistance owed back taxes. Our accountant found it. The taxes were paid by the time of the sale—it's handled—but that doesn't look good for the bottom line. The books are a mess. We'll probably be audited for real."

He means by the IRS. My eyes involuntary close. "There's time to get the books straight, right?"

"Doesn't it bother you this place was run like that? Like an afterthought?"

This stings. Hard. Jana's words float back, reminding me Joe and Prairie are flawed. They made mistakes. "It could have been an honest mistake," I point out.

He grunts. "I didn't know this place was in such bad shape. The way my father talked about it, the business sounded solid. I'd work here, get my bearings. He'd see what I can accomplish. Then I could move on and open my own place."

"You have plans beyond Resistance?"

He looks surprised at my question. "Well, yeah. Look at me. I don't fit here. I don't have tattoos or listen to old rock music or hang out with bikers. It was only a matter of time before I would move on."

It probably shouldn't shock me that Ryan isn't aiming to be a lifer at Resistance. That working here is a short-term plan before jumping into something else. I aim for a neutral tone. "Is that what you're going to do? Move on?"

"What, now? No." He appears baffled that I would ask such a question.

"So, what are you going to do?"

He paces the stretch of concrete in front of the alley. "You know what he said to me? He said, 'Your brother would have had this ship running tighter than the navy by now.'"

"Your brother was in the navy?"

By the look on his face, I can tell I've missed the point.

"It wasn't a fair thing to say to you. You'll never be able to compete with your brother."

"Right, because he's perfect." A bitter note tinges his tone.

"No, because he's gone. He'll always be memorialized and remembered for his best traits. That's what we do when we lose people. They become untouchable. That's not your fault. You can only control what you do."

He stares at the ground. "I need your help."

I want to remind him he was the one handed this opportunity, not me, and why should I bother helping when . . . but resentment feels like an old coat too tight in the shoulders. I want him to succeed. I want Resistance to succeed, with him.

Ryan's looking at me now. "I need you, Kat. Everyone here works to make Resistance what it is, but I see *you* as the center, the heart. I see it by the way people check in with you and react to you. And how that was missing this week while you were gone. You know how this place runs. If you don't know something, you know who does. I can't imagine doing this without you."

When he says I'm needed, I hear I'm valued. That I'm the center, the heart. The heartbeat. Everything in me fights against believing what he's saying, but I do believe. I want to believe.

"So the books are a wreck and we need a new freezer. And maybe replace the deep fryer. What's the bottom line? How long do we have?"

A hopeful glint hits his eye. "You said *we*. Does that mean . . . ?"

"What's the deadline?"

He walks a few steps, looks at the sky, and turns back. "My father found a buyer who's interested."

My thoughts trip over one another. A buyer. A buyer? "What? He just bought the place and now he wants to sell?"

"It's all numbers to him. Craft breweries are in demand. He found a good option and told me the six-month deal is off. It's more like two months. If that."

This doesn't make sense. "Why let you have a stab at running Resistance if he was going to sell anyway?"

"He's frustrated I haven't made more progress. I'm the one who convinced him to give this chance to me. I begged."

So it wasn't handed to him exactly. Though he still had the opportunity to be given a whole pub and brewing operation to manage on no experience.

"My parents were arguing all the time. It all goes back to losing my brother. My dad is driven by work, and it's pretty much all he does. He looks for places to invest in and turns around and sells again for profit. Meanwhile, my mom was just lost, and I felt like I needed to be around for her. Only things seemed to get worse. I thought, taking on this job—it could give my dad and me more common ground. I had no idea what I was doing."

A nagging tugs at my thoughts, how Prairie and Joe sold to a trusted friend. They probably loved the idea of a friend's son taking over. Not so much knowing an investor would flip their life's work into another sale within months.

They deserve better.

"Does this new buyer even want to keep the brewing? What if they want to raze the property and build something else?"

"I don't know." He shrugs, dejected. "Maybe it's an empty threat and there's no buyer."

He starts to say something more, but I stop him. "I want to help, but I'm not a miracle worker, Ryan. I'm a server learning to make beer. I don't have any more experience running a restaurant and brewery than you do. Why do you think I have answers?"

He's in front of me looking ground-down-to-the-pavement humble. "I'm better with you around." He makes a disgusted expression. "I owe you an apology. I didn't even ask how you were feeling. I'm an idiot. I launched into telling you to check your email and how I needed you on tables. I'm sorry."

I swallow. Truth is, I like feeling needed. I've always liked it, because it acknowledges I have a purpose. A value. I'm not in the way. I'm not forgotten. His apology covers the hurt I felt earlier. I'm not one hundred yet, but Ryan's in a fractured state and he's looking to me for help.

He places a hand at my cheek. "You're just you. That's what I like about you. No one else is like you." He leans in closer. "Can I? Is it safe?"

He wants to kiss me. I'm frustrated and this conversation is important, but I want him close too. Closer. "Yes."

He meets my lips with his, and the street falls away. I let his touch ground me. His warmth sinks into my skin, giving me new hope. This connection feels more real than anything I've felt in so long. Maybe because it's not perfect. It's alive and changing and a little bit messy.

I shift so we're pressed against each other. His hand moves to the back of my hair, to my neck. A touch so light, so respectful, but deliberate. My mind empties out, and it's bliss.

We pull apart to air thick between us. "I meant it when I said we could run Resistance together. We can turn this around and buy out my father."

The spell now broken, I want to shove him off and laugh in his face. But I like our closeness. I go with just the laugh. "With what money? I'm broke."

"We get loans."

"Banks don't give loans to people with bad credit and empty bank accounts."

"My account isn't empty. We'd do this together."

Together. Heat flashes through me. The words repeat in my head, only they don't belong to Ryan. *We do this together. First, my degree. If we don't invest in our creativity at the highest levels, the world suffers and we're all just drones . . . When I'm done, I'll have a university job and income from speaking engagements. Then it's your turn. I'll work while you're in school, and it will all even out.*

I was so stupid.

Signing loan papers with Ryan—nope. Not interested. I can't be the person I need to be if I'm tied up in a financial loan with a guy promising me the world. I don't want to make another stupid mistake just because I'm in love with a guy.

Wait—I'm not in love. It's too soon for a conversation about love. Way too soon.

"Ryan, maybe we should slow down here." Can we go back to kissing?

He nods, but not to the kissing part, since I didn't say that out loud. I should have.

"Yeah, no, yeah." Ryan shakes his head like he's shaking sense into himself. "You're right. I'll take on the loans myself. It's too much to ask of you."

"Then Resistance will be yours. What do you need me for?"

"You get going on that brewmaster thing. You run the brewing. We partner, like the last owners."

Who were married, while we're not. "You said yourself, Joe and Prairie made a mess of the books. They were in debt. Clearly, their partnership looked better on the outside than in reality." I hate to admit it, but I know too much now to gloss over the rougher details. "I don't think either of us wants to repeat their mistakes."

"Sure, I know. But your dream is to make beer. And you can. You can make the beer and I'll run the business."

Which is . . . exactly what I want. I want to focus on brewing, totally. But nothing about the current arrangement at Resistance points to that happening. "What about Kurt? He won't take a demotion."

"I'm not sure Kurt's going to work out. He and Randy can't stand each other. It's another reason I didn't want to put you in the mix with them today." He sighs, looking less confident. "My dad wants me to fire Randy."

"Randy? Not Kurt? Why?"

"Randy's main job is maintenance of the tanks."

I shake my head. "Both of them are new here. Kurt has just as much responsibility."

"I hired them because my father advised it. Now he wants me to get rid of Randy, and Kurt probably won't stay anyway."

"Wait—your dad had a say in hiring? Was he reviewing applications? I thought that was your job."

"He likes to remind me he's the investor. He likes to control things."

The invisible investor making invisible decisions with very visible consequences.

Ryan still has his hands laid against my sleeves. The denim ones. "If I went by my instincts, you would have been hired. Kurt said no to you and Dad said Kurt was a must."

Whoa, whoa, whoa. This sure is a different story than Joe and Prairie not recommending me. Suddenly, this day has gone from a successful visit with daddy investor to a shock wave of new information.

I step back from Ryan. I can't tell whether this insight is new to him, today, or if he knew all along. "You're telling me *Kurt* had a say in whether I got the job?"

He pauses. "My father said that as head brewer, he had final say. Sorry, I shouldn't have told you. It's not like anything is changed now that you know."

"I need you to tell me these things." Here I thought I'd gotten an A+ from Mr. Bennett—I'm even calling him Mr. Bennett, like he's my teacher—when he'd already determined, weeks ago, I wasn't fit for the job. Today he acted like he had no idea I was interested in a brewing job when *he's* the reason I didn't get the interview.

Worse? Ryan went along with it. He didn't stand up to his father.

This. This is exactly why I can't go into business with Ryan. Who's to say he'll stand up to his dad when it's time to sell? What if when I need him most, he bails, and I'm on the hook? A whole business, not a collection of credit cards that can be cut and pasted into a collage.

"I've got to get back." This is way too much to cover on a shift break.

He pulls me toward him again. "I'm sorry. Really. I don't want him lording over me forever. Right now, he's the one with the money."

It always comes down to money.

"Hey." He looks at me in that deep way, like he's sifting through my soul. "We can do this."

He kisses me again. I want to escape into it and empty myself out, but too many thoughts clash. I step back and head for the door.

"Kat?"

I pause, since he's not following.

"Think about it, okay?"

Tension is high when I return inside. Randy storms into the pub, letting the glass door to the brewing room fall closed behind him. The door flies open again and Kurt bursts out.

"You're done!" Kurt points at Randy, walking forcefully toward him.

Customers turn and gawk.

"You're not the boss of me," Randy fires back. His usual chill tone is heightened, his words wavering and damaged. "If I go, I go on my own."

Luiz moves quickly, putting himself between Kurt and Randy. I can't hear what he says, but I hear Kurt.

"This place is a dive! Shouldn't even have a license to brew."

Now I'm there beside Luiz. "What happened? What's going on?"

Kurt blinks. Exhaustion settles over his shoulders like sand bags. "I can't work like this."

I don't understand. "Like what? What happened?"

Behind us, Randy mutters. I turn to see him throw his hands in the air. "I don't know, man. We have different world views. I'd work for Joe in a second, but not for him." Randy shrugs his angular body into a leather coat and disappears through the revolving door onto the street.

So, that just happened.

"The guy is stoned every day," Kurt tells us. "He needs a babysitter to do basic tasks. I need my own team or I'm out."

Ryan enters and arrows toward us. "Kurt, I'm sorry." He claps a hand on the brewer's back. "Let's talk."

Kurt flinches, but agrees. The two go to the back by the tanks. The glass door seals them inside.

Alex and Magda are here now too. "You okay?" Alex asks, always looking out for me.

I mumble an affirmative response. "I can't believe we lost Randy."

Luiz sighs. "I don't think he's high at work. He's a chill guy. Kind of spacey, but he works hard. Kurt can't handle anyone who won't listen to every word he says."

I've seen it too. "If we lose Kurt, that sets us back again."

We have to replace Randy. Probably with two more brewers, like Kurt said. Ryan's expansion plans are burnt toast. Which means if impatient daddy investor gets trigger-happy with the sell-off button, Resistance is lost.

"I need a minute," I tell them, and head to the bar. I find a stool and sit.

Alex joins me and tucks his order pad into a back pocket. "What are you unsure about? Ryan's into you now, and he knows you can do the work. This is your chance."

"Kurt won't work with me." I tell him what Ryan said about his father calling the shots on hiring. How he and Kurt had final say on hires and I didn't make the cut.

Alex grows still. "I'm sorry, Kat. I didn't know."

"No one did."

I'm not sure I should tell him how bad off the books are. I don't want to worry Alex, but at the same time, if things are nose-diving, he should get out while he's ahead. It feels like betrayal to Ryan, but I've known Alex longer. So I tell him what I know. All of it.

Alex does a slow turn and leans against the bar. "Should I be looking for another job?"

"I don't know." I glance to the window where Ryan and Kurt are still talking. The two are calm, at least. A good sign.

Alex leans an elbow against the bar. "Between you and me, Kat, if you don't get the brewing job here, you should get out. Go where your talents can be used. Where you're appreciated."

My defenses activate. "I feel appreciated here. Our crew is great."

"We won't all be here forever. You have to look out for yourself."

I look back at him. "Do you think you'll leave?"

"After what you just told me? Probably." He pauses. "I've already been looking."

Good.

Huh? My first thought was *good* that Alex is thinking of leaving?

"Everything changes eventually," Alex says. "I have an offer to move into an apartment with a friend. It's closer to school. If I take it, I'll get a serving gig downtown."

I hold back a huge sigh. I'll miss him, but moving on will be good for him. More money serving at a busier restaurant; a job closer to Columbia College downtown, or nearer to an El line.

On the pub floor, Luiz looks like he has things covered for the moment. I left out a few details and want to tell Alex the rest. I keep my voice low. "Ryan asked me about partnering with him. Says that if his father sells, we could buy Resistance and run it ourselves."

Alex lets his head hang for a second. He straightens, still leaning back against the worn bar. "You know I like Ryan. I like you and Ryan together. I do. But look." He nods toward Ryan and Kurt through the glass. "They're back there making decisions while you're out here."

My throat tightens. My doubts that I've tried to squelch are pounding down the sidewalk at a full run. I have no assurance things will be different other than Ryan telling me so.

Ryan said he's a better person with me around, but I'm not an accessory. I need equal partnership if I'm going into business with someone. Right now, I don't even know what job I'm doing. Brew tours for a process that's shut down?

"It might be time for both of us to face it," Alex says. "Resistance isn't what it used to be."

CHAPTER TWENTY
CHAMPAGNE BEER

Beer made using the fermentation process of champagne.
For when you want a little bubbly.

My shift ends before closing, so I take advantage of the chance
to leave. Normally, I'd help out where needed and let someone
else cut early. Not tonight. Resistance has never felt like so much
work. Wearing rubber gloves and scrubbing tanks on my hands
and knees was less strenuous than whatever this job has become.
Even working two jobs, an eight-hour day at the office followed by
a five-hour shift serving drinks, was less exhausting.

Texts have piled up during my walk home. Ryan. Karrie. My
mom, no doubt looking for Karrie.

I don't care.

I climb into the bathtub and use a fizzy bath bomb Sadie
gifted me at the holidays. The bathroom I share with Neil has a
skinny stand-up shower, but Sadie's private bath has a claw-foot
tub. She lets me use it anytime I want. Something about those

little feet rising off the black-and-white-tiled floor feels like a slice of luxury.

When my skin prunes and the water goes cold, I towel off and get cozy in my room.

I dare to check the texts.

Karrie is still at her friend's in Bucktown. She talked to Mom and is fighting going home at all. *Called it.*

Dad chimes in with his own text, requesting I talk sense into Karrie. And while I'm at it, smooth things over with Mom, who I've upset.

Okay, next.

Sadie! She's heading to an event at the library. Cute. Typical.

Next, Ryan. He's apologizing. Kurt is staying and we can talk more.

I have another text coming in, but now Ryan's calling.

I tap answer. "Hey."

"Kat, hey. I wanted to talk, but you'd left."

I don't bother telling him he had plenty of time to catch me. "So it went okay with Kurt?"

He sighs. "Yeah. It's rough, but he's a decent guy. He just needs a good number-two."

Alex's suggestion has carved itself into my skin. Metaphorically, of course. I need to be direct, or I'll never reach my goals. "I want the job."

"Kat—"

"Kat what? I want the brewer job." Decisive. Bold. Go get it, girl. "You said you need my help. This is it. This is how I help."

"I know. It's what I wanted to talk to you about. I want you for the brewer job too. I should have hired you in the first place. I see my mistake now."

I scoot to an upright position on my bed. "Oh. Well, that's great, then. So . . . I have the job?"

"I'll need you to come in. Sit with Kurt and me, and we'll go over things."

"Kurt wants me as his number-two?" *Slow down, heart. Don't race yet.*

"I told him how great you are. He's seen you in action during the tours. It's going to be a good fit."

My mood has whiplash. "That's . . . fantastic news. Fantastic."

I get to be a brewer. At Resistance. What I've wanted from the start. It doesn't feel real. It's like I'm so used to disappointment, I don't know how to handle good news.

"Great," I say, still examining this new sensation. "That leaves you to sort the books and hire another server. And order that new freezer."

"Yeah, it's a lot. I was hoping you'd still keep tabs on the bracket promo. And follow up with the last of those breweries who want in on the promotion."

I agree to all of it. Of course I do. I'm getting what I want! Finally!

"I know you just got home, but I think we should celebrate," Ryan is saying. "Want to go out?"

The adrenaline high is gaining steam. "Do you mean check out some bars? More intel?"

"I was thinking more like a date."

I'm already at my closet looking for something not entirely black when his words hit. "A date." I trail my fingers against the fabrics hanging in front of me. Okay, maybe a *little* black.

"You're going to make me ask, aren't you?" He clears his throat. "Kat, will you go out with me?"

Okay, heart. Race all you want.

I'm wearing heels tonight. Mary Janes in deep fuchsia. The closet floor parted and they were begging: *Wear me.*

The rest of me is clothed in a long-sleeved black A-line dress that hits at my knee. A sheer layer of lace floats over the base. Black opaque tights and a necklace with a bright-pink floral charm on a strand of yellow beads. My final flourish? A vintage swing coat with a fur-lined hood, courtesy of Sadie's closet. With permission, of course.

Ryan greets me with a kiss at my front walk. Standing back, he takes in the full view. "You look amazing."

He goes for my lips again, which I've intentionally left bare, with only a thin layer of pale gloss. For this reason alone. His touch is so welcome, I want to pull him inside and not leave at all.

Instead, we part long enough to get to the car. He opens the door for me, and off we go.

We head east, toward downtown.

"Dinner first. Then wherever you'd like."

It's already fairly late, and I'm still coming off being sick, so I'm not sure how long I'll last.

Turns out I last just fine. Dinner is divine. Tender steak and roasted sweet potatoes with a chowder soup that warms me to my toes. A restaurant that's classy without being pretentious, and the food is solidly good without being an obnoxious price. Ryan did his homework on impressing me.

In fact, Ryan looks like a weight's been detached from him. He's all smiles.

"Did you talk with your dad again?" I ask over dessert. Warm blueberry pie with a vanilla-bean ice cream scoop melting at the edges of the plate.

Ryan's skin glows warm under the dimmed dinner lighting. "No, why?"

"I thought maybe he gave you more time. From his selling deadline."

He waves the thought away with a forkful of pie. "I don't want to talk about him. Besides, I have backup plans. I'm not going to let him sell Resistance. I should have been more confident from the start. I just get . . . it's like I don't think straight when it comes to him sometimes." He shakes his head. "Sorry. I said I didn't want to talk about him, and here I am talking about him."

I don't want to talk about him either.

So we don't. We finish dinner and go back to Ryan's—where we don't talk about him one bit.

It's late and I'm completely entangled with the perfect male specimen. Physically and emotionally. We've moved through various locations of Ryan's condo, our hands never long from roaming each other's bodies. Eventually, we end up in his kitchen.

Ryan, shirtless, releases me from his embrace. "Check this out." He opens the wine fridge.

Only it's not filled with wine. I point. "That's no moon."

He laughs. "Star Wars fan, huh?" He focuses back on the fridge. "I stocked up. There's beer in here I've never tried before. Found it at the liquor store down the block."

I gasp and dance over in bare feet. "This is my favorite thing."

He pulls out a few cans and bottles and places them on the counter. "Which one is your favorite?"

"No, this." I nod toward all of them. "Trying new beers. The thrill of discovery."

He runs a hand down my back, which is covered only by a strappy tank top. "It feels like there's a line about showing you a thrilling discovery just waiting to be said."

I murmur against his cheek. "Then say it."

His face scrunches. "Too corny. You deserve more than corny."

I kiss his nose. "I like corny. Feel free to corn away."

He shakes his head as his cheeks redden. "How do you manage sexy and silly at the same time? I've never met anyone like you."

I believe his observation is meant to be a compliment, so I take it as one. Which triggers immediate deflection. "Any sexiness on my part is probably just fallout from your radioactive essence."

He blinks at me. "Are you implying I have nuclear sexiness?"

I snort out a laugh. "Yes. One hundred percent. You, Ryan, are sexy at a nuclear level." I show him just how much I mean it by kissing him until he's backed against the larger refrigerator. He flinches from the cold contact but doesn't take his lips from mine. If anything, I've fueled him further.

He comes up for air first and peers into my eyes unflinchingly. The way he looks at me is evolving. When we first met, I was a fascination to him. A question with a possible punch line answer. And I assumed he was a basic sports bro. Now his gaze is filled with intent and determination. As if he's determined to know me, to see me, to breathe this life with me.

The resulting sensation is intense. A little scary. But I like that it feels real, like an intensity I can hang on to. It's not solely promises. It's us, together, figuring out how we fit.

I stroke a finger along his stellar jawline. "Every time I feel like I've nailed down the true Ryan, you do or say something that flips the script. You are quite the script flipper."

"I'll flip *your* script."

We both burst out laughing, and the intense moment dissipates.

"That was really bad," he says.

"Only if you meant for it to be serious." I look between us. We're half dressed, no socks, ready to crack open a couple craft beers as the clock inches toward a new day. "This is what sexy means to me. Right here. Like this."

He brings me closer, wasting no time or breath. I'm already close, but this is moving me from his orbit to his personal air space. Or whatever. All I know is it's sexy and cozy and I don't ever want to leave.

Ryan drops me off at home as a hazy orange glow surfaces at the skyline. Having found parking only half a block down from my apartment, he walks with me to the door. His hand feels like an extension of me. At the gate, he pulls me close again. The heat of his kiss saturates my insides. I'm tired and have no regrets.

Well, maybe I'm regretting no sleep, since our second Sunday brunch event starts in just a few hours. I pull back from him. "Are you sure you don't need me today?"

He strokes my hair back. "Everything's under control. Luiz is going in, and I'll be right behind him."

"I could still run brewing tours."

He shakes his head. "We didn't offer the tour sign-up, since you were so sick. Besides, Kurt will be in if anyone wants to go back there."

"Should I come in later so we can all talk? Get me started?"

"No. Enjoy your day off. Get some sleep. I'll call you."

"Are you sure? I'm off tomorrow too, and I don't want to delay anything." I'm antsy to get back to brewing. It's been hard to stay hands-off for so long.

He responds with another kiss. A long, lingering kiss that sends heat to my toes. I run my hand across his rough cheek. "I like the just-left-of-shaven look."

He smiles. "Good. I'll throw away my razor."

"Maybe keep a dull one."

"No beard?"

I pull back, examining his face. "You'd look good with a beard. Besides, isn't growing a beard number three in the craft-brewing handbook?"

He laughs a silent laugh. "Probably. I've got to take off. Oh, and we should see about you getting another weekend off. Michael asked when I'm bringing you up north to the lake house."

Lake house. It sounds perfect. When do I ever get a vacation? "I'm all about it. After we get my brewer job rolling."

"I'll call you in for it. I promise."

He seals his word with a kiss.

I sleep for a few hours but find I'm restless by late morning. Ignoring another text from my mom demanding I send Karrie home—how? She's not here—I realize I missed texts from Jana last night.

Jana: *How's it going, Kat? I'm off the next two days and heading your direction. Meet up?*

I respond back: *Yes! Sorry, just read this now; out late. Where will you be?*

She mentions a northern neighborhood within Chicago's city limits where she and her wife are staying with friends. They're going to a craft brewery this afternoon. It's not one of our local partners for the bracket promotion, but I'm familiar with the beer. She names a time.

I'm already getting ready.

I take a northbound bus to meet Jana at the brewery. From sleuthing the website, I know it's a taproom with a brewing operation in a separate building in an adjacent lot. It's a cute, clean little place on a block with a yoga studio and a coffee shop.

Jana and her group are seated near the door when I walk in.

"Kat!" Jana jumps up to greet me. Her long black hair swings loose behind her. We hug, and she walks me over to the table. "This is Claudette, my better half."

I wave hello. Claudette has a rockabilly style with curled short bangs and a bandanna tied in her unnaturally red-hued hair. Matte-red lipstick. Claudette is Sadie in fifteen years.

With Jana being sporty, practical, and getting the job done, I tag her as a barley wine. Strong flavor, sturdy, distinct. Next to her, Claudette is more whimsical, with big ideas and charm. She's more of a Scottish-style ale, though maybe I'm being lazy, since her family is from Wales.

"And these are our friends we're staying with—Nicole and Elena."

Nicole has on an incredible woven shawl in sunset tones that complement her dark-brown skin. Elena, black haired with a round face and golden complexion, is dressed in a zip-up track jacket and a purple tulle skirt over black boots and leggings. I'm digging the style all around. And I'll need more time to mentally match their beer types.

The group exchanges hellos. I have to be a decade or more younger than all of them, but I feel at ease almost immediately. They're all talking about beer.

"They've got a barrel club here," Jana tells me. "They experiment in small batches and parcel out those barrels with advance bottle orders. We want to do that at our place."

"Someday." Claudette gestures with her pint and a sculpted eyebrow rise. *Don't get ahead of yourself,* is what I'm getting from it.

Jana's posture is straight, confident. "Sooner than you think. Kat—we need to get your order in. What do you feel like today?"

"Good question asking on the *today*." What I want changes daily, it seems.

Or does it? I know what I like.

Nicole slides a laminated one-sheet menu my way. "Check out their sours, if you're into them. Really flavorful."

Elena makes a face at Nicole. "You couldn't pay me to drink sour beer. I like my beer like I like my men: heavy and rich or not at all."

Nicole swats her. "You are wrong for that."

"Hey, I chose not at all. No complaints." Elena clinks glasses with Nicole, and they each drink.

Their banter makes me think of Ryan. His golden ale has deepened in taste for me. The way his hands roamed, covering my body with care and attention. He's no basic drink. Okay, I'm seriously thirsty and need to order.

I go the Sadie route and choose a beer by name preference. I want something that fits my mood. Vagabond sounds too drifty, but Destiny's Arrow is compelling. Our server comes over and I choose that.

"*Destiny*," Jana says with exaggeration. "I'm feeling that word for you today, Kat."

I laugh. "I feel like things are coming together. At work, they're making me a brewer." I clasp my hands together. "I can't wait!"

Jana's brows rise and she congratulates me, as does the rest of the table. "Tell us more."

I try to keep it short, since Jana knows my story already, and fill them in on my history at Resistance. I zip through the Prairie and Joe saga and focus more on the new business owner—minus the part where Ryan and I have, um, grown closer.

"So, you're getting along better with your boss," Jana concludes.

My blush adds more detail than I intend. "He needs me. He said so himself. It feels great to be seen, you know?"

Jana makes a sound across the table, and Claudette flashes her a look. Claudette turns to me. "And you worked your way up from a server. That's *wonderful*."

Elena nods. "Great you're moving up. Make sure you get that contract in writing."

Nicole makes a *tsk*ing sound through her teeth. "Let the girl have her moment."

"No, I appreciate it." I like that they're looking out for me. "Thank you. Jana has been giving me advice already."

Elena taps her pint glass with a short, manicured nail. "Watch out—Jana comes on strong!"

They all laugh.

"Hey, I see talent and passion, I want to steer that in a healthy direction." Jana looks at me. "I'm excited for you. I really am. I hope it works out."

My beer arrives, and the table watches me eagerly. I sniff the amber brew, noting an almost leather scent. It reminds me of horses, at least. "It smells like a summer ale, but a little deeper." I sip. It's a soft flavor, but not forgettable. "It's lower hops than I usually prefer, but the flavors kind of urge me forward. I want more. I want to keep moving forward. Toward my destiny, I guess." I laugh at my own description. "Aptly named?"

"I'll say." Elena looks over the menu. "I want to try that. Get my destiny in order."

They laugh again, teasing each other in the way only close friends with history can. I mentally check out for a minute, and my mind drifts again to Ryan. To us, wrapped up in each other.

Someone comes by to check on us; turns out it's the owner. A fit woman shorter than me and cut like a blade. Short spiky black hair, a sleeve of tattoos down one peachy-skinned arm, and a makeup-free face.

Jana and the others chat with her easily.

"Want me to show you out back?" the owner is saying.

All of us excitedly agree to a personal tour. We take our beers with us and follow the owner out the back door and across a parking lot to a brick warehouse.

"We're a fifteen-barrel brewhouse," the owner says. "Not big, but we like it this size."

The others go ahead into the building, but Jana holds me back.

"Claudette and I signed a lease!" She's nearly spilling over with excitement. "We're really moving forward with our business."

I feel my jaw drop. "That's great! Is it in Chicago? Is that why you're here?"

"The place we found is a recently closed microbrewery in a small town just outside of Milwaukee. We were planning to just buy their equipment, but the space is perfect for us. This will cut our set-up time in half. Claudette's family is nearby, so even better."

"Super exciting!" Ahead of us, Claudette stands in the doorway, looking our direction. "She probably knows you're telling me about it right now," I say.

"For sure. I'm terrible at keeping my mouth shut. Our friends all know, but we're saving any announcements until we have our permits in place."

We rejoin the group and walk through the setup. I love hearing Jana's and Claudette's questions. All the things they have to consider and decide on for their own operation.

The tour doesn't last long, since the owner needs to get back to the taproom. We all thank her as we head back to a table. Ours has been taken, and business is picking up. I stay standing at the high-top table the group finds near the bar.

Claudette and Jana are talking over one another with ideas. It's fun watching them. Two partners with a shared vision.

"Myth and Muse, that's the name," Jana says to me, breaking off from her focus on Claudette.

I smile. It fits, from what she's told me so far. "Great name."

"Isn't it? And we'll probably be hiring." She winks at me.

Claudette gives Jana a stern look. "Kat has a brewer job offer."

"I'm just saying." Jana's voice ticks up. "If things don't work out . . ."

I smile nervously. "Good to know. Really. I'm glad to have friends in hoppy places."

That gets me a laugh, which I was going for.

I stay a little longer, finishing a second pint. The bus schedule on my phone app shows that my window to leave is narrowing. We say our goodbyes, and this time I get four hugs, not just one from Jana.

The ride home has me deep in thought. Starting a brewing operation from scratch seems exciting but so much work. I really just want to make beer and let someone else do the bookkeeping and marketing and staff management. Those are the things that make me feel heavy just thinking about them. Maybe it weighed down Joe and Prairie too. It weighed them down until the thoughts were so heavy, they couldn't breathe.

CHAPTER TWENTY-ONE
GERMAN BOCK

Heavy malt focus that balances sweetness with
toasted notes. A doppelbock is stronger and maltier.
And fun to say.

I'm sitting in the Resistance office with Ryan and Kurt. I'm dressed for success in a navy pinstripe blazer over a smart pant-suit. Who am I kidding? I have on the Resistance denim shirt—a size medium, thankfully, from a second, delayed shipment of shirts—black leggings, and sensible black shoes with my comfort insoles.

Ryan gets right to business. "I'd like Kat to work with you, Kurt. She shadowed Ed and Joe and knows the process. You've seen her in action doing the tours, and you've worked together a few times as she's been helping out. Kat?"

He signals for me to share—as we previously discussed—my experience with brewing and anything else I'd like to tell Kurt as we get started.

Kurt nods as I speak, even smiling from time to time. He seems pretty easygoing despite the rumors that he's difficult to work with. He nods again. "Sounds good."

I hold back a squeal. "Great. I'm looking forward to getting back to work."

"Sure, yeah. It'll be temporary, of course, until we hire someone else."

I must have heard wrong. "I'm sorry, what?"

Ryan keeps his gaze even. "Not temporary. Permanent."

Kurt chuckles, with notes of sarcasm that are hard to miss. "I don't know about that. No offense, Kat," he says to me. "But I need someone with more experience."

"Randy had more experience, and he didn't work out." I refuse to lose my chill. I will fight for this.

Ryan taps a pen against the desk. "We have an advantage with Kat because she knows our equipment. She's seasoned here at Resistance and an asset to our crew."

Kurt is shaking his head. "Experience or not, Randy's brain was fried. The guy's part zombie. Get me a couple guys and I'm set. Better yet, let me find them. I've already got a lead on somebody."

I stare at him. "Are you asking for one other brewer besides me, or two more not including me?"

"Look, to do the changes Bennett wants, we need a team." Kurt means Ryan's dad when he says Bennett. "We need to grow. I'm not interested in some patched-together operation." He waves a dismissive hand in my direction. "Again, Kat, no offense, but this is a business, not an internship."

"I agree. I expect to be paid."

He laughs. "Is that what your boyfriend promised?" He looks at Ryan.

Ryan's features turn to granite. He leans forward. "You're out of line."

Kurt settles into the chair, not looking the least bit miffed. "I've seen you two together. Cute little things running around like you think people can't see. Let me give you some advice: don't mix your business with your off hours. Never a good idea."

"Except our previous owners worked together for over twenty years," Ryan snaps. "Married."

"And you are most definitely not them." Kurt clears his throat. "Far be it from me to get in between you two lovebirds, but you need a professional operation here or you're sunk. I know about the audit. So make your choice."

Ryan's focus is knife sharp. "Kat gets a staff brewer job. You can hire a second assistant."

I watch Kurt squirm, finally. I'm boiling inside but keep it under the lid.

Kurt looks at me, then at Ryan. "Nah. That's not going to work."

It stings, like salt across an open sore. "Why? Because you want a couple *guys*?"

Kurt makes a show of rolling his eyes. "Here we go."

"We talked about this, Kurt," Ryan says back. "Kat and another assistant. That's the deal."

Kurt stays put in his chair. "If that's your deal, I walk. Your choice."

The look on Ryan's face is pure rage. He's smart enough not to let it unleash. Beneath, I see another layer scrambling to stay hidden. Fear.

My brewer job was never a done deal. Sure, Ryan is fighting for me, but he doesn't own Resistance. Not yet. If Ryan loses Kurt, it's another strike against him, and our plan. Ryan's father will use this loss to advance his own agenda. He'll offload Resistance without looking back.

And Ryan knows it.

As for me? I don't even factor in. I have literally no authority to demand anything right now. I'm a penciled-in idea. A sketch about to be erased.

Ryan's cycling through responses but won't look at me. We've lost. I've lost. And if Kurt walks, Ryan loses too—all of it.

There's only one thing I can control right now. "Ryan, take his offer. It's the best-case scenario for the business." I hate every word I'm saying, but I know it's the right option. "I'll stay out of your way."

He looks at me finally. "No. Not going to happen. I promised you—"

"Think of the business." It all comes down to what's best for Resistance, regardless of whether I was promised a job. Like what Joe and Prairie had to do when they sold. It wasn't personal; it was money and their future. "Right now Resistance needs a head brewer, or we lose time and money finding a new one. If he'll only stay with his own team, then let him hire his team."

Kurt adjusts his ball cap and has the nerve to get out his phone, looking bored. I send a sympathetic look to Ryan. *I'm sorry. Do the right thing. For now.*

At least that's what I mean to get across. Sadie is much better at interpreting my looks. Ryan's jaw tightens. The fury nearly bursts through his tightened fists.

Nothing good will come of sticking around. I stand and move to the office door. "Let me know if you need anything. I'm not going anywhere."

Yet.

The word trails quietly in my thoughts. I have options. Maybe. A future option, at least, with Jana. Or maybe not that, but another brewery in the city. Something entry-level.

I don't have to be ignored by a head brewer who doesn't want me. Or try to fix a situation that isn't mine to fix. The sight of the gleaming brew tanks sends a pang of loss through me. None of this is mine to fix. It's simply not mine at all.

Ryan storms out of the office. "Why did you do that?" His eyes are dinner plate sized, and he's gesturing wildly like how I might gesture wildly. If that's what I look like, I should maybe scale back my own gesturing. "I made a decision, and you openly went against my decision."

I walk far enough from the office door past the tanks that Kurt can't overhear, knowing Ryan will follow. He does and ends up right in my space when I turn to face him. "Kurt doesn't want me. Right now you need him more than you need me."

"That's not true. I want you back here. Brewing. You're what Resistance needs, Kat."

He's so conviction filled I almost believe him. "Stop being emotional about this and start thinking like a business owner."

That shuts him up. Ryan sputters, taking a step back. "I'm the one being emotional? You're willing to ditch your dream job just like that." He snaps his fingers. "It's like you don't care. You don't even look upset. Why aren't you fighting for this?"

I'm upset enough to fill a week of nights crying myself to sleep. But I also know better. "It isn't the right time. I needed to realize it as much as you. Besides, it's not my dream to work with a conde-scending, inflexible ass." I circle in place. "Here's the thing, Ryan. You're not running this show. Your father is, and your father wants Kurt. If we want to turn Resistance around, this is how it has to be. I don't get what I want. Maybe you don't either, but you get what you need. And you need Kurt."

He looks at me with all the intensity he had last night, when our dreams felt within reach. When he held me and made those promises, now broken. "There you go underestimating yourself. Why are you selling yourself short?"

He's not getting it. Maybe I shouldn't be surprised, because it took me a while to get here too. "If this place tanks, do you know what happens? Alex can't enroll in classes until he finds a new job. Anya can't pay her tuition. Magda can't support her husband while he's out of work—did you know her husband is out of work? She doesn't like people knowing it, so probably not. They'll probably have to delay starting a family too. And Gary. What's Gary going to freaking do? Go vape in somebody else's kitchen?"

"Gary vapes in the kitchen?"

"Pretend you didn't hear that." I'm getting derailed. "It's not worth what other people here will lose."

Ryan paces. "I don't like this."

What can I say? I don't either.

I can keep serving and doing the tours. Work out more partnerships like we did with the food truck. It will be fine. For a while.

I envision working for Jana. A haven of goddess-themed brewing—what would that look like? A space with rich tapestries and low-hanging lanterns casting cozy shadows across intimate seating. Folk music by women as the soundtrack. It's their dream, but I can see myself there. And if having an out helps me do what's best for Resistance and my friends, I'll gladly decorate that internal wonderland like it's my personal Sims game.

Ryan doesn't need to know any of that. He needs to do what his father wants until he can buy him out. Whenever that may be.

Ryan scrubs the back of his neck. "Please. Let me fix this. I thought Kurt was on board. I never would have brought you in if I knew it would go like this." He shakes his head. "You know what? He's being openly defiant. I'm his boss. I'm not going to let this go." He turns toward the office.

I grab his arm. "Ryan, don't. Letting go is exactly what you need to do. I'll be fine."

"Always accommodating other people. That's not a life, Kat."

I release my grasp as if I've been burned. "It's not for you to decide what my life is. I decide."

"You've put too much on hold for other people. That ex-boyfriend of yours, your sister. You make room for everyone else but yourself."

He's exaggerating. Everyone makes sacrifices. Here's one more concession, because it's really my only option here. "Plans don't always work out. I can whine about it, drink my sour beer, and move on."

He's shaking his head again. "I'm calling my father. Right now."

"Ryan?" Now I'm the one following.

Kurt is still in the office scrolling through his phone. Ryan circles around the desk and grabs his own phone. The dial tone fills the room from the speaker option.

"Yeah, Ryan?" His father answers in a generally friendly tone.

"I'm here with Kurt and Kat. Randy is gone, as you know." He clears his throat. "I've decided to hire Kat as a staff brewer to work with Kurt."

A few seconds of silence pass. "Kurt?" his father asks. "You all right with this arrangement?"

Kurt doesn't look up from his phone. "I am not."

"Well, it's my decision," Ryan states in a clear, strong tone.

"Son, take me off speaker. I'd like to talk with you."

Ryan's lip twitches. "I think—"

"Ryan," Mr. Bennett cuts in with a tone I recognize myself. A parent's scolding.

And that's when I know for sure who Ryan's real partner is.

I'm oddly resigned for the walk home. I'm not on the schedule today—I only came in to get my new brewing career started. Shortest career ever. I didn't even make it to signing the papers.

Strangely, I'm not upset. I can't put my finger on a specific emotion at all. The whole situation feels unsettling, but in a way I don't expect. I should feel let down because I lost the job. Instead, I'm feeling like I limited my own dreams. I've been banking on this one thing, but that thing doesn't exist anymore. Maybe it never did. Working for Kurt is not the job I want.

My world has been small the past few years. I've been in survival mode. Working, paying off debt, working some more. I don't travel. I barely leave my neighborhood or check out other pubs in the city. The past month I've done more outside my little existence than I have in probably two whole years.

When I unlock my gate, a figure rises from the steps.

"Mom?"

"Good, you're home." Before I can ask how she got inside the gate, she points to the lower-level flat. "The woman who lives downstairs let me through when she was leaving. I showed her pictures on my phone to prove we're family. I tried calling you."

"Sorry. I had my phone muted for a work meeting."

"Oh." She's skittish and doesn't say anything more.

At least she's not yelling at me. That's a plus.

"Come on." I lead her inside. Spring floral scents greet us from the candle Sadie had burning this morning. Warm light spears into the living room, highlighting a newly cleaned and tidied space.

Mom shuffles in. "This is great, Kat."

It strikes me—she's never been here. I've lived here for a year.

I swallow back hurt and take her coat.

She walks a few steps to the bay window overlooking the front walk. "You said you had a work meeting. How did it go?"

Peachy. "Mom, why are you here? I'm guessing it's about Karrie."

"I just came from seeing Karrie." She twists at her glove, which is off, but still in her hand. "At her friend's apartment."

"Oh. How'd that go?"

She lets out a soft laugh devoid of joy. "Not well. She really let me have it."

I try imagining what Karrie's version of *letting someone have it* looks like. Loud scoffing, maybe severe eye-rolling. "Yelling? Screaming?"

Mom shrugs. "Not so much. More like a reasonable plan with details and a hefty guilt trip. I wondered if you coached her, actually."

I don't know if I should be flattered or offended. "Sit down a sec. Do you want tea?"

Her attention is out the window—I don't think she hears me.

"I'm going to get the electric kettle going." I depart for the kitchen, fill up the kettle, and take out two mugs. Today is weird times a squillion. All I can do is roll with it. I'm about to dig through our impressive tea offerings when I hear Mom behind me.

"Your apartment is lovely, Kat. It's just as I would expect."

All I can see are things that aren't mine. "Oh, it's all Sadie. I just exist here and pay rent."

She picks up a blue ceramic mug. "This is yours. You had it at the house—our house. I remember when you made it at that paint-your-own-pottery place."

The mug definitely looks like teen Kat made it. Different shades of blue swirl together in a look that's whimsical but messy if you look up close.

"Sadie, that's your roommate?" she asks.

I nod. "Have you . . . you've never met her?" It feels ludicrous to say, but I can't recall a time where Sadie and my parents have been in the same space. Sadie feels like a forever friend, though I've actually only known her a few years.

Mom shakes her head. "I really have made a mess of things, haven't I?"

A many-times rehearsed response perches on my lips. One that would work beautifully, but too much time has passed and too many things have changed. The words no longer fit.

The kettle whistles, and I finish making the tea. "What did Karrie say to you?"

Mom takes one of the steeping mugs and wraps her hands around it. "I was so angry when I left that apartment. She didn't come with me, as you can see. I planned to come here and . . . blame you. For letting Karrie come out here, for not calling me back, for not convincing her to come home. I was just . . . *furious*." It's as if she's naming the emotion for the first time. "Then I was driving around this neighborhood looking for your building. I made a wrong turn and couldn't seem to get here. I kept looking for a familiar place. Only I had no idea what it looked like. And I just started crying."

Her shoulders slump. Anguish twists her face. She doesn't cry now. She stares at her hands holding the cup as soft steam rises.

"Aw, Mom. I . . ." Words fail.

The only thing I know I won't say is I'm sorry. I don't know what I'd be sorry for. I've invited both my parents here, and not just when I needed help moving. I told them they could stay here whenever they attended one of the several musicals they'd bought tickets for downtown. Or they could come out to Taste of Chicago with me and Sadie. To a special exhibit at the Field Museum. There was always a reason they couldn't. Parking would be easier if they drove straight to the event, Dad would say, or the commuter train didn't stop in my neighborhood. The El and the bus are too confusing for them.

"It's not your fault, of course," Mom says. "I truly thought I was doing the best I could with your sister. To see her in pain . . . I wished it was me. Every time, I wished I could take her pain for my own so she could live her life. I had no idea by protecting her, I was keeping her from that very thing."

I listen as my mom goes through her conversation with Karrie. It doesn't sound like it ended with hugs and tearful forgiveness. After all, Mom burned out of there with the intent to lay into me next.

Now her fire and brimstone are down to flickering embers.

She sets down the mug and looks at me directly. Her dark hair is lighter than I remember, with flecks of gray at the sides. "I'm sorry we missed your graduation. You brought that up recently. I almost didn't remember that happened. It's like a blank spot in my memory. I see the pictures from that day—the one by the mantel—and the ones you must have taken with your friends. I assumed we were there too."

She's apologizing for one day that happened ten years ago. I fight telling her it doesn't matter. Only it does matter. I need to hear the apology.

"Why didn't you ever say anything?" she asks. "I don't remember you saying a single word that you were upset. Did I forget that too?"

"Karrie went to the emergency room. I mean, how could I complain about that? It's not like you all decided to go golfing."

She makes a face, because she hates golfing even though Dad loves it. "That's too much for a young girl to shoulder. I should have seen that. I could only see Karrie's pain. I'm sorry."

"I never wanted to be mad. I never wanted a graduation party either. I really was okay with the combined party at Aunt Shelly's. Cousin Hunter got all the attention with his valedictorian self, which was fine by me. It was easier on you guys that way."

"It shouldn't have been up to you to make things easier for your parents." She sighs. "Karrie brought that up. How you took care of yourself so we could focus on her. She named examples. So many of them I couldn't believe it. I still can't. It's like this all happened to someone else."

I focus on the pattern in the aging countertop, little flecks of barely-there colors that meld into one neutral tone. "Mom? Obviously, I'm armchairing it here, but have you seen a support counselor? I think there's more going on that someone with better skills than me should talk you through." I hold up a hand. "And I'm not trying to cast you off or anything. I've seen a therapist. It really helps."

"You have a therapist?"

"Well, I don't own her. I see her from time to time."

"Because of your screwed-up family?"

I choose my words carefully. "A lot of reasons. Remember I had a bad breakup? That was part of it. General life stresses like work and debt. You know."

"Debt?"

I wave her off. "Like I said. Typical stuff."

"Your student loans?"

Shoot, I've said too much. "I'm fine. I cut up some credit cards and learned to live lean. It's Living in Your Twenties 101."

"You never asked us for money. We could have given you money if you needed, Kat."

"Look, it's not like I ever had to sleep in a car." Just the one time when I locked myself out when I was living with the creepy fingernail collector, but that's not relevant. "You had enough to worry about. I know Karrie's medical bills were bonkers for a while. You paid part of college for me—that's something."

"Do you make enough bartending? You're okay now?"

"I don't bartend. I serve drinks and, until recently, brew beer." I sigh. "As for making enough, not really, but that's another story for another day."

Tears fill her eyes. "You've done all this on your own." She gestures to the room. "All this . . . life, and we've barely been a part of it. I'm so sorry, Kat. I'm so . . . incredibly angry at myself."

I take in another round of Mom working through her hurts. It feels like ten conversations at once that we should have had separately years ago.

I have a part in this too. "I'm sorry I didn't come to you when I could have used help. I'm so used to doing things on my own. When it comes to needing something, I think of you guys as off-limits."

That really breaks open the dam. Now Mom's crying, and soon I'm crying too. We hug for the first time in ages. Not a light half-armed hug, but a real one with a squeeze.

"I think I do need a therapist," Mom tells me.

I hold up my mug for a cheers. "Don't we all."

CHAPTER TWENTY-TWO
IRISH DRY STOUT

Very dark brown to black, this stout uses roasted barley
and can feature coffee or chocolate tones. Medium to
high bitterness depending on your mood.

At my next shift at work, Ryan is clearly ashamed of following
his father's orders but won't admit it. I sense it in every awkward
interaction and every tense-when-it-doesn't-need-to-be moment. I
keep telling him he made the best choice for the business, even if
it shuts me out.

He pulls me aside. "I hate this, Kat. Every time I see you, I feel
like I need to apologize."

"So apologize and get it over with."

He holds in a breath. "That's not what I mean."

A U2 song blasts from the jukebox—"With or Without
You"—and it's feeling especially relevant. Ryan is a complication
in my life. A lethally attractive complication who's currently running warm fingers along the back of my sleeve. My denim sleeve,
which I'd like to send to an incinerator.

"Kurt will bring in his new crew, and I'll . . . figure things out."
I shrug, like the figuring-out part will come easily. "Hey. So, the
March Hopness brackets seem to be catching on over social media.
Did you see the retweet from Griffon Brewers? Tons of likes!"

He moves close, touching my hair. "I don't want it to be like
this."

I flinch. "We have to be able to talk about work. Do you still
want my help?"

"Of course. Yes." We're in view of customers, so I try to keep
professional distance. Our relationship is basically an open secret
with the staff. Heck, they seemed to know we were a thing before
I did. Ryan kisses me quickly, but with care. The kiss feels nice,
but we're not connecting. We both know it.

"What can I do?" he asks.

"Do your job. The best you can."

"Really, Kat? That's what you want from me? To do my job
and nothing else?"

I can sense the hard edges on my words and know he's onto
something. I can't seem to shake whatever this feeling is.

"You don't trust me," he says.

I open my mouth to protest and stop. "I guess I'm waiting to
see what happens next."

His gaze is drawn past me to a table of people laughing. They
look like a happy bunch, all faces I haven't seen before. A look of
mild satisfaction crosses Ryan's face.

He takes my hands. "Remember I said Michael invited us up
north to the lake house? Let's go. This weekend."

The lake house. I could really use a getaway. "The whole weekend? Away from the pub?"

"At least Friday night. No, yes. The whole weekend. Let's do it."

"What about this Sunday's brunch with Dos Islas?"

"I'll see if Luiz is comfortable running the event."

"Isn't the refrigeration system going in this week?"

"Next week. Thursday, I think."

Okay. What else? "Will Kurt—"

"Kat? Trust me. I'll get things covered."

The rest of the week passes. After losing out on the brewer job, the emotionally taxing conversation with Mom, and another loaded conversation with my sister, I'm drained. I decide not to decide anything major for the moment. I set my sights on the weekend trip. Time alone with Ryan—and a few of his closest friends. An escape is what I need right now. Some time to think things over. Or not think. Not thinking sounds lovely.

All week, I ignore what's happening in the brewing room. I ignore the two guys who look my age being shown the tanks by a satisfied-looking Kurt. I ignore their voices and their laughs from the other side of the glass.

I ignore how Alex switches two shifts in a row because he's actively interviewing at other places.

Friday arrives, and Ryan picks me up at my house early in the afternoon. The drive to the lake house is under two hours, but I feel the city and the stress of daily life fall away with each mile.

Ryan's custom music mix fills in as a soundtrack. I've been listening to oldies so long at Resistance, I barely know new music. Ryan's taste is different than mine, but I don't hate it. Bonus: we aren't talking about work.

The lake house isn't massive, but it's no rinky-dink cottage either. The narrow road we're on leads to the back of the house and the garage. Inside, a hall leads to a kitchen overlooking a great room with two stories of windows facing a lake.

"Party captain's here!" Michael gets up from a long L-shaped leather sectional.

"I don't know about that," Ryan says, and bumps fists with Michael.

"Where do you want all this beer?" I wheel the dolly we brought stacked with several cases of Resistance brews.

"Oh, no way!" Michael rubs his hands together at the sight of the beer. He opens his arms. "I'm a hugger, Kat. I hope you don't mind."

I accept the hug. I'm glad he appreciates the beer.

Someone pops in from the hall. "Hi, I'm Bethany."

"I'm Kat, hi."

Bethany has thick black hair in soft waves down her back. I'm guessing she's Korean, and when she stands beside Michael, the two look like a power couple. Fashionable, well put together, energetic.

More people arrive until a group of ten gather in the kitchen and great room. Bottle caps are strewn across the kitchen island with everyone sampling what we've brought. Michael unearths his favorite tequila. It's not even five o'clock, but I feel like I've been waiting on happy hour for ages.

These people party well. The food looks catered, laid out across large trays and in aluminum pans. We eat and drink as I get to know Ryan's friends. None of them are the bros who came into Resistance.

A blonde named April sits next to me on the couch. "I'm so interested in hearing more about you and Ryan."

Bethany is here now too, perching on the oversized ottoman in front of us. "Yes! We've barely seen him for ages. Now he's, like, running a bar and has this awesome new girlfriend."

It takes me a hefty second to realize I'm the girlfriend. I was for real about to get jealous. I can't help my shy smile. "I haven't thought of myself as his girlfriend. We haven't had the talk, you know?"

Bethany lets out a dramatic huff. "Isn't that the worst? Michael was so bad about that. We probably went out ten times before I asked him, look, is this a thing? Are you my boyfriend?"

"I just broke up with someone," April says. "I'm so over guys right now. Anyway, you are so not what I expected for Ryan, but I love it. You're, like, edgy. And you make beer. That's really cool."

"He usually dates boring girls," Bethany says.

I feel like secrets are about to be shared, and I'm not mad about it. I lean back and let the cushions further relax me.

Bethany and April share about three of Ryan's past girlfriends. The details aren't mean-spirited; it's more like general information. One girlfriend cheated on him, and another wanted to move to LA to be an actress.

"Jillian?" I ask.

"No, her name was . . . Tania or something." Bethany laughs. "They all sort of blend together."

My head spins. Am I drinking too fast? "How many are there? Exes, I mean."

April flits a hand in the air. "I don't know. Lots of forgettable ones. We've known him since college. The once-a-week-girls don't really count."

My stomach shifts. "Once a week?"

Bethany tosses her glossy hair over her shoulder. "You know, when you hook up at a party and then don't see them ever again? Or go to maybe two parties with someone and then they ghost."

My college experience was not like this, but I nod anyway.

April shifts to sit cross-legged. "Ryan was always a love 'em and leave 'em type, you know?"

I do not know.

"Like, he's there with one girl, and then next time she's got the same hair and clothes, but it's someone else!"

She and Bethany laugh.

"We lived in the same dorm freshman year," Bethany says. "That's when Michael and I met."

She goes on about their shared college memories. I let her conversation drift over me, but honestly? I'm stuck on those faceless, nameless girls he dated. How many? Were they forgettable only to his friends, or to Ryan too?

Ryan appears in the kitchen again. He's got on the plaid scarf, having just come in from outside. He catches my eye and smiles. My brain turns carbonated. I smile back like a dope and wonder how I got so lucky. All those same-girls and here I am, not-same, and he's smiling at me like that.

Ryan crosses over to us. "Hot tub?"

From my spot on the couch, I see string lights glow over the deck where the hot tub has been built into one corner. "Sure."

We head upstairs to our room on the second floor. Our room. It feels very mature to be in a lake house with my boy—

"Are we a thing?" I ask him as I take out my tankini.

Ryan slips his shirt off. "A thing?"

I've forgotten what I asked. His body is so nicely toned. His skin is a light natural tan. Soft skin with a smattering of chest hair. I'm glad he's not all oily slick and artificial. He feels real. And close. And mine. "When do you have time for the gym? You work all the time."

"There's a fitness room in my building. Why?" He looks down at his chest and stomach. "Too much beer?"

I snag him and pull him toward me. "Just enough. Maybe not enough."

He shuts the door and locks it as I fall back on the bed.

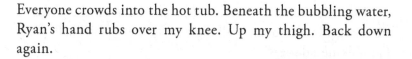

Everyone crowds into the hot tub. Beneath the bubbling water, Ryan's hand rubs over my knee. Up my thigh. Back down again.

He leans close to my ear. "I'd say this is a thing. If you want to make it official."

A small gasp falls from my mouth. "Prom too? Or do you have a promposal planned?"

He rubs his face, covering his eyes. "I actually feel sixteen again. Thanks."

I angle toward him—not that we have any privacy here. "I like that it's official." I kiss him quick on the lips. "Yes, I will be your girlfriend if I can call you Hot Pants."

"No way."

"But you look so hot in pants. Any type, really."

He kisses me to shut me up.

"Ry-*an*!" Bethany singsongs from across the hot tub. "You are so lucky to have Kat here. We were telling her earlier how we're so glad you found someone interesting."

Ryan's response mixes nervous laughter with a cold-fear chaser. "Do I even want to know what you were all talking about?"

I wonder if he can name all those girls he dated. *Stop it, Kat.*

We're still drinking by midnight, and since we started this afternoon, that's a lot of hours for inebriation. Especially given that a few Resistance brews have a high ABV. I've been drinking water and eating, but it's safe to say I'm tanked.

I check my texts and find that Jana and Claudette have an option for potential expansion to the empty retail space next door. Their one concern with the building was limited space, but they fell in love with the location.

Happy 4y I type back. That's supposed to be *4 u*. I usually hate shortening words for texts, but also, brain cells busy now.

I fumble typing a few more texts and hook up the phone to the charger in our room. Walking back to the upstairs hall, I find I'm walking sideways.

"Whoa, hey. You all right?" It's Ryan. He catches me at the elbow. "Maybe time for bed?"

I look up at his beautiful face. "You think I don't trust you."

He gently steers me into our room. "Probably not the time for a conversation like this."

The sheets and blankets are pulled back, and I'm now horizontal. "Are you coming to bed?"

He strokes my hair. "I think I might stay up a little longer. Catch up with the guys."

"Guys. Guyssss . . . not the faceless."

"Huh?" Ryan laughs.

I know he's laughing at me, not with me, but sleep knocks me out.

I wake up at an unholy hour, which is almost always the case after I drink. The sun is early in its day and the house is quiet. Beside me, Ryan's breathing comes at a slow and steady in-and-out. I roll over and glance at the alarm clock.

I try to fall back asleep and can't. I get up, take a shower and dress, then find my way downstairs.

Bethany is awake, looking refreshed. The kitchen sparkles, all traces of last night's party cleared away. Boxes of empty bottles are stacked neatly by the garage door.

"I know it's cliché," she says. "But I have to start the day with a clean kitchen. Want breakfast?"

I help her with eggs, bagels, pancakes. We make a feast. I keep trying to match her to a beer, but all I can think is top-shelf vodka. High class, adaptable, goes with lots of drinks. She's made me feel at home here and not like an outsider.

Guests trickle down while we cook. Ryan appears last. He's dressed for the day, his hair lightly ruffled from a towel-dry.

"Morning, sunshine," I tell him. "How late were you up?"

He gives me a stiff look. "Not too late. Two, maybe. Can we talk?" The last bit comes quieter.

"Is it work? What happened?" The escape this weekend from work responsibilities finally drove away the awkwardness between me and Ryan. Now the tension and worry rush back.

"How about we take a walk?"

I grab my coffee before going for my coat and shoes. We exit out the sliding doors to the deck. Ahead of us, the dirty gray lake does the opposite of glisten. Sleepy houses line the shore across the water.

Ryan progresses deeper into the yard. He stops beside a fire pit ahead of the rocky beach and a short dock.

"I know we haven't really been talking about work, but . . . I want to make sure you know how much I appreciate what you're doing. I can see what you've given up." He faces me. "I'm sorry about what happened with Kurt."

"I know—"

"Please, Kat. It's important that you hear me. I care about you. More than I've ever . . . more than I can remember ever caring. Kat, you're amazing. I really, really like you."

A blush creeps up my neck. "I've been hard on you."

"You've pushed me. People don't do that often." He starts walking toward the shore, slow enough for me to catch on and join. "Talking with my friends last night after you fell asleep—"

"That's kind. I passed out."

"You sure did—I stand corrected." He stops at the water's edge. "Talking with them made me see how much things have changed. How far a lot of us have come. Michael has a great business plan for online consulting. It was cool to hear him excited about it. It reminded me of working with you."

The blush deepens. "I'm learning a lot, too, about what I'm good at and what I want."

"When I imagine my future, you're in it. At Resistance, you and me. It excites me." He tucks a loose strand of my hair behind my ear. "I know trust is a big deal for you. You've been hurt before. I don't want to hurt you."

It feels good to hear. I want to say our future excites me too, but a hesitation nags at me. He's right. I've been down this road. Following someone else's path and being left in the dust.

Then there's that other nagging thought. "You've had a lot of girlfriends."

"I've . . . what?" He pauses. "Is this coming from Bethany and April?"

"They said your girlfriends were interchangeable. You loved 'em and left 'em and they all were forgettable."

"How many drinks in was this conversation?"

Fair point. "I'll give you that they may have exaggerated."

He steps back, then forward, moving his hands as if he can snatch a response from the air. "If it's any help at all, you are extremely memorable."

He glides a hand over my ear and down to my shoulder, letting it rest there with a light pressure. He pulls back so he's no longer touching me. I miss the sensation instantly.

"They're right, I've never dated anyone like you." He looks back toward the large windows watching us from the house. Then his focus is back on me. "I did get bored with my past girlfriends. I think I was chasing the wrong people. The wrong things. After my brother died, at least. I was at a party over New Year's—it scared me, Kat."

"What happened?"

"Some buddies of mine—different friends than these." He nods toward the house. "They invited me to a party downtown at a hotel. A huge setup with a kitchen and living room and bedrooms. Drugs everywhere. So many people were high. That's not my scene, but I tried to play it cool, you know? Just drank what was there and stayed away from everything else. This guy started freaking out. Running around this penthouse kicking over lamps and picking fights. Someone pulled out a gun." He breathes in. "Shots were fired. I hit the floor—I was fine, just scared. Next to me on the floor, someone was passed out. Twitching like a seizure."

I gasp. "That's scary."

"It's completely different than my brother, but Jesse was all I could think about. How quickly a life can pass. That guy at the party could have died. I called 911 from a bathroom. No one else called, Kat. They were all threatening each other if anyone called the cops. I took the guy's pulse, and he was alive. I looked at his ID and left to go get security."

"And the guy? Was he okay?"

"Yeah. I stayed in the lobby as the ambulance came. I asked which hospital they were taking him to and followed up. Real fun experience." He shuts his eyes to a memory only playing for him. "It was a wake-up call. I started seeing everything differently. My parents, my life. I haven't hung out with those guys again. Well, except for inviting them to Resistance that one time." He scuffs his shoe against the ground. "Which I now regret."

"The flat-screen guys," I answer immediately.

He nods. "They like to party, and who better to invite over to hype up a bar?" He laughs without humor. "When my dad offered me the chance to run the pub, it felt like fate." He looks at me again, with such intensity I can almost see the words he isn't saying. *You. You're like fate.*

"I didn't have a real sense of what I was capable of until now," he continues. "This is the hardest I've ever worked. I'm working all the time because it feels like it matters. I have a purpose turning this business around. Seeing it through your eyes is what fuels me. I want to do better, to be better, for you, Kat."

He keeps talking. "If I didn't have that drive, I'd go home to an empty condo and think of the years I wasted. For so long, I was just trying to make my parents happy by staying alive."

All the potential his brother had ended one day from a tragic accident. That's a lot to live up to, being the surviving kid. Not trying at all is one way to react to that.

As is opting out of one's own family, like me. We both have our issues. Where those intersect is my concern. The pressure on Ryan to make up for his loss means he'll bend over backward for his father. For me, I'm so intent on taking care of myself that I've shunned my own family, who could have offered help. I don't trust others.

Why would I? They haven't come through.

Time after time, the people I love just don't come through.

As if he reads my thoughts, he clasps my hand. "I don't want to let you down. I know it seems fast, but I'd like to plan—really plan with you. I have ideas and want you part of them."

My thoughts run like crazed bunnies chasing each other through the yard. A sight I've just witnessed.

"Kat? What's going on? Tell me what you're thinking."

I choose my words carefully. "I keep counting on promises that fall through. I get my hopes up and then . . ." My hopes, dashed. Time and again.

He squeezes my hand. "I'm going to fire Kurt, you know. The moment I buy out my dad, he's gone. We look for a new head brewer and add you in as their number-two. And who we hire will be *our* decision. Together."

It feels like tossing coins in a fountain, hoping the wishes will come through.

"I put a lot of faith in Joe and Prairie that probably wasn't healthy," I admit. "My friend Jana helped me see that. I looked at them like a replacement family." It's the lesson I have to keep learning in different ways until it sticks. I'm more than a relationship. I'm more than a girlfriend, or a daughter who's not chronically ill. I'm more than my job. "I don't want to call anybody out, but you might see staff looking to leave. Things are changing. Fast."

Ryan resists a big reaction. "I can understand. But for you? What do *you* want to do?"

That's the question.

"You mentioned getting a brewing certificate. I looked around online at programs. If you want to do that, I'll make it happen. A degree, an online program, more full-day courses. Whatever will help you gain confidence, I'll take care of it."

"I can't let you pay for that."

"Kat, you wouldn't owe me. It would be a business expense."

"We have too many expenses already."

"I've got money. I can help you."

It's impossible to say yes when I'm conditioned and trained to stand on my own. "I . . . will think about it."

A shy smile emerges. "It would make me happy to help you. On your terms."

Making beer has brought me the most joy I've had in years. I don't want to lose sight of that joy. Taking time to learn more on the craft is appealing. It would buy me time to figure things out. Meanwhile, I can still help where I'm needed with Resistance.

It feels like the best option yet. I stay at the place I love, at my apartment with the roommates I adore, and get to spend more time with Ryan. All while working toward what I want.

I have someone who believes in me, right here. And it feels good. Really good.

CHAPTER TWENTY-THREE
GERMAN HELLES

A simple malt lager requiring quality ingredients and excellent craftsmanship. Good brews come to those with skill.

We're not left alone long, as Ryan's friends join us outside. The snow has melted for now, so no snowmobiling. Michael, the most excellent of hosts, offers ATV four-wheelers for us to take out.

The rest of the weekend is bliss. I give myself permission to be worry-free. To live in the moment. To experience each moment. With Ryan.

When we drive back Sunday, neither of us goes into Resistance. Luiz has a handle on brunch, so we go to Ryan's condo and continue our weekend vibes. I don't leave until morning, after he's fed me breakfast.

I haven't felt this way in . . . ever? Seriously, ever.

My head is at a cumulus level—that would be cloud level—in a comfortable pattern of work and off time with Ryan for the next week.

The pub is doing well, the promotions are working, and Kurt and his Two-Male Crew are getting the job done. Yes, I'd rather be brewing, tinkering with Heartbeat or doing the everyday work with the tanks, but that's not what's available to me—yet. Instead, I work with my new boyfriend and my favorite crew.

Only the crew is changing. Alex is officially leaving Resistance for a busy, high-end restaurant in the Loop. His last week is playing out now. Anya hasn't made it official, but she has an interview for a part-time office job with consistent hours. Magda is a permanent fixture at Resistance, but she's more distant lately. I don't know if it's my time with Ryan changing us or she's occupied with her own things, but she seems to need space, so I give it to her.

It's hard to watch the changes, but I'm looking at the positives. Everyone needs to find what works for them, right? What fuels me further is registering for another full-day course at the Wisconsin brewery. With Ryan's assistance, I enroll in an online certificate course too. I'm getting closer to what I want.

Saint Patrick's weekend rolls around, which is always busy for us by default, us being a bar and all. This year we add a special from the Dos Islas food truck to the menu and have Nesto, Aaron, and another crew in the kitchen. Luiz has been a rock star getting the event together and promoting it across the community. Our clientele is looking a little different—more patrons from the Puerto Rican and Cuban families in the area. It's a change that feels suited for Resistance and not like an interference.

Monday after the latest brunch, Luiz finds me and Ryan together in his office.

I bolt from the chair. That would be Ryan's chair, which I was sitting on. With him. On his lap. Kissing his face.

"*Mrrrow.*" Luiz makes a cat noise as his walk-in theme.

I throw a wadded napkin at him, but it misses and sails to the floor. Ryan and I had been working on a business plan and looking at his loan options online. You know, until his hands started roaming and I couldn't resist joining in.

"No worries," Luiz says. "You have a minute?" he asks Ryan.

I scoot out of the way, and Luiz nods to the two chairs in front of Ryan's desk. "You can stay, gata. It's about the food truck."

Ryan is instantly alert. "Did we get them the right cut of profits?"

"They're good." Luiz sits, and so do I. "This has been a great few weeks. So great, Nesto and Aaron want to expand Dos Islas into a permanent space. They've been wanting to do it for a while, but working with us sealed it for them."

"That's awesome." Ryan grins. "Those guys are great. The corned beef Cubanos were amazing."

I flick my gaze to Luiz, because I have a feeling what's coming.

Luiz flashes a look to me. "So, it looks like we'll need to find a new partner for the brunches. They're actively looking at spaces now."

Ryan sits back. "Makes sense."

There's a good chance our new business may go with them. "Will they serve beer?" I ask. "We could get a distribution deal going with them."

We talk details a few minutes longer. Luiz checks his watch. "Got to run. Talk more later, boss?"

Ryan nods, and Luiz gets up to leave.

I'm working a shift today serving, so I also head for the door. In the staff coatroom, Luiz pulls me aside.

"Gata. I might help the guys start their restaurant. Nesto and Aaron."

"Oh, wow." I let that news sink in. He said *might*, but he wouldn't mention it at all if the option were a maybe. Not his style. "That sounds like a great fit."

"Yeah? I felt bad telling you. After Alex leaving and all."

"No, don't. Never feel bad for doing something that excites you."

He looks past me to the brewing room where Kurt and his guys are working. "I've got a cousin looking for work. I told him to come in. He'd be good here."

More change. But good change. "I'm sure I'll still see you around the neighborhood, right? They're probably looking at spaces around here."

He nods. "Oh, hey. Gary was looking for you."

"For me?" I blink. "Gary?"

He shrugs and carries on.

I find Gary out back. I let myself out, keeping in mind the brick that holds the door open a crack. "You rang?"

Gary slips his phone into his back pocket. He pulls out something from a different pocket. A paper he's unfolding. "Thought of you."

He hands it to me. It's a purple flyer for a meetup of Chicago women in brewing. *Women! Cisgender and otherwise—if you work in craft brewing, we want to connect!*

I look up from the paper, feeling genuinely touched. "Thanks, Gary."

"Figured you might need some support." He nods toward Resistance. "Not gonna find it with those bozos."

He doesn't fill in further details, like where he got this or specifically which bozos. He's seemed to warm to Ryan recently. As much as Gary warms.

"I really appreciate this. Thank you."

His nod to me is his signal we're done here.

Two weeks later I'm back at Sam Giddeon's Wisconsin brewery for another daylong workshop. I recognize a few class members from last time—older guys. None of the younger set are here. It's Jana's absence I feel most. I keep thinking of things I want to share with her as the day progresses. Which is convenient, because I'm staying the night at her house after class.

I've got Sadie's car on loan, and after the workshop ends, I head to the address Jana gave me. I'm greeted with open arms and a cold brew the moment I walk into her and Claudette's cozy Cape Cod.

"Excuse the mess." Claudette guides me past a dining room stacked with boxes. She points to one stack. "Glassware and bar supplies." Then another. "I think that's for bottling. The big stuff is coming next week. Delivered to the business."

Jana's standing in the doorway to their kitchen. "Want to see the space?"

Claudette swats her. "The woman just got here. She's been in class all day."

Of course I'm interested. "Myth and Muse? I'd love to."

"See. Toldja she'd be up for it."

The three of us get in Jana's truck and drive ten minutes into a small downtown that looks recently livened up. Landscaped walkways and park benches are tucked between strips of businesses that are a mix of old and new construction.

Their building is one of the older structures, with high ceilings and whitewashed exposed brick inside. Boxes stack in neat rows on one side of the room. Along the far wall, the existing brewing tanks from the previous owners wait patiently for new brews.

Jana walks over to the bar dividing the seating area from the brewing. "We loved how the tanks are in full view of customers."

Jana and Claudette hold hands as they describe their plans and vision. Where I see empty space, they envision ornate, vintage lighting and framed art featuring goddesses and mythological lore.

Their excitement is infectious. "It's incredible." My breath catches on the word. My whole face is screwing up like I'm—

"Kat, oh no." Jana's concern is immediate. "Are you crying?"

I wipe my eye with the back of my hand. "No."

Claudette checks her phone. "I'm going to step out." She exits the front, still in view through the picture window.

"I'm not crying," I say again for emphasis.

"What's going on?" Jana pulls two crates out and takes a seat at one.

I lower to the other. "This is beautiful. What you two have. It's so . . . inspiring. I guess I got emotional."

Harmonious is the word that comes to mind. They look and seem in sync, despite the stacks of boxes and what they shared on the ride over about stresses with licenses and permits. Maybe it's my own rosy view of their lives, but they seem content. More than that, invigorated.

I can't help but compare them to my life. I'm at the edge of invigorated but never quite there. Something is always holding me back. Telling me *not yet*.

"Tell me about today's class," Jana says. "Sorry I had to miss it."

I fill her in, but for some reason it's hard to muster my earlier enthusiasm. I mention the online certification course I just started.

She tilts her chin. "I didn't think you were going that route."

"Ryan thought it would be a good idea while we wait to make our move with Resistance." I share with her how Ryan is looking at business loans and how I'll move into a brewer role.

"Ryan is the owner's son, right? Isn't his father an investor? Why can't he work with him?"

"It's complicated." I don't want to dish Ryan's personal business to Jana, so I leave it at that. "His father is itching to sell. That's kind of his thing: buy, sell, profit, sell again."

Jana does her *mm-hmm* thing. "Wasn't the investor a friend of your mentors? What do they think?"

"Joe and Prairie—they'd be hurt, I think. I doubt they know he wants to sell already."

"Maybe you should talk to them."

The last email Prairie sent the group said Joe is doing okay but feels run-down from chemo. The vibe was hopeful but didn't leave out that he's struggling. "I think they'll be proud to have Ryan truly own the business," I say instead. "Since he cares so much."

"And your role?"

"We'll move the current head brewer and his team out once Ryan owns the business. It's better that the brewing team stays put right now for stability."

Her gaze drifts past me. "He's made you promises before."

I know she's just looking out for me. "You think I'm being naïve. That I've been burned before, and here I go again. This is different, though."

Jana waits for me to say more.

"It's different because it's my choice now. I'm waiting for the right time, and then I'll have everything I want."

She sits back, stretching her legs in front of her.

"I plan to work hard." I fill in for her silence. "Ryan has a lot of confidence that we can do this. Together."

"And you? You have that confidence?"

Okay, now I'm getting agitated. Her tone is part therapist, part parent urging a child to admit their doubts and faults. "I'm happy now. It's hard to see everything coming into play when so much is in progress, but it's exciting, and I'm okay with where I am."

The words feel like the right thing to say, but I can't get the rest of me to buy in. It's that sensation again where I'm close but the fit isn't right. I'm one size too small or three sizes too big every time.

I can tell Jana reads that sense of hollowness too, but she doesn't comment further. Instead, she stands and gives me her hand to help me up.

Claudette returns, suggesting we get burgers from the family-owned place across the street. Jana locks the front doors, and we exit through the back. I take one last look over my shoulder at the open space. At the possibilities. At the idea of what could be.

CHAPTER TWENTY-FOUR
SMOKE BEER

Lagers brewed with barley dry-roasted over an open
flame. A real smoke show.

"I'll try another lender," Ryan announces when we make it outside
the bank. A third rejection.

The sun glares so brightly, I close my eyes until I have my
sunglasses on my face again. I shrug my jacket tighter. Farewell to
the puffer; it's a lighter coat. "You gave it your best shot. Maybe it's
time to cool it on the loan pitches for now."

I joined him for the bank appointment as moral support, but
I'm not sure how much good it did.

It's been a tense week since I returned from my Wisconsin course. Luiz's cousin just started at Resistance to replace
Alex, but now Anya's gone, so we're short again. The brand-new
refrigeration system is acting up and requires the maintenance
tech to come out. The deep fryer finally gave up the fry ghost,
so now ordering a replacement is a priority. As a result, Ryan's

responses are stressed. I give him space, but those things stress me too.

Beyond those very real things, I can't help feeling wicked FOMO as I watch Kurt at work through the glass. I'm finding my own words coming clipped and tense. It happened with a customer, but thankfully a regular who I could instantly apologize to.

Ryan stops at the bottom of the bank's steps, checking his phone. "I can't stop now. We have a plan. A good one."

"There's time. Your father hasn't threatened to sell yet. Keep doing what you're doing, and he'll see how hard you've worked."

He slides his phone into his back pocket. "Maybe I should look for an investor. Other breweries do it all the time. A private equity firm who believes in our vision."

I hate to say it, but I keep thinking of Jana's comment about how he already has an investor—his father. "Maybe it's time to talk to your dad."

"You said it yourself—you'll never be a true partner with my father calling the shots. He already blocked you as brewer. Did you forget already?"

I shoot him a *get real* look. I'm not responding to that.

He seems to get that he went too far and closes the distance between us with a sweet kiss to my forehead. "Sorry. My father wants this control over me, and there's no other way to do this with him."

It feels good that Ryan is so dedicated to having me play such a large role in the future of the pub, but I can't shake the feeling we're giving his father too much power. "You should tell him exactly how you feel and why. You've got years of frustrations he probably has no idea about because you're afraid to talk to him."

"We talk plenty, and I'm telling you, he'll say no."

I match his intensity. "You don't know that."

He retracts from me. "I do. I know my father. We're not working with him. At all."

"Listening to each other was part of the agreement. You're not listening."

A car honks at us. Yes, we are that couple arguing on the street. No, I'm not about to stop.

"I need to secure my own financing." He sends a steely look at the unassuming bank. "These corporate banks use metrics to assess risk. They don't see us as real people."

"You might be better off listening to their metrics." Before he can get defensive, I tell him what I've been thinking over for weeks. "I know you want this, Ryan, but if you find yourself with a bad deal after you've been warned you're not ready, it's trouble for the both of us. Your risk factor affects me too."

He steps back, his arms wide. "After all this. You still don't trust me."

"I can't trust someone who won't listen." A bus drives past, drowning out my words. The fumes clog my nose, and I cough. "Let's get out of here."

Ryan follows. "If we don't keep trying, it's over."

I keep walking. "That's dramatic. Stop."

"You need to hear me on this, Kat." He catches up. "He gave in when I asked for this project, but he's not in this to nurture businesses. I thought I could change his mind." He laughs, dark and hollow. "I should have known. He's more ruthless now . . . after. It's like he lost part of himself." He shakes his head. "He bought Resistance for a steal. He knows what it's worth and plans to sell high."

The admission drops like lead in my gut. I stop walking. "Are you saying he paid lower than the value? Because he knew he could get away with it?"

"Yeah. That's what I think."

Prairie and Joe. Taken advantage of when they were vulnerable by someone they trusted. My chest strains at the thought. "He'll want more money regardless." It's futile. All along, there's never been a chance for Ryan's plan. Which means no brewer job for me.

"We need to cut him out. I've been saying this the whole time."

Yet again, another roadblock. None of this is making feel secure about our plans. "You and I aren't a match for an investment firm with decades of experience. Why didn't you tell me about the low offer? It's like you're always leaving something out."

Ryan's breathing comes harsh and fast. "I didn't think it mattered if you believed in us. I love you, Kat."

My head throbs. Maybe Kurt was onto something with not blending work with your off hours, or however he phrased it—

"Wait, did you just say you love me?"

Ryan's eyes have a glazed look. "I . . . yes."

The man said love. As in *love* love?

Love. I roll the word over in my mind. I should be thrilled and ecstatic and do that thing where I throw my arms around him and he lifts me off the ground and spins me in a circle. Like the movies. Only this is the exact wrong time and place for this conversation.

Or it's the exact right time and place. I don't know. Special moments don't happen to me wrapped in a Hallmark bow.

The wind sends my hair whipping across my face. It whips back, giving me a new view of Ryan's expression. It's confused. My breath is utterly stolen. That quickly, everything has changed between us. Everything.

He's telling me what I want to hear. Or what he thinks I want to hear so I'll go along with his plan. There's no way Ryan loves me. Not so soon. Not while we aren't remotely on the same page about this. We're from different worlds. If he tanks a business, he has his family's wealth to save him. I have well-meaning parents who could offer me maybe a month of covered rent. I would never put them in a position to be my backup for when I fail. Maybe that's why I hold back so much. I'm not the risk-taker Ryan is. I can't afford to be.

His breathing seems to have settled, but he's not looking particularly like someone who seconds ago declared their love for someone else.

All of this feels unnecessarily difficult. Launching a business is difficult enough, and we can't even get near the launchpad. Pedestrians stream around us; we're standing in the middle of the sidewalk. I move toward the window of a drugstore with Chicago skyline T-shirts meant to dazzle tourists. Ryan follows, seemingly oblivious to the foot traffic. Of course he's oblivious. People move for him.

That's what's wrong here. I'm still in the picture, trying to support him getting this loan. People don't move for me the way they do for Ryan.

I reframe my thoughts. "I don't like you insisting I don't believe in us when I have legitimate concerns. If you can't discuss the business without claiming I don't trust you, this won't work. It's like you're dragging my feelings for you into a business contract."

He blinks fast and looks past me. "Is that how you feel?"

"About the business? Yes."

"About us. That I'm dragging you into this."

"That's not what I said."

"It's what I'm hearing loud and clear. You don't want to do this with me. You resist at every possible point." He focuses on me with a look I haven't seen since our early encounters. Frustration. Annoyance.

What he says isn't true. The past few weeks I haven't resisted anything. In fact, the opposite. I've been fully all-in with his plan.

I've pushed my concerns aside and thought of optimistic outcomes. I felt happy, even.

Most of the time.

"I've been as open with you as I can," I tell him in a measured tone. Being vulnerable with him hasn't come easy. "I'm sorry if it doesn't seem like enough, but I've been honest with you."

It's a difficult admission. To know that even your best effort at being real with someone falls short.

"Are you sure about that?"

Cars honk at the nearest intersection. I must have misheard him. "What?"

"Are you sure there's not something you're leaving out?"

I rack my brain. "No. What are you talking about?"

I could be wrong, but it looks like guilt on his face. The look dissipates as quickly as it appeared. His hands are jammed into his coat pockets, his collar up high. I only see cheekbones and the profile of his nose and forehead against the dusty sky.

"Do you want to tell me more about Jana?" he asks.

"What about her?"

He pauses a long beat, but I don't know what he wants.

"I saw your phone. That morning at the lake house. Your friend offered you a job."

Oh. Oh no. I wrote a bunch more texts to Jana that night after saying I was happy for her, which I read later the next morning. Texts saying I wanted to work with her, but I was scared to leave my current life. How sleeping with the boss wasn't a surefire way to get hired after all. Because even my drunk texts have a sardonic air.

My heart lodges in my throat. "What were you doing reading my messages?"

He turns a quarter toward me. "It was an accident. Your phone was buzzing. I saw you'd gotten up, so I grabbed the phone to bring it to you. I saw the two texts flash on the screen as they came in."

The one before Jana's request to talk said *We'll keep a brewer spot open for you.*

"And the messages before it?"

"Your phone isn't locked." He clears his throat. "When I unplugged it from the charger, the message chain was right there."

So he saw the drunken texts. Including the one about sleeping with him not getting me what I wanted. I'm nearly bursting to explain everything, but I'm too mad he read my texts. It doesn't sound so accidental as *well, while I'm here . . .*

Ryan's staring at me now. "It's unbelievable you're upset about me seeing your messages when you kept another job offer from me. But it's not like the idea of you not trusting me is new. You've told me that a hundred ways since we met. I thought that had changed, but I don't think it has. You have a contingency plan. You think I'm going to fail. It hurts, Kat. You say you can't trust me, but how can I trust you?"

No. None of this is playing out fair. "I agreed to help you. I have helped you. I stepped back on the brewer job so you could succeed, Ryan. You think that points to wanting you to fail?"

"You do that stepping-back thing a lot, don't you? And then you wonder why life moves on without you."

It's like a slap, I'm that stunned. "Uncalled for. My hesitation here has merit. You caved when your dad told you no."

Ryan visibly flinches. I hit a nerve. And I'm glad.

"I don't know what you want from me, then." His exasperation is evident. "You told me to keep Kurt. I tried fighting for you and you told me no."

"You told me Kurt was in for hiring me when he wasn't. When that became clear, I looked at reality. That job isn't going to work for me. Not at Resistance."

He laughs without humor, putting space between us. "If you've had a backup plan all this time, that tells me all I need. Go. Do what you want."

No, not this cold response. I won't have it. "Ryan. Let's talk through this."

He isn't making a move to leave, but it's as if he's already left. He's impenetrable steel. A locked fortress.

"Ryan, you just told me you loved me. You don't want to fight for this?"

"If I have to convince you, that's the answer right there."

Numbness crawls up my skin. Maybe that is the truth. The answer I haven't wanted to face. "I told Jana no. More than once."

"So she's offered more than once."

"It's not a competition." I bite my lip. "I want to stay here, with my roommates and my job and with you."

He looks at the ground, then at me. "I can't help but notice I'm last on your list."

"You're being unfair. I didn't expect to be talking about this right now."

His impatience is audible through every sigh and breath. "It seems like this is something you should know. If you want to do this or not."

"Do the business? Or us?"

"I'm talking about all of it, Kat."

I thought these were two different things. I'm thinking now that they're not.

My chest cracks with the weight of what needs to be said. It's too much. Too much. Once I tug on this thread, the rest unravels.

He waits on me to say more. The lapse of time is deep as a canyon and loud as a sonic boom.

An odd peace, or maybe it's numbness, washes over. "I can't."

There it is. Said.

The look on Ryan's face cracks me deeper. It's as if he expected it. He isn't anguished or tearing himself apart. He's not asking me to clarify what I can't do. He's not begging me to change my mind.

"Ryan?" His name is a whisper through my unfeeling lips.

He shakes his head, slowly at first, then a quick shake like he's resetting himself. "I think you should take the job, Kat. Everything is pointing toward it. I'm only holding you back."

"That's not—"

"You know it's true."

"Don't speak for me. I make my own choices."

We look at each other. My own stubbornness can't persuade me to keep the fight up. My concerns are legitimate. My restlessness has been speaking to me for weeks, and I haven't listened. Jana's offer in my back pocket is where I've let my thoughts roam when I'm frustrated. A secret space I've created that I've kept for myself. I kept it from Ryan intentionally.

"I'm sorry," I say, because nothing else fits.

He looks sad, but not broken. Maybe too hurt, too proud, too angry. I can't tell, because he's shutting me off. He's turning away. "Me too."

CHAPTER TWENTY-FIVE

BARREL-AGED BEER

An ale, lager, or beer aged in a wood barrel. Experimental brews may involve charring the inside to bring out additional flavors in the wood. For when you want to burn it down.

It's a strange week that follows. I do things I never thought I'd do.

I put in my notice at Resistance.

I accept Jana's job offer.

I tell Sadie I'm good for next month's rent, but she tells me no way and then we cry. She also tells me not to hold back when it comes to her. We're each other's best and favorite roommate, but change is calling, and we need to hear it. I need to hear it.

Quitting my job at Resistance requires giving notice to Ryan himself. I tell him in the pub in front of the window to the brewing tanks, in full view of Kurt and his new crew doing the work I want so badly. That makes it easier. Staying here, I was always going to be on the outside looking in.

He says nothing, with the exception of two last words. "I'm sorry."

I let the words sink in. "I'm sorry too."

We've come full circle with our sad-sack apologies. They're a means of tying up the loose ends, not the start of a reconciliatory conversation. We both know it and don't bother pretending otherwise.

I find Magda immediately after and tell her. "I'm sorry to leave you."

She smirks and pours me a Prairie Wheat on draft. "I'm sorry to see you go, but you're not leaving me. I'll be fine."

"How's your husband?"

She sighs. "We're still fighting with insurance on some medical costs. The bastards."

"I hate this world sometimes."

"We'll be okay. He's doing well." She nods toward the back and Ryan's office. "Sorry it didn't work out. He's a fool."

Working my final shifts is constant confirmation it's time to move on. At one point, I try to go talk to Ryan, only to have him close the office door in my face.

I decide not to say an official goodbye to anyone, since we'll keep in touch. I'd like to say I'll be down soon for a visit, but I'm moving to another state and I don't own a car. Vague is better until I have a better grasp on my life.

Jana and Claudette offer their spare room to me, but even better, they have a lead on a small one-bedroom apartment in an old house within walking distance of Myth and Muse.

I rent a small moving truck and load my things. I don't have much beyond my bed, clothes, a few boxes of books and random belongings, and my mini-fridge for beer. Most of the apartment is Sadie's. Jana has a few pieces of furniture in storage I can use, so that helps.

I detour to my parents' house to pick up a dresser and household supplies they insist I take. They follow me the rest of the way across the state line with the intent to help unload. The gesture is unprecedented. I've had half a dozen moves in and out of dorms and apartments they haven't been around for.

They're also helping me with first month's rent. My mom, again, insisted. I agree, because it seems to be part of her own process of working through our issues. Also, money will be lean as the taproom gets started, and I need to pay Ryan back for my online certificate course. He didn't ask, but I'm sending him a money transfer.

I have a sense of peace I haven't had in weeks, even if I still end up crying four times a day. I'm definitely not numb. I'm feeling every thread of this, and it's like I've woken up after a deep sleep.

I'm ready for what's next.

Setting up Myth and Muse Brewing is the hardest work I've ever done.

I love it.

It's not lost on me that I've moved from one couple-owning brewery to another. Jana and Claudette have a different vibe than Joe and Prairie. More high strung, faster paced, with an undercurrent of worry about making it all fit. Their commitment to each other is that last step in the brew pulling the ingredients together.

The timeline for opening is aggressive but manageable (at least according to Jana), since the space is already equipped with much of what we need. We're waiting on instrument inspections. The tanks are sanitized and ready to go.

Our neighbors are a make-your-own pottery shop and a used bookstore. The family-owned burger place across from us uses locally sourced ingredients, including the cows. An office complex and the library are a block over, and an outdoor festival space behind us features a farmers' market May through September. Jana and Claudette plan to have a booth there.

With spring making way for summer, we prop the doors open, and nearby business owners stop in to share food or say hello. There have been cheese plates. Many a cheese plate.

Which I never turn down.

My apartment is a ten-minute walk from the Myth and Muse—the real selling point, since the space itself is small, with a funky layout. It's an old home, which I'm used to, divided in two, with my "half" being more like one-third of the house on a single floor while the neighbor has the remaining lower-level half plus the upstairs. I'm getting paid with the upstart money, even though we're not open yet. The financial security means a lot.

I've never lived alone. The thought struck me only after my parents waved goodbye after helping me move in.

But instead of feeling lonely, I feel like I'm where I need to be. Usually.

"Why can't I stop crying?" I ask Sadie during our now nightly phone call. She's the one who insisted on calling every day, and honestly? I'm grateful. The apartment makes creepy noises, and it's up to me to investigate or ignore them. "It's weird to keep crying, because I'm otherwise happy."

"You're in shock," Sadie responds. "This is a lot of change fast. Let yourself feel what you're feeling."

"Stop being so sensible."

"You're brave, Kat. This isn't a small thing you're doing."

I miss Sadie. I miss Alex and Magda and Luiz. I miss Prairie and Joe, especially after the latest update. Joe is sick with a respiratory infection, a bigger risk given his cancer.

I miss Ryan. I can't help missing what we started and what we could have been.

I remind myself he's a grown man who has the responsibility of running a business and I was his employee. It was never on me to fix what was wrong. Working with his dysfunctional family dynamic was never going to work.

If I had told him about the job offer, how I was thinking it over but was probably going to pass, would that have been better? Or just a lie?

Every time I think maybe I made the wrong choice by moving, I mentally review my day and the work I'm putting in. I'm proud of what we're building. I'm already tweaking recipes and working on what's next, even while we start our initial stock of Jana and Claudette's existing brews. They like my enthusiasm, and I absorb their guidance like I'm in my own master's program.

Still, my off hours are a little lonely. Sometimes I catch myself touching my lips, imagining the impression of Ryan's on mine. There's a notable absence where he filled part of my life so intensely these past few months.

"Oh, did I tell you?" I say to Sadie, after a lull in our conversation where neither of us seems ready to hang up. "I'm tweaking a new ESB."

"What's that again? The extra something . . ."

"Extra-special bitter. I'm pushing for a strong final bitter note. Claudette keeps telling me to soften the flavor, but I want this to stand on its own. I don't want it to be a beer everyone likes."

Unlike Heartbeat at Resistance, where the challenge was to please everyone, here I want my first brew to have a distinct point of view. It might alienate some drinkers, but for those who like what it offers, that's the best type of discovery. At least it is for me, and I want this first brew to reflect who I am.

I'm a little extra, maybe sorta special, and definitely a dose of bitter. Not a perfect blend, and I'm okay with that.

"Did you find a renter for my room yet?" I ask.

"Nah. I'm going to make it a craft room for myself. I already moved in a vintage dress form we picked up at an estate sale. I'm experimenting with sewing."

"That's awesome, Sadie! You could sell your clothes at the shop."

"I said *experiment*. So far I made a shirt with the right sleeve sewn shut. It also will only fit a toddler, and I used an adult pattern."

"Too soon, I'm hearing."

"Yeah. This craft room includes a daybed, so you have a place to sleep when you visit."

My throat tightens, and not for the first time today, tears show up, ready to party. "Thanks, Sadie."

We end our call, and I slide beneath the covers. An unfamiliar creak groans from somewhere inside the wall. My eyes fly open. I'm certain it's a ghost trapped in the plaster.

The wall creaks again.

"You all right in there?" I ask the room.

The creaking stops.

It's my ghost now, so I'd better get friendly.

CHAPTER TWENTY-SIX
WILD AND SOUR BEERS

Intentionally acidic, often misunderstood.

Three Months Later

Myth and Muse is doing a soft opening for friends and family, and I've invited everyone I can think of. My parents are coming and bringing friends. Karrie will be here now that school let out and she's an official college grad. She's coming with her roommate Addison.

Alex, Magda, and Luiz are driving up together.

I invited Prairie and Joe, and they sent their love. Joe isn't well enough to travel. He's stable, but they can't be too careful right now. After my call to Prairie, I sent them a card from my new address, a thank-you for all they've done for me. Writing that card was my way of closing up shop on a time in my life that feels vital to where I am now but has run its course. I've grown and I've got more growing to do, just without them as a guiding influence.

They have bigger things to deal with. I have my own family to invest in.

Myth and Muse has small batches ready to go for the grand opening. The reclaimed-wood tables are up; there's a cozy area with worn tapestries on the wall, a weathered vintage sofa Sadie will adore, and a coffee table like a living room. The rest of the taproom is table and bar seating with framed art spaced along the wall. Back by the couch, Claudette hung a framed Lilith Fair poster.

I've already seen Sadie, since she drove in yesterday and slept on my couch. After an early start, we have everything ready to go for customers, including a rose-colored ribbon draped across the front door.

We wait outside for people to arrive, and a small crowd begins to gather. The town has a downtown business bureau that's been incredibly supportive. That's all Claudette, working her charm with the community, leaving Jana and me to do the grunt work. I love it.

My Resistance crew approaches from the nearby parking garage.

"Ahh! You came!" I run toward them, arms open and flailing. We have our moment to freak out.

It's not only the three I expected either. Magda brought her husband, Alex is with a guest dressed in an incredible asymmetrical vest thing with hot-pink boots to match hot-pink hair, and Luiz is walking beside Nesto and Aaron from Dos Islas.

"What are you all doing here? This is bananas!" I'm crying, obviously. My emotions are so out of whack. Or, maybe inside of whack, a comfortable space I inhabit. "It's like a two-hour drive!"

Luiz shrugs. "You said free beer, so we came."

Nesto and Aaron have their families with them—wives and kids ranging from elementary school age to preteen. We'll have nonalcoholic options for them inside.

"I'm dying to see this place." Alex looks past me. "Also, equally as important, this is Miranda." Miranda with the pink hair says hello back.

"Great to meet you." I smile at Miranda and a millisecond after send Alex a silent *squee*.

"I want to hear everything about your job," I tell him. *And more*, I say with a look.

Everyone talks at once. My parents arrive with their friends, so I detour to greet them. Shortly after, my sister and Addison show up.

"I'm inviting myself over for later," Karrie announces. "I need to check your closet to see if you have my long black skirt. I couldn't find it when I moved."

I dismiss her claim that I may have thieved her clothes. I'm happy she finally moved out. The irony is she's only two miles from my parents, but the arrangement seems to be working for all of them.

Jana rings a cowbell to get everyone's attention. "Just a few words, and we'll get to the beer."

Cue laughter.

She goes into a speech about her and Claudette's dream of opening Myth and Muse and thanks a number of people standing in the crowd.

Jana waves me to the front. "Come here, Kat."

I shimmy through the crowd to stand beside them. "My old crew is here from Resistance in Chicago!"

They all make *whoop, whoop!* sounds and wave.

I look at the many familiar faces. "Thank you all so much for coming. It means the world."

Jana gives a few final words, and the crowd claps. She hands a pair of scissors to Claudette, who starts crying, waving her off. "No, you do it. You cut the ribbon."

They decide to both awkwardly hold the scissors and snip. There is much rejoicing.

Inside, I give the tour, kind of like the old days at Resistance, but I'm far less bitter now. Well, maybe a little bitter, but for flavor.

We open the bar. I return to the crowd for more introductions—my parents to my former Resistance friends, Jana and Claudette to Aaron and Nesto, and all of them to everyone else.

We hired day staff to serve drinks so we could mingle, but I'm still going to help serve drinks. Before I can head off, the Resistance crew huddles around me.

"There's been a lot happening," Luiz tells me. "Back home."

Worry fills the pit of my stomach. "What? What's happening?"

"We've been holding back on you, Kat," Magda announces. She's almost gleeful. No, I take that back. She is completely full of glee.

"Good news?" Maybe she's having a baby?

"Before you ask, no, I'm not having a baby." She smiles. "Hopefully soon." She glances at the door.

They're all sort of watching the door.

"WHAT?" I ask exasperated.

Alex jostles my arm. "Hold on a sec. We had this all figured out."

Magda has her phone out, texting.

If they're trying to surprise me, I'll have to keep myself busy or the suspense will be too much. "Anyone need a drink?"

I look over at the busy bar, excited that my friends and family get to see this. I turn back.

Now I see what they've been waiting for. A frame fills the door, lean and clean and more freakishly attractive than any human male deserves to be. My heart nearly disconnects.

"What's he doing here?" My insides are pudding, my brain also pudding?

Alex leans in. "It's good, Kat, I swear. Go talk to him."

I step from the huddle, the fake-it-till-ya-make-it smile in place. "Ryan. Wow, thanks for coming?" I cringe at the question in my tone, but it's what came out.

Ryan looks beyond to the gawkers, then centers on me again. "Kat, you look amazing. You look happy."

I meet him at the door. He bends with care to kiss my cheek, pausing before he does it—I imagine in case I have a last-minute urge to shove him. I do not.

"It appears they all knew you were coming." Being this close, a cascade of memories and feelings flood back. His touch, his scent, the way he's kind and thoughtful right now, same as he used to be even when I was petty and a wreck.

"I didn't have to be convinced, if that's what you're suggesting." He searches my face. "First, before anything. I'm sorry."

"You said that already. Before I left."

"I mean it in a different way now. I'm sorry for a lot of things. Not trusting you. Putting you on the spot and forcing you to make a choice." He waits a beat. "If you don't want me here, I'll leave."

I grab his sleeve. "You came here for a reason. Tell me. I'm listening."

Ryan nods to the group behind me. "Shall we?"

He progresses inside, and I follow. "Apparently, we shall."

They're waiting for us, which is seriously weirding me out.

Ryan brings his hands together. "I asked all of them not to say anything until we knew for sure, so if you're going to be upset with anyone for withholding information, be upset with me."

Hoo boy.

His eyes meet mine. "I'm no longer the acting manager at Resistance. Luiz is."

"What? Luiz!" I clap excitedly. "That's amazing."

Ryan angles back into my line of sight. "My family's investment company settled on a new buyer. Well, plural buyers." He gestures to Nesto and Aaron.

My jaw drops. "I can't believe this!" I'm shocked, a million times over shocked. "Are you huggers?" I ask them.

Nesto and Aaron laugh nearly in unison. "Are you joking?" Nesto asks. "You're asking two Latinos if we're huggers? Well, in case that doesn't answer, yes. We hug."

I hug them both. I'm dying to know the rest. "How?"

Nesto nods back to Ryan.

"I met with Nesto and Aaron about their business plan. Luiz is who suggested it, since my father came by the pub with a buyer—he waited until I was off-site to do it." He pauses for a small eye roll. "They already had a loan preapproved to move the food truck operation to a permanent space. With their history of success in the community, they seemed like a good choice. So I talked to my dad about, well, everything." He gives me a meaningful look.

A meaningful look! For me! Usually it's me giving him looks to decipher, and now I'm the lucky one on that end. This small detail excites me. A lot.

"And with an assist from my mom," he continues, "I convinced my dad to meet in person with Nesto and Aaron. They put together a kick-ass presentation on how Resistance has a community legacy and detailed their connections in the neighborhood and with surrounding businesses."

"We can't take all the credit," Nesto says. "Ryan here made it easy. Giving us advice we hadn't thought of."

Aaron rests his hand on his wife's shoulder beside him. "We plan to continue working with Kurt, to expand brewing when they can, and keep the Resistance label going."

"That's amazing!" I'm curious on the details, since Ryan said his father wasn't in it for investing in the people running the business, only focused on the bottom dollar amount. Something changed his mind beyond that presentation.

But that's all that's being said now in front of everyone, so I go with it and give a round of congratulations.

"I can't believe you all kept this from me!"

"You've been busy," Sadie offers.

"You knew too?"

She twirls a strand of hair. "Oh, you know. Maybe. Maybe not."

I want to throw something at her, lightly. "You must have been dying this morning."

She lets out a dramatic gasp. "I *hate* secrets."

My parents and Karrie lurk beyond the circle, so I bring them into the fold and fill them in, and another round of congratulations ensues.

"Mom, Dad," I say. "This is Ryan. The previous manager I worked for."

Mom shoots me a knowing look, and she's way too obvious out here with that mess. Karrie leans into Addison, no doubt filling in details I'm never meant to hear.

I'm so full of joy, and there are so many conversations I want to have right this second.

But one feels like it's risen to the top.

"Walk?" I ask Ryan.

I lead Ryan around the building. Landscaped paver steps lead to a sidewalk path to the outdoor event space. It's all inlaid brick with benches and patches of greenery and flowers.

Turning and walking backward a few steps, I throw my hands in the air. "Care to explain? For real?"

He catches up. "You're smiling, so you can't be too mad."

"I'm insanely curious. Tell me everything."

"I wasn't sure you wanted to hear from me. Especially today, since it's your day. But Alex and the others said they thought it was okay."

"I'm glad you checked with them. And it is okay." I push my pointer finger against his chest. Playful but prodding. "Well?"

"I told my dad everything. Finally. Both my parents were together, and I laid it all out. All the grief we're not dealing with as a family. How it's hurting us. My mom broke down. She had divorce papers drafted a year ago."

"I'm so sorry."

"She held on to them, hoping." He inhales and lets it out slow. "They have a lot to work through, but it was a start. Pulling my dad's other business partner in helped too. I talked to them about Joe and Prairie. Found pictures of Dad and Joe in the family albums and made my dad look. I said, 'These are the people you undercut with the sale. They trusted you.' That sort of thing. It was surprisingly effective."

My heart warms. "Your dad isn't a monster. He got lost somewhere and was only thinking of himself. And that lake-slice condo."

Ryan laughs. "I moved out, by the way. Of the condo. I know it sounds dysfunctional, but I'm living with my parents." He holds up a hand. "Before you make fun of me, I have a plan. I also have a roommate lined up, but we can't move in together yet."

"I'm glad you talked with your family. And how great is it that Nesto and Aaron are running Resistance? That's the best news." He's accomplished a lot in the time I've been gone. "What's your plan?"

He digs into a pocket and hands me a card. "Working with Nesto and Aaron felt so satisfying. Hearing someone else's business plan and helping them make it happen. In their case, they'd already done the legwork and secured financing—I can't take credit. But it gave me an idea to take what I know from my family's investment firm but do the part where you nurture the business too. Coaching and connection to community resources. There's a way to do those things where it's more hands-on with a business, and that's what I want to do. I just needed some support. A partner."

A sense of calm falls over me. He's doing okay, and I nearly throw my arms around him. I shift back, urging myself to keep cool. "Who is your partner?"

"You're going to laugh. It's Michael."

"Lake house Michael?"

"One and the same. That night we stayed up talking, he was laying it on thick that we should start our own business. He's been wanting to branch out from his own family's company for a while."

"Wow. Incredibly good timing."

He nods. "I'm driving to see him after this. At the lake house."

"Awesome. Super great." My smile is a little forced realizing this was a stop for him on the way to somewhere else. Still, I'm flattered he told me in person about the changes and consulted my friends about coming. "Well, I wish you lots of luck, then. Where will you be living?"

He rubs the back of his neck. "It's up in the air. We can do our business from a lot of places. It would be cheaper to live some-where outside of Chicago."

"Lots of suburbs to choose from."

"Another option is Milwaukee. Michael and I could live at the lake house and commute to the general area."

Milwaukee. The largest city nearest where I am.

"Or Madison," he says quickly. "We're assessing where we can best be used."

I'm too nervous to let my thoughts go where they want.

"Kat." His shoulders give out. "I gave all of it up because you were right. I was the wrong person for the job. I was hang-ing on to prove to my dad something that was never going to fix our family. I failed, and it's better for Resistance that I did. I only saw the truth because of you. To see you walk away from it all—that was powerful. All the things you thought you wanted

305

that were actually holding you back—you left them behind and started over."

He reaches for my hands with a subtle look that asks, *This okay?*

I place my hands into his, and already my mind is scribbling the story to come.

"One of the worst days of my life was the day we broke up," he says. "Maybe only second to the day Jesse died. It might sound like I'm exaggerating. It was the same dark, gutted feeling. When I told you I loved you and you looked at me like you didn't believe me—you were right. I meant it, but I used that moment to get you to side with me. I thought I could use us, the both of us and what we had, to get you to see things my way. That's what I'm most sorry about. Because you don't deserve manipulation. No one does, but especially not you after what you've been through."

I rub my thumbs along the tops of his hands. "You meant it, that you loved me?"

His features soften. "Yes. I know it happened fast, but when you know, you know. So I've heard. I feel like I know it even more now after being apart from you."

"I've missed you." I look up at him. "I wanted to call. I didn't know what to say. I figured you wouldn't want to hear from me."

"I wanted to call, but figured we both needed time. And I was afraid you'd scream at me."

"I'm more of a yeller. You should know that."

"I almost wanted you to scream or yell at me. I wanted to hear your voice." He lets go of one hand and places his hand at my cheek. "I knew actions would speak louder, so getting the deal lined up was all I could do before I contacted you."

He's right. It means everything, how he took action. He isn't here on empty promises.

"You're not mad at me for leaving?"

"Look at you. You're thriving. I was hurt at the time, but I pushed you away. I wasn't thinking straight."

"And now?"

His face is utterly serious. "My thoughts are excessively straight." The facade cracks, and he grins.

"Pointing at . . . ?"

He inches closer. "If you can forgive me, I'd love another shot."

I can't resist. "You know I prefer beer to hard liquor."

"Good thing. I know a place serving craft beer. Close, too."

I snuggle in so we're wrapped in each other's arms. Joking aside, I'm down for another shot too. One where we don't have running an entire restaurant hanging over our heads. We have our own challenges, sure, but we can face them together.

"There's a new beer you haven't tried," I tell him. "Extremely small batch. IPA, high hops, a dry note to finish. Not for everyone."

"Could be I might like it."

"Could be."

His mouth hovers over mine. "Can I get a preview?"

I break our gaze and kiss him. This time, the world doesn't fall away. Every sensation is heightened, right on the edge and waiting. Waiting to be lived and experienced. I want to experience it with Ryan.

We pull apart. "What's it called?"

"Bastet Case. After the Egyptian goddess Bastet. A goddess of a number of things, including cats."

"Goddess Kat, huh? I like it."

"On theme."

We kiss again. I have questions—logistics, what's next, are we really going to do this? I let them float aside to be answered later. Here, now, we have this moment. A chance to write the next. Together.

I break off and take his hand. "And now? We drink."

EPILOGUE

Ryan

We're on a bus. It's cold again, and we're back in Chicago, playing tourists on our way to a small-batch brewery owned by a woman Kat knows through a brewing group. We decided to make a day of it, taking an indirect route through city neighborhoods with permission to call for a stop when inspiration strikes. Just like we did last year, on that cold day when I knew for sure I was falling for Kat.

The city bus jerks to a stop at an intersection, and my whole body jerks with it. "I can't believe I ever thought riding the bus was romantic."

Kat makes a face. "*Romantic*? I'm pretty sure that slime over there trickled under our seats and congealed onto my boots. I might be stuck here. Permanently." She continues looking at me. "I can't believe I gave you such a hard time about taking public transit, like it was some sort of badge of honor. I'm such a try-hard sometimes."

"Better than a blowhard."

She snickers and jabs me in the side. Immediately, she snuggles closer. It feels good being back in Chicago with her, but I'm not sure I miss living here. Kat does, and we've discussed where we might land in a few years if we get restless.

Things have been going well living separately—me sharing an apartment with Michael on the outskirts of Milwaukee and Kat living six miles away at her possibly haunted rental house. We're together a lot, but lately I've found myself missing her more on the nights we're apart.

Someday we'll be ready to mix it all together. Maybe even someday soon.

"This is the stop." Kat stands and attempts to move, but her boots fight back. She wrangles the soles free from the unforgiving floor, and we exit the bus to the brisk winter air.

Wind sears our faces for the block-and-a-half walk to the brewery. Suddenly, Kat tugs me beneath an alcove by a door reading NO ENTRY. "Hey." She pulls me to her.

Her pink nose and flushed cheeks make her even more beautiful. "Hey yourself." I press her further into me to shield her from the wind. I want to hang on to this small moment. I'm finding I'm into small moments. They're the ones I remember most. A touch, an in-joke, a flash where I realize I love my life. And I love who I'm spending it with.

Her chilled nose lands against my neck where my scarf fails to cover it. She peeks up at me. "Before we go inside and my social self takes over, I wanted to just exist out here for a second with you."

Our lips meet. She tastes sweet, warm. I deepen the kiss and try to show her all the things I feel and can't always say the right way. "I love you," I tell her. Because I need to say it. I love saying it.

She grins and kisses me again. We part at the same time. "I think we should move in together."

"You do?" My heart races. Both of us needed time on our own, but I've waited for this.

"My lease ends in a couple months. I already started prepping Betty."

Betty is the spirit that maybe probably lives in her walls. "And?"

"Betty's chill. Probably too chill. She might be freezing me out." She blows out a breath. "Seriously, though, I'd like to look for a place. If that's what you want."

She'd definitely freak if she knew I had a place in mind already, so I try to sound casual when I say, "It could be cool to live in those rehabbed loft apartments over by the river."

Her eyes widen. "In my little town? Wouldn't you rather live in Milwaukee?"

"I want to be where you are." Always.

She gives me a steady look. "You're making this suspiciously easy."

"Suspiciously easy is what they called me in high school." I grin.

She cracks up, a loud burst of laughter that sends pure joy through my veins. "Let's get out of here and into there." She nods toward our destination, the brick building on the next corner.

I grab her hand and we cross into another moment, together.

ACKNOWLEDGMENTS

In early February 2020, I sat in a local microbrewery on a snowy night, learning how to evaluate beer in a course on craft beer judging. The fun sort of research writers love. I had no idea how much the world was about to change and that this would become my "pandemic book." Not that this book is about the pandemic, but that the story would encapsulate so many shifting emotions from that time. Thankfully, *Brew's* long road to publication has a happy ending. I'm not exactly a patient person, but have to admit, the best home for this book came about at just the right time.

Thank you to Eva Scalzo for connecting with Kat and the misfit Resistance crew so easily. You've been an incredible champion, and I love the added support from #TeamEva! Thanks also to Sarah LaPolla for helping me navigate the publishing industry as a new author and for your continued encouragement. Jess Verdi, your enthusiasm for this book is such a delight and a boost of confidence. Thank you to you and the Alcove team for the advocacy and behind-the-scenes work.

Much appreciation to Mark Fontanetta for providing resources and answering questions pertaining to the craft brewing process. Any mistakes or inconsistencies in the story are wholly mine (alas, I am a craft beer drinker and not a brewer myself). Resistance is entirely fictional and not based on any single brewing operation; instead, I found inspiration from many taprooms and microbreweries local to Chicagoland and where I grew up in Michigan (shout-out to Bell's in Kalamazoo!). I have a growing list of women-owned breweries I'm excited to visit.

Many thanks to my writing community, including my core group: Kelly Garcia, Vanessa M. Knight, Jen Bailey—can you believe we've been doing this for a decade? Thank you to Erica Chapman, Robin Kuss, Melonie Johnson, Melanie Hooyenga, Lisa Brown Roberts, and Pintip Dunn for many levels of support the past several years. I'm grateful for the dependable encouragement from Chicago North Romance Writers and the former Windy City Romance Writers. You are all my community and have shaped who I am as a writer.

Thank you to my family and friends who endlessly cheerlead my publishing achievements. To the Seasonally Booked Up reading group: you all made me a better reader. Lastly, to my husband Jason, who always encourages creative pursuits over household chores, who knows when I need space to focus and when it's time to binge the latest *Destiny 2* campaign: here's to many more long weekends working beside each other.